*The ~~Ripper~~ Was on the Loose
in London's Streets Again.
It Was A Bloody Shame
They Couldn't Catch Him . . .*

From the *London Times*:

"Another murder was committed in Whitechapel yesterday, by whom and with what motive is at present a complete mystery. At 3:45 a.m., a police constable came upon the body of a woman whose throat was cut from ear to ear. Further examination showed other fearful cuts and gashes, one alone of which was sufficient to cause death. . . ."

RIPPER

A stunning novel that brilliantly portrays the world's most infamous killer.

"Explores the psychological aspects of the case with heavy sexual overtones . . . WELL WRITTEN AND WHOLLY BELIEVABLE!"

—*St. Catharines Standard*

MARK CLARK

BERKLEY BOOKS, NEW YORK

For Mary Campeau

This Berkley book contains the complete
text of the original hardcover edition.
It has been completely reset in a typeface
designed for easy reading and was printed
from new film.

RIPPER

A Berkley Book / published by arrangement with
the author

PRINTING HISTORY
Byren House edition published 1987
Berkley edition / July 1989

ISBN: 0-425-11644-1

A BERKLEY BOOK® TM 757,375
Berkley Books are published by The Berkley Publishing Group,
200 Madison Avenue, New York, NY 10016.
The name "BERKLEY" and the "B" logo
are trademarks belonging to Berkley Publishing Corporation.

PRINTED IN THE UNITED STATES OF AMERICA

10 9 8 7 6 5 4 3 2 1

ACKNOWLEDGMENTS

I am grateful to the following: Aynne Johnston for research; Diane Yocum for manuscript preparation; Donald Redmond for checking historical accuracy; Betty Corson for editorial expertise; Professor Cathy Harland of Queen's University for lending me her copy of Nina Auerbach's *Woman and the Demon: The Life of a Victorian Myth*; Dr. Samuel Shortt for a copy of his scholarly *Victorian Lunacy;* Mary Campeau whose original idea this project was, and without whose unfailing encouragement, it would not have been completed; and finally, my wife, Liz, for her steadfast support.

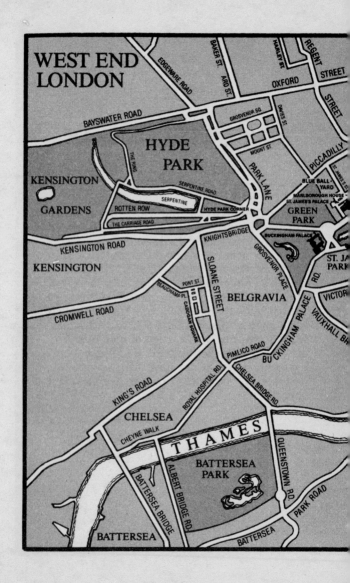

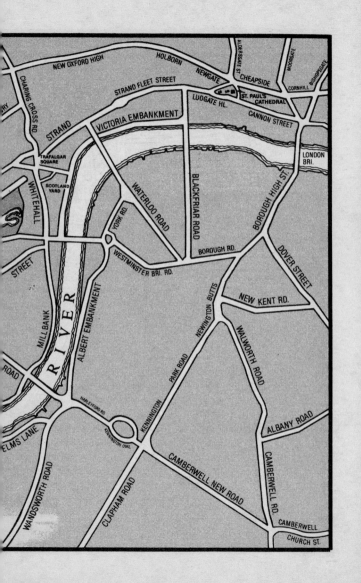

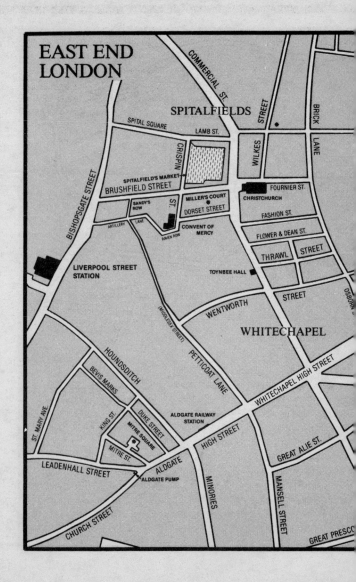

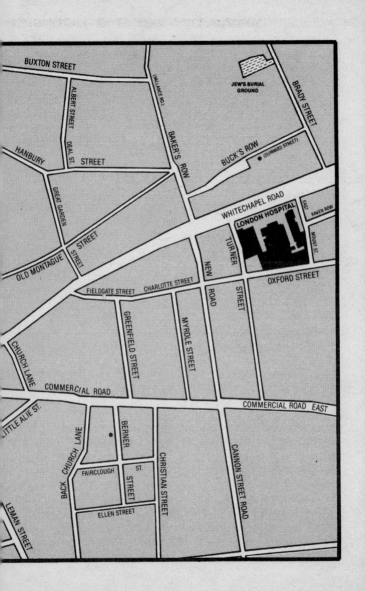

Foreword

Except for the description of historical figures and events, this narrative is fiction. The reader should, however, be aware that excerpts from the *Times,* although abridged, appear as originally published.

As the brain changes are continuous, so do all these consciousnesses melt into each other like dissolving views. Properly they are but one protracted consciousness, one unbroken stream.

William James

I am a very blessed woman, am I not? To have all this reason for being glad that I have lived, in spite of my sins and sorrows—or rather, by reason of my sins and sorrows.

George Eliot

LONDON
1888

Mary Ann Nichols

friday, august 31st

HE STOOD MOTIONLESS in a shallow recess set in the brickwork. He might have been a statue painted in lifelike flesh tones or a waxen effigy stolen from Madame Tussaud's and placed in Whitechapel to terrify passersby. He could smell the dank brick, could feel its cool moisture. The odour and dampness were that of an earthen storage cellar, but he minded neither. He felt completely at ease, as if the porous brick had somehow managed to absorb the essence of him.

He realized this was a trick of his imagination. Nevertheless, in a very real sense, he believed himself invisible. A few months ago, a remark from an overheard conversation had made an indelible impression: "Man is essentially a sightless creature. He can't see what he doesn't believe in; even more damning, he can't, or won't, see what he doesn't *want* to believe in. . . ." That insight had remained a constant; otherwise, he had existed in a state of inconstancy and struggle. Sometimes, he imagined his mind as a backwater pond. Each time a stone skimmed the surface, an unrecognizable yet hauntingly familiar image was triggered. At other times, the experience was far more unpleasant. It was as though his skull were being pried open and pricked by an imaginary needle, with competing images appearing puppet-like before his eyes. One of those faces suddenly materialized and taunted him with a phrase: *Consciousness does not appear to itself chopped up in bits*. . . . Where had he heard those words? The message was false, regardless of its author. But it didn't really matter. Not the words nor the needle nor the nightmarish images. He had learned how to stop their madness. He formed two oversized hands, brought them to the throat of the offending puppet face and strangled it. As he did, to his amazement, the face became that of a woman he thought he recognized. This so infuriated him that he tightened his grip, causing her face to mottle into patches of white on black. Then it started to disintegrate—chin, cheekbone, forehead, an eye staring in terror, floating off into an inky blackness. When it had finally vanished, he grinned savagely in the dark.

The old prostitute was walking east on Whitechapel Road. Her face was small and pinched, her skin leathery and brown from a summer out-of-doors. Yet her eyes, despite a life of deprivation, retained a defiance and sparkle that softened her features and had earned her the nickname Pretty Polly.

She wore a black straw bonnet and a reddish topcoat over a long black skirt. Her boots had been purchased in Petticoat Lane with the upper ankle supports cut off. Steel plates were fixed to the heels to prevent wearing. Her approach could not be missed, steel against stone telegraphing her imminent arrival.

She moved slowly, her arthritic joints stiff from age and too much exposure to cold, damp winters. But even if able, she would not have hurried. She was "wares for sale" and as such had always to be available for inspection. Twice she had had her doss money in hand, but each time she had squandered it on gin at the Frying Pan in Brick Lane, only a few hundred yards from the Thrawl Street lodging house where, for the past several weeks, she had been sharing a bed with another prostitute. Once, sometime after midnight, while quite drunk, she had hammered on the door of 18 Thrawl Street, demanding admittance as if she were a high and mighty queen—the alcohol had given her a sense of power and majesty. With gin in her blood she became quite gay, even vivacious, although in a weepy, sentimental way. When she was drunk, her heart was as big as the moon; she would give the keys of the kingdom to any poor soul with the presence of mind to ask. But the deputy in Thrawl Street had not possessed the same largesse, nor was he impressed with her imperious manner, although he knew it belonged to the gin. He had grabbed her by the coat sleeve and shoved her back into the street.

Now, three hours later, she was in Whitechapel Road, approaching Whitechapel Station and the sprawling mass of London Hospital on the opposite side of the street. Whitechapel Road, together with Whitechapel High Street and Aldgate High Street—the three thoroughfares following one after the other, like links in a roll of sausage—were the main traffic arteries leading to and from the East End of London. Regardless of the hour, they were always crowded with pedestrians and horse-drawn traffic. Most of the pre-dawn travellers were making their way to one of the city's early morning markets.

Prostitutes worked Whitechapel Road the way miners panned a stream for gold: with exhaustive patience, knowing that among the thousands of worthless pebbles they sifted, a nugget of precious metal was bound to turn up. It was merely a question of perseverance, a quality the old whore possessed in sufficient measure to ensure her survival. So she continued east in the road, searching for a glint of sexual hunger.

She passed public house after public house, five in one 300-yard stretch. Each caused a brief pause, a reflexive twist of her head. Outside each, she could smell gin. If she worshipped anything, she worshipped gin. Not Beefeater's or Gordon's, exquisite spirits flavoured with the delectable juice of the juniper berry. Hers was crudely distilled from potent grain mash and sold by the penny cupful. Drinking it was like swallowing fire. It raced to the pit of her stomach and settled in a steady blaze that flooded her entire body with warmth. But the fire needed to be stoked frequently or it sputtered and went out. Then her stomach and even her blood seemed filled with cold, dry ashes.

The Lord Rodney, at the intersection of Brady Street and Whitechapel Road, usually marked the turning point in her wandering. She would either cross the road and backtrack west in the general direction of Thrawl Street or travel north in Brady Street as far as the Jews' Burial Ground, a green oasis among the grimy, blackened bricks of Whitechapel. South of the burial ground was the Albion Brewery Works and, on the other side of the street, a manure works. Both enterprises operated around the clock, with scores of employees coming and going at all hours.

She hesitated at the intersection for a moment, bathed in a pool of whitish blue gaslight. She did not feel like travelling up Brady Street, nor did she feel like crossing Whitechapel Road, so she turned on her heel and began to retrace her steps. At the opening to a pedestrian tunnel, she stopped. Across the street, she read the clock set in the yellow brick façade of London Hospital: 3:30 a.m. The opening tunnel gaped like the mouth of a castle dungeon, but she did not feel threatened. Whitechapel held no terror for her, despite a recent spate of murders, each victim a prostitute.

She paused for a moment, then suddenly recalled that she had once found favour with a railway-yard watchman a few hundred yards beyond the tunnel. *How long ago had that been?* Her memory played tricks on her, had done so ever since she had embarked on a day-to-day existence on the streets of Whitechapel. It could have been last year or last month or last week. But what did it matter? If the watchman found favour with her once, he could again—and so she stepped into the tunnel entrance.

His alcove was cast in absolute darkness. Directly opposite, a narrow tunnel led to Whitechapel Road. People passed within inches of him. Some were drunk and reeked of gin or whiskey or, more often, beer. One or two had stood by the wall—not an arm's length away—and urinated, their beer piss steaming off the cobblestoned pathway. He should have been repelled by the stink, disgusted by the act itself. But he wasn't. All of Whitechapel stank of horse dung and urine; of rotted vegetable matter, butcher's blood and animal offal. Nearby were numerous Jewish abattoirs where the ritual slaughter of animals went on day and night.

Yet despite the all-pervasive stench, it was the smell of *her* that first seized his attention. The cheap perfume penetrated his olfactory system and instantly sped to his brain. At almost the same moment, he saw her, caught against the gaslit glare like a moth burned black on the glass of a paraffin lamp. The sight of her, and the scent—not of the perfume but of her underlying femaleness—triggered a response in his mind. He did not register what she looked like. He identified and marked her as *woman*.

He divined instantly that she was alone, that she was a prostitute: she wore the telltale white apron of her trade. But these observations, though isolated one from the other, were not individually processed by his mind. All of her was swept up and swallowed by his racing brain. There, the essence of her was digested, identified in a synaptic second and spit back out onto the pavement where, unaware that another's spirit had invaded her own, she continued to walk—and he stood in wait.

She came slowly toward him, her shoes scraping against the stone pathway. Each footstep jarred him, as if she were scraping nerves laid bare by intolerable tension.

The pathway from the tunnel led past him, gently arching like a Venetian bridge over a narrow canal through which ran a double line of train tracks. The tracks disappeared into Whitechapel Station, a scant hundred yards distant. The far side of the footbridge led to a school that rose several storeys above the surrounding low-lying sprawl of warehouses and other mercantile buildings.

The prostitute passed within a foot of him. He waited a second to make certain no one appeared behind her in the tunnelway, then stepped out onto the path. His rubber-soled shoes made no sound. His black suit and cape made him indistinguishable from the dark fabric of the night. Only his face betrayed him as something separate, something human. Yet his face was also of the night, like moonlight on an object in deep shadow, for it was all but hidden by a soft felt hat pulled low over his brow, the brim level with his eyes.

The knife was concealed in a newspaper hidden beneath his cape. It was a unique weapon, the blade eight inches in length and very narrow, tapering like an elegant Italian stiletto to a needlelike point. Its double-edged steel was honed to razor sharpness.

He was but a single step behind her, could reach out and strike and she would be dead before her body hit the pavement. The thought almost triggered the action, but he stopped himself. He felt a savage sense of glee, yet also of pure hatred, rise in his blood; a coalescent omnipotence almost robbed him of breath, so powerful was its onslaught —as if a powerful fist swathed in cushioning bandages had landed, THUD, on his chest, causing him to reel not in pain, not in gasping discomfort at the expulsion of air from lungs, but from the stunning shock that he could kill. Kill not just out of hatred or revenge but also for *pleasure*.

He let her cross the footbridge, measuring her progress by the slow but steady scrape of her shoes. At the instant he determined she was on the other side, he started after her. He stole across the bridge and there she was, not 30 feet in front of him, bell-shaped in her petticoats and skirt, a sideways lurch to her gait as she shifted her weight from one foot to the other.

His lips pulled back in an involuntary snarl—he was amazed at its ferocity. For an instant it seemed as though another being, crazed and enraged, inhabited his body. He wanted to protest, but then the knife appeared in his hand. And it felt *good*. Suddenly, he was running, like an animal off its leash. As he came at her, her mouth opened in terror, but he brought the knife to her throat and the scream drowned in a bloody froth. He held her upright as in a tight embrace, keeping his hand against her throat, feeling the spurting blood. Suddenly, the pumping action faltered, weakening in the same instant to a barely perceptible trickle. He was forced to his knees by the momentum of her collapsing body. He knelt beside her, the knife still clutched in his hands, overcome with such hatred and with such ecstasy that he thought he might faint.

[2]

CHARLOTTE CARLYLE SAT in composed yet ill-concealed indignation. A bird of paradise was fastened to her Persian lamb hat. Its tiny black eyes glimmered darkly as if it, too, had suffered insult. Beside her, sharing the same enclosed landau seat, were her father and mother, Sir William and Lady Lillian Carlyle. Opposite sat the object of her displeasure, her younger sister Lydia. On either side of Lydia were two gentlemen, impeccably attired in light topcoats, beneath which could be seen the black facings of tuxedos and the starched white of dress shirts. Aubrey Carsonby and Charles Randall, the latter more formally Lord Longerdale, befitting his hereditary title, Earl of Longerdale, had been the Carlyle sisters' escorts for an evening at the theatre. Upon leaving the St. James's Theatre, Lydia, flashing an ingenuous smile in Charlotte's direction, had adroitly gained the seat between the two men.

With a start, the carriage pulled away from the crowded curbside. The St. James's lay outside the heart of the West End theatre district, yet the late-night, horse-drawn traffic was no less congested. For a moment, the only sound was the rhythmic clip-clop of the two dapple greys harnessed to the landau. But the carriage was soon impeded, then momentarily halted, as it attempted to enter St. James's Street, the location of several of London's most frequented gentlemen's clubs. Without warning, the landau started up again, causing the passengers to lurch forward or backward or sometimes, as the driver jockeyed for position, sideward into forced intimacy.

The two younger couples were a foursome held together by various emotional and romantic entanglements. Aubrey Carsonby was infatuated with Charlotte Carlyle, although his feelings were unrequited. Both sisters were very much taken by Charles Randall. He was by far the more handsome of the two, with dark, tousled hair, dark skin and distinguished features to Aubrey's sandy, receding hairline, fair complexion and nondescript countenance. As well, he possessed a superior title, as Aubrey was merely an heir to a baronetcy. Charles Randall was certainly the more prized catch, but to all outward appearances, he offered no sign of preference for either Charlotte or Lydia. Both were treated with the same gentlemanly consideration. Charlotte, however, examined every gesture and nuance of speech, determined to decipher his true feeling, which, she had convinced herself, was a deep, if hitherto well-hidden, attraction to her.

Lydia's thoughts were also focused on Charles, although, unlike Charlotte's, hers were frankly sexual. As the carriage jostled over pavement and cobblestone, gently throwing their bodies together, she could sense his virility even through the layers of clothing. She wondered what he would feel like naked in bed but felt herself blush at the thought. *Damn, this will not do*, she thought in self-admonishment. What would he think were he to notice her flushed cheeks?

Lady Carlyle broke the silence as the landau fought its way through the thronging traffic. She, like Charlotte, was seething with indignation, although for a very different reason: "I can contain myself no longer," she said at last. "I found the play deplorable." She was referring to *The Dean's Daughter*, a play about a venal clergyman and his attempts to corrupt his daughter that was enjoying a profitable, if controversial, run at the St. James's. It was staged by Rutland Barrington, better known to London theatregoers as one of the producers of the immensely popular Gilbert and Sullivan operettas.

"How so, Mother?" Lydia asked.

"How so? Isn't it obvious?" Lady Carlyle was only 43, but she spoke with the acerbic tongue of a much older woman. Her conversation was laced with platitudes and aphorisms, a habit she had acquired from her sermonizing father, an Anglican clergyman. "To select a dean of the Church of England as a type that is mean-spirited and contemptible—to choose such a dignitary to illustrate self-ishness and hypocrisy as well and to pass it off as serious drama is . . ." She paused in search of an emotive phrase ". . . is as utterly untrue to life as it is wholly false to art!" She abruptly sat back as if startled at her own felicitous conclusion.

Out of the darkness, Aubrey spoke. "I take your point, Lady Carlyle, and may I say it's well made. Mr. Barrington no doubt belongs to the new school of theatre. He's all for progressive liberalism in art . . ."

"He's said as much himself. Oh, do forgive me, Aubrey, I interrupt," Lydia said. "But I read a recent interview he gave in the *Pall Mall Gazette*. He voiced his hatred of convention and his opposition to 'dramatic dogma.' I believe that was his phrase."

"Lydia! I'm surprised at you," her mother snapped. The aigrette of black ostrich feathers on her hat seemed to bristle as she moved her head from side to side. "Let us not confuse dogma, dramatic or otherwise, with what amounts to character assassination of the vilest kind. Why, take Gilbert and Sullivan, for instance. They mean to deal in extravagance and do so. They make us laugh at our silly affectations—and that is all well and good. But Mr. Barrington is wholly false to common experience in his selection of the soberest clergyman as an example of moral turpitude."

"Mr. Barrington did not *write* the play, Mother, he produced it," Lydia said peevishly.

"And is therefore even more accountable," Lillian Carlyle rebutted. "Without his support, it would never have reared its ugly head."

Charles spoke for the first time. "What you are suggesting, Lady Carlyle, if I may make this presumption, is that the stage cannot make the exception . . . the rule."

"My very point," she agreed. "It won't do. There are exceptions to every rule, of course, but the accepted rule is that the clergyman is a man of upright character. In a comic play such as *The Pirates of Penzance* or *The Mikado*, we laugh when a man of accomplishment befuddles himself with drink and mistreats his children, but in the finale, we see him in a redeeming light. He has human weaknesses as do we all. But when a dean is put on public display as the mean-spirited villain of a *serious* play . . . well, well . . . enough said. Let us move on to more appealing prospects. The new Gilbert and Sullivan opens this week. What is it called?"

"*Yeomen of the Guard*, I believe," Aubrey answered. "They were going to call it *The Beefeaters* but were afraid that when it opened in New York, the Americans might think it was a musical about beef-eating soldiers or some such nonsense," he said drolly.

"Well, whatever it's called, I'm sure it will be a delight, and Mr. Barrington will be back where he belongs."

"I cannot help but agree, Mama," said Charlotte, less because she agreed with her mother (although, as in almost everything, she did wholeheartedly) than because she did not want Lydia to jump in and monopolize the conversation.

"It is my prejudice," Lady Carlyle continued, "if such can be described as prejudice, that audiences go to the theatre for pleasure, not for unpleasant surprises."

But Lydia interjected forcefully. "That's so much nonsense, Mother. I, for one, admire Mr. Barrington's artistic courage. At least he's thrown off the fetters of convention. He could have gone on with his Gilbertian comedies and amassed a fortune. Instead, he's ventured into new territory. And aren't we encouraged by our mentors—"

"You mean our *parents*, Lydia," Charles said warningly. He had learned that Lydia and her mother rarely agreed on anything of consequence. Increasingly, their antagonism threatened to erupt into open confrontation.

But Lydia ignored him. "—to believe that a spade ought to be called a spade?" she asked determinedly.

Aubrey spoke, also in an attempt to lighten the mood. "The only spades I ever see are the wrong ones—when they are trump, and I don't have a single one in my hand."

William Carlyle stirred as if from a deep sleep. He was a stout man of average height. Beneath his top hat, his bearded face was both wizened and congenial. A lawyer by training, he had recently been appointed to the Queen's Bench as a High Court Judge. He was sparing in conversation, generally speaking only to make a point. "Well put, Aubrey," he said, stamping his brass-knobbed cane for emphasis. "The first sensible thing anyone has said all evening."

But his wife could not ignore the gauntlet thrown by her younger daughter. "I think you mistake your spades for something less admirable than forthrightness, Lydia," she said.

"And what might *that* be, Mother?" Lydia asked sarcastically.

Lillian Carlyle flinched at her daughter's tone. "For one thing, ill manners," she said, biting off every word. "For another . . . *intolerable* impertinence."

The spitefulness in her voice startled everyone in the carriage, including Lillian Carlyle herself. Every instinct, every social tenet she had been taught, rebelled at the very notion of creating an awkward situation. Yet she had done just that. *I must do something or this will become a permanent embarrassment,* she thought with some desperation. But beyond that realization, her mind refused to proceed. It was paralyzed by a single resolution: *Lydia will be punished for this.*

Charles Randall took the situation in at a glance. He hesitated for a second, then spoke. "Lady Carlyle, I must beg your indulgence," he said. "Your invitation mentioned a late supper, but I regret that I cannot join you. An elderly uncle, somewhat frail in health and forgetful, telegraphed that he was arriving in London this very night." He pulled a telegram out of an inner pocket on which could be seen, but not read, a message printed in large block letters. Beside him, Lydia could see only four letters, CONC, before Charles folded the telegram and tucked it away.

"I meant to tell you when we met at the theatre, but like Uncle," Charles's hands opened in a hapless gesture, "I forgot," he said with an apologetic smile. He leaned forward and looked out the carriage window. "We are still on St. James's, almost at Pall Mall. Uncle's club is the Athenaeum. Would it be an imposition to let me out here?"

William Carlyle was finally stirred into action. "Of course not, Charles," he said. "But the Athenaeum is quite a bit farther on. We can drive you there."

"That's very kind but unnecessary, Sir William. The walk will do me good."

Lord Carlyle nodded in acquiescence and pulled a cord that rang a bell beside the coachman. The landau immediately slowed, then came to a halt.

"Aubrey, I'd consider it a great favour if you'd help me entertain Uncle. He's not one for conversation—he's deaf as a post, uses one of those old-fashioned ear horns. He loves to play cards, though. I know he would appreciate a third hand."

Aubrey accepted the invitation with alacrity. "I would be delighted, Charles—that is if . . . if Lady Carlyle will excuse my absence, of course," he said, somewhat awkwardly. "On the other hand, I would naturally be delighted to join you at supper, Lady Carlyle—"

"Don't be silly, Aubrey," she said quickly. "Charles's uncle is far more important than our supper." She managed a brittle smile. "We must cater to our elders at every opportunity," she said, glancing meaningfully at Lydia. "Filial responsibility cannot be placed on too high a pedestal. Please pay our respects to your uncle, Lord Longerdale," she finished brightly.

Charles stepped out of the carriage, followed by Aubrey.

"Goodnight, Sir William, Lady Carlyle. Goodnight Charlotte, Lydia," Aubrey said, as if the evening had been a complete success. From within the carriage, in succession, came a chorus of "goodnights." Charlotte's was last, and it was impossible not to detect tears in her quavering voice.

Charles and Aubrey stood and watched as the Carlyles' landau turned into Marlborough Road, between the solid white-grey mass of Marlborough House, the Prince of Wales' London residence, and the blackened battlements of Henry VIII's St. James's Palace. The gaslit clock in the palace's central turret revealed the hour as approaching eleven.

"How do you account for it, Charles?"

"Account for what, Aubrey?"

"Why, Lydia of course! You're a physician, an alienist, or whatever new-fangled name you fellows go by these days. How do you explain her behaviour? Never have I been witness to such a scene, and I pray I never shall again. I have sisters, as you well know, four of them." He held up a hand, fingers spread wide, thumb tucked at the palm. "I know all about high-strung young women—what do they call it, neurasthenia?"

"Why, Aubrey, I am impressed. Have you decided to read medicine?"

"Of course not. But I'll admit to having read some Maudsley."

Charles smiled to himself. Aubrey read voraciously and possessed a retentive memory. Together with an inquisitive talent for unearthing the obscure, he was known as something of an intellectual dilettante. Henry Maudsley was reputedly England's foremost specialist on disorders of the mind. Charles thought him hopelessly out-of-date. "Maudsley is to mental illness what cave drawings are to you and me," he said.

"That may well be, but how do *you* account for Lydia? I thought Lady Carlyle might faint."

"I doubt that. Lillian Carlyle has fortitude to spare. It would take more than a display of youthful impertinence to ruin her composure."

"I thought Lydia crossed the threshold of mere impertinence," Aubrey said reflectively. "I found her outburst—"

"You mean her mother's outburst," Charles interrupted.

"That was in response to Lydia's demeaning tone."

But Charles again took exception. "She's strong-willed."

"You mean willful," Aubrey insisted.

Charles shrugged. He was wearying of his companion's sanctimonious censorship. Although Aubrey tended to see their relationship in a more intimate light, Charles regarded him as no more than an amiable acquaintance. They had met at Eton, then attended Christ Church, Oxford, together. Charles had pursued a degree in medicine; Aubrey had joined the Home Office as a civil servant. Their paths had crossed again only this summer, when Charles had suddenly entered the Carlyles' social circle.

"Lydia might well be willful," Charles agreed, "but she comes by it honestly. She inherited that trait from her mother." He paused to light a thin cheroot. "All fledglings must leave the nest. That's natural. But they're driven not so much by rudeness as by instinct. Lydia obeys that instinct, a need to test her own authority. She doesn't think; she reacts. Her age—and I will concede this point—and her nature compel her to do so."

"Charles! Frankly, you amaze me. Does this 'instinct' of which you speak leave no room for propriety? You seem to condone, even proselytise, the law of the jungle."

Charles smiled. "Proselytise? Hardly. But human nature and the law of the jungle are not always at odds. They're not interchangeable, but they do, on occasion, overlap. Now look, enough of this debate, I must be off. I can't keep Uncle waiting."

"But am I not coming? As the third hand?"

"That was only a subterfuge. Necessary in the circumstances, you understand. Actually, Uncle can't abide cards. Finds them a dreadful bore since he stopped gambling, and that was half a century ago."

Aubrey looked crestfallen. "Shall I walk with you anyway? I don't feel like turning in quite yet. The night is still young. And I'm famished. I thought we'd be sitting down to a champagne supper just about now," he said wistfully.

"That's very kind of you, but I'd like to prepare myself for

Uncle. As I've said, he's deaf—but worse, he's a bit dotty, something of a recluse and an eccentric. I have to prepare myself for our infrequent encounters. Why not have a bite to eat at Overton's?''

"I eat there all the time," Aubrey said with rare truculence. "I swear that if I eat another oyster or crab I shall take on the appearance of a crustacean, complete with hard shell and nasty claws.''

"I doubt it, Aubrey. You can't swim, as I recall.''

"Then I'll drown.''

"That's precisely what you're doing, in a sea of self-pity," Charles remonstrated. "If not Overton's, then have Toby fetch you a meat pie—''

"I detest meat pies.''

"Then chops or mutton or . . . a breast of pheasant, for heaven's sake," Charles said impatiently. "Listen, I really must be off.''

"Truthfully, do you have an uncle waiting at the Athenaeum?" Aubrey asked suddenly.

Charles stopped in midstep. "Why, Aubrey . . . how *impolitic*. If a gentleman says his uncle awaits him at the Athenaeum, then that is where his uncle is to be found.''

Although this chastisement was delivered half in jest, Aubrey felt upbraided. "Of course, you're absolutely right," he stammered. "I forgot myself. I do apologize. That episode with Lydia seems to have unnerved me." He extended a hand. "I am sorry," he said formally.

"Think nothing of it," Charles said tolerantly. "Now run along. Put something substantial in your stomach—roast beef and Yorkshire pudding, something hearty. That'll set you right. And don't waste thought on Lydia. She'll come around," he said. With those parting words, he threw his half-smoked cigar to the ground, turned on his heel and headed east along Pall Mall, in the direction of the Athenaeum.

In the carriage on the way to the Carlyle town house in Belgravia, not a word was exchanged. Lydia felt as though she were in the prisoner's dock at the Old Bailey. Opposite

sat a jury of three, those supposedly dearest to her. Yet their
collective silence loudly proclaimed a unanimous verdict of
unmitigated guilt. *Why am I made to bear the blame?* Lydia
asked introspectively. *Because it has always been this way,*
an inner voice calmly answered. The reply, although spoken
without sympathy, was accurate. Lydia knew anything said
in self-defence would only invite further invective from her
mother.

   Her father stared out the window in deep preoccupation.
That would be her lasting impression of him—a man more at
home in his thoughts than in the real world. Charlotte stared
at the floor in apparent disbelief, as if unable to comprehend
the evening's abrupt end. Paradoxically, her mother appeared the least perturbed. As the carriage passed through
lamplight, her eyes glittered like polished gemstones, reminding Lydia of the marble busts of Roman matrons on
display at the British Museum. Her mother could have been
the wife of a Caesar—haughty, oppressive, uncompromising.
But I have escaped your tyranny, Lydia thought in silence. *I
don't know how, but I have—and for that blessing alone, I
am thankful.*

Charles Randall did not have an uncle waiting for him at the
Athenaeum. In fact, he had no uncles anywhere. His father
had been an only child and, to the best of his knowledge, so
had his mother, although there had been no certainty about
that: his mother's past had been shrouded in secretive
whispers. He had only known that he had had a twin brother.
Charles had lived; his brother had been stillborn. In a
macabre ceremony, at his mother's insistence, his father had
forced the village cleric to baptize the dead infant before the
tiny casket had been sealed and buried in the family plot. His
brother's name had been Jonathan—*God Gives,* in Hebrew.
He had never known if his mother had intended the cruel
irony.

   Charles had not connected his father with his own birth.
Later, when he had come to understand the ways of
procreation, the idea of his father and mother engaging in
sexual intercourse had seemed impossible, at least in the

context of his own conception. That feeling had persisted throughout his life, surviving childhood, logic and fact. Simultaneously, he had always believed himself to be his mother's son. His difficulty had been that gestation in her womb marked the beginning of his history, and a gestation period plus a single life had not constituted a family tree, not even a sapling—only a rootlike seedling, which had been torn from some unknown soil and grafted god-like to the venerable Randall bloodline.

Charles continued east on Pall Mall, passing the Athenaeum, traversing Waterloo Place between the Duke of York's column and the brooding monument commemorating the Crimean War dead, until he arrived at Trafalgar Square. He cut diagonally across the square to the Strand, then turned south to the Victoria Embankment along the Thames, the first public thoroughfare in London to be lighted by electric street lamps. He walked along the bright embankment past Somerset House and the Inns of Court to Blackfriar Bridge. There, he hailed a hansom cab, giving the driver an address in Whitechapel, in Aldgate High Street. Fifteen minutes later, he alighted from the cab, tipped the driver generously and entered a two-storey, red brick building. On the upper floor, he pulled a key from his pocket and let himself into the darkened flat.

"You're early," a woman's voice called from a back room.

Charles took off his topcoat and hat and placed them on a cloak stand. "Your good fortune, Colleen," he called back. "Do we have some champagne on ice?"

"Yes . . . in here." The voice was melodious and beckoning.

He entered the bedroom, which was sparsely furnished with a rolltop desk, a mirror-dresser, a four-poster brass bed and a nightstand. She had wanted to decorate the flat so that it would have a homey atmosphere, but he had steadfastly refused to allow anything but the basic amenities. It was his *salon de convenance*, a place to which he could safely bring various mistresses or prostitutes, something he was in the habit of doing. The voice belonged to his most recent "acquisition," a young Irish prostitute named Colleen Murphy.

"You've been sleeping," he said. Only Colleen's head was visible above the covers. Her red hair spilled over the pillow in a satiny stain. She was very comely—lively hazel eyes, high cheekbones, an elfin smile. But her outstanding facial feature, the one that had captivated Charles at the outset, was her lips. Commonly called "bee-stung" or "cupid's bow," they were remarkably full-fleshed and capable of administering the most delicious sensations to all parts of his body.

"In anticipation of the evening," she said teasingly.

"You're the lazy wench, aren't you?"

"You never think so when you climb into bed." She sat up, drawing the sheets across her midriff just below her breasts. She wore a silver chain called a dog collar, a style of jewellery currently popular. Charles had presented it to her as a gift a few days after their first meeting.

Her breasts were milky white; the dark skin of her nipples were like two small, dark saucers. He came to the bed and sat beside her, taking a breast in one hand. It was firm and heavy. With his thumb and forefinger he kneaded the nipple until it was firm, then pinched it. Not too hard, but hard enough to hurt her. Lately, and unaccountably, he had begun to tire of Colleen.

"Ouch!" She slapped his hand. "That hurts, you bastard."

"Does it really?" he responded without much feeling.

"Of course! Would you like me to pinch *your* nipple?"

"Treat yourself." He slipped off his shirt and hung it on the nearest bedpost.

"Be serious," she said, massaging her breast.

"That's not why I come here."

"You're blunt, aren't you?" she replied, her voice still angry.

He shrugged. "Perhaps." He continued to undress, unfastening his cuff links.

"Perhaps nothing."

"You're pouting."

"I am *not*!" she said hotly.

Charles experienced a sudden flare-up of anger. Or was it a rise of tension? Whatever it was, it was an emotional pressure he could not quite understand. Nor did he want to, at this moment. He had come here to relax, to unwind, not to submit himself to self-analysis or to be subjected to Colleen's mercurial temper.

"Shall I continue undressing?" he said, his tone level yet charged with underlying menace.

"If you want to," Colleen said, either missing or mistaking the aggression in his voice.

"Don't be snide," he snapped. "Shall I open the champagne?"

"No, I will," and she swung her legs out of bed. She was completely naked. She reached for a bottle standing in an ice bucket, then took an instrument from the nightstand and expertly loosened the cork. With a hollow pop, it suddenly exploded free, hit the ceiling and caromed off a wall to the floor, where it spun crazily for a moment. She leaned over and licked the froth from the bottle top. Seeing her large, pendulous breasts, he experienced an involuntary tremor of desire.

"Pour some there," he said quietly yet with authority.

She looked at him. "Where?" she said, although she was perfectly aware of his intent.

"Don't play games with me," he said. His anger was building, like a sky filling with dark thunderheads.

"Please . . . not yet. Do at least let's have some champagne."

"I said now!" He grabbed the bottle from her hands and poured some champagne on the dark triangle between her legs.

"Oh my God!" she screamed. "It's *icy*!"

"Then let me warm you." He shoved her back onto the bed, roughly drew up her knees, and put his head between her thighs.

Charles Randall had met Colleen as a result of a conversation he had overheard in White's, one of his clubs. A fellow member had described a delirious night of lovemaking with the only *genuine* nymphomaniac he had ever encountered. This fellow had installed the woman in his own *salon de convenance* and, as a favour, had passed the key around to various friends and acquaintances, among them Charles.

His first night with Colleen had proven memorable. With virtually no introduction, she had undressed him and cleaned his entire body with a damp, warm towel, gently turning him on the bed as a nurse would her patient. She had snuffed out all but a single candle and had begun to kiss, with moist lips, every square inch of his body. She had even sucked his toes. And when she had moved up, brushing her lips in the most fleeting but exquisite contact with his testicles, he had inserted his thumb in her mouth and she had suckled it greedily, like an infant at the breast, all the while tracing trails of fire through his chest hair with her long, sharp nails. Never before had he experienced such arousal. Suddenly she disappeared, and he wondered if she were a Venus-like apparition. But she returned and took his member in her mouth, sliding it in and out in delicious rhythm, her mouth full of warm and molten . . . *honey*. He had come in a violent, shuddering paroxysm that caught her entirely by surprise, so much so that she had fallen naked to the floor, choking.

"You nearly drowned me," she had said from the carpet, coughing and laughing at the same time.

He rolled off the bed and with a savage fury that stunned him, had taken her right there on the floor, driving into her with such ferocity that he had been certain of the punishment he administered. Yet she met him thrust for thrust, pelvis to pelvis, punishment for punishment. This infuriated him, and, to his astonishment—he had never struck a woman before—he slapped her face with an open palm. The blow was neither hard nor vicious, more in the nature of a cuff. But it cut the corner of her mouth, and a trickle of bright red blood dribbled down her chin, which was already coated in honey and semen. She had looked at him in momentary shock, her tongue darting to the blood and licking at it. He stared at her in amazement, for she had then begun to laugh.

He struck at her again, a little harder this time, but she had only laughed louder. And so, to her apparent enjoyment, he had slapped her again. . . .

That was several months ago. Since then, he had removed her from the West End, his fellow club member having tired of her anyway, and installed her in this modest flat in Aldgate High Street, on the fringe of Whitechapel.

They sat up in bed afterwards, sipping on champagne. Charles's mood had lightened, but in the back of his mind, he could still feel the roiling presence of the thunderheads.

"Another prostitute has been murdered," Colleen said, "near the Whitechapel station. They say he mutilated her body. What sort of madman would do that? Isn't it enough that he killed her?"

"He's demented . . . Demented men do things that can't be explained."

"But he can't be just demented. Here, read this." She stepped out of bed and went to the dresser. He watched her with disinterest, even distaste. It seemed impossible that he had just made love to her.

Colleen returned with a newspaper, handed it to him and then lit a gas jet near the bed as he began to read the *Times* article with interest:

Another murder was committed in Whitechapel yesterday morning, by whom and with what motive is at present a complete mystery. At 3:45 a.m., a police constable in Buck's Row came upon the body of a woman lying on a part of the footway. Stooping to lift her, in the belief that she was drunk, he discovered that her throat was cut from ear to ear. She was dead but still warm. He procured assistance and at once sent to the station and for a doctor. Dr. Llewellyn of Whitechapel Road, whose surgery is not 300 yards from the spot where the woman lay, was aroused and went at once to the scene. After examination, he pronounced the woman dead. Besides the gash across the throat, she had suffered terrible wounds in the abdomen.

The police ambulance from the Bethnal-Green Station

arrived, and the body was removed. Further examination showed other fearful cuts and gashes, one alone of which was sufficient to cause death.

After the body was removed to the mortuary, steps were taken to secure identification of the victim. The clothing was of a common description, but the skirt of one petticoat and the band of another article bore the stencil stamp of Lambeth Workhouse. The police concluded the murdered woman was an inhabitant of one of the neighbourhood's numerous lodging houses. Officers were despatched to have the matron of the workhouse view the body. However, she could not identify it and said that the clothing might have been issued any time during the past two or three years. At length, it was found that a woman answering the description of the murdered woman had resided in a common lodging house, 18 Thrawl Street, Spitalfields. Women from that dwelling were fetched, and they identified the deceased only as "Polly." She shared a room with three other women in the place on the usual terms of such houses—nightly payment of fourpence each, each woman sharing a bed with one other. The deceased had led the life of an "unfortunate," lodging in the house only for the past three weeks.

However, at 7:30 p.m. last evening, a woman who is presently an inmate of Lambeth Workhouse was taken to the mortuary and she identified the body as that of Mary Ann Nichols, also known as "Polly" Nichols.

Thursday night, she was turned away by the lodging's keeper because she did not have her nightly rent. She was then the worse for drink, but not drunk, and turned away laughing, "I'll soon get me doss money; see what a jolly bonnet I've got now." She was wearing a bonnet that she had not been seen with before. A woman of the neighborhood saw her as late as 2:30 a.m., in Whitechapel Road opposite St. Mary's Church at the corner of Osborne Street. A little over an hour later she was found murdered within 500 yards of the spot. As to getting a clue to her murderer, the police so far express little hope.

Charles put the newspaper down. "The police are incompetent," was his only comment. "I'm hungry," he said. "Is there some cold chicken in the larder?''

"That's all you have to say!" Colleen exclaimed. "How can you eat after having read such an account? How can you even think of food?''

"Very easily—I'm hungry," he said. "Reading newspapers doesn't satisfy one's appetite.''

"You're cold-blooded, aren't you.''

"Colleen, do we have cold chicken or not?''

She shook her head. "I ate it.''

He looked at her in some disgust. "Before or *after* reading the newspaper?'' he said. He was rapidly, very rapidly tiring of Colleen Murphy. And on the spot, he made up his mind to do something about it. He got out of bed and began to dress.

"You're off?'' she asked in surprise. This *was* unusual. Generally, he spent the night with her. But his moodiness had been pronounced lately. Perhaps it was best he did leave early. She was about to say something uppity like "good riddance," but immediately quelled that urge. Charles (she did not even know his last name) might be turning into a proper bastard, but he still represented food in her stomach and a roof over her head, the two essentials in her life. "But you've only just got here.'' She smiled up at him. "We haven't begun to have fun.''

He did not answer her. As quickly as he could, he pulled on his trousers, shirt and shoes. He did not bother to fix his tie.

"You're angry with me," she said placatingly.

Still he ignored her.

"What have I done?'' she asked imploringly. Suddenly, she was afraid of losing him—or rather, of losing this flat, losing the money he provided for food and clothing, losing his presents, although lately, there had been none. "Was it what I said about the newspaper? Because I ate the chicken? For Christ's sake, talk to me!'' she suddenly shouted.

He turned on her. "Don't raise your voice with me, you . . . you . . .''

"Whore?'' she finished for him. "How dare you think of me as a common whore!''

"Because that's what you are," he said. She leapt from the bed and came at him. He caught her by the wrist and ripped the necklace from her throat, sending it flying into a corner.

"You fucking bastard!" she cried. She tried to strike him with her other hand, but he caught that wrist too. She brought her knee up into his groin and he doubled over in pain, letting go her hands. "You *bastard!*" she half sobbed, half screamed as she struck the side of his head.

"You goddamn whore!" he yelled at her. With a sudden backhand, he struck her with such force that she fell to the bed, then slid to the floor. She sat there in a tangle of limbs, sobbing, her hair draping her face. "By tomorrow morning, I want you out of here," he said, breathing hard and trying to regain a measure of composure. "The landlord will report to me." He reached into the same jacket from which, not more than an hour ago, he had pulled the telegram in the Carlyles' landau. He drew out a ten-pound note and threw it in her direction. "Don't drink it all," he said. He reached over to the necklace and scooped it up, then opened the door and walked out of Colleen Murphy's life.

Forty minutes later, Charles let himself into his town house in Cheyne Walk beside the Thames in Chelsea. He changed from his evening clothes to a blue silk dressing gown, then unlocked the upper doors to his carved walnut cabinet. Inside was his pharmacopoeia: phials, jars, and bottles containing his drugs and medicines. He selected two solid white jars, identical save for the handwritten labels, and poured a measure from each into a tooth glass. One contained chloral hydrate, a sleeping sedative, the other laudanum, an opium-based drug. He stepped into his study and sat down in a high-backed wing chair, waiting for the medication to take effect. In the meantime, he studied a painting on the wall opposite him, a portrait of a strikingly beautiful woman. His eyes remained on her for several moments, as if willing her to speak.

⟶⟨ 3 ⟩⟵

IN THE CARLYLES' Cadogan Square home, Lydia awoke with a start from a restless night. Before she had fallen asleep, she had relived the confrontation with her mother several times but had inevitably ended up focused on thoughts of Charles Randall. She had been unable to drive from her mind the recollection of the smouldering sensuality she had felt sitting next to him in the carriage. Soon after they had arrived home, she had spirited a dictionary from her father's study to her bedroom and had searched for words beginning with CONC. She had found dozens, starting with *concatenate* and ending with *concussion*, the only word with a medical connotation. The definition of one word, *concupiscence*, "an unusual sexual longing," had perfectly described her feelings. She had snapped the dictionary shut and a few moments later, finally fallen asleep.

Lydia rose from her bed and without fuss tied her dark hair in a bun and put on her riding costume. After a brief inspection in the mirror—she looked a little pale, otherwise no one would guess at her night of perturbation—she went downstairs. Taking two russet apples from the fruit tray and nibbling on one, she walked outside to the stable yard. Her town horse, Maude, looked majestic in the early morning light, her brushed coat glowing like amber silk. "Good morning, Maude," Lydia said, feeding her an apple. "You look magnificent." She looked at the stablehand holding the horse's reins. "Doesn't she, Darcy?"

"Yes ma'am," the man replied tonelessly.

Maude, a large horse at 15 hands, began pawing at the straw-strewn yard. "Impatient are you, beauty?" Lydia said. "Well, so am I." She placed a foot in a stirrup and with a boost from the stablehand, vaulted into the saddle. "Let's go, girl," she said, and with a clatter of hooves, they bolted out onto the street.

Lydia guided her horse north up Sloane Street to Knightsbridge and entered Hyde Park at the Albert Gate. She then crossed Carriage Road directly to Rotten Row. Morning mist still covered the grassy expanse of the park. Lydia turned her head in the direction of Hyde Park Corner but was unable to make out the pristine white splendour of Apsley House or the columned, triple gateway known as the Screen Entrance which lay in that direction. She could barely see the tree line on the far side of the Serpentine, the narrow reach of pond water that separated Hyde Park from Kensington Gardens. The clover-scented air was chill, almost invigoratingly so. She could feel it reddening her cheeks.

Rotten Row was a broad, meticulously groomed mile-and-a-half-long bridle path of red, cinderlike sand. It ran east-west and was the most prestigious riding trail in all of London. There were socially correct hours to promenade on the Row, for like any other gathering of the wealthy and elite, there were unwritten but scrupulously obeyed laws of etiquette. The "correct" hours varied from year to year; sometimes from season to season, although mid-morning and late afternoon between tea and dinner generally held sway. At such times, there could easily be a thousand horses and riders, together with hundreds of equipages and carriages, from smaller two-seat chaises, victorias and phaetons to larger landaus and broughams, all of them forming a traffic tie-up worthy of Piccadilly Circus. Lydia disdained these crowds. Her mother and sister, on the other hand, revelled in the lordly atmosphere, in season rarely missing a day's attendance in the park.

But with the arrival of August, the London season had ended. The Queen and her retinue had made their annual pilgrimage to Osborne Castle and the Cowes Regatta on the Isle of Wight, thence on to Balmoral Castle in Scotland. Parliament had adjourned until late October or early November, and what was left of the rest of society had repaired to its luxurious country estates, there to recuperate from an exhausting in-season social calendar. The Carlyles had not followed suit because Sir William was serving on the judicial committee investigating the Charles Parnell affair. Parnell, a Member of Parliament and leader of the Irish nationalist movement, had been accused of seditious activities, but much of the evidence had apparently been in the form of letters forged with his signature. The inquiry, which had not yet commenced hearings, was expected to last several weeks and as a result, Lady Carlyle had decided to remain in London with her husband.

Thus, on this mist-filled morning, Lydia found Rotten Row all but empty of riders and horses. With a sense of relish, she set off in the direction of Kensington Gardens, settling Maude into a brisk canter. Out of the mist, two officers of the Royal Horse Guards, clad in scarlet tunics and white breeches, galloped past on black horses, their bridles and halter chains shining and jingling cheerfully. They were gone almost before they could turn their heads to glance appreciatively at the young woman on the large, tawny gold horse. Lydia paid them no heed. Her mind, of its own volition, had turned to thoughts of Charles Randall and men in general.

Lydia had never lacked for suitors. Her standing in society and the aggressive socializing of her mother had ensured a steady stream of potential husbands. But none of them had interested her in the slightest; for the most part, they seemed shallow and affected. Then, three months ago, Charles had appeared in her life, and her interest in men had quickened. Since then, she had attempted to understand the nature of that interest. *Why Charles?* she wondered. *Why not another man? Why not Aubrey?* The answer to the latter was glaringly obvious. She felt no physical attraction to Aubrey. *But I am*

physically attracted to Charles. Why am I so obtuse? she
thought to herself. *The answer stares me in the face and I
ignore it.*

Lydia's mind drifted to her sister, to the differences
between the two of them. She, unlike Charlotte, had been an
inward-looking child, reading at a precociously early age.
She wondered now if this intellectual development had been
in reaction to her sister's admitted loathing of anything more
weighty than romances and, as well, to the unspoken yet
unmistakable comparison, in their childhood, of her plain-
ness with Charlotte's loveliness. Charlotte had always been a
honey blonde with grey eyes and a becoming
vulnerability—a typical English rose. Lydia, on the other
hand, had blossomed late. As a consequence, they had been
forced to nurture different gifts and talents: Charlotte, her
looks and future as mistress of a large household; Lydia,
her intellect and . . . and what? She could not envision her
future as conventional, for she knew she would languish in a
sterile marriage. Many women made accommodation with
such a fate by taking a lover. *Why shouldn't I?* thought
Lydia. But adultery involved a complicated life full of
deception and risk. *Surely I can find a man with whom I can
go to bed and, in or out of bed, discuss George Eliot or Jane
Austen?* So immersed was she in her thoughts that the
approach of a rider from behind went unnoticed. It seemed
he would rein abreast of her, for he slowed as he approached.
But at the last moment, he fell into step behind Maude.
There he stayed, with Lydia oblivious to his presence.

A row of trees appeared on the horizon as a charcoal
smudge, marking the western extremity of Rotten Row.
Suddenly, the rider darted out from behind Lydia and
dashed past. Maude immediately broke stride, pulling to the
right and rearing up, almost throwing Lydia from the saddle.
Out of the corner of her eye, as she fought to stay seated, she
saw the rider disappearing into the mist. "Rude fool!" she
shouted, pulling on the reins. "There, girl, there . . .
steady, steady . . . that's it . . . whoa . . . whoa . . ."

When Maude had settled, Lydia gave her free rein, and
the horse surged forward in pursuit of the rider who had
nearly unseated her mistress. Lydia leaned forward in the

spirit of the chase. "Let's find out who he is, Maude!" she cried aloud. In less than a minute, the wall of trees gained in substance. She was almost at the end of the cinder-red trail. Exit from the park could be made through the Alexandra Gate, almost opposite the Royal Albert Hall.

She saw the rider in the distance look over his shoulder to watch her approach. In that same instant, he whipped his horse and disappeared through dense shrubbery toward the park exit. Lydia rarely used her riding crop on Maude, but in the heat of the moment, she felt no such compunction. Jockey-like, she reached behind, giving the horse three good whacks. Maude responded smartly, increasing her pace.

At the end of the riding trail, they raced onto the north-south carriageway that marked the park boundary with Kensington Gardens. Hardly slowing, Lydia turned her horse south in a dash toward the Alexandra Gate. Wary of the sudden two-way traffic on Carriage Road, she had to slow Maude. As Lydia drew even with the Albert Memorial, she saw the rider turn off Carriage Road, dash out of the park and disappear into a rise of tall buildings. Maude began to falter, and Lydia gently reined her in. Further chase was pointless. Kensington, the neighbourhood into which the rider had vanished, was a labyrinth of narrow streets and alleyways.

The sun had begun to burn through the morning mist. Here and there, patches of blue showed overhead. Morning traffic had increased. Two yellow and green omnibuses, one heading west toward Hammersmith, the other east in the direction of Knightsbridge, passed each other, their upper decks already crowded. The eastbound bus was an older knifeboard model, with upper-deck passengers seated back to back in two rows. The outer row of passengers turned in unison to stare at Lydia.

Preoccupied with the identity and motives of the mystery rider, she turned Maude in the direction of Belgravia and started home at a leisurely pace.

Three miles east, in his rooms in Blue Ball Yard just off St. James's Street, Aubrey had also risen early, as was his habit. The Carsonby family maintained a residence in Mayfair, but it was a family tradition to close the town house for the months of August and September and take an extended holiday at their country home near Lyme Regis in Dorset. Aubrey, when he had not been able to join them in previous years, had moved into one of his clubs, either Boodle's or White's. But he had tired of the cramped accommodations and had taken rooms in an enlarged Elizabethan cottage in Blue Ball Yard, a cobblestone courtyard of private dining clubs and other apartments. He had a vestibule, a study-library, a sitting room and a commodious bedroom. There was also a smaller bedroom, accessible by a private servant's staircase for his manservant, Toby.

He liked his apartment not only because it offered more spacious living quarters—he could even have a few friends for dinner, Toby merely having to fetch the food from one of the dining clubs at ground level—but because it conferred a sense of independence from his family. Aubrey was past 30, and although very social, had come to value the privacy of his own rooms.

His study was finished with what his mother called a "cluttered bric-a-brac charm." The furnishings included a satinwood cabinet inlaid with Wedgwood plaques, an ottoman, a Hepplewhite chair, a well-stocked bookcase and an escritoire. Over the desk hung his favourite painting, a lush landscape by Alexander Cozen.

This morning, after having been shaved and barbered by Toby and after a substantial helping of poached eggs and kippers, he departed for work in the direction of St. James's Park.

A serious matter was brewing in the Home Office. The Home Secretary, The Honourable Henry Matthews, had received a letter of resignation from James Monro, head of the Criminal Investigation Division (CID) of Scotland Yard, for which the Home Office bore jurisdictional responsibility. This resignation could not have come at a more inopportune time; Scotland Yard and the CID were under increased attack from Fleet Street and the London populace, and particularly from indigents of the East End led by their outspoken Jewish Member of Parliament, Samuel Montagu. The criticism was generated by the perceived inefficiency of Scotland Yard for its failure to capture the man who had become known as the Whitechapel murderer.

The public did not know that Monro's resignation was only the leading edge of a tense situation. Increasing alienation existed between the Home Secretary and Sir Charles Warren, Commissioner of the Metropolitan Police, under whose command Scotland Yard fell. Furthermore, and something potentially more disastrous, there had been another, almost unbelievable, development. Monro, having handed in his resignation, had not quietly disappeared; he had only stepped into the background, for unbeknownst to Charles Warren, his former superior, he had continued to report directly to Henry Matthews. In effect, he had become the Home Secretary's personal spy, reporting not only on Warren's operation of the CID but on his larger performance as England's senior police officer.

Such Machiavellian intrigue was hardly unknown in the corridors of Whitehall, but there was an extra dimension to the Matthews-Warren hostility. For all intents and purposes, it had paralyzed the relationship between the CID, the police department responsible for the capture of the Whitechapel murderer and the office of the Commissioner of Police, the executive arm responsible for the operation of the CID.

It was a convoluted state of affairs, yet to Aubrey's mind an exciting one. And in a selfish sense, a rare career opportunity, for Aubrey was responsible for liaison between the Home Secretary and the Commissioner of Police. The situation was explosive; he could very well advance his career if he played his cards right or he could misplay those cards and end up looking the fool and earning a black mark on his record. But Aubrey did not lack self-confidence. In the coming confrontation, Sir Charles Warren was already at a disadvantage. His was a political appointment. Matthews was an elected Member of Parliament and a senior cabinet minister. Warren was at best a senior government appointee. If he slipped up, he would be tossed to the wolves like a chunk of hastily discarded meat. Aubrey had already placed his bets: He was, like James Monro, one of Matthews' men.

In St. James's Park, he crossed the footbridge that

traversed the pond water, smiling at the noisy honking of numerous water birds. An old lady he had seen before was tossing crusts of bread. The birds, black-faced swans with red bills, white-faced swans with orange bills, ducks of a dozen different species and plumage, battled for advantageous position. Often, he would stop and watch the silly antics of the birds, wondering who the old woman was and whence she came. She talked to the waterfowl as if they were old friends. Not for the first time, Aubrey concluded she was mad but harmless and passed her by without a second thought.

Directly ahead lay a quadrangle formed by four large buildings constructed from blocks of portland stone: the Home Office, the Colonial Office, the Foreign Office and the India Office. They possessed a Pharaonic dimension and an aura of permanence that never failed to impress Aubrey. Some men (John Ruskin for one, Bernard Shaw for another) were already prophesying the decline of the British Empire. Aubrey did not believe them for an instant. Ruskin and Shaw were both art critics. How did that qualify them to be prognosticators of approaching doom? The Union Jack, he was convinced, would fly over much of the earth for a millennium—and he would play his part in maintaining that dynastic tradition.

In the stable behind his Cheyne Walk town house, Charles brushed down Gallant, his bay gelding. He left instructions with the stablehand that the horse be watered and fed an extra ration of oats, then walked down a short laneway to the house and entered the kitchen to make himself a pot of tea.

He had risen after a restless night and gone for an early morning ride in Hyde Park. He did not know whether he had actually slept, although he did recall swallowing a potion of chloral hydrate and laudanum after his return from Aldgate High Street. Concern about the fate of Colleen Murphy had not kept him awake. But thoughts about the remarkable Lydia Carlyle had been a different matter. Never had he encountered a more intriguing woman.

Sipping his tea, he relived the morning's events. He had let Gallant have his head on Rotten Row, and they had galloped as though racing in the Derby at Epsom. When the horse had finally winded itself, he had led it at a relaxed trot up to Marble Arch at the Northeast corner of the park, then back to Rotten Row, intending to gallop a final length before heading home. But a moment later he had seen, emerging ghostlike out of the mist, the figure of a woman riding sidesaddle. He had recognized the golden horse and realized its rider was Lydia Carlyle, the veil of her flat-top riding hat floating behind her like a streamer. But rather than greet her, he had slowed Gallant so that the gelding came into step directly behind her, no more than a length from the bobbed tail. For a moment, the two magnificent animals had paraded head to tail like two Lippizaner stallions performing an intricate dressage movement. But then—inexplicably— Charles had suddenly dug his stirrups into Gallant, causing his startled horse to leap forward. They had galloped hard to the end of Rotten Row. He had half turned, seen Lydia in hot pursuit and had quickly exited the park into the close confines of Kensington.

Charles poured himself another cup of tea and began to eat a raisin-and-almond pudding. His behaviour in the park perplexed him. Yet recollection of it gave him a strange sense of pleasure, as if he had carefully planned the incident and had carried it off with particular aplomb. This was patent nonsense, of course. He had no more planned it than he had planned to be in the park in the first instance. Certainly, he had possessed no foreknowledge of Lydia's presence there. Why had he acted so recklessly? Lydia's horse could have thrown and injured her, injured her seriously. But his impulsive behaviour defied self-explanation. An old medical college saying flashed into his mind . . . *Heal thyself, physician*. But he could only make a wry grimace at that stern advisement. Besides, what was there to heal but a mild case of pranksterism? Having thus regained a measure of self-respect, he rose from the kitchen table and went up to his bedroom. He climbed into bed and fell into a deep sleep, keeping to what had become more or less habit in recent weeks: restless, dream-racked nights, followed by a few hours of peaceful sleep in the hours immediately following sunrise.

⊶⊶❪ 4 ❫⊷⊷

LYDIA ARRIVED HOME to find Charlotte in the drawing room
with Donald, the Carlyles' chef. This surprised her on two
counts: firstly, her sister was not an early riser; secondly, and
even more surprising, was the *tableau* presented by Charlotte, sitting at their mother's Queen Anne desk and Donald,
clad in immaculate whites, standing a few feet away, his
hands folded in front of him in exaggerated patience.
Charlotte had taken on their mother's mannerisms and
demeanour—aloofness with a hint of condescension implied
by the regal posture and queenly tilt of her head. How many
times had Lydia happened upon a similar scene? Her
mother, rather than Charlotte, discussing with Donald menu
selections or the freshness of last evening's fish or how the
agricultural depression was driving the price of vegetables to
intolerable levels—''How can one expect to entertain with
any degree of sophistication when the price of Belgian endive
exceeds the cost of the bone china on which it is served?''
Yet her mother treated the chef with a deference never shown
other household staff because he represented something of a
coup. Donald had been a sous-chef at Marlborough House,
residence of the Prince of Wales, and as such, might have
had royal blood running through his veins. Her mother had

not so much hired Donald as acquired him, as one would a valuable *objet d'art*. Were he a painting, she would have hung him in the dining room with the prominence of a Rembrandt or a Gainsborough.

"Good morning, Lydia. How was your ride?" Charlotte inquired cooly but civilly. She had not forgiven her sister's transgression of the night before.

"It was fine," Lydia replied noncommittally.

"I don't know why you ride so early. There is no one to be seen in the park until at least mid-morning. At least not anyone worth knowing."

Lydia looked at her sister with her usual stirrings of affection and simultaneous irritation. "I did see someone," she said.

"Oh," Charlotte replied, not listening. She wore a look that could pass for frown, fret or, in someone more artful, feigned concentration. "Ummm," she intoned in a long syllable of indecision. "I simply don't know. Poached salmon and tomato aspic or poached turbot and asparagus and celery aspic. Donald says we have an excellent Sauternes, a Château d'Yquem I believe, but only a passable Moselle. The difficulty is, I prefer the turbot over the salmon but believe the Moselle to be the superior accompaniment."

"Then have the salmon with the Moselle," Lydia said.

"But the Moselle is inferior to the Sauternes."

Lydia felt a prickle of exasperation. "Then have the turbot."

"Lydia," Charlotte rejoined, her voice edged with her own exasperation, "we had turbot only last Tuesday. Surely you remember, at Lady Ossington's, at the dinner to raise funds for the Girls' Friendly Society. Surely you recall the Earl of Meath's stirring oratory and Sarah Spencer's . . ."

"Then have the salmon!" Lydia interrupted sharply. Charlotte's self-absorbed prattling was getting on her nerves.

But Charlotte was not listening. She continued blithely on: ". . . dress. She caused a sensation, appearing in a gown not only without a bustle but with a décolletage that would have embarrassed someone of the Parisian demimonde. Worth would never have put his name to it. Did you know she claims it was designed in America—in *Boston*? I heard that from Caroline Asquith, who was as shocked as I. Would you acknowledge that a gown you were wearing was designed in Boston? Or was it New York? But what does it matter? I thought the irony *too* sublime: there we all were, gathered to promote the purity of young womanhood, and there was Sarah Spencer's dress, intended to promote heaven only knows what.''

''I thought it a fetching outfit,'' Lydia said. She had admired Sarah Spencer's daring but eye-catching gown. The absence of a bustle suited Lydia fine. They had reached the point of ridiculousness, some of them large enough to support a tea tray.

Charlotte adopted a scolding tone. ''Fetching is too polite a term, Lydia. The dress was decidedly *risqué*, more at home in a boudoir than a drawing room.'' Addressing Donald, she went briskly on. ''I think we will have the salmon with the Sauternes—one cannot risk the success of an entire dinner by gambling on the wine. Thank you, Donald, the rest of the menu will do nicely.'' With a curt nod, the chef was dismissed.

''Who did you see in the park?'' Charlotte asked suddenly.

Lydia was startled. Charlotte had been listening after all. She almost started to recount the episode of the mystery rider but decided otherwise. ''Oh, no one of consequence.''

''But you said you saw—''

''It was just a pair of Horse Guards. I didn't recognize them, but they cut dashing figures.'' The expectant look on Charlotte's face vanished, replaced by one of disinterest. If the cavalry officers had been of distinction, her sister would have recognized them.

''I'm going upstairs to change,'' Lydia said.

''Yes, do that,'' Charlotte replied distractedly, her attention on a piece of notepaper on which she was neatly printing, for her mother's approval, the results of her consultation with Donald.

Aubrey had just arrived at his office when a messenger advised him that he was required at an *ad hoc* meeting scheduled by the Home Secretary. He had 15 minutes to dispose of and, rather than dipping into the mountain of memoranda and correspondence on his desk, he began reading the *Times*, his attention caught by the headline WHITECHAPEL MURDER:

Up to a late hour Sunday evening, the police had obtained no clue as to the perpetrator of the latest murder that has so recently taken place in Whitechapel. On Saturday afternoon, Mr. Wynne Baxter, coroner, opened his inquiry at the Working Lads' Institute, Whitechapel Road, respecting the death of Mary Ann Nichols, also known as Polly Nichols. The jury was sworn in and afterwards viewed the body of the dead woman, which was lying in a shell in the Whitechapel Mortuary.

Dr. Henry Llewellyn stated that at 4 a.m. on Friday morning he was called by Constable John Neil to Buck's Row. On arrival, he found the deceased lying flat on her back on the pathway. The deceased had not been dead more than half an hour. There was very little blood around the neck, and there were no marks of any struggle or of blood as though the body had been dragged. An hour later, he was sent for by the inspector to see the other injuries discovered on the body. Llewellyn went and saw that the abdomen was cut very extensively. There was a bruise running along the lower part of the jaw on the right side of the face that might have been caused by a blow from a fist or pressure from a thumb. There was a circular bruise on the left side of the face that also might have been inflicted by the pressure of the fingers. On the left side of the neck, about one inch below the jaw, there was an incision about four inches in length. That incision completely severed all the tissues down to the vertebrae. The large vessels of the neck on both sides were severed. The incision was about eight inches in length. The cuts were caused by a long-bladed knife, moderately sharp, which was used with great violence. There were no injuries about the body except on the lower part of the abdomen. Two or three inches from the left side was a wound running in a jagged manner. The wounds were very deep and the tissues were cut through. There were several incisions running across the abdomen. There were also three or four similar cuts, running downwards, on the right side, all of which had been caused by a knife which had been used violently. The injuries were from left to right and might have been inflicted by a left-handed person. All the injuries had been caused by the same instrument.

Aubrey quickly cut out the article and scribbled some notes on a pad. He had begun to save clippings about the murders, aware that he would become increasingly involved in the case. Aubrey had always been a collector. He liked to gather information, often obscure or arcane, and file it in one of his carefully indexed scrapbooks. He had started collecting at the age of ten when his father had interested him in postage stamps. Putting his notes and the article in his file titled *Whitechapel Murders*, Aubrey hurried to the office of the Honourable Henry Matthews, Home Secretary.

Three others were present for the meeting: Godfrey Lushington, permanent undersecretary to the Home Secretary; Evelyn Ruggles-Brise, principal private secretary to the Minister, and the Home Secretary himself. Among the four men, Aubrey was the most junior.

Henry Matthews was a small man, inoffensive in appearance: balding and portly, with a round, pink face that seemed to wear an expression of perpetual surprise, as if life consisted only of the unexpected. He rarely made eye contact; his eyes shifted their focus constantly, flickering from window to door to wall and occasionally, although only for an instant, to the face of the speaker. It was a disconcerting habit, one to which Aubrey had not yet become accustomed. Matthews was a lawyer by training, yet Aubrey had never met such an indecisive and ill-disciplined mind, at least not in someone with the responsibility and political power of a senior cabinet minister. Only the year before, his bungling of the celebrated Cass case—the inadvertent arrest of a woman, apparently of respectable standing, on a charge of prostitution—had resulted in a vote of adjournment in the House of Commons. The episode had occurred on Jubilee Night, which commemorated the fiftieth anniversary of the Queen's coronation, and not only had it caused Henry Matthews and the Prime Minister, Lord Salisbury, considerable embarrassment, but, of more import, it had weakened the public image of the Metropolitan Police, whose operation was ultimately under the Home Secretary's jurisdiction.

A subsequent departmental investigation, which had revealed that the arresting constable had had reasonable and probable grounds to make the arrest, had not diminished the damage done to the force's reputation. In his wisdom, Matthews had decided not to release the details of the exonerating evidence, believing it would only inflame an already scandalous situation. That decision had not endeared him to Scotland Yard and its rank-and-file constabulary or to Charles Warren who, as Commissioner of Police, was the most visible target of public scorn and ridicule.

The Minister opened the meeting without looking up from his desk; he seemed to be speaking to his ink blotter or to the letter he held in his hand. "We've all had time to consider a replacement for Monro," he said, glancing up for a brief second. He held the letter up for inspection. Aubrey had seen it before:

Scotland Yard
Criminal Investigation Division

Personal & Confidential

Home Office, Whitehall
Office of the Home Secretary

To The Honourable Sir Henry Matthews

Dear Sir:

I regret that I am no longer able to fulfill my duties and responsibilities as Head of the Criminal Investigation Division, Metropolitan Police. I therefore humbly request that you accept my resignation, tendered herewith.

Your obedient servant,

James Monro
Assistant Commissioner of Police

Beneath the signature block were three sets of initials, two made by Godfrey Lushington, the other belonging to the Minister himself. Beside the *H.M.*, he had angrily scrawled a question in the purple ink he favoured: *Is he serious?* Directly underneath, Lushington had penned the tersest of replies: *Yes*.

The Minister continued, his eyes now fixed on a pair of Purdey duelling pistols mounted on the wall opposite the fireplace. "The Whitechapel murders complicate the significance of his resignation. His sense of timing was . . . *is* awful. Why did he have to resign *now*?" The question was obviously rhetorical because he continued without pause. "Lushington had a go at changing his mind. So did I. But his mind was made up. He was adamant. But we cry over spilt milk. It's done, a *fait accompli*." At this, he dropped the letter, which floated to his blotter like a dead leaf. "We must move on replacing him as best we can. He was, *is*, a good man, you know. Damn his intransigence anyway." The Minister's eyes flickered from the ceiling to contemplation of his steepled fingers.

"What do you think of Anderson?" he asked of no one in particular, referring to Sir Robert Anderson as Monro's possible replacement.

Godfrey Lushington cleared his throat. "I believe he fits the bill, Minister. He has considerable departmental experience . . . and he certainly has tact—"

"You mean he'll get on with Warren," Sir Henry interrupted, sounding doubtful and facetious in the same breath.

"As best he can, sir," Lushington said, echoing the Minister's sentiments with his own. "But there is one problem, Minister . . ."

At the word *problem*, Matthews jerked his head up.

"Nothing serious, Minister," Lushington hastily added. "I have this note from him, sir." He extended a cream-coloured sheet across the desk.

"What does it say?" the Minister said impatiently, waving the letter off as if it were a pesky fly.

"He requests a period of extended leave."

"*Now?*" The Minister was incredulous.

"Yes, sir. He hasn't had his leave this year—"

"He has two months?" Matthews interrupted.

"Yes, Minister."

"Well, he can't have two months. Not now. What about a fortnight?"

"He'd like to travel to Switzerland."

"*Switzerland*. Does he have to go that far? Why not Wales or Scotland? Some place not too far away, so that we can communicate with him easily."

"He always takes at least a month in Lausanne, sir."

There was silence in the room for a minute. Ruggles-Brise spoke for the first time. "As you know, Minister, he replaced Erskine this summer. You may recall that Erskine's doctor diagnosed a case of nervous prostration, which he attributed to overwork. Apparently Anderson is fearful of the same fate, should he take over from Monro immediately."

Matthews pursed his lips and half swivelled his chair so that he could look out the window behind his desk. "I wouldn't mind a holiday in Lausanne myself. Or Bad Ems," he said petulantly. "Assuming we let him go, what then? What do we do with the CID?"

"The press will have a field day, Minister," Aubrey warned.

Matthews turned in his direction with a baleful glare. "The press can be damned for all I care. Besides, does Fleet Street have to be apprised of his leave? This predicament wouldn't even be newsworthy if the *Times* had not reported Monro's resignation. What is happening to the *Times* anyway? I thought one of its aims was to *enlighten* public opinion, not agitate it.

"This," he said, tapping Monro's letter, "puts us in a very awkward position. He resigns the very day that woman is murdered. You saw the headlines: WOMAN MURDERED! CHIEF OF CID RESIGNS! The public immediately connects the two events as though one triggered the other. I thought Monro had more foresight."

This last remark baffled Aubrey. He couldn't help saying, "I don't think he foresaw the murder, sir."

"No, I suspect not," Lushington said in a wry tone.

"Why in damnation can't the police catch the man responsible? As if we don't have enough trouble on our plate already. Look at this." He indicated his desk piled high with papers and file folders. "Haven't we got enough constables? What is the strength of the police force, anyway?" He looked expectantly at Aubrey.

"Fourteen thousand, sir."

"*Fourteen thousand.* My God, that's an entire army. Surely with such manpower we can catch a single miscreant. You read the *Times*. There were policemen all around, watchmen, neighbours, pedestrians, workers. The constable on the beat testified he walked right by the place of the murder minutes before it happened. Where did the killer go? Did he just melt into the darkness? Slink into a hole like a snake? No wonder the press howls like a pack of wolves."

"Well, that's my very point, Minister," Aubrey persisted. "If the CID's new chief goes away on leave, won't they howl even louder?"

"And I repeat, they don't have to know. We will simply keep his appointment a secret—let the press think we're still deliberating over Monro's replacement. The position has become a key one, after all. We can't be expected to rush the decision merely to appease the press."

Aubrey tried another tack. "In the meantime, what do we do about the CID, and the Whitechapel investigation?"

"About the CID, we inform the Senior Inspectors; about the Whitechapel murder, we leave that in the hands of the division detectives—and in the hands of the Commissioner —after all, we can't play detective. This murderer is Warren's responsibility, not ours. Enough said. Inform Anderson his leave is granted."

"The full two months, Minister?" Godfrey Lushington inquired.

"Why not? Lausanne is a long journey, and the Alps are quite stupendous this time of year. Let Anderson have a good restorative leave. He'll come back full of vim and vigour, and by then, the Whitechapel murderer will be tucked safely away inside a prison cell, awaiting his appointment with Her

Majesty's gallows. That will be all.''

Matter-of-factly, the Home Secretary reached for the top file on his desk. Aubrey could see the words SALMON FISHERIES printed in neat block letters.

Charles had narrowed the scope of his medical practice to such an extent that he was as much medical scientist as he was practitioner. He saw patients only on a referral basis. Soon after graduating from the University of Edinburgh with a degree in medicine (after an undergraduate degree at Oxford), he had moved to London and opened an office in Harley Street. This seemed to be a logical step in starting his career—Harley Street was beginning to gain a reputation for housing the finest physicians in all of England. Although he had expected the more established members of this august, fraternal group to look askance at a young doctor, particularly one who was also an earl, he had not expected to be ostracized. Yet that was exactly what had happened.

Harley Street physicians generally catered to the aristocracy and the upper classes. Although this group suffered the same physical ailments as the rest of the population—tumours, ulcers, palsies, gout and kidney stones—Charles knew they liked to think their afflictions were different from those of the lower classes. A lord's kidney stone was not the same as one passed by a Billingsgate fish porter. The peer's stone might be kept as a peculiar yet sentimentally valuable heirloom. Like letters or photographs, it could be handed down from generation to generation, for it offered tangible and anecdotal evidence of an ancestor's existence.

"Do you see this?" a duke had once said to him. "As a medical man, I'm sure you'll appreciate it." He opened a tiny jewellery box to display an object that appeared to be a fine gem. "It's great-great-*great*-grandfather's kidney stone. He passed it in 1741, during the reign of George the Second . . . remarkable, isn't it?" he had said, as if displaying a diamond of rare distinction.

But Charles did not deal in kidney stones or other "organic" diseases. He was an alienist—a physician whose specialty was the treatment of mental disorders. Aberrations of the mental processes had always held a special fascination for him—the result, he believed, of watching, at very close quarters and over what seemed to be an interminable period of time, his father's gradual descent into madness.

The spectre of lunacy terrified Charles's peers, more so than the spectre of cancerous tumors, which, although potentially lethal, had a physical presence that was perversely comforting. The growths could be operated on, could be excised from the body. Even if the patient's prognosis remained hopeless, there remained some consolation in the fact that the ''enemy within'' had at least been attacked, and, to some extent, itself been hurt.

Insanity was far more difficult to deal with. It could not be seen, at least not the physical *being* of the beast. One could see its symptoms readily enough: outlandish behaviour, catatonic states, epileptic fits, drooling mouths, tremors, wild staring eyes. The eyes were worst: they seemed to exist in a state somehow detached or apart from the face in which they were set, as if they had departed and taken up residence in a supernatural world. To become insane was to face a living death. There was no worse fate or stigma. Those afflicted were hidden away in homes and asylums, scarcely to be acknowledged as family members for the rest of their lives. It was rumoured that even Queen Victoria hid such skeletons behind royal closet doors.

Upon arriving at this sad truth about his fellow man, Charles had quietly closed his Harley Street office. He might as well have announced himself a specialist in the treatment of leprosy, for as far as Harley Street was concerned, that was essentially what he had done.

He believed he would enjoy the challenge of research and so had travelled to Paris, where he lived for several months while studying at the famous Salpétrière Institute for the Insane. He also worked with Pierre Janet, who was making a name for himself with his research into the phenomenon of desegregation, Janet's term for the division of human consciousness into more than one personality.

On his return to London, Charles had reopened his practice in his Chelsea town house. A specialist in mental diseases in Chelsea raised an occasional eyebrow, but more generally provoked only mild curiosity. Insanity was acknowledged in a tolerant, almost avuncular manner. It was an acceptable disease, and the afflicted were to be accorded the same degree of sympathy as any sufferer of illness. Charles believed this enlightened attitude stemmed not from a deeper understanding of human nature but from the rather eccentric character of the individuals who lived in Chelsea. The neighbourhood contained some of England's most free-spirited writers and artists. To the inhabitants of Chelsea, the insane were merely extreme manifestations of their own eccentricity and, in effect, formed a microcosm within their neighbourhood, just as Chelsea was seen as a larger microcosm of eccentricity by the greater London populace.

The name of the patient sitting opposite Charles in his Cheyne Walk office was Lucie Rhinegold. She reminded him of his mother. She had the same delicate bone structure, the same pale skin, the same soulful brown eyes and the same mane of lustrous, chestnut-shaded hair. She was in the process of freeing her hair from a circumspect bun. It tumbled to her shoulders in undulating waves, the edges of which caught the sunlight in thin strands like finely spun copper. She smiled at him, revealing teeth as white as porcelain and an intent that was purely wanton. This aura disturbed Charles considerably, as if his mother, and not Mrs. Rhinegold, were attempting to seduce him.

With her fingers, she played at the buttons that fastened the lace top of her dress. "One little piglet," she said in a girlish voice, as a button popped free. "Two little piglets," and the second button came unfastened with an accompanying giggle. Her tongue ran slowly over her lower lip. "You know . . . you are a very attractive man. I'm sure you know that. I'm a very lucky woman to have you." She toyed with a third button. The skin of her exposed neck was flushed. "Three little piglets," she said with throaty laughter, and a third button came undone. "Now we have a problem, don't we." Her voice was husky, and she spoke with a slight slur as if she had been drinking. The forefinger on her left hand quickly tapped each remaining button, finally coming to rest directly on the swell of her bosom. "There are only three piglets in the story. Yet I count five more buttons. What are we to do?"

Lucie Rhinegold had been sent to Charles after being diagnosed as neurasthenic, a blanket term that covered a wide range of female "nervous" conditions, from hysteria to melancholia to problems with menstruation. She had been referred to several specialists, but not one had been able to make a precise diagnosis. Her symptoms had been admittedly vague. Headaches, upset stomach, nervousness, insomnia, anxiety. One doctor had referred her to Tunbridge Wells for the mineral waters, another to a German spa where she had taken several hour-long baths each day. But after two weeks, complaining that she had not been cured, and having contracted an annoying skin condition, she had returned to England. Another specialist had prescribed a far more radical treatment than spa baths, one with more serious consequences than dermatitis—a clitoridectomy. But Lucie Rhinegold had not been about to surrender to a surgeon's knife, although Charles knew the surgeon had been on the right track. Charles carefully examined Lucie on her initial visit and had discovered her labia majora and labia minora swollen and inflamed. The irritation had not appeared to have an organic pathology, and keeping in mind her other complaints, Charles had concluded that she was a chronic masturbator. That deduction had proven accurate when later confirmed by her husband Fredrick. Although the poor fellow had squirmed in discomfort, Charles had learned that Lucie had not been receptive to sexual advances. The remarkable thing, according to Mr. Rhinegold's acutely embarrassed account, was that his wife had enjoyed sex *before* marriage, but shortly after "the nuptials," as her husband had put it, she had "gone frigid." Not only that, but in recent months, she had started staying out till all hours of the night, sometimes *all* night, returning home after daybreak, "like a tomcat."

On her very next visit, Charles persuaded Lucie to

undergo hypnosis. At first, she was resistant to the idea, believing it another form of medical quackery. In actual fact, hypnosis as a form of treatment had not yet been endorsed by the British medical community. France was the centre of investigation into the phenomenon, and it was there that Charles had learned how to use hypnosis on patients. He overcame Lucie's reservations with the words, "no worse than a spa bath, far less painful than a clitoridectomy," and she had then proven an easy and willing subject. In the hypnotic trance, Charles was able to verify what he had suspected: Lucie Rhinegold had not one but two distinct personalities.

Charles had started today's session by drawing out the "hidden" personality, the one who craved sexual satisfaction.

"Lucie, would you please fasten your buttons."

"I don't want to."

"It isn't acceptable behaviour," Charles said firmly.

"I don't give a damn about what's acceptable and what's not. I want to undo all of my buttons. And my bodice. I want you to see my breasts. I want you to touch them. I want you to kiss them." She suddenly smiled lasciviously. "In fact, I want to undress. Right now. Right here. I want to take every stitch of clothing off. I want you to take me to your bed, Fredrick." She closed her eyes and her head lolled slightly to one side. Her face became flushed, her voice tremulous. "I want you to take me to your bed . . . and I want you to put your tongue inside me . . . inside me there . . . lick me hard, Fredrick. Will you lick me hard? Gentle at first," she said in a sudden breathy rush. "But then hard. Very hard and fast," she said, her voice now demanding.

Charles felt sudden revulsion. He had hypnotized women before and had been intrigued by their sexual confessions. Generally, they had been uninhibited in the sleeplike trance, discoursing openly and at length about their most private fantasies. Occasionally, he had felt like a voyeur peering into the very private world of individual sexuality. But Lucie's graphic eroticism angered him in an odd, inexplicable way. He had to discipline himself to be detached and clinical, as he continued to probe her psyche.

"Lucie, listen to me carefully. We are going to go backwards in time. We are going back two years. You are now 23. It is 1886. June 20th, a Saturday. Do you remember that date?"

Lucie, who now sat still, hands in her lap like an obedient schoolgirl, nodded her head. "Yes. I remember. June 20th, 1886."

"What is happening today?"

"I'm to be married to Fredrick Rhinegold."

"Are you excited? Happy?"

She hesitated. "Yes," she finally said.

But Charles caught the tentativeness in her voice. "Does anything trouble you?"

She cast her head down. "I worry about tonight."

"Why?"

"It's my marriage night."

"Why does that trouble you?"

Lucie hesitated again. "It means the end."

"The end of what?"

There was a moment of long silence. "The end of the fun," she eventually said.

Charles pressed her. "What fun?"

Lucie paused, wringing her hands nervously.

"What fun, Lucie," Charles persisted.

"The fun in bed."

"Do you mean sexual fun?"

"Yes," she said softly.

"Why does the fun end *after* marriage?"

"Because God forbids sex, unless it is to procreate."

Charles briefly pondered his next question. "Who told you that?" he asked.

"My mother. The Bible. The vicar. Everybody tells me."

Charles waited a moment before continuing his probing. "Lucie, have you ever had sex with Fredrick?"

Lucie's cheeks flamed, and she fidgeted noticeably in her chair. "Yes," she said, in a barely audible syllable.

"Does God permit sex *before* marriage?"

This had been the stumbling block in each of three previous visits. Charles had learned that Lucie the wife was frigid, a fundamentalist when it came to the Bible. She attended church regularly and nightly read a passage from the Scriptures. That was Lucie Alpha. The second personality, Lucie Beta, had emerged soon after the marriage. She was a sultry woman with an active and, in Charles's opinion, a healthy sexual appetite. But Lucie Beta had become promiscuous. In one way, the explanation for this was simple. Lucie Alpha had been brought up within a strict moral code but possessed a strong, incompatible sexual drive. Lucie Beta had emerged to allow expression of this sexual need, yet she could only find gratification through extramarital activity. For some reason, her moral frame of reference had been turned inside out. Charles's difficulty lay in bringing the two Lucies together into a single, integrated personality, thereby resolving her dilemma.

"God does not permit sex before marriage," Lucie said piously.

"But you have had sex with Fredrick."

"I have—"

"And with others? Before him?"

"I have sinned. I am not a clean woman—"

Charles adopted his authoritarian tone. "You must answer my question, Lucie. Have you had sex with someone other than Fredrick?"

"Yes."

"Who?"

She stared disconsolately at the floor.

"You must answer the question. Who did you have sex with before Fredrick."

"No one of account," she said in sudden stubbornness.

"But he is of account. You *must* tell me."

"He is of no consequence and therefore not worth mentioning," she said with finality.

Frustrated, Charles leaned back in his chair. *I am the physician,* he muttered under his breath. *I shall decide who is and who is not of consequence*. But he had arrived at the same dead end before and had been unable to penetrate Lucie Rhinegold's obdurateness. Once again, he was forced to concede temporary defeat, and so he concluded the session by ending her hypnotic trance.

Annie Chapman

saturday, september 8th

﹢﹢[5]﹢﹢

LIVERPOOL STREET STATION was the busiest train terminal in all of London. It catered to the suburbs that had sprung up east of the city, north of the Thames in the direction of the Lea Valley and Epping Forest. More than a hundred trains a day left for places like Walthamstow, Chingford, Edmonton, Enfield and Loughton—villages soon to be known as bedroom dormitories of London.

The railways were seen as a panacea, a way to clear out the urban slums of Spitalfields, Whitechapel and Bethnal Green to the north. The government had encouraged the migration by enacting the Cheap Trains Act, whereby companies such as the Great Eastern, which controlled Liverpool Street Station, had been compelled to provide workmen with inexpensive fares between London and their outlying communities. Two hundred and fifty thousand passengers had been ticketed through Liverpool Street Station on Whitsunday alone.

Overcrowding on the workmen's trains was notorious. Ventilation was poor. In winter, travellers froze; in summer, they suffocated from the heat and choked on the acrid smoke emitted in poisonous clouds by the coal-burning locomotives. Nor was the rolling stock built for comfort, outfitted as it was with only straight-backed wooden benches, no more endurable than oak church pews, yet with an added degree of discomfort: unlike the church pew, the train bench moved, jarring every bone in a passenger's body as cars clattered over uneven tracks and switches.

The station itself was a kind of purgatory. For in Liverpool Street, man had made his own vaulted heavens, constructing it from glass and delicate lattice-thin ironwork, which seemed to belong more to an elaborate gazebo than to the roof of a vast railway station. Rows of thick iron girders stretched upward, bent like the arms of strongmen labouring under impossible strain. The grandiose architecture was meant to inspire, but the air was befouled with coal dust, steam and sulphurous gases. Beneath this manmade sky, the contemplation of stars and distant galaxies was beyond human ken. Out of the station stepped not the conquering race of giants whose imagination had seen to its erection; the men of Liverpool Street were a puny, tight-lipped, mean-spirited race, men who didn't look to the future because they didn't believe in one. They lived for food, sex and drink and not much else mattered save a day's labour to pay for those primitive needs.

Yet another train departed, destined for Broxbourne at the eastern end of the Lea Valley, where it emptied into the Thames Estuary. At the open-air entrance to the station, billowing clouds of steam rolled skyward as the locomotive fought for momentum. Inch by resistant inch, the train cars obeyed the tug of their locomotive. Quite suddenly, the entire train began to move as a unit, breathing a relieved sigh as iron wheels glided over iron track. An abrupt blast of wind brought warm steam vapour against his face, the microscopic mist smelling faintly of a kettle at the boil. When he moved his tongue along his upper lip, it tasted of salt, as if he had spent a day at the seashore.

A phrase flashed to mind, *idolatry to our machines, bondage to our locomotives,* immediately followed by three names he did not recognize: *Macaulay, Arnold, Emerson.* This unsettled him, as if he had been presented with both sides of an equation he could not balance.

He turned and pushed his way up the staircase to the pedestrian bridge that led to Bishopsgate Street. The evening traffic flowed down into the station, and his ascent was like swimming upstream against a strong current. At the exit, he finally fought free of the jostling crowds, relieved to step out into fresh air. Almost opposite him stood Bishopsgate Police Station. Outside the gaslit entrance, two officers, one with a sergeant's chevrons, were engrossed in conversation. He had read in the *Times* that, since the Whitechapel murders, leaves had been cancelled and all constables had been assigned extra beat hours. To his right, the street led south in the direction of the City and London Bridge; to his left, north to Bethnal Green. Bishopsgate was bustling with people and horse-drawn traffic of every description. He watched for a moment as a crossing sweep, a young boy of eight or nine armed with a bristle brush, scooped up a load of horse dung and, darting underneath a hansom cab's horse, deposited it on a pile at the curbside. Later, a wagon from a manure works would appear to collect the dung for use in a leather-softening process.

He crossed Bishopsgate, passed the police station and Dirty Dick's public house, then turned into Widegate Street, a roadway that admitted a two-horse tandem wagon and nothing an inch wider. Two hundred yards later, Widegate narrowed to a passageway called Gun Street, which he continued along, coming out in Crispin Street in front of the Convent of Mercy. Inside the convent, the Sisters of Mercy offered succour to the homeless and the hungry. They had arrived mid-century from County Wexford to minister to their Irish Catholic brethren, who had been driven out of their homeland by the great potato famines. In the moonlight, the brickwork glowed like pale yellow gold. He stood on the corner watching nuns in black-hooded habits scuttling to and fro like industrious but furtive black beetles—or monks or druids or black-frocked rabbis. For what did their faith matter? What did they count for in the crushing tide of destitute humanity in the East End? They themselves were grains of sand, particles of human dust blown here by distant storms and political upheavals. They would have their moment in history and be gone.

Diagonally across the street from the corner on which he stood, Christ Church, Spitalfields, dominated the skyline, a solid, prosperous-looking structure that seemed out of place in the grime and squalour of East End London. Once the church had stood in the midst of a prosperous neighbourhood, populated by Protestant Huguenots who had fled France at the beginning of the 18th century to escape religious persecution. They had settled in great numbers in Spitalfields and Whitechapel, bringing with them their silk-weaving industry and the profitable secret of how to give lustre to silk taffeta. But a hundred years later, the introduction of cheap calico had depressed the market for raw silk, which had to be imported all the way from China. Then steam-driven looms had made handlooms obsolete. The prosperity of the Huguenots had plummeted like a bankrupt's stock; so, too, had real estate values in the East End. Then the migrant Irish had arrived. But now, like the silk weavers before them, the Irish Catholics were being driven out of Spitalfields and Whitechapel by a new wave of immigrants, another swarm of ravaging human locusts: the Jews. These latest arrivals had also fled religious persecution, coming from Russia and Poland, from unpronounceable villages like Gyergyoszentmiklos and Dneiperpetrovsk, driven out by a series of savage pogroms following the assassination of the Czar in 1881 by a revolutionary group called the People's Will. From his corner, he counted eight synagogues within a three-minute walk. Since the Jewish influx, four Anglican churches had been forced to close their doors.

He moved on, heading for Spitalfields Market, London's largest fruit-and-vegetable emporium. There, in subterranean storage rooms, could be found pineapples from Bermuda, oranges and lemons from Spain, bananas and coconuts from Barbados and Jamaica, pomegranates and figs from the Aegean and eastern Mediterranean. And at ground level, every vegetable known to man could be purchased. The marketplace was a favourite haunt for the hungry and the down and out, for they could scrape from the pavement a crushed pineapple, a stalk of celery or a rotten turnip disdainfully thrown away but still good for a tramp's stew.

It was not only scavengers who could be found loitering around the glass-roofed marketplace. Prostitutes flocked to it like flies to honey, for the market, which continued throughout the night, employed labourers, porters, barrow pushers, costermongers, men by the hundreds. And surrounding its five-acre grounds were gin and beer shops by the dozen.

He left the market and walked east in Hanbury Street to Brick Lane, passing dozens of Jews and listening to their chants, intended to ward off the evil eye—*To long years, until a hundred and twenty, I am well*. He passed a bearded Schnorrer, nail scissors attached to his frayed coat lapel and used to clip out Torah quotations in Hebrew or Yiddish; a bagel salesman screamed in a guttural voice, "Bagels! Bagels! Hot bagels!"; beside him, a street vendor pulled live eels from a zinc tank and chopped them into two-inch lengths, the individual portions still contorting as they were dropped into a pot of boiling fat.

He moved down Brick Lane past the Frying Pan public house, past the entrances to Flower and Dean and Thrawl Streets, which had gained notoriety because Mary Ann Nichols had left this neighbourhood before travelling to her death in Buck's Row. Indeed, that was all the neighbourhood prostitutes talked about: how Pretty Polly had had her throat cut and—so the rumour went—her private parts mutilated. Those who had seen her in the mortuary shell, naked, with black cat-gut sutures running up her abdomen, painted a ghastly picture of the corpse. *She looked like a sewn-up doll only with the straw torn out*, or, *she looked all shrunken, like she had no insides*.

That was not what he recalled of the old prostitute. He remembered only the orgasmic sense of power and hatred that she had inspired. And now that feeling had begun to return, a buildup of pressure that was at first tentative in its hold, but grew progressively more assertive. He could not resist the corresponding rise of aggression, nor the struggle for control of his mind.

At 2 a.m., Annie Chapman, Dark Annie to her acquaintances, had been forced to leave her lodging house at 35 Dorset Street because she lacked the money for her bed.

Dorset Street opened at one end in front of the Convent of Mercy, and at the other in Commercial Street, the main north-south artery through Spitalfields and Whitechapel. She was not feeling well and had been trudging the streets for what seemed like hours. She had stopped in the park beside Christ Church, but the benches had all been occupied by tramps. She had made several trips around the perimeter of Spitalfields market, which officially opened for business at 5 a.m.—which hour it must now be, because she could see customers beginning to make purchases. At the corner of Lamb Street on the northern boundary of the market, she decided she would cross over to Hanbury Street, then walk down Brick Lane to Flower and Dean Streets where she had friends who might be able to sneak her into a kitchen. She had a black eye and several bruised ribs that ached when she walked, the result of a fight with another prostitute over a piece of soap. Dark Annie was past her prime, but she had retained her spirit; no young whore could steal *her* soap with impunity. But the other woman had been not only younger but stronger. She had fought like a hellion and given Annie a good mauling. The morning air was chill and a touch of warmth would be like a healing salve.

He finally stopped wandering and hid in the doorway of a vacant house in Hanbury Street. He pulled his felt hat over his eyes so that in the blackness of the doorway, he appeared faceless. He waited for an hour, the Christ Church clock striking each quarter-hour, and, in the opposite direction, the clock in the Black Eagle Brewery sounding on the half-hour. Occasionally, a gust of wind brought the warm, yeasty smell of fermenting hops into Hanbury Street.

As time wore on, he became agitated. Dawn was in the air, dew casting a sheen on the cobblestone pavement. Soon the sky would soften into pinks and greys, and the cover of night would be lost.

He could feel the folded newspaper underneath his arm and the solid presence of the knife between the folds. Feeling its presence calmed him, for they were two friends bent on a common mission of retribution. All of the knife's weight and substance seemed concentrated in its handle. Forged from iron, it was shaped like a flat ellipse with an added hilt at the base no more than two inches wide. The top of the handle was silver and shaped like an egg sliced vertically in half. Between the hilt and the silver egg half, the handle had been sheathed in black onyx. Although it was not a thing of beauty, he could stare at it for hours, pondering its crude, almost primitive symmetry and wondering at its terrible efficiency. It was what it purported to be: an instrument of death, its lethality in no way disguised by its ornamentation.

So absorbed was he in this thought that he almost missed the prostitute. She was walking opposite him on the far side of the street. He hardly had a moment for reflection. Daylight was beginning to break, the sky now more grey than black. He could make out a hint of colour in her dress, and for some obscure reason, that decided her fate: despite the risk, he would kill her. He stepped out of the doorway and crossed the street in one stealthy movement. At her side, he took her firmly by the elbow. She started, and he saw the sudden fright in the whites of her eyes, so he smiled and put his finger to his lips. The smile seemed instantly to reassure her, and he guided her into an open doorway. Tenement houses in Hanbury Street kept their front doors open all night. The houses were terraced, and all were built to the same plan. A central passage led from the door to a small backyard.

Keeping her in front of him, still holding her by the arm, he steered her toward the backyard. He could hear sounds as if they were amplified. The cough of an infant. The creak of a mattress. The meow of a cat. It seemed the very structure of the house breathed in laboured sleep. In an instant, they were on the steps at the backyard door. She almost fell forward, but he grabbed her by the shoulder and roughly pulled her back. She turned, her mouth open in protest. He punched her, and she was knocked momentarily senseless. *Clumsy, thoughtless whore.* He shoved her to the ground, and her head almost collided with the fence. A red handkerchief was knotted at her neck. He grabbed it and slashed at her throat.

LYDIA SLIPPED NAKED out of bed and pulled on a silk peignoir, which she tied at the waist. Earlier in the evening, the Carlyles had hosted a dinner party to honour the members of the Parnell Inquiry. Unbeknownst to her, Charles Randall had been invited by her mother. Since their flare-up after the outing to the theatre, mother and daughter had observed an undeclared truce. Yet all the while, her mother had been plotting her revenge, and Charlotte had been a more-than-willing partner to the scheming: she had arranged the seating as well as the menu, naturally placing Charles beside herself. Lydia had ended up at the far end of the table, sandwiched between the Attorney General, Sir Richard Webster, and the President of the Parnell Commission, Sir James Hannen, two very distinguished but otherwise very staid gentlemen. Each, she knew, had been smitten by her appearance. But beauty, she also knew, was a double-edged sword; depending on the personality of the beholder it either made him tongue-tied or precipitated a loquaciousness that could tie up a conversation for minutes on end. Sir Richard had been loquacious—she had learned volumes about Irish nationalism and the obstructive filibustering tactics of Mr. Parnell and his home rule MPs. Sir James, however, had spent most of the dinner in poker-faced silence. Only once, during the soup course, had he turned to her and managed, "There is only one thing more powerful than a beautiful woman."

At his pause, she was obliged to say, "And what is that, Sir James?"

"A beautiful woman with *ambition*," he replied instantly, the answer obviously poised on the tip of his tongue. He had then lapsed back into silence as if the effort of uttering that single sentence had exhausted him.

On her other side, Sir Richard had added with a smile, " 'A witty woman is a treasure; a witty beauty, a power'— George Meredith, a very quotable fellow. And one who knows of what he speaks."

What are these two men saying, she had wondered at the time. That beauty is a dangerous prize?

Charlotte had dressed for the evening in the very sort of daring shoulderless gown she had condemned only a few days before. Her curled coiffure, with its crimped bangs and low chignon, emulated the famous Lillie Langtry, actress and inamorata of the Prince of Wales—allegedly the most beautiful woman in the world. She and Charles had engaged in earnest conversation, and Lydia could not help noticing how his eyes kept straying to Charlotte's half-exposed breasts. She had not thought her sister capable of being such an immodest coquette. But then again, she had to remind herself, this was *love*.

Occasionally she had felt her mother's eye on her, alight with self-satisfaction. Once, on impulse, Lydia had met her penetrating gaze with a broad, spontaneous smile. Her mother had flinched as if at a painful muscle spasm—one in her derrière, Lydia hoped.

Throughout the evening, Lydia did not have a single opportunity to speak with Charles. He had remained in the dining room with her father and the other men for obligatory brandy and cigars. She had been forced to join the women and the condescending smugness of her sister, whose blushing glow was so transparent as to invite invidious comment.

Only by an act of supreme self-control had Lydia managed to bite her tongue. She had, with barely concealed impatience, listened to gossip (the latest liaisons of society's three reigning libertines: the Prince of Wales, Henry Cust and Wilfred Blunt); a lecture on the usefulness of woollen brocades and an announcement that velvet and satin reversible ribbon had returned to favour, moiré and fancy ribbons having grown common—and on and on, ad infinitum.

When the last guest had finally departed, she fled to her bedroom, pleading a splitting headache. Charlotte's fawning solicitude had almost been the end of her, but finally, she had closed her bedroom door on the world.

Her room was dark. She walked to the window and opened the drapes slightly. A crescent moon threw pale, silvery light on Cadogan Square. Inside the square was a tree-lined park with benches and pathways, the larger path forming an extended oval that encircled the park lawn like a miniature racecourse. As a child, she had often stolen out of the house and down to the park to sit and stare at the moon. Its alien and desolate beauty had entranced her, so much so that she sometimes thought she preferred the world under moonlight.

Across the square, no windows betrayed the presence of burning candles. At either end, gas lamps flickered in the darkness like torches held aloft by unseen sentries. In a far corner, a single electric porch light shone brightly. Lydia had decided she did not like electric light. It was too harsh and intrusive. But she knew it was the future. Whole streets and houses would soon be lit by electricity. Magnus Volk had demonstrated his electric train at Brighton this summer, and the St. Catherine's lighthouse on the Isle of Man was now equipped with an electric light equivalent to the intensity of six *million* candles.

She walked away from the window and sat down at her desk. Her leather-bound diary lay open, and a copy of her favourite novel, *Return of the Native* by Thomas Hardy, stood on end, as did a collection of George Eliot's essays. A tasseled bookmark had been placed in the latter to mark the start of a retrospective essay that Eliot had written on

Margaret Fuller, an American, and Mary Wollstonecraft, a British writer, both of whom had published important works on the role of women in their respective societies. The Eliot essay was to be the starting point for a lecture that Lydia had been asked to deliver at Toynbee Hall in Whitechapel, where she did volunteer work. Toynbee was a spiritual retreat and learning centre that had been founded by Samuel Barnett, a clergyman. His wife, Henrietta, had approached Lydia with the idea. In the asking, she had said, "You're a lovely role model for the new woman, dear. It would benefit the women of Whitechapel to hear your vision of what their future could be." Lydia had been both flattered and surprised to hear herself described as a 'new' woman. She had not seen herself in that light, although her education—Cheltenham Ladies College and her current status as an undergraduate at Girton College, Cambridge—marked her as unusual.

She had actually attempted to start her research by committing an excerpt from Mary Wollstonecraft to a notebook. She pulled open a drawer and read her notes:

> Men of fancy, and those sanguine characters who mostly hold the helm of human affairs in general, relax in the society of women; and surely I need not cite to the most superficial reader of history the numerous examples of vice and oppression which the private intrigues of female favourites have produced; not to dwell on the mischief that naturally arises from the blundering interposition of well-meaning folly. For in the transactions of business, it is much better to have to deal with a knave than a fool, because a knave adheres to some plan, and any plan of reason may be seen through sooner than a sudden flight of folly. The power that vile and foolish women have had over wise men who possessed sensibility is notorious.

She could scarcely believe that this excerpt had been written by a woman. Wollstonecraft's work, *Vindication of the Rights of Women*, had been published almost a hundred years ago, in 1792. Lydia disagreed wholeheartedly with the notion of blaming the course of human history on the meddlesomeness of women. *I have been Cleopatraed to death,* she thought. The evening's earlier allusions to the dangers of beautiful women did not help. On impulse, she tore out the page, crumpled it tightly and threw it into the wastepaper basket.

She picked up her diary. A compulsive diarist and an intensely emotional one, she wrote what she felt at the moment, pouring out feelings rather than reflections. She knew that writing in her diary was more a form of catharsis than an attempt to chronicle life's daily experiences. She read what she had written earlier in the evening:

> *I cannot deny my attraction to Charles; nor can I deny that attraction is a strongly physical one. My error has been to attempt to intellectualize what I feel—imagining that somehow I can neutralize his physicalness with lofty platonic thoughts. This is sheer rubbish—I am drawn to him as much out of desire as anything else. Why do I try to run from that desire?*

Lydia sat back: *Is it because if I surrender to that desire, I will think myself less a woman?* She stood and walked to the floor-length mirror that stood beside her commode. Letting her dressing gown slip to the floor, she pulled at her braided hair and unfastened the ribbon by which it was tied. She ran her fingers through the soft tresses and tossed her head back and forth until her hair fell over her shoulders. She was naked, save for a teardrop solitaire diamond she had been given on her sixteenth birthday. The diamond rested against her skin like a single, brilliant star. For a moment, she became lost in unself-conscious contemplation of her reflection.

What she saw pleased her. She was shapely, even voluptuous: high, firm breasts, narrow waist, flat stomach, graceful long legs and pleasing thighs. The composite portrait was of a desirable—and desiring—woman. But she was suddenly piqued, not at her self-admiration, but at how even subconsciously she had seen herself as a sexual object. *But damn it,* she thought, *that is how I feel at this moment. I want Charles, and nothing else matters.* "I must have Charles," she said aloud to her mirror-image. "Then you shall have him," the image appeared to answer matter-of-factly.

She put her peignoir back on, returned to her desk and quickly scanned the diary entry. She considered tearing out the potentially damning page, something she had never done before. *No,* she thought, *that would be another form of sacrilege.* She closed her diary, not bothering to lock the clasp.

Charles sat bolt upright, his heart pounding from a nightmare. It seemed someone's fist was inside his chest wall, hammering unmercifully as if desperately at a door. And then, he suddenly realized someone *was* pounding at his. door. He had taken his usual dose of chloral hydrate and laudanum before retiring, and now he shook his head violently in an attempt to clear it. Reaching for his dressing gown, he got to his feet, almost stumbling. *Who could be calling at this hour?* he thought. *What was the hour, for God's sake?* A clock was ticking on the mantel, but he could not bring its face into focus. With difficulty, he made his way to the front door and swung it open—but no one was there. The air was chill and foggy, impregnated with the ineluctable smell of the river. The odour had the immediate effect of recalling his nightmare.

He had been at the very precipice of a thundering waterfall. Within an instant, he knew he would be swept over and pulverized on the hidden rocks that lay far below. The noise had been deafening, as if all the elements in the world had been reduced to a single cyclone of terrible sound that threatened to propel him over the falls. But at the very brink, the water had suddenly become calm, and the deafening crescendo had abruptly vanished. Nothing had remained but the swift flow of water; the current, like an executioner confident in his guillotine or gallows, knew it could not be denied. He was doomed. The blade would drop, the trap door would open—he would plunge over the falls. But at the precise moment death seemed certain, he had been awakened by the hammering on his door. That pounding returned him to the present, and he realized his caller was at the side of the house. In haste, he made his way to his office and opened the door. A figure was in retreat.

"What do you want?" Charles shouted.

The figure stopped and stiffened. A man of slight build and average height turned and faced Charles. He was dressed in evening clothes and wore a top hat. River mist clung to his features like transparent muslin. "I thought no one was home." He spoke in a cultured voice with a vaguely foreign accent.

"I was sleeping," Charles explained.

The man appeared to smile, although his eyes looked sunken and haunted. He was dark-skinned with fine, patrician features, but a thin black mustache gave him a rakish look. "Of course," he said. "Please forgive my unannounced visit. And the hour, naturally. You are Charles Randall? Dr. Charles Randall."

"I am."

"The alienist?"

Charles nodded, drawing his dressing gown close. The chill in the air caused him to shiver, yet oddly did nothing to clear his still numb mind. "Please come in," he said.

But the man did not move. "I can make an appointment."

"But . . ."

"Now that I have seen you, the urgency seems to have vanished. Listen, you must go back indoors. You'll catch your death—I'll make a proper appointment . . . tomorrow." He turned to leave.

"What's your name? How did you find me?" Charles called out.

But the stranger was already walking down the laneway toward the river and the Chelsea Embankment Road. Completely mystified, Charles made his way back to bed. But to his disgust, he was unable to sleep. When his nocturnal visitor had awakened him, his mind had refused to function with any degree of clarity. Now that he wanted to relax and return to sleep, his mind was becoming increasingly alert and active.

He lay perfectly still for several minutes, thinking about the stranger. *What did he want?* Charles wondered. *Why choose such an ungodly hour to consult a physician?* He reached for his watch on the night table. It was almost 5 a.m. The night was all but over. With a groan of disgruntlement, he sat up and after a moment, climbed out of bed, walked over to his washstand and splashed cold water on his face. He worked up a lather from his soap, quickly shaved and then dressed in a loose-fitting white linen shirt, pulling on trousers and braces and his riding boots. Donning a woollen jacket and a straw panama hat, he stepped outside. On the eastern horizon, he could see the fiery cusp of the sun as it rose over the Thames, turning the river into a lava stream of red gold.

The Thames was not always so majestic, although it never ceased, for unfathomable reasons, to cast a spell over Charles. It was a river of many moods, and in an anthropomorphic sense, a river of many appetites. In daylight, it appeared brown and green, as sluggish as a giant python removed without warning to the chill of temperate England. At times, there was something strangely malevolent about it, as if its sluggishness resulted not from unaccustomed chill but from a full stomach. Its character changed with the tide; at the flood, it became brooding and watchful, the current no longer meandering but purposeful.

Charles walked by the river in the direction of the Embankment Gardens and the grounds of Royal Hospital. There was a becoming "oldness" to Chelsea—a ruinlike sense of ghosts stealing down streets and laneways, a place where they still felt welcome. Henry VIII had once lived in a Chelsea manor house. Mulberry trees still grew in a garden nearby, said to have been planted by his daughter, Elizabeth I. And the ghosts of George Eliot and Dante Gabriel Rossetti, whose madness Charles had treated before his death, still lingered.

The neighbourhood was overgrown with clinging vines and creepers. Flower boxes were everywhere, on doorsteps, windowsills and pathways. In season, they burst into brilliant colour. Plant life that had no business growing in England's sometimes harsh climate flourished in Chelsea. Orchid-like lady's-slippers, oleander bushes and profusions of rhododendron scented the air as if it were a tropical arboretum. To

Charles's mind, the better comparison was to a zoo since Chelsea was also filled with a menagerie of assorted exotic animals: marmosets, raccoons, armadillos, peacocks, wombats and even a small, black bull that someone had managed to import from India. The noise from these creatures could be awesome, reminding one not of civilization but of the Amazon or Congo rain forest. But with the seasonal retreat of the sun, a change overtook the neighbourhood. The animals fell silent, and the plant life withered and died. It was then that the Thames took over, river fogs stealing inland, cloaking people's comings and goings, masking the sound of their footsteps and conversations. This Chelsea was infused with a shivery kind of magic, invaded by the nightmares and dreams of its eccentric inhabitants, and Charles knew, as summer now deferred to fall, this Chelsea was gradually coming to life.

When Charles returned home, he made himself a breakfast of tea, cheese, rolls and fruit. He ate quickly, his mind on the Carlyle dinner party of the night before. Lady Carlyle had worked a swift revenge on her daughter. He could tell from Lydia's reaction that Charlotte and her mother had not told her he was invited. He had exchanged only formal salutations with her; the remainder of the evening had been spent in idle chatter with Charlotte, the only diversion being her arresting décolletage. Brandy and cigars with the other "gentlemen" had been a test of his patience. Never did he want to hear another word about the infamous Charles Parnell and the Irish Question.

Charles walked into his study and sat down at his desk. Years ago, Rossetti had given Charles a portrait of Jane Morris, his famous model. Charles had had the portrait framed and glassed to protect it from the dampness. He had hung it in his study over the fireplace and it had become his most prized possession. Lydia reminded him of Jane Morris as Rossetti had painted her 20-odd years before, in the full blush of youth. Both women were possessed of uncommon, un-English looks.

As Charles stared at the black-haired Jane, long-necked, languorous, yearning, beckoning, he found himself staring at

Lydia. She did not float off the canvas to disappear teasingly into thin air, like the ethereal women of other painters. Lydia Carlyle looked down at him and was not a dreamy image that could be blown or swept away like a miasma of smoke. She stood her ground, rooted in a kind of psychic reality. Once she had him, he knew he would not be able to banish her as he had Colleen Murphy and so many others. That, he thought, would be part of the challenge in his conquest of her.

As a diversion, Charles picked up a letter from his desk. It was from William James, the American psychologist who taught at Harvard. Charles and James had been exchanging letters for more than a year in which they discussed case histories. They were to meet in Paris at a symposium on abnormal psychology at the end of October. Charles was scheduled to present a paper entitled "The Phenomenon of Double Consciousness."

This letter, which he had received in the latest post, described in detail the bizarre history of a patient at first thought to be suffering from amnesia. The patient's name was Ansel Bourne, and he was from Rhode Island. James wrote:

> . . . *he was brought up to be a carpenter, but in consequence of a sudden temporary loss of sight and hearing, he was converted from Atheism to Christianity just before his thirtieth year and has, since that time, lived the life of an itinerant preacher.*
>
> *He has been subject to headaches and temporary fits of depression during most of his life and has had a few fits of unconsciousness lasting an hour or less. Otherwise, his health is good. He is of a firm and self-reliant disposition, a man whose yea is yea and his nay, nay; no person who knows him for a moment will admit the possibility of his case not being perfectly genuine.*
>
> *On January 17th of last year, he withdrew some money from a bank in Providence to pay for a lot of land and some outstanding bills.*
>
> *This is the last incident which he remembers.*

He didn't return home that day, and nothing was heard of him for two months. He was announced in the papers as missing, and foul play being suspected, the police sought in vain his whereabouts. On the morning of March 14th, however, at Norristown, Pennsylvania, a man calling himself A.J. Brown, who had rented a small confectionery shop six weeks previously without seeming to be unnatural or eccentric, woke up in a fright. To a boarder, he said his name was Ansel Bourne, that he was entirely ignorant of Norristown, that he knew nothing of shopkeeping and that the last thing he remembered—it seemed only yesterday—was withdrawing the money from the bank, etc., in Providence. He wouldn't believe that two months had elapsed.

The people of the house thought him insane and so, at first, did a doctor, whom they called in to see him. But upon telegraphing to Providence, confirmatory messages came, and presently a nephew arrived upon the scene, made everything straight and took him home. He was very weak, apparently having lost over 20 pounds during his escapade.

The remarkable part of the change is, of course, the peculiar occupation "Brown" indulged in. Mr. Bourne has never in his life had the slightest contact with trade. "Brown" was described by the neighbours as taciturn, orderly in his habits and in no way odd. He went to Philadelphia several times, replenished his stock, cooked for himself in the back shop, where he also slept, attended Church regularly, and once, at a prayer meeting, made what was considered a good address, in the course of which he related an incident which he had witnessed in his natural state of Bourne.

Charles underscored this observation.

I induced Mr. Bourne to submit to hypnotism to see whether, in the hypnotic trance, his "Brown" memory would come back. It did, with surprising readiness; so much so that it proved impossible to make him remember any of the facts of his normal life. He had heard of Ansel Bourne but "didn't know as he had ever met the man." When confronted with Mrs. Bourne, he said that he had "never seen the woman before," etc. On the other hand, he told of his peregrinations during the lost fortnight and gave all sorts of details about the Norristown episode.

The whole thing was prosaic enough, and the Brown personality seems to be nothing but a rather shrunken, dejected and amnesic extract of Mr. Bourne himself.

Charles also underlined this passage, and to it he added an interlinear observation: "'Brown-Bourne' personality an amalgam of individual personalities of Brown and Bourne. Can the same be said of Lucie Rhinegold and her alter ego?"

He gives no motive for the wandering except that there was "trouble back there" and he "wanted rest." During the trance, he looks old, the corners of his mouth are drawn down, his voice is slow and weak, and he sits screening his eyes and trying vainly to remember what lay before and after the two months of the Brown experience.

"I'm all hedged in," he says. "I can't get out at either end. I don't know what set me down in Norristown, and I don't know how I ever left that store or what became of it."

His eyes are practically normal, and all his sensibilities are about the same in hypnosis as in waking. I had hoped by suggestion to run the two personalities into one and make the memories continuous, but no artifice would avail to accomplish this, and Mr. Bourne's skull today still covers two distinct personal selves.

Charles underlined this passage and made another note: "Contiguous personalities side-by-side on the continuum of consciousness but 'before' and 'after' on the continuum of experience."

Charles put the letter aside and considered what this case was telling him about the human mind. Opening a notebook, he dipped his pen in the inkwell and began making notes:

The human mind is:
   1. At least bi-partite.
   2. Layered in varying degrees of consciousness.

3. Is (or is not) compartmentalized like the cargo holds in a ship. Are they watertight? Does seepage from one compartment to the other occur? Could a "persona" in one compartment be unaware of the existence of "another," even though separated by only the thin restraining wall of consciousness?

4. A part of the brain functions like a railway signalman; if neural points are shifted left or right, the course of consciousness will follow the path selected. But how is that accomplished? What triggered the change in Ansel Bourne? Lucie Rhinegold has no memory of Lucie Beta, yet under hypnosis, Lucie Beta has some knowledge of Lucie Alpha. What catalyst triggers the appearance of the second Lucie?

Charles put down his pen, went to the window and parted the drapes. The sun had risen over the horizon and its brightness made him squint. He wondered if Lucie Rhinegold would end up as Ansel Bourne, her skull forever covering two disparate selves.

---»+[7]+«---

THE SAME SUNSHINE that greeted Charles found Lydia at her window. In the square below, she could see a nanny sitting on a bench watching her charge, a toddler dressed in a blue Little Lord Fauntleroy costume. Lydia felt sorry for the overdressed youngster with his plumed hat, velvet suit and lace collar.

She quickly put on a morning dress and joined her family for Sunday breakfast.

"Good morning, Lydia," her mother said, not unkindly. "Sleep well?"

"Yes, thank you," she glibly lied.

"You look a little peaked to me. Are you feeling poorly?"

"Not at all. Actually quite the contrary, thank you. I'm starved."

Sunday breakfast in the Carlyle household was an informal affair. Lydia went to the sideboard and helped herself to a plate of sliced tongue, sausage rolls, an oyster pattie, eggs Benedict (adding an extra spoonful of hollandaise sauce) and, in a final flourish, a fruit compote.

Her father looked at her brimming plate in wonder. "You *are* hungry. Didn't you eat last night, or do you have a hollow leg?" he said with a warm smile. Lydia and her father maintained an arm's-length but cordial relationship. His natural reserve forbade displays of affection, but Lydia knew that she was his favourite and that he was secretly proud of her intellectual interests and academic achievements.

"To be perfectly honest," she said, sitting down to snow-white linen and shining silverware, "I can't explain my appetite."

"Well, if you ate like that every morning, Lydia, you'd wake up one day to find yourself a whale or a walrus," Charlotte said, picking at a piece of tongue. She ate like a bird, maintaining her weight at exactly 100 pounds. The gain of a single ounce was enough to make her fast on tea and toast for a day.

"Did you enjoy last evening?" Her mother inquired brightly. "I thought the conversation quite scintillating. You were very fortunate to be seated beside Sir Richard. Imagine! How many young ladies can claim to have dined with the Attorney General of England by their side. Did he say anything of particular interest?"

Lydia swallowed a mouthful of eggs Benedict, then brought a napkin to her lips before speaking. "He did say something about beautiful women—"

"Oh . . . what?" Charlotte asked, her interest suddenly piqued.

"I couldn't quite put it together. Something about women, beauty and wit. Or was it ambition? Anyway, whatever his phrasing, he said they were a dangerous combination."

"Dangerous?" Charlotte asked in honest puzzlement. "Whatever did he mean?"

Lydia shrugged. "How am I to know? What do you think, Mother? What *did* he mean?"

Lillian Carlyle stiffened perceptibly. She aggressively cut into a piece of ham, her knife scraping on the Wedgwood plate. "I couldn't begin to guess," she said. A small square of ham disappeared into her mouth, where it was aggressively chewed. After a moment, she said, "I find that kind of remark odd. Particularly if made in the company of a young lady—"

"I must say," her husband interjected, "coming from Sir Richard, I'm equally surprised. Did he elaborate?"

"No. We moved on to Charles."

"Charles?" Charlotte again voiced surprise. "Charles Randall?"

"Of course not, silly . . . Charles Parnell." Lydia sipped from a glass of chilled orange juice. *"That* Charles was the focus of the dinner, was he not? . . . albeit uninvited."

This game of innuendo bypassed Sir William Carlyle. "I have it!" he said suddenly. "Of course. Sir Richard was referring to Mrs. O'Shea."

"Mrs. O'Shea?" His wife sounded perplexed. "What do you mean, dear?"

"His remark about beauty, ambition and dangerous women. He meant it in the context of Mr. Parnell and Mrs. O'Shea."

After a few seconds of awkward silence, with Lillian Carlyle glowering across the table at her husband, Charlotte innocently inquired, "Who is Mrs. O'Shea?"

Lydia, before her mother could say a word, answered. "Mrs. O'Shea is Katharine O'Shea, the wife of Captain O'Shea. Isn't he an Irish M.P., like Mr. Parnell? They say she is very beautiful—"

"Lydia," her mother cut in ominously.

But the words were already out of Lydia's mouth. "Mrs. O'Shea is Mr. Parnell's mistress and, oh yes," she said, ignoring her sister's open mouth and her mother's baleful glare, "there was one other thing Sir Richard mentioned. Not directly to me. He was actually speaking to Sir Henry. He said another prostitute had been murdered in Whitechapel, near the Spitalfields market. Apparently, her throat had been cut."

"Oh dear me." Charlotte cupped a hand to her mouth. The sensitivity of her stomach to distressing news was acute. She suddenly turned pale and pushed back her chair.

"Charlotte! Are you going to be—"

By now Charlotte was standing, her face stricken. "Oh dear," she repeated helplessly, and with a gentle hiccup, up came her breakfast.

"Oh Charlotte!" her mother cried with considerable irritation. But Charlotte didn't hear. Already she was fleeing to her room, a napkin clutched to her face.

Lillian Carlyle looked Lydia square in the face. "I trust you are satisfied."

"Satisfied with what, Mother?"

"At what you managed to accomplish."

"I'm sorry, I don't follow you."

"Look what you did to Charlotte. All this talk of mistresses and prostitutes. It is *not* fit conversation for the table. And we don't call them prostitutes. They are 'unfortunates' or some other less crude term."

"I must retire to my study," said Sir William, rising from his chair. "I must get in an hour's reading before Church. That will give you time to change, won't it, my dear? And you, too, Lydia." Intercession between his wife and daughter was becoming a regular feature of family life. He might as well be in the courtroom attempting to arbitrate between two unruly and hotheaded barristers. Still, on quick reflection, his daughter was "junior counsel" and therefore deserving of some chastisement. "Prostitute" was perhaps too impolite a term for the table, at least where his wife and Charlotte were concerned. In Lydia's presence, the word somehow seemed inoffensive.

"Lydia," he began mildly, "I must agree with your mother. That word—"

"Which one, Father?" Lydia interrupted.

Sir William was taken aback. His daughter really was on her high horse. "You know very well which one," he said sternly.

"Prostitute . . . or mistress?"

"Both!" her mother snapped.

"Yes, both," her father joined in. He suddenly felt that he *was* sitting on the bench. He knew how to handle lawyers who threatened to get out of hand. "I will not tolerate any more such impertinence. Decorum is called for at the table"—he almost said *bar*—"and if you are unable to adapt to this code of conduct, you shall"—he almost found himself saying *you shall be held in contempt*—"you shall . . . you shall have to take your meals elsewhere," he finished, stalking out of the room as he spoke.

"Or we shall revoke your privileges at Cambridge," her mother added, shooting an arrow far closer to the mark.

Lydia bowed her head. She did not want to lose her privileges at Cambridge. She knew her father would not withdraw his support, but her mother was a different matter, "I'm sorry," she said. She *was* skittish these days. A manifestation of love, she wondered? "Too little sleep—"

"And far too few manners," her mother snapped.

Lillian Carlyle found her husband in his study, a sanctuary she rarely invaded. "Lydia is becoming impossible. She has too much freedom and not the wherewithal to handle it," she said abruptly.

"It's just a phase she's going through," Sir William said, although doubt gnawed at his words.

"It's more than a phase, I fear," said his wife. "It's her nature. She won't, or can't, answer to authority. She's involved with the likes of socialists and other political agitators whose sole goal in life is to change the way things are. She is capable of betraying her class . . . her birthright. I know that seems terrible to contemplate in the context of one's own daughter." She began to pace. "But there is a destructive quality to Lydia that I can't quite place. Does she get these . . . *foreign* notions from school? Is this the by-product of permitting women a university education?"

Sir William pursed his lips and furrowed his brow. "I don't know, my dear," he said with heavy resignation. "The principle is sound in theory but perhaps unworkable in practice. Although we mustn't forget that rebelliousness is not confined to the female gender—"

"But it's far more unbecoming in women," his wife interrupted, "and the consequences are more onerous. Men can be rebels and maintain some kind of standing in society. They are not held accountable to the same standard of morality. Or to conventional political or social beliefs. Female rogues are ostracized. Mrs. O'Shea is a perfect case in point. She is invited nowhere. She lives in adultery and agitates for Irish nationalism, but society is a closed door to her. I don't want that door slammed in the face of a daughter of mine—even if sometimes it seems Lydia deserves that fate."

* * *

Aubrey Carsonby arrived back in London by train from Lyme Regis, where he had joined his family for the weekend. News of the latest Whitechapel murder had not reached him until late Saturday afternoon. Railway service to the old Dorset port was intermittent, and as a consequence, he had not been able to make a connection until early Sunday morning.

During the journey, Aubrey had had time to reflect on his interest in the Whitechapel murders and on his position within the Home Office. Aubrey belonged to the Criminal Department, which oversaw the operation of the prison system and, in less well-defined terms, acted as a legislative watchdog over the operation of British police forces. It was the latter operation to which Aubrey was assigned.

The workload in the Home Office had become staggering. Benjamin Disraeli's Conservative government of 1874—80 had produced the largest crop of social legislation yielded by any British administration, and the Home Office was still feeling the effect because it was charged with regulating this legislation. The onslaught of paperwork had crested to new records: 1862—18,000 pieces of paperwork; 1872—30,000; 1880—44,000; 1888—over 50,000 to date. Departmental officials were now making unprecedented decisions and judgements. Aubrey knew his plate was full, yet he wanted to increase his involvement in the Whitechapel matter. He wondered if his curiosity was morbid and ungentlemanly. But today was Sunday, and it was his to do with as he saw fit.

On arriving in London, he sent Toby with their baggage directly to Blue Ball Yard and then hailed a hansom cab and travelled to Whitehall. He was surprised to find no one in the Home Office; the place was as silent as a mausoleum. He had anticipated a beehive of activity, at least in the upper corridors of power, despite its being the Sabbath. After all, another heinous murder had been committed, and if the devil did not cease his activities on the Lord's Day, why should the custodians of law and order?

Not for the first time, Aubrey wished he had a telephone. The first exchange in England had been installed several years ago on a nine-line circuit in London. But the powers that be had not deemed Mr. Bell's invention of sufficient worth for installation in the Home Office or Scotland Yard. Communication between the Yard and outlying police stations was by runner, horse or telegram, an experiment involving carrier pigeons having failed.

Aubrey left the Home Office, walked up Whitehall and five minutes later was at Police Headquarters. There he made his way to the offices of the CID. Again, he noted the absence of activity, although here, at least, a small staff was on duty.

"There's been another murder in Whitechapel," he said to the duty sergeant, a red-faced, barrel-chested individual whose brass buttons strained at his tunic as much out of self-importance as girth.

"That's right, and may I ask who's inquiring?" he said officiously.

"My name is Aubrey Carsonby. I work in the Home Office. I'm a personal assistant to The Honourable Henry Matthews. He sent me here to be briefed on the latest information concerning the murder," Aubrey replied, a tone of authority disguising the nervousness he experienced when telling a falsehood.

The sergeant's demeanour at once became respectful. "I see, sir. Well, no one is here at the moment."

"Is Sir Robert Anderson available?" Aubrey interrupted.

"Sir Robert *who*, sir?"

"Robert Anderson, the new chief of the CID."

The sergeant looked at Aubrey with a blank face. "I've never heard of him, sir."

"Would the Commissioner be in?"

"Sir Charles Warren?" the sergeant asked skeptically. "It's *Sunday*, sir."

Aubrey's impatience was growing. "Who is in charge at present?"

"I am, sir."

"Is there not an officer who is working on the Whitechapel murders?"

"As I said," the sergeant replied with some exasperation, "no officers are on duty at present. Perhaps if you checked with H Division, that's the Whitechapel Division, you might receive some assistance.''

"Has a report been filed?''

The sergeant studied Aubrey with uncertainty. Police incident reports were confidential.

"I possess the necessary authority," Aubrey said. "I come here directly from the Home Office.''

"Just a moment, sir," the sergeant finally said. He disappeared inside an inner office and returned with a handwritten report. It was brief, and Aubrey quickly scanned the salient points. The victim's name was either Annie Siffey or Annie Chapman. She lived in Dorset Street and had been killed in the backyard of a lodging house at 29 Hanbury Street, not far from Christ Church, Spitalfields, in the early morning of the 8th. *"The body had been mutilated in the area of the groin and stomach."* Aubrey swallowed hard and read on. *"The injuries are of a nature compatible with that of the Buck's Row victim of 31st August. There would appear to be no doubt the perpetrator is one and the same man."* The report was signed by an Inspector Frederick Abberline.

Aubrey handed the single page back to the duty sergeant and left Scotland Yard. He walked down to the Victoria Embankment, crossed the roadway and leaned against an iron railing, watching a coal barge make its way up the Thames. What kind of madman would want to get inside a woman's stomach? It was not a question Aubrey could begin to answer.

Across the river he could see Lambeth Palace, London residence of the Archbishop of Canterbury. To his right, beyond Westminster Bridge, he could see the Parliament Buildings rising from behind a mass of green trees. The intricate stonework reminded Aubrey of the fussy miniature patterns of the fossils that could be scraped from the flint beds of the Lyme Regis undercliffs, as if tiny coral-like creatures had risen from the river and gone to work on the stones of Parliament and over the centuries left their indelible and precisely tooled handiwork.

He turned and began walking east beside the river. Why had the Sergeant not heard of Sir Robert Anderson, his own superior? And where was he? His travel plans to Switzerland had not been completed as of Friday. Surely he hadn't simply left. On impulse, in front of Cleopatra's Needle, the Egyptian obelisk beside the Thames, he waved down a hansom cab. "Commercial Road, please," he told the driver.

Lydia did not intend to join her family in Sunday worship as she usually did. Despite her parents' displeasure, she had decided to visit Toynbee Hall.

Toynbee Hall had been premised on a philosophy similar to Oxford House, another East End experiment in social work. Both centres combined a spiritual and a secular function: staff were recruited from various universities (in the case of Oxford House, both undergraduates and graduates from the university whose name it bore) and were dedicated not only to saving souls but to improving the education and the quality of life afforded East End indigents.

Lydia checked the schedule of activities for coming weeks in her appointment book. Today's events included an ethics lecture titled simply "Socrates" and a travelogue presentation on "Normandy" (photographs to be presented by means of a magic lantern, a footnote added). The remainder of the week's fare included meetings of the Toynbee Shakespeare Club, the Elizabethan Society, the Reading Society and the History Club, as well as language classes in Latin, German, Italian and French; classes in wood carving, clay modelling and shorthand and, finally, lectures on an eclectic mix of subjects from Venetian art to the physiology of the starfish and political economy and trade unionism.

Lillian Carlyle disapproved of Lydia's volunteer work at Toynbee, but she could not be too vehement in her opposition because the work was charitable, and Lady Carlyle was a community leader in the matter of charitable organizations. This high-mindedness was a matter of *noblesse oblige*. Lady Carlyle sat on any number of boards and ensured that the Carlyle charitable subscriptions were of such cumulative amounts as to be noticed by other less generous donors. Due to her fund-raising efforts on behalf of the Girls' Friendly Society, the next shelter to be acquired by the Society was to be named in her honour. Of this she was very proud, although one factor was of some annoyance. The proposed

site for Carlyle House was right in Whitechapel, hardly a
stone's throw from Toynbee Hall. Lillian Carlyle had never
set foot east of Aldgate Pump, the boundary between the
City of London and the East End. But she would have to do
so in order to attend the ribbon-cutting ceremony, an event
she both anticipated and dreaded. She could not abide the
thought of having to breathe the same air as the squalid and
dirty masses of Whitechapel, let alone actually walk through
their vermin-infested slums.

As Lydia drove her cabriolet alone through the streets of
London, she was somewhat apprehensive, not about her
safety but about her peace of mind. She had been to
Whitechapel before but had never really *seen* it because she
had never really opened her eyes to look. Usually, chauf-
feured by one of the Carlyle coachmen, she had never
bothered to peer outside once the carriage entered the East
End. And as soon as the carriage arrived at Toynbee Hall,
she would step out quickly and just as smartly step into the
red brick building that resembled a university chapel.

William Booth, founder of the Salvation Army, had
prepared a survey of the East End. Each street had been
graded according to its fitness as a place to live and rear a
family. The various categories were colour-coded, black
representing the worst environment, red the healthiest. A
black street was described as "an awful place; the worst
street in the district. The inhabitants are mostly of the lowest
class and seem to lack all idea of cleanliness or decency. Few
of the families occupy more than one room. The children are
rarely brought up to any kind of work but loaf about and no
doubt form the nucleus of future generations of thieves and
other bad characters. The property is all very old, and it has
been patched up and altered until it is difficult to distinguish
one house from another. Small backyards have been utilized
for building additional tenements. The property throughout
is in very bad condition, unsanitary and overcrowded. A
number of the rooms are occupied by prostitutes of the most
pronounced order." On the map accompanying the survey,
Toynbee Hall was boxed in, in black.

Once inside Toynbee, Lydia relaxed and enjoyed herself. That was because once the East Enders were in the hall, it somehow conferred a civilized and sanitized status on them. Many of them still looked hungry (most of them *were* hungry), and most looked as if bathwater and soap were either beyond their means or their knowledge of hygiene. Still, they came to learn and be entertained, and except for the parasites and frauds who endured the lectures in order to have access to the soup kitchen, she felt affection for these people.

But her visit today was to be a very different matter. She intended to "look" at Whitechapel. She even intended to visit 29 Hanbury Street, where the last murdered prostitute had met her fate.

Aubrey stepped down from his hansom cab in front of H Division Headquarters in Commercial Road. Inside, somewhat to his surprise, for he had started to believe that no one else was interested in the capture of the Whitechapel monster, he found Inspector Frederick Abberline. The inspector was a small, portly man with a quiet, unflappable manner. His face was traitless, the only distinguishing features being a neatly trimmed moustache and shrewd but world-weary eyes. He was wearing a homburg and a black-and-white checked suit.

Abberline showed no surprise at Aubrey's visit. The two men sat down in a small interrogation office outfitted with an olive-coloured table and two wooden chairs. On one wall hung a portrait of a young and moderately attractive Queen Victoria and in a corner, a faded and dusty Union Jack stood on a floor-mounted pedestal. A Bible, the words *Holy Book* boldly embossed on the cover, lay on the table. Aubrey wondered if such blatant appeals to God, Queen and country actually encouraged criminals to speak the truth. Outside, the steady clip-clop of horses' hooves and the rattle of iron-rimmed wagon wheels could be heard.

"This is a terrible business," Aubrey said, by way of opening.

"Terrible," Abberline agreed forthwith.

"Do you have any clues? Any idea as to the identity of the person responsible?"

Abberline removed his hat and scratched at his scalp in a universal gesture of frustration. "I wish we did, Mr. Carsonby, but so far, we've drawn a total blank. We have murders all the time in this district, over 30 this year so far. We don't always catch the man . . . or the woman," the Inspector quickly added, "but we always know the motive. Robbery, jealousy, revenge. We've seen it all before. Those murders fit into some kind of a recognizable *human* pattern. Take the stabbing of the Trabham woman bank holiday last. Thirty-nine stab wounds. One of them would've finished her off. She was a prostitute like the last two victims. We think her murderer was ambidextrous and that he had a knife in each hand. He did her in by stabbing at her with both hands going at the same time." The Inspector moved both of his hands up and down like two pistons. "At first, I thought the man who killed her was also responsible for the Buck's Row and Hanbury Street murders—"

Aubrey interrupted. "But you don't think so now?"

The Inspector shook his head.

"Why not?"

"First, the stab wounds to the Trabham woman were centred around the chest area. Second, *two* weapons were used. Third, and most importantly, although we haven't found the killer, the killing fits into one or more human motives, probably jealousy. Or maybe she cheated her old man out of some of her earnings. So she was killed, viciously I'll admit, but in a context I've seen a hundred times before."

"And the last two murders?"

"They've been done by a madman. You see, he mutilates his victims. Doesn't just cut their throats. It seems he's after something." The Inspector paused and glanced out a window. "After something *inside* their bodies. And I'll tell you something else, Mr. Carsonby. He seems to know where to look—"

"Are you suggesting he's a doctor?" Aubrey's shock was immediate.

"Not necessarily. He could be a butcher. There are thousands of butchers in and around this area. He could be a mortuary assistant. Or someone used to the dissecting room of a teaching hospital. But I don't happen to think so."

Again Aubrey asked, "Why not?"

The Inspector tapped his nose. "Call it intuition, I guess." He took off his homburg and turned it in his hands. Aubrey could tell it was a habit because the brim looked soiled and dog-eared. "I have this theory. It can't be substantiated, of course. But I believe he's a Jew. Killing for religious reasons."

"But why on earth a Jew?"

"Because he's cutting something out of each body. For religious purposes."

"But what, for God's sake?"

The Inspector replaced his hat and looked down at the table. "We think it might be a kidney."

Aubrey was incredulous. "A *kidney*? Why a kidney?"

"Because that's what the doctors tell us."

Aubrey felt his stomach churn. "This is all too horrifying," he said.

"It is that, sir, it is that."

"Have you questioned anybody?"

"Of course, sir. We've questioned hundreds. We've searched lodging houses, public houses, private houses. We've been searching for 36-odd hours straight."

"And you've found nothing?"

Inspector Abberline once more turned to the window. "Nothing," he admitted, resignedly. After a moment's silence, he continued. "Did you know the Jews call their butchers *shochtim*? They use a special knife called a *khalef*. These shochtim are addressed as 'Reverend' . . . like we address our clergymen. They're a damn peculiar race of people, the Jews. I've been doing some studying, sir. Both August 31st and September 6th fell on Jewish holy days. They started their New Year on September 6th—"

"And August 31st?" Aubrey quickly interjected.

"The 24th day of Ellul. A day of piety. They say prayers for all their sins, apparently beat themselves about the chest, berate themselves for misdeeds.''

"Have you mentioned this to anyone?"

"Do you mean the Commissioner?"

Aubrey nodded.

"Yes, sir."

"And?"

"He told us to search the abattoirs and question the shochtim. Which we're doing."

"Do you mind if I take a look at Hanbury Street?"

For the first time, Inspector Abberline looked surprised. "If you can get near the place."

"What do you mean?"

"They're charging admission."

"I don't understand."

"The owners and the neighbours have got a regular little business going on. Penny gets you a window overlooking the yard where it was done. For sixpence, you can go into the yard and see where the body was lying—get to feel along the fence where we washed off the blood."

"You can't be serious."

"Oh, I'm serious, yes sir, very serious. This is Whitechapel, after all. We don't have the refinements of the West End out this way."

Lydia turned off Bishopsgate into Brushfield Street, which ran in a straight line past Spitalfields Market to Christ Church. In front of the church, she saw a steady parade of people heading east. The air seemed festive, as if the day were a special holiday. She found the street so crowded that she could not get her cabriolet through, and so she climbed down and led the horse by hand back to the church. She saw a pleasant-looking young man in a brown suit leaving a side entrance. A shock of brown hair, which perfectly matched his clothes, was swept back high over his forehead.

"Excuse me, sir. Where might my horse and cab be safe?"

He appeared taken aback by the appearance of a lady of breeding in his neighbourhood.

"Do you have business with the vicar?" he asked.

She smiled. "No," she said and told him a simple lie. "I'm from Toynbee Hall. I'm paying a visit to a student in Hanbury Street."

His face lit in instant understanding. "This might not be a propitious moment to go there, ma'am. The streets are overrun with curiosity seekers. It might not be safe."

"What has aroused their curiosity?"

"You don't know?"

"No," she lied again.

He paused, uncertain whether to tell her about the murder. She might faint . . . although on second thought, despite her attractiveness, she looked a formidable young woman. And she did teach at Toynbee Hall. He concluded that she could not lead a completely sheltered life. "There was a murder," he said, "just one street over, in Hanbury Street. They're all trying to visit the scene of the murder. It's like a carnival."

"How horrid," Lydia said.

"Yes, indeed. Reprehensible behaviour, but I suppose nothing less than can be expected from these people," he said with considerable distaste.

Lydia looked downcast. "That is a pity. I promised my student a spelling tutorial. I am quite determined not to disappoint her."

"But you'll never get through the crowds, and your person may come to some harm," he said firmly. "It simply isn't safe."

"Would you serve as my escort, then?" Lydia said with a sudden, disarming smile.

Aubrey, after much man-handling, had arrived near 29 Hanbury Street from its Brick Lane entrance. The crowd was as boisterous and unruly as Inspector Abberline had forewarned. There were several uniformed constables in attendance, but they stood in pairs simply watching the goings-on, making no effort to control the crowd that, to Aubrey's mind, was more like a mob.

He had found Brick Lane eerily quiet and deserted save for roaming groups of young toughs. They were looking for Jews, a goodly number of whom lived in Brick Lane.

Abberline had mentioned that Jews were being blamed by the local populace, and several had been assaulted. At the end of their conversation, Abberline had also confided that the police were on the lookout for a Jew known as Jack or John Pizer, also called Leather Apron.

There was a long line-up going into 29 Hanbury Street. Abberline had said he would have two constables escort Aubrey, "as a senior government official," to the site. But Aubrey was having second thoughts about his voyeuristic quest. What good could he do by actually inspecting the site? He paused in his deliberations and looked over the crowd. Never had he seen such a collection of down-and-outers, men, women and children. Dressed in tatters, they stared at his finery with envious eyes. Suddenly, Aubrey wanted to run, and then he caught sight of someone he recognized: Lydia Carlyle.

That evening, Lydia was still excited over her excursion into the East End. Benjamin Disraeli had been right: England, or at least London, *was* two planets. By the simple expediency of a half-hour carriage ride, she had made an interplanetary journey, landing in a world as alien to her and her Belgravia home as would be distant Mars or Jupiter.

Jeremy Barnthorpe, nephew of the vicar of Christ Church, had served as her guide. And what sights she had seen.

First, she had persuaded the reluctant young cleric-in-training to accompany her into the backyard of 29 Hanbury Street. He had even generously paid the price of admission. The backyard itself had been a disappointment. What had she hoped to see in a square patch of dirt and stones, hemmed in on all sides by a high fence or brick wall? In a physical sense, nothing. But there had been a distinct otherworldly atmosphere in that backyard, as if she were visiting a shrine that held a religious relic, like the bones of a saint or a sacred talisman.

Outside the house, a lively babble and carnival atmosphere had prevailed. There had been calliope players, a hurdy-gurdy grinder with a monkey outfitted in a dress and a papier-mâché crown set with glass jewels. "Queen of the

Monkeys!'' the owner proclaimed. ''Watch Her Majesty do a pirouette for a penny!'' There had even been a penny-gaff clown and a snake, sword and knife swallower. And street vendors had been everywhere, selling everything from hot ginger beer to pickled whelks, sherbets and ices.

But once inside the house—down the narrow hallway, through which the killer and his victim had stolen, with its scabbing paint, creaking floorboards, malodorousness and, even in mid-afternoon, its cave-like gloom—a strange silence had fallen. The ears shut out all street sounds. In fact, all of the senses suddenly seemed focused on re-creating the moments of the terrible tragedy. Lydia had felt gooseflesh on her arms, hair prickling at the nape of her neck. And when she stepped *down*—two steps only, but the motion somehow created the illusion of stepping *up* as a condemned man climbs to the gallows—the sensation had sent a tremour of cold terror up and down her spine.

Inside the backyard, all had been hushed, whispers carrying like those of worshipful visitors huddled in the Poet's Corner of Westminster Abbey. Only here, the worshipful whispered not of genius but of the life of a common prostitute. Yet Lydia could not help feeling that in the horrid and sensational nature of her death, Annie Chapman had assumed a status that transcended her miserable existence on this earth—her spirit would somehow be kept alive, not in celebration but in remembrance of an unspeakable travesty.

From Hanbury Street, Barnthorpe had taken her, at her insistence, to Petticoat Lane, where every square inch of sidewalk space had been converted to stalls or given over to wagonloads of goods backed into the street. Never had she witnessed such crowds, such frenetic activity. Barnthorpe had stood close by her side, not out of attempted intimacy but out of a need to protect her from the crush of humanity. She had been buffeted on all sides, prodded by arms, shoved forward, sideward, backward, never with an apology, more often with profanities she had never heard before. But after ten minutes of exposure to the language, she had ceased to hear it at all; it simply became part of the loud, almost deafening, background noise. Vendors had hollered at the top of their lungs, shouting until they were hoarse, and their purchasers had bartered just as loudly.

She recalled listening to the exchange between a frowzy-looking woman in a worn bonnet and tattered shawl and a Jew with earlocks and a yarmulke perched on his almost cleanshaven skull. The object of barter had been a battered but apparently still serviceable oil lamp.

"Eightpence!" the Jew had barked.

The woman rolled her eyes and looked away in disgust.

"Sevenpence!"

She shook her head.

"Sixpence—"

The woman had started to turn.

"Fivepence . . . *four*pence! Fourpence, you steal from me," the man had said in a thick Eastern European accent.

"Fourpence, you steal from *me*!" The woman had snapped back. "Threepence, not a penny more."

The Jew had studied the oil lamp for a moment. Then, in a sudden angry flurry, he began to wrap it in an old newspaper, cursing under his breath. The woman's face had broken into a gap-toothed grin as she had reached for her purse. Lydia had smiled to herself and moved on.

The wares for sale had been unimaginable. There were garments of every description, for this was the Jews' used-clothes exchange: costume jewellery, telescopes, patent medicines like corn salve, wart remover and female "purgatives" and rubber sheaths laid out on a table as plain to see as any other merchandise. She had never seen such a device before. On either end of the stall, two had been filled with water. "Leak proof they are, lady!" a Cockney voice had shouted at her with a dirty leer when he caught her staring. Some were even coloured or decorated with cartoon-like faces. Barnthorpe had quickly steered her away, his face transparent with acute embarrassment.

They had passed by parrot, canary, rabbit, fish and guinea pig vendors, a stilt vaulter, a street juggler and a Scottish piper and his "blind" dancing daughter, before they had finally been free of the crowds.

After Petticoat Lane, they had passed by a socialist

meeting in Wentworth Street. Lydia had insisted they stop and listen. The speaker, a man with a heavy-set face and full beard, had been a fire-and-brimstone orator. She could recall, almost word for word, his ringing denunciation of *her* world: "Private property leads to class war and places personal interest above the interests of society. Your future does not lie in the old commandments of the past, which have long since lost their moral value. Emancipate yourselves from the lust for power that is fundamental to privilege. Stop praying to gold and light! Away with the cult of the past! Ally yourselves with the people and their true friends! Oppressed humanity is organising to regain its rights and liberties. The Social Revolution has raised its banner and calls you to the community of labour, the free fraternity of workers of all lands, the removal of all rule by force and of everything that is opposed to the demands of justice. Human brotherhood knows no division according to nations and races; it knows only useful workers and harmful exploiters. Against these, the working people must fight!''

And then a Salvation Army band had passed them by, cymbals clashing, trumpets braying, French horns blaring, the polished instruments shining like sunlight on breastplates and shields. On an impulse, Barnthorpe still in tow, she had followed the band to its Citadel. A Salvationist speaker, Bramwell Booth, son of William Booth, had matched the anarchist orator's fervour. So impassioned had he become that he tossed off his tunic, stripping down to a red undershirt soaked, as was his face and brow, with perspiration. He had exhorted the crowd of 40 or 50 enthusiasts, "COME TO JESUS! JESUS SAVES! JESUS *LOVES*!'' The band then struck up the hymn *"Come to Jesus,"* and soon the small hall had resounded with the sound of voices.

Finally, she had allowed Jeremy Barnthorpe to buy her a lemonade at a respectable establishment in Bishopsgate Street before she had headed home, arriving well after teatime to a round of scowls from her family. After dinner, Lydia had retired to her room, spending the better part of the evening committing the adventure to her diary.

She recalled how Barnthorpe had been critical of everything they had seen, even the Salvation Army. "Booth has turned religion into music-thumping, breast-beating hysteria. True religion springs from the intellect, not from emotionalism. One reflects on the goodness and wisdom of Christianity from within the decorum of Church of England pews and from spiritually uplifting sermons, not from the circus atmosphere of a Salvation Army Citadel. It is my contention that the 'Army' is not really a church. Mr. Booth now measures his progress according to how many tons of bread and potatoes he has distributed to the poor, not by how many souls he has saved—"

Lydia had interrupted, "But does not the work of the Lord encompass feeding the needy?"

"Spiritual nourishment must come first, Miss Carlyle," he had responded admonishingly.

Of the socialist, Barnthorpe had said, "A misguided, godless man preaching a message of false hope and fallacious philosophy."

Lydia had heard of political philosophies such as socialism, egalitarianism and utilitarianism but could not profess a deep understanding of any of them. Their messages seemed similar: that personal conduct should be motivated toward securing the greatest amount of benefit and welfare for the greatest number of people possible. In a sense, this message was the poorer people's definition of *noblesse oblige*. But Lydia was finding it increasingly difficult to reconcile the soul-saving, sanctimonious charity of her class with the sweeping social changes espoused by the likes of the socialist orator she had heard in Whitechapel. A refrain from a childhood hymn came to mind:

> *The rich man in his castle*
> *The poor man at his gate*
> *God made them high and lowly*
> *And ordered their estate.*

It was her mother's sentiment put to the music of godliness. To Lydia, it had suddenly become a lyric of prejudice and injustice.

AUBREY CARSONBY'S MANSERVANT Toby was a young man of 21. He was of diminutive stature, had sandy hair and a lightly freckled face that habitually wore a gamin's grin which charmed mothers and daughters alike. His father had been a Carsonby butler for years, and Toby was being groomed to follow in his footsteps. Baronet Carsonby, Aubrey's father, had decided to begin Toby's training by making him his eldest son's manservant, an arrangement that suited Toby perfectly. His master was easy to get along with except for a punctilious attitude when it came to entertaining or when the two of them were travelling in public. Then Toby was expected to observe strictly all formalities attendant to their master-servant relationship. This bothered Toby not in the least. He had grown up under his own father's careful tutelage, and according respect to his social superiors was second nature to him.

Fortunately for Toby, his master was addicted to his work, often remaining at the Home Office or in his study from first light to dark. Aside from running occasional errands, Toby had his days pretty much to himself. Although he hated rising at 5 a.m. in order to fetch Mr. Aubrey's breakfast and prepare his toilet and wardrobe, he was free to return to bed, which invariably he did, to catch up on his sleep for a couple of hours as soon as his master left for work.

Toby's first mission this morning was to fetch a copy of the *Times*. Mr. Aubrey often read the paper propped up in bed, sipping his morning tea. Toby knew his master wanted it with special urgency this morning to read about the Whitechapel murders, which they had discussed on their journey from Lyme Regis yesterday. Toby did not read the *Times*, it being "all words and then more words." He was following the story in papers like the *Illustrated Police News* and the *Star*, which featured gruesome drawings and sensational headlines like STREETS OF WHITECHAPEL RUN RED WITH PROSTITUTES' BLOOD. That, in Toby's opinion, was how news should be reported, "with the blood and guts steamin' off the ink." Although the truth was that, in its reporting of the murders, even the staid *Times* was tending to be sensational—and Mr. Aubrey, Toby knew, was enjoying the thriller tone of the articles.

When Toby returned with the *Times*—he had stopped on the way to chat up a dollymop in a nearby baker's shop—he found that Mr. Aubrey was beside himself with impatience.

"What took so long, Toby?"

"I got sidetracked for a moment, sir."

"Sidetracked," Aubrey said dubiously, fumbling at the newspaper. "How could you get sidetracked? It's only just daybreak, for heaven's sake."

"The bakery was open. I stopped for some sweet rolls."

"I never eat sweet rolls for breakfast, Toby. You know that. Next time, the *Times*. Nothing else. Oh, here it is. Another cup of tea, if you will," and Mr. Aubrey was lost in his newspaper:

Whitechapel and the whole of the East End of London have again been thrown into a state of intense excitement by the discovery early on Saturday morning of the body of a woman who was murdered in a similar way to Mary Ann Nichols at Buck's Row on Friday last week. In fact, the similarity in the two cases is startling, as the victim of the outrage had her head almost severed from her body and was completely disembow-

elled. The latest crime, however, surpasses the other in
ferocity. The scene of the murder was at the back of 29
Hanbury Street, a street that runs from Commercial Street to
Baker's Row, the end of which is close to Buck's Row. The
house is let out to various lodgers, all from the poorer class. In
consequence, the front door is open both day and night, so
that no difficulty is experienced by anyone in gaining admission to the back portion of the premises. Shortly before 6 a.m.
on Saturday morning, John Davis, who lives with his wife in
the top portion of No. 29 and is a porter engaged in
Spitalfields Market, went down into the backyard, where a
horrible sight presented itself to him. Lying close up against
the wall, with her head touching the other side wall, was the
body of a woman. Davis could see that her throat was severed
in a terrible manner, and that she had other wounds of a nature
too shocking to be described. The deceased was lying flat on
her back with her clothes disarranged. Without nearer approaching the body but after telling his wife what he had seen,
Davis ran to the Commercial Street Police Station, which is
only a short distance away. An officer, having despatched a
constable for Dr. Baxter Phillips, the divisional surgeon,
returned to the house, accompanied by several other policemen. The body was still in the same position, and there were
large clots of blood all around it. It was evident that the
murderer thought that he had completely cut the head off, as a
handkerchief was found wrapped around the neck, as though
to hold the body and head together. There were spots and
stains of blood on the wall. One or more rings seem to have
been torn from the middle finger of the left hand. When the
police emerged from the house with the body, a large crowd,
consisting of some hundreds of persons, had assembled. The
excitement became very great, and loud expressions of terror
were heard on all sides. At the mortuary, the doctors made a
more minute examination of the body, after which the clothes
were taken off. The deceased was laid in the same shell in
which Mary Ann Nichols had been placed. A telegram was
sent to Inspector Abberline, at Scotland Yard, apprising him
of what had happened.

On Saturday afternoon, Dr. Baxter Phillips, aided by his
assistant, made a most exhaustive post-mortem examination,

lasting upward of two hours. Although, of course, the exact details have not been made public, it is known that Dr. Phillips was unable to find any trace of alcohol in the stomach of the deceased, thus disproving reports that when the woman was last seen alive, she was the worse for drink. The deceased was a little over 5 feet in height and of fair complexion, with blue eyes and dark brown wavy hair. A singular coincidence about the corpse was that there were two front teeth missing, as was the case with Mary Ann Nichols. On the right side of the head was a large bruise, showing that the deceased woman must have been dealt a heavy blow at that spot. There were also other bruises about the face, and finger marks were discernible. The latter indicate that the murderer must first have grasped his victim by the throat, probably in order to prevent her from crying out.

The police believe that the murder was committed by the same person who perpetrated the Buck's Row murder. That person, whomever he might be, is doubtless labouring under some terrible form of insanity, as each of the crimes has been of a most fiendish character, and it is feared that unless he can be captured speedily, more outrages of a similar class will be committed.

Great complaints have been made concerning the inadequate police protection in the East End, and this want is even admitted by local police authorities themselves, but they are unable to alter the existing state of affairs. On Saturday and yesterday, several persons were detained at the various police stations in the district but were freed after proper inquiries had been made; up to the present time, the police have no clue to the murderer and lament that they have no good ground to work upon.

Aubrey called out to Toby for another pot of tea. "Not orange pekoe. Something stronger, Lapsang Souchong, perhaps." Toby obeyed with a quizzical look on his face. Mr. Aubrey rarely mixed teas, and Lapsang Souchong was a very strong Chinese blend, one his master drank only when he was under strain.

While Toby was attending to his tea, Aubrey leaned back

against his pillows for a moment. He could only agree with the *Times'* conclusion that more "outrages of a similar class will be committed." Inspector Abberline had admitted as much himself. The "great complaints" already being voiced about police protection would gain momentum with another murder. That would increase pressure on both Henry Matthews and Sir Charles Warren and, indirectly, on him.

Yesterday, he had gone to Scotland Yard and the East End out of some kind of morbid curiosity. That he was prepared to admit; he assumed that the same curiosity had brought Lydia Carlyle into Hanbury Street. She really was quite extraordinary, not simply in her appearance but in her unladylike, *unwomanly* conduct. She ignored rules and proprieties as if they did not exist. How else could one explain her presence—in the company of a stranger—at the site of a day-old murder? Her sister was surprisingly just the opposite, a composite of all the feminine virtues. But thinking of Charlotte did not soothe an underlying sense of unease. Charlotte Carlyle frazzled his nerves almost more than a trying day at the Home Office did. The first time he had seen her, she could only have been eight or nine, and he had fallen in love. He had waited patiently until she grew into womanhood to make her his betrothed. Yet to date, his patience had been for naught. Charlotte was stalling, and he did not know why. Even more distressing, if he was being honest with himself, he had no idea how to press home his suit.

Toby appeared bearing a fresh pot of tea, and Aubrey returned to his *Times:*

Detective Inspector Abberline of Scotland Yard, who had been detailed to make special inquiries as to the murder of Mary Ann Nichols, at once took up the inquiries with regard to the new crime. He held a consultation with Detective Inspector Helson, J Division, in whose district the murder in Buck's Row was committed. The result of that consultation was an agreement in the belief that the crimes were the work of one man only and that, notwithstanding many misleading statements and rumours—the majority of which in the excitement of the time had been printed as fact—the murders were committed where the bodies had been found and that no gang were the perpetrators.

It having been stated that the woman must have been murdered elsewhere and her body deposited in the yard—the house door giving access to the passage, and the yard never being locked—the most careful examination was made of the flooring of the passage and the walls, but not a trace of blood was found to support such a theory. It is, moreover, considered impossible that a body could have been carried in, supposing no blood had dropped, without arousing from their sleep Mrs. Hardiman and her son, past whose bedroom door the murderer had to go. There is no doubt that the deceased was acquainted with the fact that the house door was always open or ajar and that she and her murderer stealthily passed into the yard. Although, as in the case of Mary Ann Nichols, only a very small quantity of blood was found on the ground (leading to the supposition that the murder was committed elsewhere), its absence is accounted for by the quantity absorbed by the clothing.

The deceased had no time to raise a cry, and the tenants of the house agree that nothing was heard to create alarm. The back room of the first floor, which has an uninterrupted view of all the yard, is a bedroom and was rented by a man named Alfred Walker and his father, neither of whom "heard a sound." John Richardson, the son of a woman living in the house, stated that he entered the place when on his way to work at Leadenhall Market, and at that time—4:50 a.m.—he was certain no one was in the yard. The police, however, have been unable to discover any person who saw the deceased alive after 2 a.m., about which time she left the lodging house, 35 Dorset Street, because she had not fourpence to pay for her bed. No corroboration of the reported statement that she was served in a public house at Spitalfields Market on its opening at 5 a.m. could be gained, nor of the sensational report that the murderer left a message on the wall in the yard, which was made out to read, "5; 15 more, and then I give myself up." Nevertheless, the police express a strong opinion that more murders of the same kind will be committed before the miscreant is apprehended.

Soon after the murder was discovered, a woman of the same class reported to the police that a man had accosted her in the streets of Spitalfields at an early hour that morning but that she tried to avoid him. Thereupon, he began to knock her about; she screamed, and he ran off. He gave her two brass medals for half sovereigns. She was asked to describe the man, but her description was not considered clear. Still, the police determined to follow up the matter, more particularly because the woman has stated that the man seemed ready to kill her. The woman's description did not answer the description of a man for whom they have been searching in connection with the murder of Mary Ann Nichols—a man known as "Leather Apron"—and they incline to the opinion that, after the hue and cry raised about him during the past few days, he would not have ventured into the neighbourhood of Spitalfields, where he is so well known.

Aubrey folded the newspaper in half and put it aside. This second account reported nothing that he had not learned from Inspector Abberline yesterday. He was relieved to see that no mention had been made of Sir Robert Anderson.

His usually hearty breakfast appetite had deserted him on reading the descriptions of the woman's injuries. If the *Times* was so graphic, what would be the tone of today's *Star*? He would find out tonight, from Toby. Still wearing his mono-grammed pyjamas, he sat down at his escritoire. Out of a drawer, he pulled a pair of scissors and a small pot of glue and neatly clipped out the *Times* accounts and pasted them into his scrapbook, the most recent clipping joining the reports of the Mary Ann Nichols murder. *Pretty Polly, Dark Annie,* he mused to himself. I wonder what the sobriquet of the third victim will be?

Aubrey arrived at the Home Office at 8 a.m. Before he could remove his hat, Ruggles-Brise appeared to advise that the Minister would like to see him at his *earliest* convenience, a communication Aubrey correctly interpreted as a summons rather than an invitation to be exercised at his discretion.

The *Times* was spread out on Henry Matthews' desk. The Minister's face, always flushed, was more florid than usual. He plunged into the matter at hand without preamble or formality. "You've read of the latest outrage?"

Aubrey nodded. "I have, Minister."

Matthews' eyes darted from the newspaper to a point somewhere over Aubrey's head. "Carsonby, there is something very rotten in Scotland Yard. We have thousands of policemen. I believe only last week I referred to them as an *army*. We have at the head of this army a former military officer, an officer with considerable field experience in India—"

"Egypt and the Sudan, sir," Aubrey interjected.

"India, Egypt, what does it matter? The point is that Warren has field experience. Plenty of it. Now I'm speaking in *his* terms, Carsonby. In the view of Sir Charles—a view I find untenable—he, as Commissioner of Police, is in the position of a colonel of a regiment. As such, for general purposes, he operates under a higher authority: substitute Home Secretary for commander-in-chief. But the actual day-to-day administration and discipline of his 'regiment' remains completely within *his* authority. Do you understand, Carsonby?"

Aubrey was a bit at a loss for words, not fully comprehending the exact thrust of Matthews' point. "Sir Charles . . . believes—" he began tentatively.

"That he is *still* in the army! Exactly my point, Carsonby," the Minister exclaimed excitedly, "my point precisely. That is the root of his problem. He must stop thinking of himself as a colonel of foot soldiers and start thinking like a policeman. That is the first step in apprehending this murderer, this madman loose in the East End." The Minister tapped his *Times*. "You're familiar with the sorry details?"

"I am, sir. I met with Chief Inspector Abberline yesterday."

Matthews' eyes met Aubrey's for a fraction of a second and then flicked back to his newspaper. "Yesterday . . . was Sunday," he said, as if uncertain.

"Yes, Minister."

"I'm not a strict Sabbatarian, Carsonby. You understand that, of course. But I believe Sunday to be a day of rest."

"I believed there was some urgency to the matter. I was unable to locate Sir Robert—"

"Sir Robert has gone. Left yesterday. Can you believe the coincidence? He leaves for Switzerland, the murderer strikes. It begs explanation, particularly in light of Monro's inauspicious departure. You may recall my prediction. If we had announced Anderson's appointment . . . well, coupled with the events of Saturday, Fleet Street would now be in an uproar."

"Perhaps Sir Robert should have postponed his trip," Aubrey suggested.

The Minister snorted. "Nonsense! Again, you make the mistake of connecting two unrelated events."

"I'm thinking of the future, Minister. Actually, the here and now. My point remains the same. The CID is without a head."

"Not exactly, Carsonby. We have Monro, who maintains regular contact with the detectives of the CID. This is strictly confidential, of course. If Warren were to find out, there's no telling what he'd do. Resign. Or write a letter to the editor of the *Times,* for God's sake. He's capable of such insubordination. But this leads me to your involvement in this matter. We must have an acting head for the CID in Anderson's absence. Monro must, of necessity, remain very much in the background. I'm appointing you to that position. Until Anderson's return, you are to act as the *de facto* head of the CID."

"But, Minister—"

"No buts, Carsonby. You're the only man. Ruggles-Brise is the only alternative, but he's swamped."

"Sir, I have no qualifications as a police administrator."

"Nor does Anderson. Nor, for that matter, as I've just carefully explained, does Warren."

"Perhaps Monro would agree to come back in a temporary capacity—until Sir Robert returns."

"He won't," Henry Matthews said tersely. "He detests

Warren, couldn't work another day with him. No, your temporary appointment fits the bill nicely. You say you've already met Abberline. You know Sir Charles Warren through previous liaisons. You know me, Carsonby, and of course the converse is true: you might say we know each other," he smiled ingratiatingly. "We're on the same side of the wicket, even if Warren is not."

Aubrey left the Home Secretary's office in a daze. The CID operated out of Scotland Yard. Would he have to move lock, stock and barrel out of Whitehall? Or would he maintain his Home Office connection by remaining in his present comfortable surroundings, an office with a fine view of St. James's Park and, more importantly, immediate access to the powers that be? Aubrey had been a bureaucrat long enough to know that the road to promotion was paved by direct access to the decision-makers, men who held genuine power. In his case, those men were the Minister and Godfrey Lushington, the Permanent Undersecretary. If he moved to Scotland Yard, he would be distancing himself from the men who counted. He was also troubled about how Warren would view the promotion. Did Sir Charles even know of Anderson's appointment, let alone his departure for an extended Swiss holiday? Certainly, he knew nothing of Monro's hidden role in the CID.

Aubrey liked Monro. He was a qualified police officer, having worked in India as director of the Bengal Police. In fact, Monro was one of the few men who came to Aubrey's mind as competent enough to operate a detective department. But the Home Office had continued to appoint military commanders to responsible positions within the Scotland Yard hierarchy, primarily because the police were seen as guardians of law and order, *preventers* of crime rather than members of an agency that caught and prosecuted criminals. Of course, that function also existed within the police force mandate but in clear subordination to its role as a keeper of the peace. In this context, some logic existed for a paramilitary police image: some 60-odd years ago, when Sir Robert Peel had formed the original Metropolitan Police Force, he had organized it into quasi-infantry divisions.

During the intervening years, nothing much had changed save the evolution of the CID, a cadre within the force that became essentially crime solving in nature. In recent years, this relatively small department had undergone a further transformation with the creation of the Special Branch. This group of plainclothes officers had been formed to combat the Fenians, a group of Irish revolutionaries who, among other acts of violence, had attempted to blow up the Houses of Parliament and Scotland Yard. But other than the CID and the Special Branch, the image and role of the "beat copper" retained its paramilitary identity.

Two years before, Sir Charles Warren had further entrenched that ideology after taking over command of the force. One of his first executive orders had been the issuance of a manual to every constable entitled *Field Exercise and Evolutions of Infantry*. And his annual reports focused not on crime statistics but on how much bootblack the force expended in maintaining its spit-and-polish parade-ground appearance.

The approach had served Warren well in the past. In November of 1887, a year after his appointment, some of the worst rioting since the Chartist uprisings of half a century before had occurred right in Trafalgar Square. Aubrey dated the animosity between Matthews and Warren from that period. Warren had urged the Home Secretary to close the square to the "demagogues, agitators and criminal scum" of London, a description that had been an extreme exaggeration. A new term, "the unemployed" (many of the so-called demagogues had been out of work for the first time) seemed more appropriate. Aubrey had read some of Warren's correspondence concerning the matter: "It is in the highest degree impolitic to allow a hostile mob to perambulate the streets day and night, even under police supervision. They will soon get out of hand." But Matthews had been unable to reconcile the public's right to freedom of voice with the perceived threat to law and order. Aubrey had, for the first time, seen the vacillating nature of Henry Matthews: he was like a man with two heads, each arguing a different point. He had solved his problem by burying both heads in the sand.

And, after days of "shilly-shallying," the Commissioner's prophecy had come true—a mob did get out of control on Sunday, November 13th. Warren's men, some 7,000 strong, dispersed the rioters, and Henry Matthews closed the square thereafter to public gatherings, an edict that was still in effect. The day became known as Bloody Sunday, and while Warren's stock rose in the public's estimation (the *Times* lauded his handling of a deliberate attempt to terrorize London), Matthews' reputation had tumbled. The Home Secretary had suffered a severe embarrassment at the hands of the Commissioner of Police, and Aubrey was convinced that from Bloody Sunday on, Warren's days were numbered, the Home Secretary bent on his destruction. Aubrey wondered if the Whitechapel murderer was, however inadvertently, expediting the delivery of Warren's head to Henry Matthews on a silver platter.

Charles's desk was cluttered with papers. He was in the process of composing a letter to William James. He had organized his thoughts, outlining the contents of the letter in draft form, but was not quite ready to begin the actual writing. He stood, stretched and then pulled on his woollen jacket. He left the house and walked to Battersea Bridge, where he absent-mindedly watched the traffic for several moments. He then returned home, poured himself a glass of claret and sat down at his desk. He quickly scanned his draft letter and, after thanking James for his latest correspondence, began to describe one of his own recent case histories:

> *The patient, Mr. S., age 24, is an active, intelligent and healthy young man. Though coming of a somewhat nervous stock, there is no actual psychosis in the family. On Friday evening, June 2nd, he retired as usual. Next morning, as he didn't appear at breakfast, a member of the family entered his room and found him unconscious in bed. Gas was escaping from a leak in the pipe. (There was no reason to suspect an attempted suicide.) The patient's lips were blue, his eyes open, his respiration slow, sometimes almost ceasing. The family physician, a Dr. Rodenstein, was called, and he worked over*

him for three hours before the breathing became natural and his life seemed out of danger. He was partially conscious by 4 p.m., and he talked rationally to a clergyman who had been called.

Next morning, he recognized his sister and father and said he thought he was losing his mind. In the afternoon, he became somewhat delirious. He slept that night but during the succeeding six days, his mind wandered, and he was apparently distressed and excited. He was obsessed with the idea that someone wanted to take him away and do bodily injury to him. Four days after the accident, he was seen trying to read a newspaper upside down.

On the eighth day, he was taken to Dr. Granger's sanitarium. He went without trouble, though he was somewhat excited and maniacal. That night, he slept and next morning awoke free from any signs of mania. He was quiet and sane in every way.

From this time, the evidence of his amnesia and changed personality were apparent. He dressed himself neatly and with his usual attention to his toilet. He showed by his conversation that he didn't know who he was or where he was, and that his conscious memory of everything connected with his past life was gone.

His vocabulary at first was very limited; he could use only familiar words and could understand only language of the simplest character, such as that bearing on those things immediately about him. He did not know the names or uses of the things in and about the house, though he at once remembered and never forgot any name told him. He had a German attendant and pronounced many of the new words with a German accent. Everything had to be explained to him, such as the various articles about the house. Yet he would sit at the table and eat his meals with his former neatness, preserving also the courtesies and amenities of a gentleman, although he could not understand why he did certain things until they were explained to him. He did not recognize his parents, sisters or fiancée, though he said he had always known the latter and that his great desire and longing was to have her with him. He did not remember the slightest detail of his former relationship with her and did not know what marriage meant or the significance of the filial relation.

His vocabulary gradually increased, but even two months after his accident, he could not read a newspaper with understanding, except simple accounts of everyday happenings. He was slowest in understanding abstract terms. He learned figures and arithmetic very quickly and could soon do ordinary arithmetical computations easily. He had been accustomed to playing billiards a little but played the game badly. He very soon learned to play again and before long became much more skilful than he had ever been in his former state. He had always been clumsy with his hands and had never liked mechanical work or shown the least capacity for it; he never could draw or carve. With a little instruction from another patient, he soon became very skilful in carving. He showed a much greater cleverness with his hands and finer development of muscle sense than he had had before.

He had formerly played and sung a little. About six weeks after the accident, he picked out a tune on the piano that he had known long before but had not heard or played for a year. He did not know what it was, nor did he associate it with any early memory. He sang some of his old songs and played a little on his banjo. The old musical memories were there but were dissociated from any thought of the past.

If one were to meet him and discuss ordinary topics, he showed no evidence of being other than a normal man, except that he might betray some ignorance of the nature of uses of certain things. His conversation ran chiefly to the things he did every day and to the new things he was learning.

He was exactly like a person with an active brain set down into a new world, with everything to learn. The moon, the stars, the animals, his friends, all were mysteries that he impatiently hastened to solve.

On three occasions, I hypnotized him. On the second and third trial, I put him in a light degree of hypnotic sleep. During this, I told him that after waking at a specific signal, he would go through certain acts, such as rubbing his eyes, walking about the table, opening the door and giving a certain greeting to his mother. Also, that at a certain hour in the evening, he would remember the past. He did everything I suggested except the last. At the time named in the evening, he simply said without suggestion, "Dr. Randall told me to remember something, but I can't do it."

On the day of my scheduled return to London, he went to see his fiancée. She thought, after the interview, that he was rather worse, less like himself. She cried that night when he left, thinking he would never get well. While riding home with his brother, he said he felt as though one half of his head was prickling and numb, then the whole head, then he felt sleepy and was very quiet but did not fall asleep. When he arrived home, he became drowsy and was carried to bed, where he fell asleep. At about 11 p.m., he woke up and found his memory restored. He remembered distinctly the events of three months ago: his visit to his fiancée, his supper at the club afterward, his journey home, his shutting his bedroom door and getting into bed. His memory stopped there. He could not recall a thing that had occurred during his "amnesic" state.

Charles interrupted his writing to pour himself a second claret, then returned to his desk. He read what he had written and then glanced through James's Ansel Bourne letter. What similarities existed between Mr. S. and Mr. Bourne? He thought of Lucie Rhinegold and rephrased his question to include her. The two male patients had lived part of their lives as different persons—in effect, had lived two lives. But they had done so in an interrupted sense, returning permanently to their former selves. Lucie Rhinegold was a different matter. Her two personas recurred at regular intervals. Charles picked up his pen: *I have under my care another patient, a Mrs. R.* As briefly as he could, he sketched a case history of Lucie Rhinegold and then concluded his letter with a request that Professor James give the case of Mrs. R. some study, expressing the hope they could, in six weeks' time, discuss it in Paris.

⊷⊶[9]⊷⊶

CHARLES WARREN PACED his Scotland yard office like a caged animal. He was wearing a blue serge uniform that, with its military collar and red leg piping, seemed too resplendent for that of a police officer. He was a formidable-looking man, broad-shouldered and straight-backed, with piercing eyes, a walrus moustache and closely cropped, iron-grey hair. He looked every inch a commander of men, which coincided perfectly with his self-image. Prior to his appointment as Commissioner of Police, he had been administrator of Bechuanaland, an African dependency.

Warren had read the *Times*' account of the latest murder at breakfast with the rest of civilized London, and so he knew he would be in for a rough day. The murderer was proving as elusive as the proverbial slippery eel, seemingly able to come and go at will; apparently, in the latest outrage, even in broad daylight. The Commissioner believed he knew a great deal about eels—the *human* variety. To quote himself exactly, "They were the veriest scum in all London." He was used to dealing with them, by the hundreds or by the thousands, and did not worry about one or two that somehow slipped through the mesh and escaped back into the sea. That was his

analogy for the Whitechapel miscreant and the furor caused
by his killings. ''For the sake of Christ,'' he had bellowed in
the general direction of Inspector Abberline only an hour
before, ''they are only common prostitutes. He is not
murdering the Royal Family one by one!'' Yet that was how
the press was treating the matter. What were the police
supposed to do? The scum of which he spoke congregated in
Whitechapel like maggots in a carcass. Was he responsible
for interviewing every single one, every *individual*? A
preposterous and impossible suggestion. More importantly,
the murders had deflected public attention, and that of Henry
Matthews *(not a particularly difficult task,* he thought acid-
ly), from the true danger that lay within the bosom of the
East End: the socialists, anarchists, unemployed and other
potential troublemakers. London was a hotbed of foreign
intrigue. Political exiles from all over Europe congregated
there, free from harassment and persecution, thereby making
a flattering statement about British democracy but causing
untold headaches for Sir Charles. Karl Marx had founded the
activist International Working Men's Association in London.
And the Russian Peter Kropotkin, who had encouraged
''permanent revolt by word of mouth, by writing, by the
dagger, the rifle, dynamite, by whatever means necessary,''
had lived in Whitechapel. While the Salvation Army sang
''Onward Christian Soldiers,'' the revolutionaries sang their
own parodied anthem:

> *Onward Christian soldiers! Duty's way is plain,*
> *Slay your Christian neighbours or by them be slain.*
> *Pulpiteers are spouting effervescent swill,*
> *God above is calling you to rob and rape and kill.*
> *All your acts are sanctified by the Lamb on high,*
> *If you love the Holy Ghost, go murder, pray and die.*

Even the *Times* was breathing down his neck about the
murderer. Had everyone forgotten Bloody Sunday in the
midst of the hue and cry for one demented felon? On
impulse, he stopped his pacing, reached into a desk drawer
and pulled out a yellowed newspaper clipping dated Novem-

ber 14, 1887. It was taken from the *Times,* and he read it
with considerable pride:

Sir Charles Warren receives this morning the congratula-
tions and thanks of the whole law-abiding population of this
country for his complete and effectual vindication of that law
which is the sole bulwark of public liberty. Thanks to his
masterly arrangements and to the ability and devotion with
which they were carried out by the force under his control, the
determined attempt made yesterday to place the metropolis at
the mercy of a ruffianly mob was totally and signally defeated.

Then he reached down to his desk and reread this morning's
Times:

Two arrests were made yesterday, but it is very doubtful
whether the murderer is in the hands of the police. Members
of the Criminal Investigation Department are assisting the
divisional police at the East End in their endeavours to
elucidate the mystery in which these crimes are involved.
Yesterday morning, Detective Sergeant Thicke of the H
Division, who has been indefatigable in his inquiries respecting the murder of Annie Chapman at 29 Hanbury Street,
Spitalfields, on Saturday morning, succeeded in capturing a
man whom he believed to be "Leather Apron." It will be
recollected that this person obtained an evil notoriety during
the inquiries respecting this and other murders recently
committed in Whitechapel, owing to the startling reports that
had been freely circulated by many of the women living in the
district as to outrages alleged to have been committed by him.
Sergeant Thicke, who has had much experience concerning
thieves and their haunts in this portion of the metropolis, has,
since being engaged in the present inquiry, been repeatedly
assured by some of the most well-known characters of their
abhorrence of the fiendishness of the crimes, and they have
further stated that if they could only lay hands on the
murderer, they would hand him over to justice. These and
other circumstances convinced the officer and those associated
with him that the deed was in no way traceable to any of the

regular thieves or desperadoes in the East End. At the same time, a sharp lookout was kept on the common lodging houses, not only in this district but in other portions of the metropolis. Several persons bearing a resemblance to the description of the person in question have been arrested but, being able to render a satisfactory account of themselves, were released. Shortly after 8 a.m. yesterday morning, Sergeant Thicke, accompanied by two or three other officers, proceeded to 22 Mulberry Street and knocked at the door. It was opened by the Polish Jew named Pizer, alleged to be known as "Leather Apron." Pizer was charged with being concerned in the murder of the woman Chapman, and to this he made no reply. The accused man, who is a boot finisher by trade, was then handed over to other officers, and the house was searched. Possession was taken of five sharp long-bladed knives—which, however, are used by men in Pizer's trade— and also of several old hats. With reference to the latter, several women who stated they were acquainted with the prisoner alleged he has been in the habit of wearing different hats. Pizer, who is about 33, was then quietly removed to the Leman Street Police Station, his friends protesting that he knew nothing of the affair, that he had not been out of the house since Thursday night and that he is of a very delicate constitution. The friends of the man were subjected to close questioning by the police. It was still uncertain, late last night, whether this man remained in custody or had been liberated. He strongly denies that he is known by the name of "Leather Apron."

Warren had sent Abberline to interview Pizer, instructing him to use every effort to verify or contradict the man's alibi. If Pizer was the Whitechapel murderer, it would be a mixed blessing. The police would likely be congratulated on his arrest, but feelings against Whitechapel Jews were already running high. Individual Jews had been beaten, some so viciously that they had had to be hospitalized. If Abberline and his cohorts were not careful, Pizer would be lynched, and a pogrom could begin in the East End. He had already been approached by the chief rabbi about increasing police protection for Jews, a request he had passed on to the Home Office in conversation with Lushington. Henry Matthews had received this communication with his customary "ostrich" approach, refusing to believe that Englishmen were capable of acting against the Jews in any organized fashion. Warren had experienced a sense of déjà vu, recalling his similar warning about the Trafalgar Square mob. If another Bloody Sunday were to occur, it would mean the end of Matthews' political career. *And good riddance*, Sir Charles thought to himself.

He replaced the laudatory *Times* clipping in the file folder where he kept correspondence of a congratulatory nature: letters and clippings he was saving for an autobiography he was contemplating writing upon retirement. He quickly shuffled through the letters: one from Sir Francis Knollys, Equerry to the Prince of Wales; another from H.R.H. the Duke of Cambridge, Field Marshall Commander-in-Chief. Both letters complimented him on his handling of the huge crowds that had attended Queen Victoria's Golden Jubilee on June 21, 1887. There was a third letter appended to these two. He read it with smug satisfaction:

Sir,

    In obedience to the Queen's express commands, I have great satisfaction in signifying to you Her Majesty's entire approbation of the excellent manner in which the arrangements for preserving good order were made by you and executed by those acting under your orders, on the occasion of Her Majesty's visit to Westminster Abbey to attend the Special Service of Thanksgiving for the attainment of the Jubilee year of her reign.

It was signed: *Henry Matthews, Home Secretary.*

Warren replaced the letter, wondering if it might not become a useful article of negotiation in any future confrontation he might have with Matthews.

Chief Inspector Abberline was at his desk in Scotland Yard. In front of him sat the same Home Office official who had visited him only yesterday, Mr. Carsonby, a slight man with a self-effacing manner and an interrogative mind. Abberline had been informed by Godfrey Lushington that Mr. Carsonby was, in a more or less official capacity, assuming "some" responsibility for the operation of the CID until Sir Robert Anderson's return.

To Abberline's pragmatic mind, "assuming some responsibility" was an equivocal term. One either had the responsibility or one did not. There was no middle ground. Although he was tempted to put this directly to Mr. Carsonby, he decided not to—it might be interpreted as a hostile challenge. Abberline had a finely tuned sense of who belonged where in the power hierarchy, and the civil servant sitting opposite was obviously on the rise. Instead, he asked, "What has happened to Mr. Monro?"

"Oh, he'll be in and out. But in an unofficial capacity."

Abberline nodded his head sagely, although it was obvious that no one had assumed official control of his department.

"Apparently, you've circulated a notice concerning a description of the murderer," Aubrey said.

"Yes, sir." Abberline pushed a notice across his desk:

Description of a man who entered a passage of the house at which the murder of a prostitute was committed at 2 a.m. on the 8th—age 37; height 5 feet, 7 inches; rather dark beard and moustache. Dress—shirt, dark jacket, dark vest and trousers, black scarf and black felt hat. Spoke with a foreign accent.

"To whom has it been circulated?"

"Every police station in the country, sir."

Aubrey nodded in approval. "Do you believe the description to be an accurate one?"

Abberline deflected the question. "It could fit half the male population of England. But we have nothing else."

"What about this Jew, Pizer?"

"He apparently has an alibi. We're attempting to verify his story."

"Which is?"

"Concerning the Nichols murder—that he wasn't in London."

"And the Chapman murder?"

"He was at home, hiding because he thought someone might hang him from a tree. Which they might have."

"But if he didn't know he was a suspect before the Chapman murder, why would he hide?"

"Because he's a Jew, for one. Because he does go by the nickname 'Leather Apron.' And because he does knock about whores—begging your pardon, sir, prostitutes. He's known to the division constables as something of a terror when it comes to prostitutes."

"Do you think he's the man?"

That question earned a skeptical look from the Inspector. "Possible, but not likely. We took his knives into custody. You know he's a boot finisher? Well, the surgeon says none of them could be the murder weapon. Something else: he also works on ballet slippers. Said that if he wanted to hurt a woman he'd crush her feet. Said there are 50 or 60 bones in the human foot. He's a damn peculiar sort, but I don't believe he's our man."

"There is a rumour circulating that he was identified in a lineup."

"That's true. But the man who identified him is a crackpot, a half-Bulgarian, half-Spaniard reprobate named Emanuel Violenia."

"But they say he went right up to Pizer." Aubrey had gathered his information from a conversation he had overheard between two constables as he had entered Scotland Yard.

Abberline nodded in agreement. "He did, sir, but the line-up was a little irregular. A description of Pizer had already made the rounds after his arrest. Street talk had him pretty much pegged."

"Then why bother with a line-up in the first place?"

"What if Violenia had picked someone else out?"

"Seems a small chance of that."

"At this point, sir, with respect, any chance is one we can't afford to miss."

"Yes, of course," Aubrey said. "And there is no other news?"

Inspector Abberline shook his head, and for the first time, Aubrey realized how exhausted and shadowed his eyes were. He was tempted to mention something about proper sleep but thought better of the idea. He did not want to cross the proper bounds of the "employer-employee" relationship he believed he had begun to establish.

On his return to Whitehall, Aubrey picked up an early edition of the *Times*, his eye caught by the headline: BLOODY TRAIL OF MURDERER FOUND:

An important discovery that throws considerable light upon the movements of the murderer immediately after the committal of the crime was made yesterday afternoon. In the backyard of 25 Hanbury Street, the house next to the scene of the murder, a little girl noticed peculiar marks on the wall and on the ground. She communicated the discovery to Detective Inspector Chandler, who had just called at the house in order to make a plan of the back premises of the three houses for the use of the Coroner at the inquest, which will be resumed today. The whole of the yard was then carefully examined, with the result that a bloody trail was found distinctly marked for a distance of five or six feet in the direction of the back door of the house. Further investigation left no doubt that the trail was that of the murderer who, after finishing his work, had passed through or over the dividing fence between Nos. 29 and 27 and thence into the garden of No. 25. On the wall of the last house there was found a curious mark, between a smear and a sprinkle, which had probably been made by the murderer who, alarmed by the blood-soaked state of his coat, took off that garment and knocked it against the wall. Abutting on the end of the yard of No. 25 are the works of Mr. Bailey, a packing-case maker. In the yard of this establishment, in an out-of-the-way corner, the police yesterday afternoon found some crumpled paper almost saturated with blood. It was evident that the murderer had found the paper in the yard of No. 25 and had wiped his hands with it, afterward throwing it over the wall into Bailey's premises. The house at

No. 25, like most of the dwellings in the street, is let out in tenements direct from the owner, who does not live on the premises and has no direct representative therein. The back and front doors are therefore always left either on the latch or wide open. The general appearance of the bloody trail and other circumstances seem to show that the murderer intended to make his way as rapidly as possible into the street through the house next door but, being frightened by some noise or light in No. 29, retreated by the way he came.

Aubrey finished the article while walking to his office. Now he sat down in anger. Why hadn't Abberline mentioned the blood-stained paper? Because it led nowhere? But that was immaterial. The Inspector would have to be made to understand that in future, when asked if there were "new" developments, he must give full answers; Aubrey would decide on their significance.

I don't know what I shall say, Lydia thought to herself. She was in her room researching her Toynbee Hall presentation, and had been reading George Eliot, beside whose name, in brackets, she had written "pseudonym, Marian Cross," as if to remind herself of the writer's gender. But the going was tedious. From Eliot she had copied: "A really cultured woman, like a really cultured man, will be ready to yield in trifles. So far as we see, there is no indissoluble connection between infirmity of logic and infirmity of will, and a woman quite innocent of an opinion in philosophy is as likely as not to have an indomitable opinion about the kitchen."

Reading when the heart is not in it is like hoeing a weed-infested garden, Lydia had decided. One worked through paragraph after paragraph to arrive at a clear understanding or conclusion. She had worked tirelessly all morning and where was she? *What was George Eliot saying?* she pondered. *That women, according to men, lack logic? But don't suffer from lack of will? And therefore, because women possess will, they must, perforce, possess logic? I am adrift in a sea of illogic,* she thought, in growing frustration. *How can I speak with authority on a subject matter I myself am not capable of comprehending?*

"George Eliot is too obtuse," she wrote, then quickly stroked out the sentence, following it with, "I am too obtuse." This was much closer to the truth. Would the women who attended her lecture even have heard of Eliot? Would they find her philosophy too intellectual in content and therefore her lecture dry and dogmatic?

One fascinating fact she had uncovered about Eliot was that her skull circumference had exceeded that of any other skull measured, save that of Napoleon Bonaparte. It even dwarfed Darwin's, and what brighter man had the century produced? This was more like it, she decided. She must season her speech as one did a soup. Start with a basic broth, then add seasoning: peppery insights about women with superior skull circumferences.

And what had she just read in the *Illustrated London News*? That the Empress of Japan had decided that European Court gowns were to be worn at state functions. And that a group of prominent American ladies, including the President's wife, Mrs. Cleveland, and the widow of the late President Garfield, had sent a letter encouraging their Japanese sisters to pause before exchanging their "loose" national costume for "our ungraceful, inconvenient and unhealthy fashions." Yes, this, too, was a bread-and-butter issue to which any woman who had been strapped into a whalebone could relate.

And then there was Walter Pater. That misogynist had provoked her wrath with his famous essay on the Mona Lisa. She quickly thumbed through her diary, for so incensed had she been when she first read it that she had vented her anger through the medium of her pen. She found the entry in March, written at Girton College, Cambridge:

> *Mr. Walter Pater, spiritual leader of the aesthetes, has outdone himself. He has taken Da Vinci's Mona Lisa and likened her to the vampire who has been dead many times and learned the secrets of the grave. This pronouncement, for such is Mr. Pater's stature that everything he writes rings with the authority of a royal proclamation, strikes me as remarkable.*

Yet Mr. Pater is not satisfied with the likes of mere vampires. He pours into this most inoffensive and benign of women the animalism of Greece, the lust of Rome, the paganism of the pre-Christian tribes—even, with his most elegiac of imaginations, the sins of the Borgias.

He writes: Set 'it' beside one of those white Greek goddesses or beautiful women of antiquity, and how troubled they would be by the Lady Lisa's bewitching beauty—through the soul of which all maladies have passed.

And Mr. Swinburne, the poet, enters the fray, although as an avowed sensualist, he can almost be forgiven his comment that Mona Lisa is a "woman beautiful always beyond desire and cruel beyond words, fairer than heaven and yet more terrible than hell, pale with pride and weary with wrongdoing." This is so much prattle, yet it passes for the insight of genius.

Man puts a woman in a frame or on a pedestal, as he would a painting or a statue. Then he subjects her to critical scrutiny under the magnifying power of his own prejudice, finally to proclaim his interpretation of what the Creator intended by this particular rendering of the female. Women are the medium by which men exorcise their own demons. . . .

Lydia sat back and took stock of what she had just read. The notation fairly smoked with anger. But simultaneously, and for the first time, she felt uncomfortable about the nakedness of her emotionalism. Now, although only half a year older, she was fascinated by her own development, from uninhibited youth to assiduous maturity.

She reached in a bottom drawer of her desk and pulled out another diary, the year 1881 stamped in gold on the blue Moroccan leather. In an upper desk drawer, she found a small music box. When she unlocked and opened it, the bright, plinking notes of Tchaikovsky's *Polonaise* filled the silent room with music. She removed a tangled mess of string, keys and tags, found the right key and managed to open the diary. In 1881, she had been 12 years old, a child. She closed her eyes, opening the slender volume to no page in particular, feeling strangely queasy, as if she were actually walking backward in time, trespassing on the private mind of a young girl who had died prematurely. She opened her eyes to:

April 27th, 1881

> *Today it rained. Not a warm shower but cold, hard drops of rain like hailstones. The tulips were battered, poor things. But the sun came out in the afternoon, fiercely hot, as if in competition with the dreary chill of morning, and the tulips recovered nicely.*
>
> *A fight with Mama. I have to write a homily about parental respect. . . .*

Lydia stopped reading. *What had the fight been about?* she thought. *God only knew; there had been so many over the years.*

A sharp rapping on the door startled her, and she hastily shut the diary.

"Come in," she called.

The butler, whose name was Dawkins, opened the door. In one hand, he carried a small silver salver on which rested a beige envelope.

"A correspondence for you, Miss Lydia," he intoned formally in his rich bass voice.

Lydia could not help blurting out an undignified "For me?" Dawkins had never delivered a "correspondence" to her before, let alone a mysterious envelope on a salver as if it had originated from Buckingham Palace, embossed with the royal seal.

Dawkins, with his balding scalp, coattails and swelling chest, reminded her of a plump swallow. "Yes, Ma'am. It bears your name. Lydia Carlyle," he read from the envelope.

She thanked him and he retreated from her room. As curious as she was, she could not simply tear the envelope open. Letters were treasures to be savoured, like a Christmas or birthday present delayed in its opening. She smelled it (the vellum stationery seemed to have a masculine scent), held it up to the strong window light (the envelope was thick and completely opaque) and finally held it up to her forehead, attempting to divine its contents and author. But the envelope steadfastly retained its secrets.

Finally, she could restrain herself no longer. With a letter opener, she slit the envelope and removed a card. It was an invitation, handwritten in an elegant sweeping script, the penmanship unmistakably male yet displaying an almost feminine flair:

> *Lydia,*
>   *Would you attend with me a performance of Jekyll and Hyde at the Lyceum this Saturday evening?*
>
> *Charles*
>
> *RSVP Cheyne Walk, Chelsea*

Lydia pressed the card to her bosom. On the outside was a lush watercolour of golden yellow honeysuckles and vibrant red roses. *Roses and honeysuckle. My God,* she thought, *how audacious of Charles. What if Mother had intercepted the card?* But Lillian Carlyle was out, attending one of her innumerable teas. Lydia was well aware of the language of flowers. The Germans called it speaking *durch die Blumen*. Secret desires were often communicated by means of symbolic flowers. The marigold and lily for sweetness of person and purity of soul, the scentless camellia for worldly vanities and the rose and honeysuckle for sensuality and sexual attraction. Charles, with the card she held in hand, had declared not only an interest in escorting her to a theatre outing but. . . . Abruptly she stood and walked to her mirror. But that was a mistake, for the mirror gave a visual presence to the somersaulting turmoil in her mind. There before her stood a young woman blushing deeply, but moreover, a young woman with desire in her eyes as transparent as a glass-enclosed corsage of roses and honeysuckle.

At Cheyne Walk, Charles was having no difficulty writing the introduction to his paper. It had been handed to him gift-wrapped, courtesy of Robert Louis Stevenson's *The Strange Case of Dr. Jekyll and Mr. Hyde*:

It chanced that the direction of my scientific studies, which led wholly toward the mystic and the transcendental, reacted and shed a strong light on this consciousness of the perennial war among my members. With every day, and from both sides of my intelligence, the moral and the intellectual, I thus drew steadily nearer to that truth, by whose partial discovery I have been doomed to such a dreadful shipwreck: that man is not truly one, but truly two. I say two, because the state of my own knowledge does not pass beyond that point. Others will follow, others will outstrip me of the same lines, and I hazard the guess that man will be ultimately known for a mere polity of multifarious, incongruous and independent denizens. I for my part, from the nature of my life, advanced infallibly in one direction and in one direction only. It was on the moral side, and in my own person, that I learned to recognize the thorough and primitive duality of man; I saw that, of the two natures that contended in the field of my consciousness, even if I could rightly be said to be either, it was only because I was radically both; and from an early date, even before the course of my scientific discoveries had begun to suggest the most naked possibility of such a miracle, I had learned to dwell with pleasure, as a beloved daydream, on the thought of the separation of these elements. If each, I told myself, could but be housed in separate identities, life would be relieved of all that was unbearable; the "unjust" might go his way, delivered from the aspiration and remorse of his more upright twin; and the "just" could walk steadfastly and securely on his upward path, doing the good things in which he found his pleasure and no longer exposed to disgrace and penitence by the hands of this extraneous evil. It was the curse of mankind that these incongruous faggots were thus bound together—that in the agonised womb of consciousness, these polar twins should be continuously struggling. How, then, were they dissociated?

Charles reread the passage, noting the appropriateness of his underscoring. Somewhere—he had forgotten the circumstance—he had heard that Stevenson had dreamed the plot to Jekyll and Hyde. Charles doubted that a spontaneous dream had been his sole inspiration. The last word in the opening scene, *dissociated,* convinced him of that. That word, for Charles, existed in a scientific and medical vocabulary and not one of common usage. Charles was certain that Stevenson had talked with someone knowledgeable about the work of the French psychologists Janet and Binet and that when he wrote his thriller, he had been aware of the genuine phenomenon of double consciousness.

The paragraph that Charles wrote, following the Stevenson excerpt, flowed without difficulty:

> *Dissociation of the personality of the same individual, that is separation into "two" distinct consciousnesses, belongs not to the realm of fiction, not to the febrile imagination of a writer such as Robert Louis Stevenson, but rather to the realm of reality, to the no less inventive mind of that all-pervasive "entity" we know as Mother Nature.*
>
> *Pierre Janet has given scientific credence to the concept of dissociated personalities, which he interprets to be a system of ideas that has split apart from the major personality, which can then exist as a subordinate presence. This is an unconscious presence, but it is capable of becoming conscious; in fact, it is capable of subordinating the major or principal personality. Max Dessoir has written a treatise "Das Doppel-Ich" (The Double Ego) in which he identifies two streams of mental activity, an "upper" and a "lower" consciousness. This is strikingly similar to the stream-of-consciousness notion theorized by William James—that consciousness does not consist of discrete, distinctive and disconnected mental elements but rather flows continuously like a stream. The stream provides a medium in which every thought, image and feeling is immersed.*
>
> *Alfred Binet has concluded that "the division of consciousness is not a sharp line of demarcation, yet the division leaves unimpaired the independence of split-off mental images and memories. Each ego knows only what transpires in its own domain."*

Charles stopped for a moment and collected his thoughts, then continued to write:

From these individualistic interpretations, a consensus can be formed. If this consensus proves empirically verifiable, it will shake the foundations, not only of the medical establishment, but of how man perceives himself—that he is a multilevelled self, an aggregation of consciousnesses.

Charles put down his pen and tried to analyze the impact of what he had written, not wanting to overstate his case. Just 30 years ago, Charles Darwin had all but destroyed the God-given authority of the Bible, meeting the Creator thunderbolt to thunderbolt. The world had not been the same since. *And who stands taller?* he wondered. *It appears society is soon going to have to weather another attack on its sense of order within the universe.* But Charles suddenly became impatient with this polemical diversion. He picked up his pen and quickly sketched out the conclusion to his paper:

1. The elements (day-to-day events) entering into the normal "memory" of self may exist in a state of dissociation.
2. A consciousness continues to accompany these happenings, although the self loses knowledge of it.
3. Sometimes under pathological (or experimental) conditions, these elements organize themselves into a second personality.
4. These separate personalities need not be aware of each other's existence.
5. An individual can fall asleep one man and wake up another.

⊶❧[10]❧⊷

THE CARLYLE SISTERS were entertaining Charles and Aubrey in the drawing room of their Cadogan Square home. Lydia sat opposite Aubrey; Charlotte faced Charles. The foursome sat at a green baize card table with dark oak trim and ornately carved legs. At Charlotte's instigation, they had been drawn together to play whist. The game had been in progress for the better part of an hour.

Lydia, who had said nothing about Charles's invitation to either her sister or mother, felt under some strain. Charles had given no hint that he had received her reply to his note: *"I am delighted to accept your invitation and look forward to an evening at the theatre,"* it had read.

Lydia's message had been followed, that afternoon, by Charlotte's invitation to an evening of cards. Charles had given serious thought to declining but could not bring himself to pass up an opportunity to be near Lydia, even if in the tiresome company of Charlotte and Aubrey.

"Have you been following the story of the Whitechapel murders?" Aubrey asked of no one in particular, as he led an ace of clubs.

"It's absolutely horrid. It makes my skin crawl," Charlotte said. "I actually had a nightmare about it last night."

"There's nothing for you to worry about," Aubrey said with concern. "As demonic as this monster seems, he would never cross over into the West End."

"Why not, Aubrey?" Lydia asked, as he took the trick.

Aubrey glanced at her uncomfortably and then studied his cards. He had decided not to mention the fact that he had seen Lydia in Hanbury Street unless she brought it up in conversation. "Why not? Why because his . . . ah . . . his victims are generally not to be found here."

"That's not quite true, Aubrey," Charles contradicted. "His victims have also been known to frequent the Haymarket, the Strand, even Sloane Street, just around the corner."

"Charles! Are you trying to frighten me?" Charlotte exclaimed. She laid down a low trump on Aubrey's king of clubs.

"That wasn't very kind of you," he groaned.

"How many tricks do we have now, Charles?" Charlotte asked.

"I believe the hand is ours."

"A battle lost, but the war yet to be won. Don't despair, Lydia. We shall rise from this defeat." Aubrey was enjoying himself. With the burden of being responsible for the CID weighing heavily on his mind, he found tonight's entertainment a welcome distraction. He was among friends, in fact sitting with the woman he hoped one day to make his wife. "Have you been keeping track of the murders, Charles?" he asked conversationally.

The question caught Charles off guard; he had read the *Times* but was reluctant to pursue the subject in the company of Lydia and Charlotte. "Not really, Aubrey. I see enough 'demonic' behaviour, as you style it, in my practice."

"Some of your colleagues are following the case quite closely. Here, read these," he said, reaching into his pocket and taking out what appeared to be newspaper clippings. "I thought you might have missed them."

Charles picked them up. Both were letters to the editor of the *Times*. The first consisted of a single sentence:

TO THE EDITOR OF THE TIMES

Sir,

I would suggest that the police should at once find out the whereabouts of all cases of "homicidal mania" who may have been discharged as "cured" from metropolitan asylums during the last two years.

Your obedient servant,
A Country Doctor

He handed it over to Lydia, then unfolded the second, longer clipping:

TO THE EDITOR OF THE TIMES

Sir,

My theory having been circulated far and wide with reference to an opinion given to the authorities of the Criminal Investigation Department, I would like to qualify such statements in your columns.

That the victims in the Whitechapel deaths have been murdered by one and the same person, I have no doubt.

The behaviour in the whole affair is that of a lunatic, and as there is "method in madness," so there was method shown in the crime and in the gradual dissection of the body of the latest victim. It is not the work of a responsible person. It is a well-known and accepted fact that homicidal mania is incurable but difficult to detect, as it frequently lies latent. It is incurable, and those who have been the subject of it should never be let loose on society.

I think that the murderer is not of the class of which "Leather Apron" belongs but is of the upper classes, and I still think that my opinion given to the authorities is the correct one—that the murders have been committed by a lunatic lately discharged from some asylum or by one who has escaped. If the former, he is doubtless one who, though suffering from the effects of homicidal mania, is apparently sane on the surface and consequently has been liberated and is following out the inclinations of his morbid imaginations by wholesale homicide. I think the advice given by me to be a sound one—to apply for an immediate list from all asylums who have discharged such individuals with a view to ascertaining their whereabouts.

I am your obedient servant,

L. FORBES WINSLOW
M.B. Camb., D.C.L. Oxon.

"Well, what do you think?" Aubrey asked.

"I suppose the point about the lunatic asylums is well made."

"Has that been done, Aubrey?" Charlotte inquired.

"Truthfully, I don't know," he replied pensively. "I've been placed in a position of some responsibility in this matter. I am overseeing the Criminal Investigation Department, at least in a manner of speaking, I am."

"How do you mean?" Lydia asked, still holding the longer of the two letters.

"The chain of command between the Home Office and Scotland Yard is not all it could be. And tension, real tension, exists between Henry Matthews and Charles Warren. This is all very confidential, of course. What I say is among the four of us."

"I don't believe you're breaking any confidences, Aubrey. The Warren-Matthews animosity is public knowledge," Charles said.

"Not the degree of it," Aubrey riposted. "The public mistakes their animosity for petty jealousy, but I can assure you that it is more than that."

"Oh come, Aubrey," Lydia interposed. "They are politicians, behaving like politicians."

Aubrey looked at Lydia with displeasure. "Sir Charles is not a politician."

"He's the closest thing to one," Lydia replied. "I heard two fellows discussing politics at Toynbee last week. One asked the other if he knew the difference between a Liberal and a Conservative government. His companion said he didn't. 'The difference between a jackal and a hyena,' was the reply."

Charles laughed aloud at this sally.

"That sounds anarchistic to me," Aubrey said.

Charlotte spoke. "What exactly is anarchy? I've never really understood the term."

"In its mildest form, it's the wrangling of men like Matthews and Warren," Lydia said.

"Or, on a slightly grander scale, Question Period in the Commons," Charles added.

"You're both being irresponsible," Aubrey said.

"Don't take yourself so seriously," Lydia admonished. "I heard an anarchist speak in Whitechapel last Sunday. His speech was quite riveting."

Charlotte frowned. "Why you visit that horrid place is beyond me, Lydia."

"What did he say?" Aubrey asked.

"That he and his followers are going to tear down society," Lydia replied.

Charlotte made a derisive face. "And where will that leave them?"

"Undoubtedly at the top of the heap," Charles said.

"But there has to be some order in the world, Charles."

Aubrey nodded in agreement. "I endorse you wholeheartedly, Charlotte," he said. "The East End is overrun with his kind. The Whitechapel murderer is a case in point."

"But Mr. Forbes-Winslow thinks otherwise," Lydia said, tapping his letter. "He thinks it's someone from the upper classes."

"That's pure nonsense," Aubrey scoffed. He turned to Charles. "Do you know Dr. Winslow? He hounds not only the detectives at Scotland Yard but also constables on their beats. He's determined to be a one-man vigilante committee. What do you make of his point about the man being sane on the 'outside' but a homicidal maniac on the 'inside'? Isn't that sort of thing right up your alley?"

Charles did not reply for a moment. "It's a plausible explanation. Yes, I know of Dr. Winslow. He's something of an eccentric—"

"With an eccentric's theories, I fear," Aubrey interrupted. He lit one of his infrequent cigarettes. The game of whist had been forgotten.

"Listen," Charles said suddenly. "I haven't given these murders much thought, but I do have some knowledge of the diversity of the human mind. Look at it in the sense of two city-states, each with its own laws and social norms, different but recognizable and understood as such. I think it possible that another 'mental' state, other than that known by us, can exist. A state of mind where madness and genius, sadism and kindness, coexist, side by side, yet leave no line of demarcation visible to the eye." Charles sipped coffee from the cup by his side. He was enjoying talking about the very topic in which he was so deeply involved and was almost unaware of the others' rapt attention.

"The human mind has its twilight zone—and so, in a larger sense, does life. But beyond this twilight exists a form of human darkness. Within this darkness, all of our frames of reference, our laws, manmade and otherwise, suddenly lose their meaning. Nothing is more terrifying than the absence of the ability to reason. With no rationale, we are plunged into the abyss, the very heart of human darkness. In this darkness exists the fiend from the East End—or the West, as Dr. Winslow has said. He's quite at home there, and I daresay he is enjoying our outrage and horror immensely, and our inability to comprehend his very existence."

The conclusion of Charles's exegesis was greeted with silence that, after a moment, was broken by Aubrey. "How do you propose we stop such a monster?"

"I don't propose anything. That's probably quite impossible," Charles said.

Aubrey frowned. "Do you mean . . . ?"

"I mean precisely what I said," Charles interrupted with a trace of asperity. "The murderer might as well be possessed of supernatural powers. In a sense, he is. And as for his detection, well, that seems beyond our power. The police and the Home Office are unfairly maligned."

"Do you mean we can't stop him?" Aubrey said, unable to restrain his trepidation.

"No, I believe he can be stopped. But it will involve luck, and unfortunately luck, as we all know, comes in two varieties. It seems this man-monster has a monopoly on the good kind,'' Charles said thoughtfully. ''But don't worry. The killings will come to an end, if not by good fortune then by the man's own volition. He'll tire of his sport.''

Charlotte shivered. ''What an awful thought! It chills me to the very marrow.''

''Sport indeed!'' Aubrey snorted.

''There you go, Aubrey, falling back on your own frame of reference, for which you are completely excused, of course.''

''But this is madness,'' he said.

''Not to him. To him, it's genius,'' Charles replied. ''Charlotte, do you have something other than coffee to quench a fellow's thirst? All this talk and theorizing has left my throat dry.''

Charlotte undressed in her room with the assistance of her maid, Anna-Marie. The evening, which had been orchestrated with such care, had been a failure. The plan had been simple: a foursome for whist, she paired with Charles, Aubrey with Lydia. But her motive had been ulterior, the evening staged to perpetuate a relationship with Charles Randall. Whist had been her Mother's suggestion: ''A game of perfect innocence, yet one that can be used to advance a suit, if you will pardon my weak pun, dear. Whist is to love what cannons are to war. That is how my own dear Mother used to put it.''

''Do be careful,'' Charlotte snapped at Anna-Marie, as the maid attempted to unfasten the clasp on a string of pearls. Charlotte had spent all afternoon preparing herself for the evening. *It's amazing,* she thought in a moment of distraction, *hours of preparation, and the entire effect can be undone in minutes, even if one didn't have a maid with fumbling fingers*. ''Anna-Marie!'' she scolded, ''are your fingers in knots?''

''Sorry, ma'am.''

''Tonight was a disaster.''

''Yes, ma'am,'' Anna-Marie said, thinking that nothing could have been plainer.

"You've seen Lord Longerdale?"

"Yes, ma'am."

"Aubrey Carsonby?"

"Yes, ma'am."

"What do you think of them?"

"Beg your pardon, ma'am?" Anna-Marie said in surprise.

"For pity's sake, *who* is more handsome?"

Anna-Marie remained silent. Obviously, Lord Longerdale was. And he was a Lord. The other gentleman was only a Mister. And because the answer was so obvious, the question momentarily stumped her.

"Anna-Marie!" Charlotte stamped a stockinged foot.

"Lord Longerdale, ma'am," the maid answered quickly.

"Of course he is. What took you so long?" Charlotte said testily. She stepped out of her last crinoline, revealing a chaste chemise, silk and white.

"Shall I undo your hair, ma'am?"

Charlotte always took great pains with her honey blonde hair. It was not peroxided, a process that many women were resorting to now that blondness had become almost *de rigueur* in society. Tonight, her hair had been swept up into a braided crown, held in place by pink rosebuds and a tiny rice paper fan, with a delicate curl dropping over her forehead like a golden honeycomb. The coiffure alone had taken three hours to create. Now the forehead curl drooped like the tail of a forlorn poodle.

"No," she snapped at Anna-Marie, "I'll do it myself." She suddenly wanted to be alone with her thoughts. "That will be all, thank you."

After the maid left, Charlotte pulled the rosebuds and fan from her hair. She would leave it pinned up for the night. She slipped out of her chemise and into a thin cotton night shift, then climbed into bed beside her French doll, Angeline. The doll had its own tiny pillow onto which its own blonde ringlets cascaded. Charlotte kept a diary, but unlike her sister, she did not make entries on a daily basis. Angeline, as often as not, was her nightly sounding board—the doll did not talk back, something a diary entry sometimes did, particularly if one was not guarded in one's written confessions.

Charlotte was troubled and perplexed. A very unpleasant realization was dawning: Lydia was attracted to Charles—hardly an earth-shattering discovery—but it appeared that the attraction was reciprocated.

"How can that be, Angeline?" she said softly in the dark. "Lydia is so outspoken. Surely the recent scenes with Mother have left an unfavourable impression. She is so forward. I don't say these things in spite, you understand," she added quickly, "but what can Charles possibly see in her that he can't see in me?"

She sighed and lay in silence for a moment. "It's an impossible situation, really. Lydia, Countess of Longerdale," she whispered. "No, Angeline, that will not do."

She calmed herself, conjuring up the image of herself on the arm of Charles Randall. She was dressed in a magnificent white wedding gown, the train held by 12 petite bridesmaids. The wedding procession made its way up a cathedral aisle, she and Charles, man and wife; Lydia's tear-stained face looking on.

"Confound Lydia!" she suddenly said aloud. "She does not know where she stumbles, who she hurts. She must be corrected and made to set an example. If she will not heed Mama, she will have to contend with me."

Down the hall from her sister, Lydia quickly undressed. She had been offered a maid on her sixteenth birthday but had declined, to her Mother's annoyance and disapproval. "A maid is not a privilege for a lady of breeding, Lydia, she is a necessity—a fact you will shortly recognize as your social agenda grows in scope and responsibility. Then you will rue your decision." Lydia had occasionally regretted her judgement, but never to the extent of reversing it.

She sat down at her desk and made a note in her diary:

Most men's interests, in which I would include their political, moral and other beliefs, can be measured on a horizontal

plane—they have breadth. We say a man is "catholic" in his
tastes, eclectic in his outlook. Such a man is the prototypical
homo universalis. He's as polished as the high gloss of a
mirror, but, unlike the looking glass, he reflects the image of
others, not himself. That is because there is no self. He is a
composite of others. I think Aubrey falls into this category,
although to say so may malign him. Charles is cut from a
different cloth, and that is one reason why he fascinates me.
Not only is he well-read and accomplished in a professional
discipline, but he also has an impenetrable quality, a depth.
Tonight, we made eye contact and a kind of frisson occurred.

She paused in her writing, pushed aside the diary and pulled
the rose and honeysuckle card from the bottom of her drawer.
The lush watercolour reminded her of James Whistler's
work. For a moment, she studied it in the candlelight and then
put it beside her diary pages as if comparing it to what she
had written. *They seem to be saying the same thing,* she
thought, putting the card in her diary and closing it.

She reached for Thomas Hardy's *Return of the Native* and
took it with her to bed. She had met the author at the same
botanical fête where she had first seen Charles, but had been
disappointed in his appearance. Hardy's novels contained
some of the most sensual and provocative writing in all of
England, and somehow she had expected him to look like
one of his characters: leonine, handsome, slender yet muscu-
lar, virile yet gentle—the very qualities she saw in Charles
when he had appeared ten minutes later. But the novelist had
proved to be a stuffy sort, taciturn and ordinary in appearance. She had managed a few laudatory words about his
work, compliments that seemed not to move or interest him.
As gracefully as she could, she had slipped away.

She had read *Return of the Native* several times. Now she
sat leafing through the book and reading passages at random:

"Wildeve gave her his arm and took her down on the
outside of the ring to the bottom of the dance, which they
entered. In two minutes more they were involved in the figure
and began working their way upwards to the top. Till they had

advanced halfway thither. Eustacia wished more than once that she had not yielded to his request; from the middle to the top she felt that, since she had come out to seek pleasure, she was only doing a natural thing to obtain it. Fairly launched into the ceaseless glides and whirls which their new position as top couple opened up to them, Eustacia's pulses began to move too quickly for longer rumination of any kind.

Through the length of five-and-twenty couples they threaded their giddy way, a new vitality entered her form. The pale ray of evening lent a fascination to the experience. There is a certain degree and tone of light which tends to disturb the equilibrium of the senses, and to promote dangerously the tenderer moods; added to movement, it drives the emotions to rankness, the reason becoming sleepy and unperceiving in inverse proportion; and this light fell now upon these two from the disc of the moon. All the dancing girls felt the symptoms, but Eustacia most of all.''

Lydia stopped reading and lay the book on her breast. The scene was almost too intense. For a moment, the book on her chest moved up and down, synchronous with her rapidly beating heart. Unself-consciously, she reached between her legs, parting the soft hair and moist yielding lips. She could not resist inserting her fingers and gently caressing herself for a brief second of exquisite intimacy. But they were suddenly pulled away, as if she had been grabbed by the wrist.

To still her aroused state, Lydia thought of Eustacia and Wildeve's mutual fate: death by drowning. This ending satisfied society, for their love was illicit, each married to another. Hardy had originally conceived the plot of *Return of the Native* as one of crude violence and passion. Eustacia had been cast as an actual witch, and the overall tone of the original draft had been satanic rather than romantic. But Hardy's editors would have none of it. Thus Eustacia, passionate in nature, bewitching in beauty, a perfect foil for an unyielding puritanical society (*A fictional me*, Lydia thought) was destined for tragedy. Somewhere in the novel, she had cried: ''I was capable of much; but I have been injured and blighted and crushed by things beyond my control." On first reading, this *cri de coeur* had gone directly to Lydia's heart. Hardy had been condemned for dismantling conventional morality, substituting instead the immorality of nature. As her mother had once put it, "Mr. Hardy has replaced life as it is, with nature as it *seems*."

Lydia lay in deep thought for several minutes. Rereading the story of Hardy's lovers prompted her to consider seriously her forthcoming evening with Charles. She knew she was envisioning the loss of her virginity with a surprising detachment—like a Brontë heroine swept up in the drama of romance yet distanced from it, as if she were manipulating the players. Propelled by this thought, Lydia slipped out of bed and walked over to her dresser, where she began to brush her hair.

She wanted Charles's physical passion, his embrace, his caresses, his whispered endearments, yet she wanted more. The rhythm of her brush stroke gained momentum. *I want to know what goes on in his mind,* she thought. *Therein lies the greater prize,* and her brush fell still as she realized she was analyzing Charles as men had always analyzed women. Charles would be a victim, a plaything and specimen, a key to the larger masculine society. It may have been cold-hearted, but she wanted rapture, and in an odd retributive sense, revenge—for Eustacia and for her sex.

Charles was awake, roused from sleep by the recurrent nightmare he called the river dream. He could recall a narrow river and a swift current that broke around large rocks. He thought he could discern mirage-like creatures sitting on the rocks. They appeared to be water-soaked women, but their features were partially obscured by mist.

He had stripped naked and slid down a muddy embankment. He had no fear of the river or the misted thunder of distant falls. The water was warm and shallow, the bottom soft and alluvial. He could sink into it up to his knees. The water was strangely thick and golden, like molten toffee. It was an exquisite sensation—like being immersed in a viscous oil that had been perfumed and warmed to body temperature. The current had gently pulled him 20 or 30 yards downstream. He had breaststroked to shore and, upon touching solid ground, he had awakened.

Charles wondered if the origin of the dream lay in his memory of the Nile. After his mother's death, he had accompanied his father on a journey around the world, spending several weeks in Egypt. He recalled a story his father had told him as they had watched the body of a fellah, an Arab peasant, being fished from the water. His father had described how the peasant had carelessly fallen from a muddy bank and been swept downriver.

"And can you guess what, Charles?" his father had said. "It wasn't the body of a man after all! It was a woman's, a living doll torn asunder." His father had laughed. "This was a major event for the natives. Had it been a man, there would have been no fuss. Men die in the river all the time but women only rarely. She was seen as a sacrifice. Everyone was exceedingly happy with her timely and auspicious end. Isis, the Egyptian goddess of fertility, was pleased. These natives are entirely pagan, Charles," his father had continued, "but don't be fooled. They have their own kind of wisdom. Sacrificing women is one of them." With this remark, his father had slapped him on the shoulders with a hearty laugh. The cruel jest had not seemed out of place because, although Charles was only 12 or 13, he had grown accustomed to his father's contemptuous denouncements of women.

Charles closed his eyes and attempted to settle his mind, which was in a strange slow-motion turmoil, when, suddenly, he heard the distinctive CLAP of his brass door knocker several times in succession. He managed to climb out of bed and make his way to the door, where he was greeted by the mysterious stranger who had called several nights before. He was dressed in the same costume, top hat and evening clothes. Charles motioned him through the doorway into his drawing room. They sat facing each other in comfortable wing chairs, as if they were old friends, reunited and enjoying a night of reminiscing.

Charles believed there were two windows into the human mind. One was the eyes; the other, the hands. Hands told a

tale to those skilled in reading their expression, so Charles
first studied those of his visitor. Although the stranger was
slight in stature, his hands were disproportionately large and
distinctly masculine. He was dark-skinned and dark-eyed,
and in his eyes Charles detected what he believed to be a
form of ocular dysfunction—his pupils appearing to remain
in a fixed state of dilation. Charles immediately thought of
syphilis, sight impairment being a symptom of the disease.

For a moment, Charles was distracted from reading his
visitor's eyes and hands; he found observing the man sitting
opposite him a little like seeing a mirror image of himself.
He was experiencing a strangely narcissistic pleasure in
beholding his look-alike.

"Rossetti," the stranger said, observing the painting
above Charles's fireplace.

"Yes. Do you like it?"

"How did you come to acquire it?" he asked, sidestep-
ping the question.

"Rossetti was a patient."

"He died mad," the stranger said, with the finality of a
tombstone inscription.

"Yes, that's true, he did," Charles agreed.

"She's very beautiful, but in a repulsive way," the
stranger commented.

Charles was surprised at this remark. "How so?"

"Like a snake," his visitor said. "Snakes shed their skins;
women, their purity. Snakes are hypnotically beautiful, as is
a beautiful woman. A cobra can spit in your eye and paralyze
you, a woman can *look* in your eye—the danger is the same.
Look at her hands. They are coiled, serpent-like. And she is
holding a pomegranate, the Greek equivalent of Eve's apple.
She is Proserpine, daughter of Zeus and Demeter. Hades
seduced her and made her Queen of the Underworld,
permitting her entry into our world but once a year."

This outburst momentarily overwhelmed Charles. He did
not know how to respond, but the man opposite hesitated
only a fraction of a second before resuming his diatribe.

"You know that Rossetti's wife died of an overdose of
laudanum. Suicide or accident? No one knows, but I suspect

the latter. And no doubt you are aware that he took an overdose himself. *Not* by accident. He placed a notebook of poems in his wife's coffin and years later exhumed the body to retrieve it:

'Love's all penetrative spell
Amulet, talisman and oracle
Betwixt the Sun and Moon a mystery' "

he repeated from memory.

But the poem was quickly forgotten. The stranger continued to speak rapidly, his hands opening and closing repeatedly in tightly balled fists of anger.

"He had hallucinations at the end. Heard voices from walls, trees, stone greyhounds, from *everything*. The world became a buzz of conspiratorial voices mocking, jeering him. Even his paintings, his women, came off the canvas on which he had painted them. The painted women and the models gathered in one room. Imagine. Proserpine and Jane Morris, Lucrezia Borgia and Sidonia von Bork, the latter both murderesses—witches in fact—and 'Fazio's Mistress,' you know, Fazio degli Uberti, the poet? His mistresses with their amorous, beautiful mouths and 'white *easy* necks.' What did he mean by that, I wonder? Fanny Cornforth was the model for that painting. You know she was a *whore*? Gave Rossetti a disease that caused his testicles to swell to the size of coconuts. He couldn't wear trousers for a time."

Abruptly, the stranger stood as if he intended to start pacing, but immediately, he sat down again. "So many women are whores. I don't mean the ones in the Strand or the Haymarket or Whitechapel. I mean the women who were whores and have rehabilitated themselves. Their betrayal is worse. Imagine lying in the arms of a woman who has lain in the arms of God knows how many men." He suddenly leapt to his feet. "*All* of these women, some real, some composed of oil paint"—he paused to point at the Rossetti painting—"and some only of bones picked clean by the centuries, their spirits all gathered in the same room, hissing like a nest of agitated snakes, pouring their venom into poor Rossetti whose only sin was to fuck them, then paint them so that they could be hung on the wall like trophy heads.''

Charles listened to this staccato outpouring in stunned silence and wondered whether his visitor, his name still a secret, was suffering from syphilitic dementia. How had he learned so much about Rossetti's private life? Not just about his career and lifelong infatuation with beautiful women, but details, exact in their description—his decline into madness, his fits of terrifying paranoia. ''You seem to have a thorough knowledge of Rossetti's life and career,'' he managed to say.

''Yes, that is a fact I can't deny,'' the stranger said cryptically.

''You knew him?'' Charles pressed.

''That is of no consequence,'' was the quick retort.

''Why are you here?'' Charles said brusquely, offended by his rudeness.

The stranger pursed his lips and shrugged. ''You're a physician, someone who specializes''—he paused—''in the mental''—and again he hesitated—''in the processes of the mind—'' he finally finished, looking at Charles as if he expected a comment.

Charles was taken aback by the directness of his gaze. ''My field of expertise is a narrow one. I don't see many patients. Research consumes most of my time.''

''I'm aware of those factors,'' the man said tersely. ''And they are why I am here. If you will bear with me, I would like to recite a tale, a story you may find both interesting and instructive.''

''Tonight? At this hour?'' Charles asked, suddenly aware that it was the dead of night.

The stranger smiled. ''No. Not tonight. But I must address one further issue. This matter is of extreme sensitivity to me,'' he said.

''You need not fear the indelicate with me,'' Charles said. ''You may also be assured of my professional discretion.''

As he uttered these words, Charles felt as if he were being subjected to the most intensive scrutiny. Like a blind man's hands, the stranger's eyes searchingly touched his face, ran over every inch, probing, testing and analyzing. Finally, his eyes came to rest on Charles's, and another extraordinary phenomenon occurred: his eyes seemed to penetrate into Charles's brain. Charles experienced a distinct tingling sensation, as though their minds had met. It lasted only a moment, but there remained a sense that the stranger had left a presence within him that would measure pressures and truths, his experiences against the stranger's. The visitor stood and reached across the desk, hand extended.

"You leave . . . now?" Charles expostulated. But the stranger just looked at him, his face strangely placid. "Never fear, Doctor, we have just begun our journey together. By the way, my name is John Castrain," he said casually. And with that belated introduction, he stood and let himself out.

-✦❪ 11 ❫✦-

LYDIA WAS ALONE in the drawing room. It was the start of the weekend, and her mother, father and sister had left for a brief holiday in the Sussex countryside. Over the strenuous objections of her mother, Lydia was remaining in London—her assignation with Charles was tonight. Not yet allowed to attend social functions unchaperoned, she had feigned a bout of flu. Her mother had greeted this disclosure with considerable suspicion, yet it was not something to which she could take exception. Accepting her daughter's illness at face value had left her two alternatives: cancel the weekend in the country or leave Lydia to recover alone in the quiet of Cadogan Square. But her mother had invited weekend guests, and Lydia, aware of that fact, had shrewdly played down the severity of her symptoms. The family's decision to travel to Sussex without her had been fully expected.

To distract herself temporarily from thoughts about the coming evening, Lydia picked up the *Times* and started to read an article headlined ST. PANCRAS CORONER'S COURT:

The deceased Emma Wakefield, aged 21, described as a well-conducted girl, worked at Mr. Homan's shell-box factory and was engaged to be married to Thomas Price, a young man employed at M'Corquodale's printing works.

She had lodged with her married sister, Mrs. Burrows, for six weeks prior to her death during her mother's absence in the country. On Sunday evening, after being out with her sweetheart for an hour and a half, she returned to her sister's house and retired to her bedroom, ill. The next night, she consulted Dr. Kennedy, who treated her for a severe cough and cold, but she gradually grew worse and expired on the following Saturday. A post-mortem examination revealed that the deceased had been enceinte, and Dr. Kennedy and Dr. Jones, a colleague, were agreed that blood poisoning, following abortion, had caused the death.

Thomas Price stated that he had "kept company" with the deceased for five years and that they were to be married next Whitsunday. He earned one pound per week and helped to maintain her mother. He emphatically denied that he was responsible for the deceased's condition and added that he was wholly unaware of it until after the post-mortem examination. He had no reason to suspect that she was on terms of intimacy with any other man.

The deceased's sister and Thomas Price's mother were in attendance with the girl during her illness. Both denied any knowledge of the real cause of the girl's illness or of her previous condition.

The jury found that the deceased died from the effects of blood poisoning following an abortion, caused by the illegal use of instruments, and they were of the opinion that some person or persons at present unknown were guilty of causing her death. They expressed their dissatisfaction with the evidence of some of the witnesses.

The coroner said the verdict was tantamount to one of wilful murder. He stated his belief that perjury had been committed.

Lydia put the paper aside with a shudder of revulsion. *Poor woman*, she thought. *Abortion in a back-street hideaway*. Yet the fate of Emma Wakefield was hardly unique, though not one she thought possible for herself.

She walked upstairs and sat down at her desk, picking up George Eliot; but within a minute, she closed the book with a dull thud. She opened a drawer and pulled out a small mother-of-pearl jewellery box, removing two drop-cluster diamond earrings. From the same drawer, she removed two royal-blue velvet pouches, both knotted at the neck with a yellow silk cord. She untied the first and let a diamond choker fall into her hand. She flattened the velvet on the desk top and placed the necklace on it, then opened the second pouch and lifted out an elegant diamond and amethyst-encrusted coronet. She placed it beside the choker. Both pieces of jewellery belonged to her mother. She had cajoled her father into letting her keep them in her room overnight. "I like to look at them in the moonlight," she had explained disingenuously last night. This morning, she had conveniently forgotten to return them, and her father, distracted both by his impending journey south and by his concern for her health, had not mentioned them.

She had chosen the coronet and choker, together with the earrings, to wear on her evening with Charles. The coronet featured a large hexagon-shaped diamond mounted in a delicate swirl of gold. She marvelled at the gem's blue-white fire for a moment, turning it slightly from side to side so that the inner light moved too, although it seemed to be trapped within the diamond. This illusion had the unwelcome effect of recalling the *Times* article.

Prior to doing volunteer work at Toynbee Hall, matters such as abortion and contraception had belonged to the ugly underside of a world Lydia scarcely knew existed. In her society, even the word "pregnancy" was frowned upon, the French term *enceinte* being eminently more tasteful. But her experience at Toynbee had shed light on the more unsavoury aspects of life in the East End, including the practice of back-alley abortions and the difficulty of securing reliable contraceptive devices. Birth control was a highly controversial issue, one about which Lydia knew virtually nothing. She was aware of the two schools of opinion that existed: the small but vocal minority who favoured wide distribution of contraceptives, led by the likes of social crusader Annie

Besant, and the large majority that lobbied against their use, of whom the chief spokesman was Thomas Manning, brother of Cardinal Manning, England's senior Catholic prelate. To inform herself more fully about this contentious debate, Lydia had set out in search of a book she had heard about at Toynbee Hall entitled *The Wife's Handbook*. Written by Dr. H.A. Allbutt, it had caused a sensation because of its detailed description of a variety of contraceptive methods.

Having managed to purchase a copy in a chemist's shop in Commercial Road, she had learned for the first time of such devices as the intra-uterine stem, also called the stem pessary, "a mushroom-shaped object," and of the new mensinga diaphragm. She read that Casanova had provided his mistresses with a pessary-like apparatus that consisted of wire and three small spheres of gold soaked in an alkaline solution which he believed to be spermicidal. Mention was also made of *coitus interruptus,* or, as the French said, *la chamade,* the retreat. And also of the douche and other means of natural contraception—including one based on the uncertain prediction of a woman's fertility cycle.

She had also picked up a pamphlet edited by Annie Besant and Charles Bradlaugh, and had thumbed through the introductory pages, which contained a denunciatory miscellany of prevailing attitudes toward female sexuality:

> "As a general rule, a modest woman seldom desires any sexual gratification for herself. She submits to her husband's embraces, but principally to gratify him. To use any means whereby the masculine and feminine elements cannot unite are unnatural practices, clearly akin to the solitary vices which are so abhorrent and so destructive; and there is no doubt that every practice of this kind is a physical injury. For conjugal onanism is not only criminal in men, it must tend to demoralize women.
>
> If you teach them vicious habits, and a way to sin without detection, how can you assure yourself of their fidelity when assailed by a fascinating seducer? And why may not even the unmarried woman taste of forbidden pleasures also, so that your future wife shall have been defiled ere you know her?"

Yet the worst insult had been saved for last, written by no less an authority than Elizabeth Blackwell, England's first female physician:

> The active exercise of the intellectual and moral faculties has the remarkable power of diminishing the formation of sperm and limiting the necessity of its natural removal, the demand for such relief becoming rare under ennobling and healthy influences.

Lydia had greeted the notion that the potency of sperm was susceptible to the mind-over-matter argument with a great deal of skepticism. In fact, on reflection, it had seemed scarcely credible.

Recalling that passage brought forward with rude impact thoughts of making love with Charles. Surely, she reasoned, a man of honour would not risk pregnancy with his lover. After all, even so notorious a debauchee as Casanova had concerned himself with that possibility. However, linking Charles to Casanova's reported reputation for considerateness did little to pacify her mind, which could be obstinately pragmatic if she did not control herself. But in exercising that control, part of her mind revealed an agile, evasive quality. When confronted with an unwanted and weighty dilemma, her mind was capable of squirming out from underneath, just as a child wriggles out of an adult's unwelcome grasp. Lydia was aware of this tendency yet was often incapable of correcting it, and as she once again contemplated her jewellery, thoughts of Charles and Casanova and contraceptives conveniently receded.

Lucie Rhinegold sat opposite Charles and studied her primly folded hands. She had missed her last session, which had been scheduled for the week before.

On first meeting Lucie, Charles had thought her hair a glossy chestnut shade, but now it appeared as a shoulder-length cascade of shimmering luminescent reddish gold; her eyes were growing ever more lustrous—in fact, they reminded him of his own mother's on her deathbed. They were huge, staring eyes, so deep and mysterious that to look into them was to stand on the edge of a very deep well, the surface of which did not reflect images but rather absorbed them. Lucie had lost weight, and it seemed that as her hair and eyes grew in lustre, her skin assumed a more fragile, translucent quality.

At the outset of Lucie's treatment, Charles had experienced no difficulty in eliciting, under the influence of a hypnotic trance, the presence of her two distinct personalities. That was not the case now. Somehow, the two Lucies had merged to form a third "hybrid" personality that was neither obsessively chaste nor obsessively promiscuous but rather an amalgam of the two.

"Lucie, describe your mother for me."

"She is . . . a good woman."

"Can you please be more specific?"

"She is a front-pew person. A 'Nearer My God to Thee' sort of person."

"She is very religious?"

"Earnestly so."

"Describe her, please."

The question appeared to puzzle Lucie. "Are you asking what she looks like?"

"Yes," Charles said.

She answered in a supercilious tone: "Like a mother should."

Charles persisted, "And how is that?"

"Do you like the Queen?"

"I find her dowdy."

"What do you mean?"

"She dresses dowdily, always in black. She reminds me of a black cloud, always hovering on the horizon but doing nothing else. Why can't it just rain and be off? She means to pass life in mourning, as if it doesn't begin until the hereafter."

"And do you agree with that? Or with her?"

Charles observed the struggle on Lucie's face. "She is my Queen," she finally answered.

"We are not compelled to like our Queen."

"It is our duty to honour her."

"As we must our mother?" Charles enquired.

"Yes." Lucie responded without a trace of emotion. And then, "I've started to paint. Still life. Fruit. An apple and a peach. Trouble with the fuzz on the peach and the shine on the apple. I like to open the peach with my fingers. The flesh is succulent, the juice sweet. I like to eat the flesh, feel the juices run down my chin. I love the intensity of the colours, the texture. I don't like apples. You can't open an apple with your thumbs; you have to cut it with a knife. And you can't suck the juice from it like you can a peach. There is no colour to the inside of an apple."

Charles listened to this rambling discourse with rapt attention. The next question would be critical. "Does . . . does your mother favour a particular fruit?" he asked quietly.

Lucie answered, "My mother *is* an apple."

"Does she enjoy peaches?" Charles quickly countered.

Again, a struggle distorted Lucie's face. "She preserves peaches. We eat them in the winter. 'To get a taste of summer,' she says."

"But does she like them?"

"She eats them in the winter, I said!" Lucie snapped. "That *must* mean she likes them."

Suddenly, she looked exhausted, and although Charles wanted to pursue this line of questioning, he reluctantly ended the hypnotic trance. After she left the office, he quickly jotted down a note in her file: *Physically weaker, inner struggle evident, mother key? Judgemental persona has emerged that appears to have some knowledge or recognition of two formerly predominant personalities*. Charles pushed back his chair, reflected for a moment and added a postscript to his notation: *Third persona appears to be diluted extract of former personalities, the extremes appear quiescent, yet they linger somewhere in her consciousness, and until they are drawn out and reconciled, her struggle will continue*.

Charles closed the file and looked at his watch in surprise. *Where had the afternoon gone?* he wondered. He was due at Cadogan Square within two hours, yet he felt the need for a breath of fresh air. He deliberated for a moment and decided he could still go for a brisk walk and have time to prepare for the evening. So he donned his woollen jacket and stepped outside into the crisp air and the soft roseate light of early dusk.

Lydia had chosen her dress with great deliberation. Three alternatives had presented themselves: a modest but still stylish green silk Directoire dress; a slightly decadent pale peach costume such as that favoured by the outer fringe of society, a creation without a bustle but with a fluid drapery effect, like a Japanese kimono; but she had chosen the third dress, a high-waisted gown that was on the leading edge of fashion, the style inspired by Sarah Bernhardt's costumes in Sardou's *La Tosca*, a production of which was playing in London. The lustrous fabric was of a violet colour; a mauve silk sash added a dramatic touch. When she pinned the coronet to her hair, put on the rest of her jewellery and inspected the result in the mirror, she thought she had never looked more beautiful.

She knew she had no time for further reflection, for it was half past seven and Charles was punctual by habit. She glanced out of her window and saw a cabriolet pull up in front of the house. She watched as Charles alighted, straightened himself and briskly strode up the steps to the door. Draping a silver fox stole over her naked shoulders, she went downstairs to greet him.

Charles was ushered in by Dawkins. He found the house strangely hushed, as if unoccupied, although he had anticipated meeting both Sir William and Lady Carlyle. *Do they know I am calling for Lydia?* he wondered.

"Miss Lydia will be down in a minute," the old butler said warmly.

Charles smiled at him. He was obviously an ally of Lydia's. At the same time, he became increasingly curious about who else in the Carlyle household knew of his visit. But such speculation was abruptly pushed from his mind. Lydia was descending the staircase, and she looked positively enchanting.

He had escorted many beautiful women in his time. In the last decade, they had been called "Beauty," as if it were a professional title. "Stunner" was now in vogue, and Lydia Carlyle was certainly that. What was it about her that so captivated and intrigued him? She was more than the sum of her parts. There was an aura about her that radiated not merely loveliness but a vital quality, an intensity that in a man would be called charismatic but in a woman . . . for a moment, his mind was defeated. Lydia remained a mystery, but he was determined to solve the riddle by night's end.

"Lydia, you look truly ravishing," he said.

"Why thank you, Charles, and you look very suave," she replied. *And he does,* she thought. *Suave and elegantly handsome in his perfectly tailored dress jacket and silk-lined cape.*

The carriage ride along the Strand to the Lyceum Theatre passed with hardly a word exchanged; conversation suddenly seemed superfluous.

To Lydia, it seemed she was sitting beside a magnificently proportioned black lion, like one of Landseer's spectacular bronze sculptures at the base of Nelson's column, which their carriage was just now passing. Her lion, too, sat immobile yet poised to spring at the slightest command or signal. It was the same sensation she had experienced sitting beside him on the night of *The Dean's Daughter.* She could feel the tension in Charles, a nervous tension, but there was an extra dimension she could not define. It entered her body like a galvanic current and ran up and down her spine, penetrating her entire nervous system and making her feel giddy and weak-kneed.

As they alighted in front of the theatre, heads turned on every side. Lydia Carlyle and Lord Longerdale would now be linked by a network of gossip that functioned not only with the smooth efficiency of a well-oiled engine but with head-spinning alacrity. *The irony,* Lydia thought, not for the first time, *is that Mother will gain by the gossip.* "Imagine," she could hear wagging but envious tongues, "Lillian Carlyle"—for credit would go to her mother's matchmaking skills, not to any initiative on Lydia's part—"is to be the mother of a Countess. She must be crowing in her sleep."

They had centre seats in the stalls, six rows back from the footlights. Charles became engrossed in the play immediately. To a minor degree, he was curious about the acting ability of the American Richard Mansfield in the dual roles of Jekyll and Hyde. His talent, in inverse proportion to the increasing notoriety of the Whitechapel murderer, was depreciated by London critics. As a consequence, attendance had started to drop.

But Charles's primary interest lay in the mechanics of the drama itself, in the portrayal of the duality of human nature. And in the final analysis, as the play came to a conclusion, he found himself disenchanted not so much with Richard Mansfield as with the stereotypical rendering of the good in man wrestling with his base and evil nature. Charles decided on the spur of the moment that he would rewrite the introduction to his paper. *Jekyll and Hyde* was not about states of double consciousness or "dissociation," despite the author's use of that psychological term. The book, and the dramatic adaptation, was a morality play, a clever one but ultimately only a reinvention of the age-old struggle between good and evil.

Lydia hardly paid attention to the play. The actor, as Hyde, capering and lurching about the stage like the deformed hunchback of Notre Dame, did not frighten her in the slightest. She found the effect almost comic. Besides, her mind was not on the stage, save for brief moments. All of her mental faculties had been taken prisoner by the proximity of Charles.

When they were leaving the theatre, he asked, "What did you think of it?"

She could only fumble for words.

"I thought it . . . it had its moments," she said lamely. To cover her embarrassment, she quickly turned the question. "And you?"

"All cleverness and cliché," Charles said.

"You seemed absorbed."

"A trick of my profession."

"But you do believe an individual can actually be two people?"

"Yes." Charles answered simply.

"How is it possible?" Lydia asked. "It defies my understanding."

Charles replied with a smile. "Mine too. We are just beginning to acknowledge that the phenomenon exists. The research has hardly scratched the surface. One thing is certain, though. The human mind is stratified. A paleontologist can go into the field and study a cliffside that has been stripped clean by wind and erosion. He can examine the layers of the cliff and tell us something of the earth's history, of the creatures that once existed at the time one of those layers was forming. If we could see the human mind in the same manner, by removing layers of consciousness, we would see the history of the individual."

"Is that how you use hypnosis?"

"Yes, but it isn't that simple. You never get a clear picture. In a sense, you do get a chance to scrape away one of the 'layers,' but unlike the preserved state of a cliffside, the human mind is dynamic. The layers of consciousness are always shifting. Hypnosis lets you inside the mind, but sometimes I feel I am inside a large underground cavern with a single and very feeble candle. And to make matters worse, it often seems the earth overhead is in constant and threatening motion."

"You make it sound like dangerous work."

Charles laughed. "Only to the patient," he said.

"Can you hypnotize anyone? Could you hypnotize me?"

"Why, Lydia," Charles said teasingly, "I thought I already had."

Later, at a restaurant in Sloane Street, they were seated in a private room. Its location, midway between Cheyne Walk and Cadogan Square, amused Lydia. "Did you choose this place because of its neutrality?"

Charles did not take her meaning. "Neutrality?"

"It's equidistant between Chelsea and Belgravia. Are we two negotiators bent on forming a treaty, neither of us to have the advantage of home ground?''

Charles smiled because he *had* chosen the location of the restaurant with care. He could have taken her to any number of private dining clubs closer to the City, but that might have risked her reputation. He had chosen this place because it was respectable and because, depending on how the evening unfolded, it was within five minutes of each of their homes.

''And what would be your terms for such a treaty?'' he asked, twisting the stem of a champagne glass, looking from the swell of Lydia's bosom to the live sparkle in her deep and dauntless blue eyes.

''Oh, the usual. A mutual non-aggression pact. Free trade, an exchange of missions. Something the Foreign Office would press for.''

''Why, that sounds the very apotheosis of fairness. Surely you seek to secure some advantage. A special concession, perhaps?''

''As a matter of fact, I do, Charles. How perceptive of you.''

''And what is that?'' he asked, a smile playing on his lips.

''A first-rate supper,'' Lydia said, and Charles laughed. ''But that's not all,'' she continued.

''No? What else?''

Lydia paused for a moment. ''You must create for me a special memory. This is my first evening out alone with a man. I want to remember it always. Treasure it always.''

Charles stared at Lydia for a long moment, pondering the intent of her remark. ''You force hard terms,'' he finally said, ''but what choice do I have? As the French say, *'Coûte que coûte,'* cost what it may, I capitulate. You shall have your special memory.''

Lydia had imagined the evening would be spent in engrossing conversation. She wanted to talk about anything and everything under the sun: Socialism, George Eliot, Toynbee Hall, the horrors of Whitechapel. She had even thought of a way to bring up contraception anecdotally, by mentioning Casanova's three gold balls. Yet the conversation, if their verbal exchanges could be characterized as such, was curiously truncated. They might make a start on a particular topic, but they did not progress far, perhaps a few sentences, before one of them changed the subject. It seemed that neither was in the mood for serious conversation—and if one of them headed in that direction, the other quickly moved on to a different, more lighthearted topic.

Certainly, that was how Charles felt. Rarely, in recent weeks, had he been so relaxed, so unpressured by the demands of his practice and work. He did not want to think, did not want to exercise his brain at all. He wanted only to feast his eyes on Lydia, to imagine what she would look like naked in his bed. How long had it been since he had had a woman? A beautiful virginal woman? Too long.

After a supper of prosciutto and melon, lobster bisque and chicken florentine, followed by a rich praline glacé—Lydia had not eaten all day and ate every morsel—Charles raised a glass of champagne. "To a goddess," he said.

So grand and sudden was the compliment that Lydia was at first flustered. "A Greek one, I trust," she managed to say.

"You would have stopped them cold in the streets of Athens. Hearts would have fallen like stars from heaven."

"Charles! Such extravagant praise. You cause me to blush. And actually, I thought the Greeks preferred boys."

"Your beauty would rewrite history, Lydia," Charles said, meaning every word.

"And you, the book of flattery," she replied. Yet her heart rejoiced like a love-struck schoolgirl's. *Steady,* she said to herself. *You cannot just throw yourself at him.* But that was what she wanted to do. The champagne had gone to her head as though it were ambrosia. So had Charles's handsomeness, his virility, his flowery paean to her beauty.

Half an hour later, she was undressed in his arms in his Cheyne Walk bedroom. *His physical presence is like a potent stimulant,* she thought. *I cannot get enough of the smell of him, or the warmth of his skin. I seem to draw him into me with each breath that I take . . . all of this is intoxicating,* and she had to fight down a sudden flare-up of panic. A distant corner of her mind steadfastly resisted the ground swell of passion. Detached and observant, it registered everything that was happening to her and remarked, in displeasure, at her apparent helplessness in the face of Charles's seductive technique: *He is practised, he has done this a thousand times before, you mistake lust for love and ardour*. But these tiny echoes were easily dismissed. *His hands are softer than I imagined, his tongue rougher*, she thought. His hands were everywhere, and where they weren't, his tongue caressed her with deft stabbing skill. Its rough texture drew wave after wave of intense pleasure to the surface of her body. The feeling began to invade her mind, sweeping before it every vestige of rational thought. Charles entered her, and she gasped at the hard thrust, yet it was exactly what she craved, and she began to move with him in an urgent primal rhythm.

Elizabeth Stride
Catherine Eddowes

sunday, september 30th

⊶[12]⊷

HE WAS WATCHING the Whitechapel strongman, Hunder-weight Tony. A flamboyant exhibitionist, Tony had once hoisted a wheelbarrow of pig iron onto his shoulders. Another time, he had pulled a locomotive out of Liverpool Street Station with a steel cable clenched between his teeth. Tonight, he was putting on another show by piling "'ores" on his brawny arms and shoulders. For every prostitute lifted over six, a small Irishman had agreed to give him a slug of whiskey. The strongman now had nine women on his shoulders and outstretched arms, all of them squealing like pigs at market. Tony was bellowing for a tenth and more whiskey when a dwarf-like woman stepped out of the noisy crowd and started to climb up his leg.

"I'm being cheated!" the Irishman bellowed. "No dwarfs or midgets allowed!"

"She's an 'ore, ain't she?" Tony screamed back to loud applause.

"Friggin right!" an anonymous voice shouted from the crowd. "But a damn lousy one!"

"You're cheat'n!" the Irishman insisted. "Put Long Liz aboard an' you'll earn your whiskey." A tall woman in black on the edge of the crowd started to giggle, and the boisterous crowd took up the chant, "Long Liz! Long Liz!"

But the strongman suddenly dropped his arms, and the pyramid of women collapsed like a house of cards. He lunged toward the Irishman, who nimbly stepped aside and darted into the laughing crowd.

The two men ran past him, and then he stepped back and turned into a side street, leaving the crowd behind. Five minutes later, he was sitting in a flat, moodily contemplating his own existence.

He was coming to the East End more and more frequently. Actually, he did not come so much of his own volition as out of a powerful compulsion that he failed to understand. He did not mind the crushing poverty, the abject squalor. Perversely, he found great delight in it all. Yet he could not be intimate with the inhabitants of this ungodly world. He was a visitor—silent, invisible and aloof—and did not join them in any form of social intercourse. This was an alien land, and he was an alien among its inhabitants. Yet they were his neighbours, and although it was a contradiction, he knew he needed these people and felt at home with them.

He realized the East/West London demarcation existed in his mind as something more than a geographical and cultural boundary. It symbolized the innate polarity of the human mind, for he tended to construct mental tandems—concepts, emotions or physical descriptions of objects. He reduced everything to a couplet of irreconcilable opposites: truth-lie, lightness-darkness, pleasure-pain. When he formed one of these inviolate pairs, inevitably his mind was drawn to the darker of the two. He did not know when this process had started to evolve, but it seemed he had played it for ages—this word game—like two children engaged in a running battle of wits.

"I'll say one thing, you another, first thing that pops into your head. No thinking allowed. Come on, try it! Up."
"Down."

"In." *"Out."*

"Cat." *"Dog!"*

"Round." *"Round what?"*

"Round the world." "*Round the corner. Round the mulberry bush. Pop goes the weasel! The cow jumped over the moon. Little Jack—*"

"Frigging!" "*Fucking!*"

"Love!" "*Hate!*"

"Woman."

Silence.

"I said woman."

Silence.

"WOMAN! for Christ's sake."

"*WHORE!*" he had finally screamed, but only this past summer, years after the association had been made.

He picked up the *Times* and read the Coroner's conclusion to the hearing concerning the murder of Annie Chapman:

> The body had not been dissected, but the injuries had been made by someone who had considerable anatomical skill and knowledge. There were no meaningless cuts. The organ had been taken by one who knew where to find it, what difficulties he would have to contend with, and how he should use his knife to abstract the organ without injuring it. No unskilled person could have known where to find it or could have recognized it when found. No mere slaughterer of animals could have carried out these operations. It must have been someone accustomed to the post-mortem room. The conclusion that the desire was to possess the missing abdominal organ seems overwhelming.
>
> It has been suggested that the criminal is a lunatic with morbid feelings. That may or may not be the case, but the objective of the murderer appears palpably shown by the facts, and it is not necessary to assume lunacy, for it is clear there is a market for the missing organ.
>
> Within a few hours of the issue of the morning papers containing a report of the medical evidence given at the last sitting of the Court, the Coroner received a communication from an officer of the London Hospital Medical College that he had information which might have a distinct bearing on the Inquiry. The Coroner attended at the first opportunity and was

informed by the sub-curator of the Pathological Museum that, some months ago, an American had called on him and asked him to procure a number of specimens of the organ that was missing in the deceased. He stated his willingness to give 20 pounds apiece for each specimen and said that his objective was to issue an actual specimen with each copy of a publication on which he was then engaged. He was told that it was impossible to comply with his request; still he pressed home his need. He wished them preserved, not in spirits of wine, the usual medium, but in glycerine, in order to preserve them in a flaccid condition, and he wished them sent directly to America. It is known that this request was repeated to another institution of a similar character. Now, was it not possible that the knowledge of this demand might have incited some abandoned wretch to possess himself of a specimen? It seems beyond belief that such inhuman wickedness could enter into the mind of any man; but, unfortunately, our criminal annals prove that every crime is possible. The Coroner at once communicated his information to the Detective Department at Scotland Yard but did not know what use had been made of it.

It is a great misfortune that nearly three weeks have already elapsed without the chief actor in this awful tragedy being discovered. Surely, it is not too much to hope that the ingenuity of our detective force will succeed in unearthing this monster. It is not as if there is no clue as to the character of the criminal or to the cause of his crime. His objective has been clearly divulged. His anatomical knowledge carries him out of the category of a common criminal, for that knowledge could only be obtained by assisting at post-mortems or frequenting the post-mortem room. Thus the class in which the search must be made, although a large one, is limited. In addition to the former description of the man, they should know that he is a foreigner, more than 40 years of age, a little taller than the deceased, of shabby genteel appearance, with a brown deer-stalker hat and a dark coat. The police are confronted with a murder of no ordinary character, committed not out of jealousy or revenge or for the purpose of robbery but from motives less adequate than many that still disgrace our civilization, mar our progress and blot the pages of our Christianity.

He finished the article, scarcely believing what he had read. First, they thought he was a doctor, then a collector of anatomical specimens, an American buying uteruses for medical colleges. But always a Jew, of course. An American Jewish physician, killing Christian prostitutes for their wombs, which were then to be sold like Shylock's pound of flesh. He felt anger at the ludicrous conclusions. The authorities were unable to grapple with him in the abstract and therefore could not begin to grasp his true motives.

The public had begun to call him Jack the Ripper. One newspaper had said he was like a Pawnee Indian. Another said he had the terrible soul of a tiger. Letters were pouring into Fleet Street and the Central News Service faster than they could be counted. Many claimed credit for Jack's handiwork. Some even announced, like a playbill, the date, time and place of his next appearance. A nursery rhyme couplet came to mind: *Jack be nimble, Jack be quick.* He was both quick and nimble, but he did not jump over candlesticks or the moon, a supernatural power the terrified public was starting to believe he possessed.

From a narrow leather case, he removed the knife and stroked it several times against a honing stone. He then slipped it into the *Times* and, in a strange sense, into himself, for there on the thin sheets of newsprint was his life history. He paused in thought for a moment. He was a man without an identity, without a past. Even the flat offered no clue to who he really was. It was like a hotel room, a place where he stayed each time he came to the East End. He changed his clothes there, like an actor costuming himself for a night's performance. *Am I an actor?* he thought. *If so, where is my script, my audience?* He started to laugh aloud and soon found himself unable to stop, wave after wave of uproarious mirth shaking his entire body and bringing tears to his eyes. The warm tears rolled down his cheeks, and then he could taste the saltiness in the corners of his mouth—and then he was sobbing, great wracking sobs that emanated from somewhere deep inside. But the sobbing was almost immediately displaced by new, violent spasms of laughter, until they, in turn, gave way to another convulsion of sobbing.

Long Liz was walking east in the Commercial Road. She was dressed almost entirely in black, except for the grey feather trimming of her jacket and her grey crepe bonnet. A fog was brewing, and its long vaporous limbs reached everywhere. Her pace was desultory. She was sober, hungry, a little tired, mildly dispirited, but to her surprise, mildly horny. She did not devote much thought to cerebral matters, but an instinct told her that hungriness and horniness went hand-in-hand—when her hunger was relieved, the appetite for horniness would be whetted.

He saw her fog-shrouded figure and recognized her instantly as the prostitute he had seen earlier in the evening. Stepping out of his hiding place, a drumbeat of excitement thrummed inside his temples. He shook his head, but the cadence remained, muffled like the approach of a faraway army.

Commercial Road was still crowded, the main intersections choked with horse-drawn traffic and late-night revellers. Although he was indistinguishable from the dozens of men in the street, he did not feel comfortable on this mainline thoroughfare. He began to follow the woman, keeping several yards behind. Her gait remained steady as she proceeded down the centre of the broad sidewalk. She paused to peer into a milliner's window and, ten yards away, he stopped to stare at an outfitter's display. She turned to look at him, and he returned her stare. The orgasmic flood of power, the overwhelming urgency to be at this woman's throat, returned. But to take her in a doorway in Commercial Road was unthinkable. He decided to set a trap.

Turning on his heel, he started south down a side street in the direction of the river, his pace swift and purposeful. A narrow alley running parallel to Commercial Road opened to his left. He darted into it and, almost running, travelled its length in seconds. It opened into a schoolyard, the school rising several storeys into the inky, fog-enveloped sky.

Running across the yard, he came to Berner Street, a low-lying thoroughfare that ran down toward the London, Tilbury and Southend Railway. There, he turned north. He was a short distance from Commercial Road now. Could she have managed to get ahead? He doubted it. His detour had not taken more than a minute, but she could have found another customer. He was almost at the intersection when he passed a building out of which raucous male laughter spilled onto the street like the rowdy notes of a music hall piano. Curbside of Commercial Road, he stopped. A small sign screwed into a brick facing read *Berner Street*. He turned in the direction the woman had been travelling, and there she was, whorls of thin, yellowish fog trailing her every step. He had not seen another soul between the school and Commercial Road. The distance had been a tunnel of darkness—no gas lamps burned, and no windows threw light into the street.

The woman was almost abreast of him when he whispered his customary greeting: "Will you come with me?" She stopped and looked at him, her eyes, almost level with his, filling with foolish surprise. A slack grin creased her face.

But he was seized with impatience. She must come with him *now*! They were standing in plain view of the street traffic, pedestrians coming out of the foggy darkness and quickly disappearing. No one gave them a second glance, for the area abounded in prostitutes, and Commercial Road was a choice area in which to ply their trade. He guided her firmly by the elbow into the yawning mouth of Berner Street, and instantly, they were swallowed. In this black cavern, he felt immediately at home. He held her tightly on his right side, hugging close to the brick walls.

She hesitated, feeling her way, her eyes unaccustomed to the sudden darkness. She reached into an apron pocket, feeling for her breath mints, groping with her fingers but unable to open the packet. She had hoped they would have a drink before getting down to business. It was all so much easier then, the tongue and spirits loosened by the magic of alcohol. And she was hungry, famished, in fact. What had she had to eat all day but some cheese and potatoes? And she wanted to talk, to have some fun. Then she would nestle down and show him a thing or two.

He stopped beside two tall wooden doors that were wide enough to admit a horse-drawn wagon. A small Judas gate was set in one, and he pushed it partially open to an empty black courtyard. Across the street, he saw what appeared to be a deserted warehouse, on which a weathered sign read: *Messrs. Hindley, Sack Manufacturers*. Beside the warehouse stood a stable. He tested the wooden doors, and with gentle pressure they yielded, hinges groaning, the sound exaggerated in the stillness. He took the woman's hand and led her through the opening. A tenement house ran down one side of the yard and on the other was a clubhouse, three illuminated windows facing the enclosure. From behind the windows came an intermittent babble of sound. Over the buzz of conversation, he could hear a chorus of male voices singing a rollicking beer-hall song in a foreign language. The tune ended abruptly amidst much backslapping and laughter.

She smiled. The gaiety of the party goers was infectious. She wanted to join them in some bawdy songs and laughter, toss back a few drinks. But she was here for business, and he meant to have her here, on the courtyard pavement. She'd been taken in worse places—although never within shouting distance of a hundred partying men.

Suddenly, he shoved her in the chest, propelling her in the direction of the courtyard wall. In the same fluid motion, he grabbed her neck scarf and yanked her toward him, bringing the knife against her outstretched throat. The blood spurted immediately, a fountain of warm, gushing liquid. He leaned her body against his, and she sank to her knees, as if in supplication. He could see the liquid spilling like paint, the colour brilliant and intense: orange-red and sunlike, it blossomed in *his* sky, radiating the most remarkable warmth.

But just then the sun was eclipsed. Everything became black, very still and extraordinarily quiet. Then, ten feet distant, he saw a man staring at him, his face apprehensive and perplexed. He was sitting on a barrow hitched to a pony. Both the man and the pony seemed petrified, and then he realized the driver could not see him. The pony's behaviour was perplexing the man. *It smells the blood,* he thought.

He stepped quietly back, flat against the wall. The pony started forward but took only a step before halting again. The man clucked and brought a whip to the animal's rump. The pony started to move into the yard but shied away.

He remained absolutely still, each breath seemingly drawing him farther into the brick.

The barrow driver was opposite him, perched high on his seat. He could actually smell the man's beery breath. The body of the woman was at his feet, the wheel of the barrow not more than two feet from it, not more than five from where he stood. The pony's nervous shying continued to puzzle the driver. Then the animal suddenly jerked a few feet forward, unbalancing the driver, who swore and pulled hard on the reins.

At that moment, he made his move. He stepped from the wall and stole directly behind the barrow, swiftly moving through the open doors into the safety of Berner Street. The fog had thickened, and it materialized from everywhere—from the brickwork, from the cobblestones and pavement, from the trees and houses, from the pedestrians, from everything living and lifeless, it slowly seeped. In hushed silence, its glaucous presence stole through every street and alleyway. Into this ether, he insinuated his own eerie presence, and so disguised, he travelled west toward Aldgate Pump, still armed with his knife and murderous intent.

⊷❈[13]❈⊷

THE HEADLINE OF of his *Times,* which was propped against a
pitcher of milk, caused Aubrey to choke on his kipper as if it
were a chicken bone. He gagged so noisily that Toby ran into
the room. "Are you all right, Mr. Aubrey?" he asked in
consternation. Gulping on a mouthful of orange juice,
Aubrey managed a nod.

He was just home from Lyme Regis, having taken his first
weekend off in three. The Whitechapel murderer had apparently taken a holiday (it was three weeks since the last
killing), and Aubrey had decided to do likewise. The
political brouhaha the murders had created, if not completely
over, had considerably abated. Henry Matthews' attention
had been diverted by the formation of the London County
Council, a municipal authority that would have broad
legislative powers beyond the historic square mile of the City
of London. Matthews was happy with this development, but
he wanted to ensure that the Council did not surpass the
Home Office's greater prerogatives of power. And Sir
Charles Warren had a new bee, or rather two new bees, in his
bonnet: an outbreak of rabies and a less serious, although no
less vexing, outbreak of littering. London consumed more

oranges than any other capital in the world, and at the first sign of autumn, Londoners went orange-mad. The fruit was sold from every street and park corner, the sweetly acidic scent sometimes overwhelming the odour of horse dung.

London also had one of the world's largest dog populations, and rabies was a recurring problem. An anti-litter law for orange peels and a strict muzzle law for dogs: these two pressing matters occupied the Commissioner of Police. Under those circumstances, Aubrey's weekend departure for Lyme Regis and the Dorset seacoast had seemed beyond reproach.

But it appeared Aubrey was not the only one to have noticed waning interest and relaxed vigilance concerning Jack the Ripper, the Whitechapel murderer. The creature himself had read the signs and, as if overcome with jealous rage, had wreaked a terrible vengeance for the inattention. He had killed again. Not just once, but twice—one killing within an hour of the other:

In the early hours of yesterday morning, two more horrible murders were committed in the East End of London, the victims in both cases belonging to the same unfortunate class. The police have no doubt that these terrible crimes were the work of the same fiendish hands that committed the outrages which have already made Whitechapel painfully notorious. The scenes of the two murders just brought to light are within a quarter-hour walk of each other, the earlier-discovered crime having been committed in a yard in Berner Street, a thoroughfare out of Commercial Road, while the second outrage was perpetrated within the city boundary, in Mitre Square, Aldgate.

In the first case, the body was found in a gateway leading to a factory, and although the murder, compared with the other, may be regarded as of an almost ordinary character—the unfortunate woman only having her throat cut—little doubt is felt due to the position in which the corpse was found that the assassin had intended to mutilate it. He seems, however, to have been interrupted by the arrival of a cart that drew up close to the spot, and it is believed that he may have escaped behind this vehicle. The body was removed to 40 Berner Street, which is near to the now-notorious Hanbury Street. These premises are occupied by the International Workmen's Club. The victim, according to official details, appears to have been a woman of low character, aged about 35. Her height was 5 feet 5 inches and her complexion and hair dark. She wore a jacket made of black cloth with feather trimmings, a black skirt, crepe bonnet and white stockings.

The second murder was committed under circumstances which show that the assassin appears to be free from any fear of interruption while at his dreadful work. Mitre Square is entered from three places: Mitre Street and passages from Duke Street and St. James's Place, through any of which he might have been interrupted by the arrival either of ordinary pedestrians or the police, although the square is lonely at nighttime, being occupied chiefly for business purposes. The constable's beat, moreover, is patrolled every 15 or 20 minutes, and within this short space of time, the murderer and his victim must have arrived and the crime been committed. The beat is in the charge of a man who is regarded by his superiors as thoroughly trustworthy, who has discharged his duties efficiently for several years and who reports that when he went through the square at about 1:30 a.m., he noticed nothing unusual and no one about. Plainclothes constables also occasionally patrol the square.

An hour after reading this account, Aubrey was seated opposite Henry Matthews who, for the first time Aubrey could remember, looked him squarely in the eyes. That rattled him; the Home Secretary's eyes were watery and pink, as if slightly inflamed.

"Carsonby, I'm astounded by the Ripper and confounded by the incompetence of the police. Only an hour before her death the last victim was in custody for drunkenness. They released her into the night without apparent concern for the danger she faced. It defies belief. Can *you* explain it?" he asked, holding a file on which was marked, in bold black letters, "WHITECHAPEL MURDERS."

"No, I can't, Minister," Aubrey answered truthfully.

"Nor can anybody else," the Minister said. "Anderson is on his way back. He arrives tomorrow, poor sod. But he can't complain: three weeks in the Alps while you and I and everybody else have been mired up to here," Matthews put a hand over his head, "with this Ripper thing. I don't envy Anderson, but perhaps his fresh eye will help. I want you to continue in your present assignment. Monro has been something of a disappointment; not that he can be blamed."

"No, Minister." Aubrey had had no contact with Monro over the past three weeks.

"The City Police are in on it now, too. Maybe they'll have some luck. It'll be fitting if they capture the man when all of Scotland Yard has failed." Matthews' eyes had long since left Aubrey's face and were again flitting around the room.

"I want you to keep an eye out for the City Police-Scotland Yard rivalry. I don't want them at each other's throats. It's not something I want to have to deal with. Politically, it would be better for the Yard to make the capture. You know what I'm saying, of course. Cooperate and conquer rather than divide," the Minister said. "Now I must confide in you, Carsonby, a matter that is of the utmost sensitivity." Matthews moved closer to Aubrey and leaned on the corner of his desk, continuing in hushed tones. "I want you to be an emissary to the Jews. Lord Salisbury spoke to me yesterday. A number of Jewish leaders, men such as Lord Rothschild and Samuel Montague, have communicated with him. They are most upset about the mistreatment of their people in the East End." Matthews walked back to his leather chair and sat down. "It's a nasty business, very nasty. Have you heard about the message found on a wall in Whitechapel? It was written in bloodstained chalk, apparently by the Ripper creature himself, and mentions something about the Jews. I'm not certain of the wording. Sir Charles ordered it scrubbed off. That caused a hell of a row with the city detectives, but I think, for once, that he did the right thing. Carsonby, I want you to communicate directly with the chief rabbi. His name is Adler, Nathan Adler. His son is the 'delegate' chief rabbi because the father is semi-retired or some such thing. Assure him, or the son, that we're doing everything in our power to curb any anti . . . any anti-*foreign* activities. We British should be very proud of how we treat our Jews. We've even had a Prime Minister of Jewish descent. Jews can sit in Parliament, in the House of Lords. There is not another place in the world where they can live so free of prejudice or molestation.''

Matthews stood and walked to his window, hands clasped behind his back. After a moment, he turned and said, ''You are to visit the chief rabbi's office in Finsbury Square. Tell them we don't believe the Ripper is Jewish, although, in all confidence, many think he is. And remember this, Carsonby: the Jews are a very powerful group. They have a history of getting their way. I say this man to man. It's their wealth, of course. Keep that in mind. Remember also that you are an unofficial plenipotentiary of Her Majesty's government. The Prime Minister himself is the impetus behind your visit. You might mention that fact. The responsibility is a large one, but you're up to it. And by the way, please give my compliments to the chief rabbi. We met once at a social function, and I thought he was just another gaitered bishop. He didn't look Jewish. Thought he was Episcopalian. Fooled me completely. That will be all,'' he said abruptly.

Back in his office, Aubrey stared out the window. From his fourth-floor vantage point he could see down the length of St. James's Park to Green Park and, in the distant foreground, to the grey, thinning trees of Hyde Park. Acre upon acre of parkland. In fact, if he narrowed his vision to a tunnel-like aperture, he could see only grass, pond water, shrubbery and trees. He might have been perched on the upper branch of a tall oak situated in the middle of a vast country estate. But as he widened his field of vision, the buildings and monuments of the world's largest city crept into sight, destroying the illusion of pastoral splendour, and it was not so difficult to accept that within a mile radius of where he stood, more than a million people lived out their daily lives—among them, the Ripper.

Thinking of the Whitechapel killer brought him back to

the present, to his meeting with Henry Matthews, and that reminded him of an old political axiom of his father's: "A politician is a hydra-headed creature, Aubrey, never forget that. One head belongs to the party, be it Whig or Tory, and speaks the party line. Then he has his own head, the one that speaks out of self-protection and self-aggrandizement. And when in the Cabinet, he wears a third head that speaks the government line about matters of state, that sort of thing. It's a bit of a juggling act, but you have to remember to keep all three in sight." Experience had confirmed the wisdom of his father's words. To Aubrey's mind, being surrounded by politicians was like being surrounded by scavengers; one never knew which one to keep one's eye on, but one knew that all of them were dangerous.

Charlotte had planned her shopping expedition with care. First, she travelled by carriage to Swaine, Adeney & Sons in Piccadilly, where she took delivery of a walking stick intended as a surprise gift for her father; she then browsed briefly in Fortnum & Mason, simply because she enjoyed the piquant aromas of the famous food emporium, then moved on to the House of Floris, where she purchased an expensive perfume. Finally, she visited Harrods, the prestigious Knightsbridge department store, where she was recognized and greeted with elaborate courtesy by a senior clerk.

"Good morning, Miss Carlyle. May I be of assistance?" he inquired, ceremoniously.

"I wish to purchase a game," Charlotte replied.

The clerk was mildly surprised. "A game, madam. A parlour game?"

Charlotte took exception to the word "parlour." "Something similar," she said, with faint condescension. "It must be suitable for the drawing room. It is intended as an evening's entertainment . . . a *divertissement*," she said in accentless French.

The clerk inclined his head slightly. "Of course, madam, please follow me." He sat her at a desk and disappeared, returning moments later with an assistant whose arms were stacked with several boxes. He reached for the uppermost one and removed the top with a small flourish. "Backgammon," he said. He deftly opened the leather-encased board and unfolded it. "The board is made of interlocked ivory and onyx. The craftsmanship is truly excellent. It was manufactured in India."

Charlotte deliberated for a moment. The clerk, sensing her indecision, spoke up. "The leather is of the finest quality. The markers and dice are handcarved from elephant tusk and ebony."

"Yes," she said, "the workmanship is quite splendid."

"The object of the game—"

Charlotte cut him off. "I am aware of how the game is played," she said cooly. "What else do you have?"

The clerk swiftly opened a second box. "Dominoes," he said. "The pieces are carved from cherry wood."

"Dominoes is a child's game," Charlotte said impatiently. "I am looking for something more novel, more exotic."

The clerk, wearing an uncertain frown, parroted her, "*Exotic,* madam?" He thought for a moment. "Would madam consider Tarot cards?"

"They are occultist," Charlotte corrected him sharply.

The clerk's assistant spoke for the first time. "There is a game that's just arrived from the Continent, from Paris, I believe. It's called Ouija."

"Ouija?" Charlotte repeated.

"Yes, madam. I believe it comes from the French and German. It means yes—yes."

"How does it work?"

"On the same principle as the planchette."

"The planchette?" Charlotte interrupted. "Do you have a planchette?"

"We do, madam," the junior clerk replied.

"That will do perfectly," she said. "Please wrap one. I wish to take it with me."

Charlotte arrived home to find her mother taking tea in the sitting room with Lady Ossington, a family friend and president of the Girls' Friendly Society.

"That looks like an interesting package. A present for someone?" her mother asked archly.

"It certainly looks like one," Lady Ossington said. "Is someone celebrating a birthday, Charlotte?"

Charlotte answered with some discomfort. "Actually, it's for me."

"Well, jolly good for you. I buy presents for myself all the time. I don't think a woman can spoil herself enough, especially at Harrods. What do you think, Lillian?"

"Oh, I quite agree. A present for oneself is the perfect countermeasure to a downcast mood. May we know what it is, Charlotte?"

"Nothing much. A game, that's all."

Her mother was surprised. "A game? What kind of game?"

Charlotte could feel the inquisitive eyes of both women fixed on her. She had unintentionally piqued their curiosity and was at a loss for words because she did not want to divulge the package's contents. At that moment, a maid entered the room bearing a tray of petits fours, and Charlotte seized the opportunity to make her exit. "They look delicious," she said. "I must change and have something to eat. I feel a little faint, and I do believe it's hunger."

Her mother was instantly alarmed. "Well, do have a sandwich and some tea," she said.

Charlotte helped herself to a delicate watercress tea sandwich. "I'll eat this in my room, if I may. Then I'll change and join you in a few minutes. Would that be all right?"

Her mother responded with affection. "Of course, dear, you run along and change."

In her room, Charlotte nibbled at the tiny sandwich without much appetite. She had not been fabricating when she had mentioned feeling faint. *Mother is very perceptive,* she thought. *She has been watching me and accurately divined my despondency. But surely she cannot guess the cause of my moodiness. Or can she?* Charlotte wondered. She placed the planchette, still wrapped in its package, on an upper shelf in her closet among her many hat and shoe boxes. As she unfastened her dress, her thoughts turned to Lydia and Charles.

Almost certainly they were involved in some sort of romantic *rapprochement*. Lydia was not to be found in the house much these days since she was spending all of her time at either Cambridge or Toynbee Hall. When she was home, however, she either hummed, as one in love, or kept to herself, looking glum and preoccupied, as one *troubled* in love. Charlotte much preferred this Lydia to the contented, humming one.

Perhaps the planchette will give me an answer, Charlotte thought. A heart-shaped piece of wood with two casters and a small pencil mounted on the underside, the planchette was apparently able to communicate with the spirit world. Its operation was simple. Players placed their hands on the board, preferably in a darkened room, closed their eyes and posed questions to departed spirits. Answers came back in written form, courtesy of the pencil.

Charlotte was uncertain about the existence of spirits, but she did believe in ghosts and the like—the Bible, after all, was chock-full of spiritual and supernatural goings-on. Although the instrument appeared perfectly harmless, she felt that she was taking a very courageous step in deciding to "play planchette." If it were charged with otherworldly powers, she could wield it to her advantage. The planchette would reveal the true state of affairs between Charles and Lydia, and the true direction of Charles's heart.

Feeling somewhat more resolved, Charlotte finished changing and left her bedroom to join her mother and Lady Ossington. Passing by her father's study, she noticed the *Times* folded on a chair, and the sight of the newspaper caused her to pause. In a move toward self-improvement, she had decided to become better acquainted with the world she knew existed beyond London. Lydia's decision to pursue her studies at Cambridge had once been a subject of mild derision, just another manifestation of her idiosyncratic personality. But now, Charlotte suspected that there was some method in Lydia's ways: men—including Charles—

seemed to enjoy conversing about worldly affairs. But two could play that game, and so she decided to have a quick look at the *Times*. Her eyes found the start of a paragraph:

According to the report of Police Constable Watkins, when passing through the square at 1:45 a.m., he found the murdered woman lying in the southwestern corner with her throat cut and her intestines protruding.

Oh my God! Charlotte thought, bringing a hand to her mouth. Her stomach rose in her throat, but she continued to read:

He immediately sent for Dr. Sequeira of Jewry Street, who arrived ten minutes later. The deceased was found lying on her back, her head inclined to the left. Her left leg was extended, her right bent; both her arms were also extended. The throat was terribly cut: there was a large gash across the face from the nose to the right angle of the cheek, and part of the right ear had been cut off.

Protruding intestines. Ears cut off. That was too much for Charlotte. She threw the paper to the chair and fled back to her room.

Charles lay in bed, a pot of tea and a plate of warm crumpets on a breakfast tray beside him. He buttered a crumpet and covered it with a thick spread of apricot marmalade. He took a bite, savouring the tart but sweet flavour of the preserve. It was the first food he had had in 24 hours.

Yesterday, he had awakened with a migraine severe enough to keep him bedridden, dozing on and off, for the entire day. Sometime last night, he had heard evensong from the church near the Albert Bridge. Or had it been voices raised in song from the nearer King's Head & Eight Bells public house? Whichever, he had risen, swallowed some more laudanum and fallen back into his recurring dream world.

Each evening, he slipped into the river to bathe in the

exotic sensation of the golden water. But as the sequence of dreams remained constant, so did the tameness of merely floating or playfully gamboling in the current. He found himself gazing downstream toward the rising plumes of mist that signalled the plunge of the falls. Night by night, he allowed himself to drift closer to those plumes and to the cataclysm they heralded. He savoured the growing strength of the current and continued unafraid, the air suddenly tingling and crackling with unseen danger. This only heightened his enjoyment. He had not thought about the nymphs and mermaids for several nights, but last night, they had reappeared, lolling in the distance on the rocks. They were naked, although through the veils of mist, their images had been shadowy and insubstantial. Were they real? The river was real—he could feel the water. He could flutter his fingers and feel the gentle turmoil. The falls were not imaginary; he could hear the rushing torrent. He had listened carefully and thought of the roar of a speeding train. He could see clouds of fine spray billowing above the chasm and the rocks on which the women-creatures rested. Of them, there was not a shadow of doubt. The rocks stood near the drop of the falls, as solid as stone griffins guarding a palace entrance. But he had not ventured any closer. He had climbed out of the river and, as always, immediately awakened.

Charles poured another cup of tea and recalled his evening with Lydia. Their night together had been like one stolen from another world. He had revelled in her young body and her lustful, uninhibited lovemaking, for her boldness had taken him by surprise. Charles was used to aggressive women, but generally they were either prostitutes or lower-class women he had seduced with ridiculous ease. He had also had more than one encounter with an upper-class adulteress, a woman seeking pleasure outside the confines of her marriage. One respectable lady of society had stated her clear intention to have knowledge of every peer of the realm. "And I do not mean to pick their brains, Lord Longerdale," she had sweetly said, slipping out of her chemise. "I mean to sleep with each one. Now, if you will kindly oblige me"—she was by then stark naked—"I will oblige you by crossing your name from my list.'' The motivation that lay behind this well-bred marchioness's ambition had intrigued Charles. He had wondered whether she sought revenge for infidelity on her husband's part, whether she suffered from some form of sexual imbalance or whether peers of the realm were simply her fetish. ''Not at all,'' she had explained. ''It's simply a matter of ambition. I don't think of it as trophy-hunting. It's not even really sexual. Oh, I'll admit I enjoy it. You've just seen evidence of that. But it's what they tell me in bed. I am the most informed woman in all of England. I like to know things. But take all of that away, and I suppose it has something to do with power. Do you know I could probably pass an Act of Parliament,'' she had said, stretching provocatively. ''One day, perhaps I shall. Certainly, I'll write my memoirs. But don't be alarmed, your review will be a splendid one. Now, I would be deeply grateful if you'd do it to me again. Then, I shall put two ticks beside your name.''

There were elements of this obsessive and calculating nature in Lydia Carlyle if one looked beyond her youth and loveliness. Originally, he had not fully intended their first night to be a night of conquest but rather a setting of the stage for the future. Lydia had ended up rewriting the drama, excising several scenes and acts to arrive at the *finale* almost before things had gotten properly under way.

He was wary of emotional involvement with her, as he was with any woman, but there was no denying she had burrowed under his skin like a tiny, seductive microbe, with the intent of becoming a much larger presence in his life. Microbes could be dangerous and parasitical, using someone else's flesh and blood to feed their own needs—just as the marchioness did.

He finished his tea, then bathed and shaved. As he stood before his mirror, carefully scraping at his two-day growth, it crossed his mind that his nocturnal patient, the mysterious John Castrain, had not revisited him, and he wondered as to his whereabouts and general health.

After dressing, he checked his appointment book, confirming that Lucie Rhinegold was due within half an hour.

He went downstairs to review his case notes but was interrupted by a sharp rapping at the door. He opened it, and there stood Mrs. Rhinegold and her husband, both looking ill at ease.

"May I have a word with you, Doctor? Alone, if possible," Fredrick Rhinegold asked.

"Of course," Charles said, covering his surprise at the husband's appearance. "Please come in. Lucie, if you will kindly be seated"—he indicated her customary chair— "I'm certain this won't take long. Please come with me, Mr. Rhinegold," and Charles showed him into the study adjoining his office.

Charles did not know a great deal about Lucie's husband, only that he had inherited a sizeable estate and a prosperous clay-tile business from his father. He offered him a chair and sat down opposite. At first, Mr. Rhinegold was silent, nervously fidgeting in the chair as he plucked invisible pieces of thread from the trousers of his worsted suit. Charles observed that his eyes were bloodshot from lack of sleep, and his complexion was pale beneath a shadow of stubble. When he finally spoke, he said, "She's not improving, Doctor. I'm not a scientific man; I don't profess to have knowledge or understanding of the more . . . modern medical treatments available. But I am concerned that the hypnosis is not working. Rather, to my uneducated eyes, it seems to be having a . . . deleterious effect. It is weakening her stability."

Charles digested this information, then asked, "How is she less stable?"

"She weeps more, is prone to more hysteria. She has joined the Ladies Ecclesiastic Embroidery League. Before that, it was painting. Now, interspersed with bouts of crying, she spends her waking day embroidering, praying and reading the Bible. Always the same verses—"

"Which are?" Charles interrupted.

"Those pertaining to adultery. She seems fascinated by the Biblical penalty of stoning the guilty woman to death. I asked her, 'Is that not barbaric?' She answered only that the penalty must fit the crime."

"I take it, then, that she no longer leaves the house at night?"

Mr. Rhinegold fell silent for a moment, his head slumped forward. "No, she doesn't," he answered. "I suppose I should be grateful. But Doctor," he continued, his voice raised in anger, "I did not marry . . . *that* Lucie," he said, pointing a finger at the closed door. "She is not the same woman. Is there not some medicine?"

"What was her relationship with her mother?" Charles asked suddenly.

Fredrick Rhinegold looked at him in surprise. "What has that got to do with anything?"

Charles ignored the question. "Did you know her well?"

"We were . . . acquainted," he answered noncommittally.

"Her father?"

"He died when she was a child."

"She comes from a good family, then?" Charles asked directly.

Fredrick Rhinegold suddenly stood up. "Her stock is mentally sound, if that's what you are driving at. I am aware of no history of mental . . . infirmity in the family."

"I see," Charles said.

"I shall be back in an hour to fetch my wife, Doctor. I trust an hour will suffice for her session."

"It will, Mr. Rhinegold."

"Then I shall see myself out, thank you," he said with a perfunctory bow and left the study.

Before Charles returned to his office, he spent a moment assessing what he had been told by Mr. Rhinegold, noting his sensitivity to questions about his wife's family history. The man was hiding something, and Charles instinctively knew that it was integral to the successful treatment of his wife.

Charles returned to his office and placed Lucie in a light hypnotic trance. He decided to investigate further the peach-and-apple symbolism and its relationship to her mother. But almost immediately, he ran into a problem: His patient would not cooperate. Although Lucie was hypnotized, her puritanical personality remained dominant. Usually the second personality, Lucie Beta, was easily accessible in a trancelike state. In answer to a direct question about what had "happened" to that Lucie, Mrs. Rhinegold answered, "She has gone away."

"Where?" Charles asked gently.

"To certain perdition," Lucie Alpha responded sanctimoniously.

Charles was momentarily baffled. "Can we visit with her? Souls in jeopardy are our concern. We must do what we can to rescue them."

"That is too late. She is a fallen woman."

"No fall is final." Charles almost grimaced: he sounded like a bloody evangelist. But he had no choice; he had to play whatever part necessary to re-establish the persona of Lucie Beta.

Lucie looked at Charles, holding her hands in her lap and clutching a pair of kid gloves. Her eyes seemed defeated, yet defiant. Charles had never seen her so pale; her face looked as if it belonged to an alabaster figurine. "That Lucie has gone," she repeated with weary resignation. "I'm sorry. We shall both miss her, but it's for the best. I didn't know her well, but what I did know, I didn't like. She was not a woman of refinement. Her morals had lapsed into a deplorable state. It's better this way."

Charles sat back and evaluated this statement. Lucie Beta had obviously been banished. He had not integrated the two personas, but he had somehow managed to reintroduce a single personality in the form of the puritanical Mrs. Fredrick Rhinegold. He could hardly describe this development as a cure, yet he did not have any clear idea of how to resolve the impasse.

Lydia entered Liverpool Street Station followed by a servant carrying her luggage. As always, the concourse was crowded with passengers arriving and departing. From every direction, she was assaulted by the cry of newspaper vendors announcing lurid details of the latest Whitechapel Murders: RIPPER DRUNK ON BLOOD! KILLS AT WILL! POLICE

HELPLESS! Lydia ignored the shouting and pushed her way clear. Her train to Cambridge was scheduled to leave in 15 minutes. At the track gateway, she turned to the servant. "I shall take my luggage from here," she said.

The servant stopped in mid-stride. "Madam?" he said in surprise.

"I shall carry the luggage myself," Lydia repeated, reaching for her handgrip and a larger plaid-patterned valise. Ignoring the servant's surprise, she turned, walked along the platform and entered a first-class coach. Keeping the handgrip and valise at her feet, she sat down and waited exactly ten minutes. Making certain the servant had left the station, she signalled a porter, paid him a shilling and instructed him to deposit her luggage in the baggage claim office. She then walked to the front of the station and hailed a hansom cab, giving the driver Charles's Cheyne Walk address. *I am either a fool or a woman in love,* she thought as the cab pulled into the swarming traffic at the entrance to Bishopsgate Street and headed west in the direction of the City and Chelsea.

In her purse, Lydia carried a small antique hourglass encased between two dolphins made of wafer-thin gold. She had purchased it in Venice and now used it at Cambridge to monitor the progress of her study periods. Looking at a watch did not convey the passage of time, but watching the downward spill of sand reminded her that time was wasting, and she used this inducement to keep her mind focused on her books. Since her night with Charles, however, the hourglass had come to symbolize something more than time lost in daydreaming. The grains of sand represented the future, and Lydia had resolved that it would not be wasted. Her life would not be an accumulation of lost opportunities, and with that in mind, she had decided to visit Charles for an afternoon of lovemaking and conversation. And as the hansom cab neared Chelsea, she wondered which she hungered for more.

A quarter of an hour later, she arrived at Charles's home, paid the driver and walked to the side entrance. As she raised her hand to knock on the door, it was opened by a woman. Lucie Rhinegold refused to meet Lydia's eyes, hurried down the stairs and disappeared down the laneway like a distraught spirit.

"Lydia!" Charles said, suddenly appearing in the doorway. "What a surprise!"

"Not an inconvenient one, I trust," Lydia managed to say. Had she interrupted a tryst?

"Good God, no. You're the most pleasant surprise I could imagine. Come in, come in."

"Who was she?"

"A patient."

"She's very beautiful," Lydia said, removing her hat and handing it to Charles.

"Do I detect a note of jealousy?" he asked.

"Yes, you probably do," Lydia said forthrightly.

"Well, you have my assurances that my interest in her is purely professional. But enough of her. How did you manage to come here? I thought you were off to Cambridge for the week."

"I was. But I decided to take a detour in the direction of Cheyne Walk, on the off chance that you might be home."

"You could have sent a message."

"I have no message save this," she said and reached up to kiss him.

After they had made love, Lydia roamed Charles's bedroom, fascinated by its unassailable masculinity. It reminded her of her father's study: shelf upon shelf of books as if the wall were constructed of book spines, overstuffed maroon chairs matching heavy maroon drapes, heavy polished wood, a pedestal-mounted globe.

Charles also kept souvenirs from trips he had taken with his father. Wood carvings and grotesque-looking masks from Africa, a mounted kudu head and a jade statue of the monkey god.

But the most interesting memento was a 6-inch tall fertility idol that was all thick lips and erect penis. It was as smooth as satin and waxen in colour. "Ivory?" she had asked on first seeing it.

"Rhinocerous horn. The natives believe that as a woman

rubs it, the man she thinks of will respond. Something like a voodoo doll.''

"How droll. Does it work?"

"Try it,'' he had challenged.

So she had caressed the little idol, all the while watching Charles. To her great amusement, it had worked.

She returned to the bed and began tracing patterns on his chest, running her fingers through a thick forest of dark hair. "We must use some protection now that we have formed a *liaison dangereuse*,'' she said.

For Charles, the sensation was exquisite. Sometimes her fingers dropped below his navel to the even thicker forest of groin hair. There, at the base of his penis, the fingers drew circles and other geometric designs. In his youth, so distant yet so close, such tantalizing caressing would have stimulated the growth of a very tall, very upright tree in that forest. And his one urgent need would have been to plant it in the moist, fertile vulva of the woman lying beside him. But he was older now, if being in one's thirties qualified one as older, and their lovemaking had made him drowsy.

"Protection?'' Charles murmured. "For whom? Or rather, from whom?"

"From the enemy within,'' Lydia said.

"I don't take your meaning.''

Lydia took all of his penis in one hand and gently squeezed. "I mean from this,'' she said, thinking that while when shrunken it might feel like a harmless chick, it could quickly transform itself into something of an altogether different and more consequential character.

"If you keep taunting it like that, you'll bring it back to life, and I won't be responsible for what it does,'' Charles groaned.

"That is my very point.''

Charles noted the change in Lydia's tone. After making love, she became introspective, the opposite from its effect on him. He only wanted to nap or to eat. "Will you stay for supper?'' he said, feeling suddenly hungry. "I have a leg of lamb and some cheese—and a bottle of Pouilly-Fuissé.''

The invitation distracted Lydia from her train of thought. "I'm tempted," she said, "but I'm expected in Cambridge."

"Take a train in the morning."

"What if I am seen?"

"What if you are seen this evening? I don't see the difference."

"I will say I missed this afternoon's train."

"But you were seen to board that train," Charles said. "Face it, Lydia, if you are found out, tonight or tomorrow, no alibi will be sufficient to prove your innocence. The die is cast."

Lydia said, "I must say, you're very cavalier about my situation. If I am found out, you will surely be implicated. Don't you have concern for *your* reputation?"

Charles laughed, almost harshly. "I have no reputation. You mistake me for a gentleman."

"And you're not?" Lydia asked.

Charles raised himself on an elbow and looked at her flushed face. *From earlier arousal or present anger?* he wondered. Whichever, he suddenly experienced an urgent need to have her again. He touched a breast and leaned forward, taking the nipple in his mouth. Lydia pushed at his shoulders. He looked at her in surprise, then roughly pinioned her with his arms. She opened her mouth in protest, but he covered it with his own and took her with a violent passion that both frightened and exhilarated her.

⊶⊷【 14 】⊶⊷

LYDIA AND CHARLES ate supper on a quilt spread out on the floor in his bedroom. The late-afternoon air had chilled, and Charles had thrown several logs on the fire, which were now blazing and crackling cheerfully. Lydia was wearing Charles's velvet smoking jacket and knee-high socks, and Charles wore a loose-fitting flannel nightshirt. Afterwards, an amicable silence fell between them, Charles smoking a cheroot while Lydia stared into the fire, sipping a glass of wine. Although her expression was placid, even contented, Lydia's mind was full of worrisome thought. *I have known this man only a few months, yet I feel I have known him a lifetime . . . I could tell him everything . . . yet tell him nothing.* This emotional ambivalence was both irritating and puzzling. She stood and walked over to Charles's desk.

"Where are you going?" he asked.

"Nowhere," she replied pensively as she perused the collection of papers and open books scattered about. She sat down at the desk and read the first sentence that caught her eye: "It is a matter of curious observation that remarkable ability sometimes goes along with signal eccentricity. An extraordinary development of one part of the mind is by no means incompatible with an irregular and unstable condition of other parts of the mind." Lydia flipped the book closed and noted Henry Maudsley's name on its cover. Picking up a crumpled piece of paper, she asked, "What's this?" and worked patiently to open it. An almost illegible name was scrawled on the paper.

"Who is John Castrain?"

Charles looked up in surprise. "Do you know him?"

Lydia shook her head.

"He is the oddest fellow," Charles said, tossing his cheroot into the fire. He leaned on an elbow and stretched his legs. "Calls only at night, always dressed to kill, and he tells the damnedest stories. I don't know whether to believe him or not."

"Is he insane?"

"To be honest, I don't know. I can't seem to diagnose his condition. I can't cure all of my patients, but only rarely am I at a loss to understand the nature of their disorders. Unfortunately, this Castrain fellow has fallen into that category for the moment."

"Do you see many patients?"

"Not a lot. At any given time, perhaps ten or eleven. They're all referrals, patients whom other physicians have given up on."

"Do most suffer from double consciousness like Jekyll and Hyde in the play we saw? That woman I ran into here this afternoon, for instance?"

"Yes, she does. I call her Lucie Alpha and Lucie Beta."

"How extraordinary," Lydia said.

"Yes, isn't it."

Lydia mused for a moment. "It must also be very convenient," she added.

"How so?"

"Well, wouldn't we all like to be two people? One fun-loving and free-spirited, able to do or say whatever we feel. The other could be as strait-laced as the vicar's wife."

Charles interrupted. "That's astonishing," he said, "you have just described the two Lucies. Those are the very personalities at odds within her."

"Why can't she reconcile them?"

"Would that it were so easy," Charles said depreciating-ly. He stood and lit another cheroot, then lay down on the bed, his feet crossed at the ankles. He patted the mattress beside him. "Come," he said.

Lydia made a wry smile. "Again?"

"Again."

"You are a satyr."

"If by that you mean insatiable, I must plead guilty."

Lydia left the desk and crawled into bed beside him. "We can't go on as we are, Charles," she said, alluding to something Charles was obviously unable to comprehend.

"What do you mean?" he said.

"We risk pregnancy."

Charles was suddenly fully alert as he tried to decipher her exact meaning. The word "we" had struck an immediately discordant note. "Pregnancy?" he said, sounding as casual as he could. He had never given consideration to that possibility before. Contraceptives were a female problem. "What do you propose?"

"You're the physician. I thought you might propose some device."

"Such as?" Charles inquired. He was surprised that Lydia was so well informed, and this caused him to wonder again about her previous sexual experience.

"For heaven's sake, Charles, you are the doctor."

"I'm not as versed in these matters as you presume."

Lydia sat up in displeasure. "You're avoiding the issue," she said.

"Not at all."

"Then answer me. You didn't wear a sheath."

Charles climbed out of bed and pulled on his dressing gown. Sitting in a chair, he looked at Lydia, who was also sitting and hugging drawn-up knees, a blanket thrown over her shoulders.

"No," Charles said, a little cooly. "I didn't. Nor have I ever."

"Never? But haven't you risked a pregnancy?"

"I'm not a father. At least not to my knowledge."

"That is all you have to say? That is your defence?"

"It is a statement of fact. Make of it what you will."

There was a moment of strained silence. Outside the window, a collier was travelling up the Thames, a cloud of coal smoke pouring from its funnel. On the ground, a sundial threw an elongated, evening shadow across the lawn.

Lydia had not anticipated Charles's reluctance to discuss contraception. She also found it discomforting that a mood of intimacy could evaporate so quickly. Still, she felt attracted to him as he sat opposite her, his face as dark as the smoke that was wafting inland.

She had begun to contrast Charles with Aubrey since each of them had been a frequent escort over the past several weeks. She had concluded that there was a bloodlessness about Aubrey. He was bred to the insular world of his family and class and felt at home with the established order of things. This was not to say that he lacked ambition or intellect. But nonetheless, he was the spaniel type with not a streak of meanness to his personality. "Bloodlessness" could never apply to Charles, however. Lydia had come to sense that there were mean streaks in Charles, plenty of them. Instinctively, she knew that he could hurt, be ruthless, even cruel. Charles had not betrayed that potential before this moment, but now she could see it in his tense posture and dark, brooding eyes.

"If you won't wear a sheath," she finally said, "then could you fit me for a diaphragm?"

Charles stood up as if shocked. He walked to the bedroom door where he stood with his back to her.

"Lydia, where did you learn of such . . . such devices?"

"In a book, *The Wife's Handbook,* by a Dr. Allbutt."

"Oh yes, Allbutt. He's from Leeds. Do you know what the General Medical Council did to him? They struck him off the Register. He can't practise."

"Why? Is he a quack?" Lydia was alarmed. His book had seemed honest and lucid in its advice.

"Not at all, but he breached professional ethics."

"Professional ethics? How so?" Lydia cut in.

"By making available to the public, cheaply available, information about birth control."

Lydia was unbelieving. "That's a sin?"

"Well, think of it from the Medical Council's perspective. Here we have this country doctor who took it on his shoulders to sanction contraception for the sole purpose of encouraging risk-free sex. That was his sin. In a way, he usurped the role of the Council."

"It's *their* responsibility to sanction contraception?" Lydia asked.

"They seem to think so. Let me speak plainly, Lydia. Take the diaphragm for example. How is it to get *in* . . . in where it's supposed to be. The council has nightmarish visions of thousands of doctors' fingers in thousands of vaginal cavities. What is becoming of the medical profession's sense of decorum, they wonder. 'Is there no stone of shame left unturned?' to quote one of the council members."

"And in the meantime—"

"Things will change," Charles interrupted, "but change, we both know, moves at a snail's pace."

"In the meantime, women suffer. I read of one who died from blood poisoning following an abortion," Lydia said, restraining the urge to raise her voice.

"She's hardly the first," Charles replied matter-of-factly.

Lydia looked at him, scarcely believing his unperturbed comment. "You don't find that criminal?"

"Of course it's criminal. But it's been a fact of life since the dawn of creation and will continue to be until the end of time. Life has always had and always will have its ugly side, and there is nothing you or any other person can do to change that, no matter how dedicated or committed you are." Charles reached over and stubbed out his cigar in an ashtray on the bedstand. He then slipped back into bed and rolled over to embrace Lydia, holding himself above her by his outstretched arms. "Life will remain as it always has: full of evil, greed, horror, deceit . . . and passion," he said, as he lowered himself onto her.

Aubrey had been presented with two problems or, as he had complained to Toby, with "two explosive political problems: the Jews and the police. Not just explosive in the sense of flying mud and other harmless debris, like someone else's career, but a kind of Guy Fawkes eruption in which *my* career could go up in flames.''

Toby had handled these colourful remarks with his customary surefootedness: "More likely Sir Charles Warren and Mr. Henry Matthews, but not you, sir. Not a chance. The way I see it, their names are the ones people see in the papers. It's *them* that will go up in flames, not you, sir.''

"That's very astute of you, Toby,'' Aubrey had said. "Let's trust the future confirms your intuition.''

Aubrey's first problem, dealing with the Jewish community, would take all of his tact. It required a walking-on-eggshells kind of diplomacy since the prevailing Jewish situation—or alien question, as it was called in Whitehall—was highly sensitive.

Over the past six years, a veritable flood of Jewish refugees had fled Russia and resettled in London. It was impossible to count their total number, but estimates placed it somewhere between 30,000 and 40,000. The Jewish influx did not sit well with East End inhabitants. The labour market was already depressed, and the newcomers would work for next to nothing in order to secure a financial toehold. Furthermore, they refused to anglicize themselves, fraternizing only with their own kind. A vicar, well laced with claret and under a full head of steam about the "alien" problem, had once explained to Aubrey: "When visiting the poor, I often hear the complaint, 'It's them Jews.' Time after time, I hear that lament. Many men and women, *English* men and women, struggle to keep a roof over their heads but are driven out of work by the foreigners. 'I would live on less,' they say, 'and would take less, but what's the use? The Jews are coming by the thousands, and there will be nothing left.''' The cleric, draining his glass of claret as if it were water, had leaned toward Aubrey and continued conspiratorially: "Truth compels this sentiment: wherever the Jews settle in any numbers, that neighbourhood speedily drops in character, in morals . . . their very virtues seem prolific of evil.'' The old cleric had delivered his peroration full of wine, righteous invective and transparent anti-Semitism. Aubrey knew too well that the vicar spoke for the majority of his countrymen.

Aubrey's second problem, the rivalry between the City Police and Scotland Yard, also required the skills of a consummate diplomat. The Lord Mayor ruled the square mile of the City of London as though he were a feudal lord. Its police force existed totally separately from Scotland Yard. Its constables were better paid, educated, trained and pensioned than their metropolitan brethren. City Police boots came in more than two sizes; the Metropolitan Police boots were only available in large and small. It had been said with some seriousness that a man got into the City Force with his brain and into the Metropolitan Force with his feet. As a result of this one-upmanship, the City Police were able to recruit the cream of the crop.

Henry Smith, the acting Commissioner of the City Police, was a professional policeman. He considered his Scotland Yard counterpart, Charles Warren, a bumbling amateur. Because the Eddowes woman had been murdered within the boundary of the City, it came under Smith's jurisdiction. For the first time, the two forces were officially joined in the hunt for the Ripper. The difficulty would be in coordinating their efforts; Aubrey knew Henry Smith to be as headstrong as Charles Warren.

After enjoying an oyster dinner at home, Aubrey walked the short distance to Brooks's in St. James's Street. He was sentimentally attached to the club because his family had maintained at least one membership since its founding in 1764. It had a reputation for dullness, undeserved to Aubrey's mind.

In the card room, the players often gambled for high stakes, the traditionally popular games being faro and macro, although whist and backgammon were also played regularly. Aubrey stepped into the large sitting area known as the great subscription room and picked up a *Times*. The room's only sources of illumination were oil lamps and beeswax candles, which gave it a Rembrandtesque sense of ambient light and dark shadow. He pulled a chair close to a lamp and began to read a detailed account of the latest murders:

The scene of the first crime is a narrow court in Berner Street, a quiet thoroughfare running from Commercial Road down to the London, Tilbury and South-end Railway. At the entrance to the court are a pair of large wooden gates in one of which is a small wicket for use when the gates are closed. At the hour when the murderer accomplished his deed, the gates to the yard were open. There is a dead wall on each side of the court, the effect of which is to enshroud the intervening space in absolute darkness. Further back, some light is thrown into the court from the windows of a workmen's club, but such illumination, being from an upper storey, falls on the cottages opposite and would only serve to intensify the gloom of the rest of the court. It is believed that the murderer threw his victim to the ground and severed her throat from ear to ear with one gash. The body was found lying as if the woman had fallen forward, her feet a couple of yards from the street and her head in a gutter that runs down the right-hand side of the court. The condition of the corpse and several other circumstances prove conclusively that only a short period elapsed between the committal of the murder and the discovery of the body. In fact, it is generally conjectured that the assassin was disturbed while at his ghastly work and made off before he had completed his design. All the aspects of the case connect the tragedy with the one that took place 45 minutes later, a few streets distant. The obvious poverty of the woman is entirely opposed to the theory that robbery could have been the motive, and the secrecy and dispatch with which the crime was effected are also good evidence that the murder was not the result of an ordinary street brawl. At the club referred to above—the International Workmen's Educational Club, which is an offshoot of the Socialist League and a rendezvous of a number of foreign residents, chiefly Russians, Poles and Continental Jews of various nationalities—it is customary on Saturday nights to have friendly discussions on topics of mutual interest and to wind up the evening's entertainment with songs. The proceedings commenced on Saturday about 8:30 p.m. with a discussion on the necessity for socialism among Jews. That kept up until about 11 p.m., when a considerable portion of the company left. Between 20 and 30

remained behind, however, and the usual concert which
followed did not conclude when Louie Diemasebutz, the
steward of the club, advised that a woman had been murdered
a few yards from the club. No one heard anything in the nature
of a scream or a woman's cry of distress.

Aubrey raised his head from the newspaper. His attention
had been interrupted by two older men, one with muttonchops and an incipiently choleric expression, the other a thin
fellow with an angular face, who had sat down a chair's-
width away. They were smoking cigars, sipping port and
discussing the Whitechapel murders. Although eavesdrop-
ping was strictly against unwritten club etiquette, Aubrey
found himself drawn into the conversation as an unwitting,
silent participant.

"The Jews and the Irish are both benighted races," the
man with muttonchops said in a rasping voice. "Both are
inbred, almost incestuously so, promiscuous and fanatical in
faith, on which each blames his persecution. They speak in
strange tongues—Gaelic on that green but cursed isle, the
Jew his incomprehensible Yiddish. But, although alike, they
are also vastly different. Money sticks to a Jew's hand, never
to an Irishman's. Give the Irishman a shilling, and within an
hour he is besotted with drink; the Jew, however, would lend
his coin at usurious interest. The Irishman gets drunker, the
Jew richer."

His companion murmured some reply, which Aubrey did
not catch, and the man continued to expound on his theory.
"The Jew's downfall is his avarice, but what about the
Irishman? Is it a propensity for violence? The Irish will
slaughter one another or an Englishman at the drop of a hat.
A form of racial fratricide. But what about the Jew?" He
swallowed a mouthful of port but did not give the other man a
chance to respond. Instead, he answered his own question.
"Never. Jews do not kill Jews. Over the ages, their race has
been slaughtered and massacred at regular intervals. Witness
the present Russian and Polish pogroms. Does he retaliate?
Rarely, if ever, it seems. It's as if he's fatally indifferent to
the spilling of his own blood. If a particular Jew is

victimized, he merely shrugs his shoulders, mutters 'so be it' and goes meekly to his death. The taking of human life—even in self-defence—has proven repugnant to the race. History and logic, therefore, dictate the unlikelihood that a Jew is the East End murderer."

"Unless an unbalanced one. One who seeks revenge in the ritualistic slaughter of gentiles," responded his thin companion, finally getting a chance to speak.

"But why women? And why common prostitutes?"

"Easy targets. Perhaps he had sexual intercourse with one and feels defiled."

The fellow with muttonchops took umbrage at the comment. "Would a sense of defilement create an animalistic thirst for revenge? To such a degree that a man would literally rip apart a woman? There is a lust for blood here that is beyond explanation. Take the Irish, who are prone to violence and who have committed the most horrible atrocities in the name of Home Rule. Some of their crimes are bloodcurdling: The Phoenix Park murders, for example. Cavendish and Burke were hacked to death with surgical knives. Political motivation, however deeply rooted, seems merely an excuse to satisfy a primitive need: the spilling of human blood."

Aubrey attempted to return to his newspaper, but he could not ignore the conversation. The other man, who was relighting a cigar, offered no comment to his companion's last remark.

"A Jew can think in the abstract," he went on. "Not the Irishman. His mind moves directly forward. No detour, no convoluted twists and turns. He is motivated to murder, and he does murder. So let us apply that logic to an Irish Ripper. He possesses a pathological hatred of the English that has been bred into him. He despises us like a slave does his master. He cannot strike out at authority, at the House of Commons, the army, the police. Do not take me literally now," he interrupted himself, lifting a pointed finger. "I speak in a broad metaphysical sense. He has planted his bombs outside the House of Commons and Scotland Yard, but to what avail? He has provoked a sensation, but he has not spilled the English blood for which he lusts. But does that lust simply dissipate? No, it is malignant, it must have *expression*. He could kill a policeman with a pistol shot but would probably be captured and end up dangling from a noose. Contrary to their own estimation, the Irish are not a martyring race, so there we have him: a Fenian caged in a mental prison of his own design.'' He inhaled hungrily on his own cigar, then noisily vented through his nostrils, the smoke joining that of his companion's to form a single bluish cloud.

"How does he break out?'' he continued. "By slaughtering a useless whore, that's how. He satisfies his blood lust, but accomplishes more, much more than that. Read the *Times,* the penny dreadfuls, read what you may. Of what do the headlines scream? Of unspeakable horror, horror that translates into public terror. Never has public confidence in its protectors, our esteemable police forces, been so shaken. The public's perception of its own safety has taken a beating, and so the terror, which was the object of the Fenian outrages against Parliament and Scotland Yard, has been achieved a thousandfold by the butchering of cheap whores. There is a grotesque and immeasurably cruel logic to this. What other topic dominates the press and occupies the minds of every thinking, self-respecting citizen at this very moment?''

"The Parnell Inquiry,'' his friend responded.

"Of course. There are only two newsworthy matters afoot right now, Parnellism—''

"And the terrorism of the Ripper,'' the thin man interrupted. "But would the Fenians commit such atrocities? You have said the Irish are not given to Byzantine stratagems. I agree wholeheartedly. Yet, if what you postulate is true, political motivation as the cause of these murders is completely Byzantine. It begs explanation.''

"Not if one views the perpetrator as a demented Irish Fenian.''

"It seems too incredible a set of circumstances.''

"But doesn't that precisely summarize the activities of the Ripper?''

"Not necessarily. Take the Polish Jews,'' the thin man

said in sure tones. "They migrate westward, and with every mile travelled, the gulf between their culture and Western civilization increases. In a very real sense, these Polish Jews are stepping out of the Dark Ages into an enlightened world—and they do so overnight! That is our modern age. Steam has transformed the face of society as no other force of nature. Like a time machine, the steam engine transports whole populations directly into the future without their undergoing the metamorphosis from savage to civilized man. Now, relate this to the butcher in the East End. The gulf between his atrocities and the behaviour of a civilized man is parallel to that which exists between an immigrant Polish Jew and an Englishman today."

"What are you driving at?" the man with muttonchops said irascibly.

His companion replied: "At the moment, we are confounded by his savagery. Our mistake has been to superimpose our own frame of reference on his. No Englishman, even an insane one, would commit such butchery. Yet the barbarianism of the Slavic people is legendary. Mark my words: when the murders are solved, our man will be found among the Polish Jews who so recently have inundated our East End."

Aubrey found himself gritting his teeth at the bigotry of the two men. During the Middle Ages, England had been the first country to order a wholesale banishment of the Jews. It was Cromwell who had permitted their return. But as Sir Edward Coke, the great English juror, had stated in the 17th century: "Between them, as with devils, whose subjects they are, and the Christian, there can be no peace." That sentiment had died, at least as a matter of historical record, only 30 or 40 years ago, when Lionel Nathan de Rothschild had been the first person of the Jewish faith to be elected to Parliament. Once there, he had refused to swear a Christian oath, and that courageous stand had forced Parliament to pass a bill whereby one's Jewish ancestry could no longer be used as a legal weapon against an Englishman.

Aubrey stood and left the two men to their port, cigars and prejudices. Outside, across St. James's Street, moonlight

glowed on the famous bow windows of Boodle's, where once
the Duke of Wellington had sat and watched the world pass
by. Aubrey wondered what his thoughts would have been had
he overheard the conversation in Brooks's: his defeat of
Napoleon had been bankrolled by Jewish money.

John Castrain was sitting opposite Charles Randall in his
study. *What time is it?* Charles wondered. *Two, three, four
a.m.?* He was shivering and had drawn his chair up close to
the hearth, wishing the fire would throw off more heat. He
had the distinct feeling of having lived this moment before,
not once but several times. The hour was the same, the
wide-awake posture of Castrain, his unannounced arrival, all
of these recurring factors, including shivering before a fire,
led Charles to conclude that his study had become a
miniature stage—and he and Castrain the cast of a two-
character play. *How can I chase the man away,* he thought
sleepily, *or have him make sensible arrangements for a
consultation?* These visits robbed him of sleep and drained
him emotionally.

"Tahiti would be a pleasant interlude," Charles said. He
did not mention that he had been there once, when he had
circled the globe with his father.

"The heat there is fierce, but the women, the *wahines*,
make it worthwhile. Rousseau can have his lake in Switzerland. You have not seen nature until you have sat at night
beneath a firmament of blazing stars and contemplated
Moorea across the Sea of Moons. The Polynesians are so
sensible about sex. It's a natural function, not an amoral
act."

What could Charles remember of Tahiti? Black sand
beaches that sucked at him like quicksand; a merciless sun
that broiled him lobster-red; old men with elephantiasis; the
scent of frangipani trees . . . his father wearing a straw
boater, his face flushed and damp, pants rolled up to his
knees, yet still wearing a tie for propriety's sake, telling him
that "here on this sunstruck island, perhaps God has made
His peace with women." Recollection of that observation
prompted another: a sound originating from the next room in

the hotel where they had stayed in Papeete. He had heard his father's lovemaking, violently shaking the fastenings of corroded bedposts, the prostitute crying out in pleasure . . . then, inevitably, the sound of his father's hand as he slapped her. Charles had thought at the time that God might have made His peace with women on Tahiti, but his father had not.

"Did you spend much time there?" Charles asked of John Castrain.

"Not enough. I was circumnavigating the globe. Like a gypsy, I stayed in no one place longer than a month. But I shall never forget Tahiti or its women. I confess I have slept with women of every race on the face of this earth. Yet I shall never forget the Tahitians. What do you call a man who collects women?" But he did not expect a reply. He was delivering another soliloquy, and his question was rhetorical, posed as if having spent a lifetime in pursuit of a particular theory he was now at a stage where he had to make sense of it.

Lydia, who had left for Cambridge several hours before, was constantly on his mind. Their relationship would develop into a whirlwind of clandestine sex, of that he was reasonably certain. He had withstood countless such whirlwinds in the past. Some had become quickly tempestuous; in such circumstances, he had simply extricated himself from the situation just as he had with Colleen Murphy. Recriminations could be acrimonious, but they always passed. Passion moved the heart and senses to an intense degree, a phenomenon that made the rest of life seem dreary. But passion had a relatively short life span. It was essentially cannibalistic, feeding on its own energy. At some point, it simply ran out of emotional fuel and sputtered to a halt. That would happen to him and Lydia.

His gaze fell on Rossetti's "Proserpine." He was beginning to comprehend his attraction to the painting subject. She represented a certain female ideal. She was beautiful, but there was a compliant quality to her as well. She was passive. You could strike her, abuse her verbally, be unfaithful, be a complete and uncivil swine . . . and she would not raise her voice in complaint. She would simply retain her beatific composure. But if Lydia Carlyle, not Jane Morris, had posed for Rossetti, the result would have been startlingly different. Lydia would be witchlike as queen of the underworld, her attractiveness subordinated to the will and vitality of her mind.

"You are lost in your Rossetti," John Castrain said.

Charles started. "Forgive me, I must plead the hour," he said.

"Odd, isn't it?" his visitor said. "We each seem to have our own internal clock. I should travel exactly halfway around the globe—Tahiti perhaps—where it would be midafternoon and my habits would be deemed normal."

Charles, upon first seeing him, had immediately thought he suffered from syphilis. A different facet of Castrain's appearance or behaviour seemed to confirm that diagnosis on each subsequent visit. Syphilis was known to be a generalised systemic disease caused by a *spirochete treponema pallieum*. Once this microscopic organism invaded the body, death was almost certain. Mercury or potassium iodide kept syphilis in relative quiescence, but over this period of time, the disease was actually going about its deadly business. The symptoms included memory loss, delusions, disorientation, hallucinations and, on the physical side, drooping eyelids, chronic suppuration about the ears and weight loss.

Castrain presented some of these symptoms. He did tug at his left ear fairly regularly, and his penetrating green eyes often remained in a state of fixed dilation. This was most peculiar because the only source of light in the study was the fireplace, yet Castrain's vision seemed unimpaired. Charles concluded that he must possess extraordinary night vision.

It also crossed his mind that English might not be Castrain's mother tongue: his diction was precise, almost perfectly so. His vocabulary was extensive, and he was obviously well-read. A curious feature about his voice was its flat, tonal modulation. He spoke in a hurried manner, his sentences rushing together like a stream abruptly narrowing and confronting a sudden drop. His thought patterns were, at first utterance, disjointed, but he invariably pulled the threads of an apparently disorderly train of thought into a rational, if sometimes amazing, conclusion.

"Didn't Tennyson write something about a hunter of women?" John Castrain was saying. "Didn't the Northern King declare that men hunt women—I believe I repeat this verbatim—'for their skins'? Now we have the Ripper hunting them for their wombs. I myself am something of a hunter. I don't want to shock you, Doctor. I warned at the outset I was of . . . an 'eccentric' nature. But being who, or rather what, you are no doubt inures you to curiosities the likes of me, so pray, let me continue. From every woman I've slept with I have taken a pubic hair. That's not as extraordinary as it may sound. Countless sailors have sealed away in an envelope a wisp of their sweethearts' hair. Even the Queen has a lock of her beloved Albert's hair. And one can buy a lock said to come from the scalp of Napoleon. Well I, too, have my hairs, a charming collection and every one of them mounted, catalogued and graded according to a pleasure scale I devised myself. Would you like to see a sample index card?"

He rose and handed Charles a piece of paper three inches square. It was sepia-brown with age:

1868 (30/9)

Edwina Hap-Song, 18. Baptized Christian by British missionary. Deflowered by same. Brown skin, black glossy hair, agate eyes. Very slender, slip of a woman. Moorea, warm, on beach. Performed fellatio. Pain: stoic.

No. 145

Charles handed the card back. The date, 20 years ago, raised a question. In 1868, Castrain would have been hardly more than a teenage boy. But he had no opportunity to quiz him; already he had moved on to another topic.

"I have a brother. A *bête noire*. He is a member of a secret society of flagellants. They birch whores and girls destined for whoredom. My brother's society meets monthly, as do many such gatherings of gentlemen. All members have standing in society. Not a *parvenu* among us." Charles noted the slip into the first person. "I could name six gentlemen of whom frequent mention is made in the *Times*.

"Our birches are divided into 20 classifications. Number one is the thickest, perhaps as thick as a rawhide whip; a 20 is almost as slender as a blade of grass. Birching is really an art. There are variations, of course. Sometimes the play becomes a little rough, but no one has ever died. And the wenches are well compensated. Their living quarters are spacious, well appointed. When it's time for them to move on, most actually protest."

As Charles listened to this remarkable testimony, he felt drawn into a kind of psychic energy field generated by John Castrain. *In truth, he . . . frightens me,* Charles thought. At the same time, the man's air of familiarity irritated him. Charles was developing a moribund fascination for Castrain, but also a concomitant dislike for and aversion to him.

Charles decided that he had heard enough for one night and that if Castrain wished to continue his consultation, it would be on his terms. "The hour grows late," he said. "I have an early appointment tomorrow—or I should say *this* morning."

"I have overextended my welcome again—a habit I must break." Castrain stood.

"You will be back?" Charles inquired.

"Most certainly." He smiled and extended a hand. "These sessions are of enormous help to me."

Charles almost recoiled. His grip was bony and cold, like the emaciated hand of a cadaver.

-–►❧[15]❧◄–-

AUBREY WAS IN his office carefully reading the notes made
by Police Constable Alfred Long, whose notebook had been
delivered to the Home Office because it contained, in the
opinion of the Home Secretary, politically sensitive material. Matthews was becoming increasingly wary of anything
with potential political repercussions. To Aubrey's mind, the
Ripper had turned him into his personal marionette: every
time he committed a murder, Matthews jumped as if
attached to strings. Matthews the marionette, Warren the
martinet, that seemed to be a succinct summary of the two
men.

It appeared that the murderer, upon finishing his ghastly
work in Mitre Square, had fled east out of the City and back
into Whitechapel. A piece of bloody apron found in
Goulston Street had proved to belong to Catherine Eddowes.
But someone, presumably the murderer himself, had written
a message on a nearby black-faced wall. It was the political
implications of those words that alarmed Henry Matthews. It
read, as reported in the *Times:* "The Jews are the men that
will not be blamed for nothing." The grammatical construc-
tion of this phrase made interpretation ambiguous. Had the

constable misplaced the word "not"? Should the sentence read: The Jews are not the men that will be blamed for nothing? If so, the author was attempting to absolve the Jews of blame for the murders. As the sentence stood, it appeared it was not for nothing the Jews were blamed. The constable had stated it was written in a good schoolboy hand, and this created more ambiguity. Was it written by a schoolboy? Or did the constable mean that it had been written with care, so that its meaning could not be mistaken or the message itself missed?

And there was a further complicating factor: the spelling of the word Jews was not as had appeared in the *Times,* but according to Constable Long's notebook, had been spelled J-U-W-E-S.

Sir Charles Warren, upon his arrival at the scene and despite the strenuous objection of the City Police, had ordered the sentence scrubbed from the wall so that it could not be studied further. The City Police had been powerless to intervene. Goulston Street lay outside the City and inside Whitechapel and was hence within Warren's preserve. Later in the morning, when pressed to explain his decision, he had stated that the neighbourhood was already crowded with people setting up stalls for the nearby Petticoat Lane market. In such circumstances, he was concerned about a riot against the Jews. "A pogrom on English soil is no more remote a possibility than it is on Polish or Russian." This comment had proved to be politically difficult for Matthews to rebuff. He knew the Jews of Whitechapel were under assault and were, in fact, suspected of harbouring the Ripper. At the same time, the possibility of a pogrom seemed to stretch credibility—and it also tarnished the image of all Englishmen.

Regardless of the political implications, the only record preserved of the controversial inscription was that contained in Constable Alfred Long's notebook.

The office of the chief rabbi was in Finsbury Square on the northern boundary of the City, near Liverpool Street Station and Mitre Square. Two men greeted him: the chief rabbi,

Nathan Marcus Adler, and the delegate chief, his son, Hermann Adler. The elder Adler stood with difficulty, supported by a stout cane. His hair was snow-white, the whitest Aubrey had ever seen. He had obviously dressed with care for the interview, his black rabbinical costume clothing him from head to toe. His facial skin was pink and wrinkled like that of a day-old infant, but his eyes seemed as ancient as those of an Old Testament prophet. They were the wisest, most gentle eyes that Aubrey had ever looked into, and they possessed none of the sly profundity attributed to Jews by gentiles.

His son was dressed in an identical costume, and Aubrey estimated his age to be 45. Wire-rimmed glasses were perched on the end of a large hooked nose, and his salt-and-pepper beard was precisely trimmed, the sides forming a perfect isosceles triangle. He gave Aubrey the impression of being a man of formidable intellect and strength of will. His expression was welcoming but stern—a man prepared to listen politely but equally prepared to go on the offensive at a moment's notice.

The elder Adler spoke first, so softly that Aubrey had to lean forward to hear him. "Thank you very much for coming to our office, Mr. Carsonby. Please convey our gratitude to the Home Secretary for his efforts to protect us during this difficult time."

The old man moved slowly and sat down behind a large desk, the surface of which was polished to a high gloss. His son took a chair not quite beside his father, crossing his knees and resting one elbow on a corner of the desk. On the wall behind them, a wooden plaque carved in the shape of the Star of David gave testimony to the founding synagogues of the United Synagogue, the first organized alliance of Anglo-Jewry. The date, 1870, was etched in gold. On either side of the desk stood floor-to-ceiling bookshelves; on the desk itself was a leather-bound copy of the Torah.

Aubrey was aware that Nathan Adler had been chief rabbi of the Great Synagogue since 1845 and that, together with the first Baron Rothschild, he had been a pivotal figure in the creation of the United Synagogue. But he also knew the elder

Adler had surrendered much of the day-to-day management of the chief rabbi's office to his son and, in declining health, had retired to the sea breezes of Brighton.

"The Minister sends his compliments, sir," Aubrey began. "I am also instructed to convey the good wishes of the Prime Minister, Lord Salisbury."

The younger Adler inclined his head slightly to acknowledge the greeting, then moved directly to the matter at hand. "The events of the past few weeks have been a great stress," he said, as he turned toward his father. "To the chief rabbi, to myself and to all members of the Jewish community. We have no wish to aggravate a situation already of grave dimensions. But naturally, we are very concerned about the great harm being done to our reputation. You must understand that the acts of this monster are as reprehensible to Jews as they are to any Englishman. They are an outrage against humanity."

Aubrey nodded his head in agreement but said nothing. "Large numbers of Jews have been assaulted in recent weeks. Many of our people fear to go outdoors. We hear it repeatedly asserted that no Englishman could commit such heinous crimes, that they must have been done by a Jew—"

Aubrey interrupted. "I am aware of these unfortunate incidents. Special squads of police have been formed whose sole purpose is to prevent such . . . such altercations—"

"With respect, Mr. Carsonby, they are not altercations. They are assaults, vicious in nature." The younger Adler's voice was growing heated.

From behind the desk, his father spoke in a dulcet whisper. "My son means no offence. But his point must be taken. Even the *Times* has published reports of a Jew arrested near Cracow and charged with the ritual murder of a Christian woman."

The elder rabbi pulled open a desk drawer, and from a vest pocket slowly fitted reading glasses to his eyes. He then began to read from a paper retrieved from the desk: " 'The man was acquitted, but the evidence touching the superstitions prevailing among some of the ignorant and degraded of his co-religionists remains on record' "—here the old man mournfully shook his head—"and was never wholly disproved.'"

"Then we have this letter, again published in the *Times*, from a doctor, no less," said Hermann Adler, reaching in front of his father to pick up a letter clipped from a newspaper. He handed it to Aubrey, who read:

> I cannot help thinking that these Whitechapel murders point to one individual and that that individual is insane. Not necessarily an escaped or even as yet a recognized lunatic. He may be an earnest religionist with a delusion that he has a mission from above to extirpate vice by assassination. And he has selected his victims from a class that contributes pretty largely to the prevalence of immorality and sin.

"Note the use of the phrase 'earnest religionist.' There is no doubt that he means earnest *Jew*," Hermann Adler said with disgust. "I can assert without hesitation that in no Jewish book is such a barbarity even hinted at. Nor is there any record in the criminal annals of *any* country of a Jew having been convicted of such a terrible atrocity . . . the tragedies enacted in the East End are sufficiently distressing without the revival of moribund fables and the importation of prejudices abhorrent to the English nation. Two of our *shochtim* from our kosher abattoirs were detained for questioning. It wasn't until a police surgeon confirmed that their *khalefim* could not have been the knives used by the assassin that they were released."

"Such sensationalism is as abhorrent to me as it is to you, gentlemen," Aubrey said quickly. "This message was found chalked on a wall, apparently by a bloodstained hand, near the last murder site." Aubrey stood and handed a sheet of paper to Nathan Adler.

> *The Juwes are*
> *The men That*
> *Will not*
> *be blamed*
> *for nothing*

"This is exactly as it appeared?"

"It is copied from a constable's notebook, sir."

"Let me see it, Father." The son took the sheet. "I've seen this. It was in the *Times* and other papers. Sir Charles Warren communicated with me directly on this matter. I have already sent a response by hand." Hermann Adler appeared surprised that Aubrey had no knowledge of this. He rose to his feet. "We make copies of all correspondence sent out from our office. Please excuse me."

He returned with a large ledger-like book and placed it in Aubrey's lap. "There," he said, tapping an entry made in the careful handwritten script of a copy clerk:

Dear Sir Charles,

I was just about to write to you on the very subject named in your note. I was deeply pained by the statements that appeared in several papers today, in the Standard *and the* Daily News, *for instance, that in the Yiddish dialect the word Jews is spelled 'Juwes.' This is not a fact. The equivalent in the Judao-German (Yiddish) jargon is 'Yidden.' I do not know of any dialect or language in which 'Jews' is spelled 'Juwes.' I am convinced that the writing emanated from some illiterate Englishman who did not know how to spell the word correctly. . . .*

My community really appreciates your humane and vigilant actions during this critical time.

I am convinced that no Jew, unless he be a maniac, could be connected with the horrible outrages. There is nothing that a Jew is taught to view with greater horror than the mutilation of a dead body, whether it be that of a Jew or a gentile.

With sincere regards,

Nathan Adler

Aubrey placed the book on the desktop. "I will see that the Minister obtains a copy from Sir Charles. It perfectly answers the question." What would these two obviously intelligent men think when he had left? That the left hand knew not what the right was doing? Why had Sir Charles not advised the Home Secretary of his direct communication with the chief rabbi's office? It breached internal government protocol. Of that, he was certain. Regardless, Henry Matthews would be livid.

Aubrey would well remember Adler's line, thanking Warren for his "humane and vigilant actions." Yet everyone thought Warren a jackass for erasing the chalk scrawl—everyone except the Jews and their chief rabbi.

Charles was watching Lucie as she nervously played with her hands. They were clenched, the fingers interlocked, the knuckles showing white. "I am concerned about my husband," she said, without detectable emotion. Her face was very pale, even her lips seemed bloodless. Lucie Rhinegold was slipping away from him, as if an unseen leech were draining her of life-sustaining fluids. *Have I made her worse?* Charles thought. *Am I that leech?*

He decided not to attempt a hypnotic trance. He would let the woman who had first visited him speak her mind. Perhaps she could provide a clue as to her own rapid decline.

"Why does your husband concern you?"

"He is not well."

"Physically?"

She shook her head. "No. But he doesn't eat . . . he has started to drink. Actually, he has been drinking heavily for several weeks. He will finish a bottle in one sitting, drinking himself senseless. You must see this." She reached inside her purse and handed Charles a piece of notepaper on which had been written a single sentence. The penmanship was almost illegible, as if written by a hand under the influence of drink or overwrought by despair. It read, "I am Jack the Ripper."

"He wrote this?"

"Yes."

"How can you be so certain? It's almost a scrawl."

"I recognize the hand, the notepaper—they are his."

"But you say he drinks."

She nodded. "Like a man trying to forget."

"But, surely you don't believe—"

"Believe he is the Ripper?" She looked at Charles.

Her direct gaze momentarily unnerved him. *She has become all eyes,* he thought. *Like my mother, her eyes consume her. Her eyes are the leeches: to stay alive they devour the rest of her. It can't be possible. Her husband the Ripper? Was that the secret torturing her?* "But it can't be," he found himself saying.

"Why not?"

"Has he said anything? Done anything? Written anything else that would offer proof?"

"When he drinks, he mutters about hating . . . hating . . ."

"Hating whom, Lucie?"

"Whores. He talks about 'buckling' whores, complains that the Ripper is doing *his* work. He reads the newspapers as if he's reading about himself."

"This is the very worst kind of speculation, Lucie. It can lead to no good."

"I found a blood-spattered collar."

"You what!" Charles exclaimed.

"A shirt collar with blood all over it. I hid it."

Charles stood and walked over to a table. "You've said nothing of this to the police?"

"Nothing."

"Why not?"

"It might mean nothing, as you suggest. And he is my husband. He talks of doing himself in. 'I'll drown myself,' he says. 'Or I'll hang myself.' "

"Is he seeing a doctor?"

"He refuses."

"Will he see me?"

"He doesn't trust you."

Charles turned to look at Lucie: "Why ever not?"

"He . . . he believes—" Lucie Rhinegold pulled a hand-kerchief from her sleeve and began to weep quietly.

"*What* does he believe?" Charles asked.

"That your intentions toward me are not honourable."

"But that is preposterous!" Charles said, jumping to his feet.

"Not to him. He says I've gotten no better since I started seeing you. That I've gotten worse. That I can't be two people. That you belong to a group that investigates the supernatural."

"Supernatural!"

"The Society for Psychical Research."

"But we are all scientists and reputable artists—Yeats, Conan Doyle, to name only two, are members," Charles protested. "Our research is serious." *This is madness,* Charles thought. *She and her husband are both mad. And what does this mean?* he wondered, picking up the notepaper lying on his desk. *I must extricate myself from this situation. This woman can't be helped. And what if her husband is the Ripper?*

"You must take this back, Lucie," he said. He held out the paper to her.

She shrank back. "I don't want it."

"Then throw it away."

"No. Do with it what you will." Again she began to cry, dabbing at her eyes with her lace handkerchief.

"Lucie, soon I must leave for Paris—"

"Paris?"

"To a symposium. I am presenting a paper—"

"How long will you be gone?"

"Several weeks. For that reason, I must refer you to another—"

"I will not go."

"But you must—"

And suddenly, before Charles's disbelieving eyes, Lucie Rhinegold underwent a transformation. A mischievous smile played on her face, replacing the haunted, driven look with one of craftiness. Even her voice underwent a change, becoming husky, beguiling. "I know your game, Doctor. You're frightened of that other woman, that other Lucie. She's driving you away. She loves you. She's done her best to keep me at bay as long as she could." Lucie Beta started to laugh, "I haven't been to bed with a man, not for—for, well, it must be days. But that will change, change tonight, in fact."

Charles was stunned. Where had Lucie Alpha gone, the woman teetering on the edge of madness, her physical appearance almost corpse-like? Colour was back in Lucie Rhinegold's cheeks, and her eyes fairly danced with life.

"Don't try to rescue her, Doctor. No hypnotic trances. I'm here to stay. Once she said I was 'gone away.' I was, but I'm back. Now it's *she* who has gone."

Lydia had been part of a remarkable conspiracy, the creation and smuggling of a petition into Buckingham Palace, right into Queen Victoria's bedchamber. The document was the idea of Henrietta Barnett. With the assistance of Lydia and others, she had managed to obtain the signatures of more than 3,000 women living in the East End. The petition, addressed to "Our Most Gracious Sovereign Lady," stated:

> *Madam, we, the women of East London, feel horror at the dreadful sins that have been lately committed in our midst and grieve because of the shame that has befallen our neighbourhood. By the facts that have come out at the inquests, we have learned much of the lives of our sisters, who have lost a firm hold on goodness and who are living sad and degraded lives.*
>
> *While each of us will do all she can to make men feel with horror the sins of impurity that cause such wicked lives to be led, we also beg that your Majesty will call on your servants in authority and bid them put the law that already exists in motion to close bad houses within whose walls such wickedness is done, where men and women are ruined in body and soul.*

It was signed:

> *We are, Madam, your loyal and humble servants*

The arrival of the Whitechapel petition did not offend Victoria's sense of royal protocol. The old Queen had been closely following the horrible events in the East End; she even had her own theory as to who the murderer might be. But she also knew that it was not her constitutional place to meddle in Parliamentary affairs, much less in the operation of an individual government department. Nevertheless, the Queen had made it her concern to keep her finger on the pulse of the nation's business ever since her accession to the throne more than 50 years ago.

The Queen laid the petition aside for the moment and became engrossed in that morning's *Times* as if it were a detective novel:

Diemasebutz, who is a traveller in cheap jewellery, found the body. He had spent the day at Weston Hall near the Crystal Palace on business and had driven home at his usual hour, reaching Berner Street at 1 a.m. On turning into the gateway, he had some difficulty with his pony, the animal being apparently determined to avoid the right-hand wall. For the moment, Diemasebutz did not think much of the occurrence, because he knew the pony was given to shying, and he thought, perhaps, some mud was in the way. The pony, however, obstinately refused to go straight, so the driver pulled him up to see what was in the way. Failing to discover anything in the darkness, Diemasebutz poked about with the handle of his whip and then discovered the body. He entered the club by the side door higher up the court and informed those in the concert room upstairs that something had happened in the yard. A member of the club named Kozebrodski returned with Diemasebutz into the court, and the former struck a match while the latter lifted the body up. It was at once apparent that the woman was dead. Both men ran off without delay to find a policeman, and after some search, a constable was found in Commercial Road. With the aid of the policeman's whistle, more constables were quickly on the spot, and in a few minutes, Dr. Phillips was also at the scene of the murder.

The fact that another murder had been committed soon became known in the neighbourhood, and long before day-break, the usually quiet thoroughfare was the scene of great excitement. Extra police had to be posted along the street, and even with this precaution, locomotion from an early hour was a matter of extreme difficulty. A large crowd followed the body to the mortuary, and here again it was necessary to take unusual precautions to keep the crowd back.

The following description of a man seen with the deceased Saturday evening has been circulated by the police: Age 28. Slight. 5 feet 8 inches in height. Dark complexion. No whiskers. Black diagonal coat. Hard felt hat. Collar and tie. Carried newspaper parcel. Respectable appearance.

Mrs. Mortimer, living at 36 Berner Street, four doors from the scene of the tragedy, has made the following statement: "I was standing at the door of my house nearly the whole time between 12:30 and 1 a.m. on Sunday morning and did not notice anything unusual. I had just gone indoors and was preparing to go to bed when I heard a commotion outside and immediately ran out, thinking there was a row at the social- ists' club. I went to see what was the matter and was informed that another dreadful murder had been committed in the yard adjoining the clubhouse. On going inside, I saw the body of a woman lying huddled up inside the gates with her throat cut. A man touched her face and said it was quite warm so that the murder must have been committed while I was standing at the door of my house. There was certainly no noise made, and I did not observe anyone entering the gates. It was just after 1 a.m. when I went out, and the only man I saw pass through the street previously was a young man carrying a black, shiny bag, who walked very quickly down the street from Commercial Road. He looked up at the club and then went round the corner by the Board school."

At 3 p.m. yesterday, a meeting of nearly 1,000 persons took place in Victoria Park, under the chairmanship of Mr. Edward Barrow. After several speeches concerning the con- duct of the Home Secretary and Sir Charles Warren, a resolution was unanimously passed that it was high time both officers resign and make way for some new officers who would leave no stone unturned to bring the murderer to justice, instead of allowing him to run riot in a civilized city like London.

"This is too much!" Victoria exclaimed aloud.

She had cross-examined her Prime Minister, Lord Salis- bury, on more than one of his weekly visits. Of all her Prime

Ministers, she had liked Benjamin Disraeli the most; William Gladstone the least. She did not like or dislike Lord Salisbury for, simply put, she did not know how to take him. His blood was almost as blue as hers, and he was the ninth earl and third marquess of his line. He was a burly bear of a man, well over 6 feet 4 inches tall, and so he towered over her (she was under 5 feet). But she was not intimidated. She did, however, feel somewhat uncomfortable in his presence because he was never at ease. She knew that he was subject to "nerve storms" and periods of deep melancholy; that he was so short-sighted he regularly failed to recognize members of his own Cabinet and that during the summer, he always fled to his villa at Beaulieu, on the French Riviera—a practice she considered almost unpatriotic.

When she had pressed him about the Whitechapel "matter," he had only hunched his rounded shoulders and mumbled something to the effect that "the investigation was in the hands of those best trained to handle it." This evasive response had annoyed her. Action was required: *her* government must know of her displeasure. And so she composed an indictment of *her* detective department. The Whitechapel miscreant might escape because of police incompetence; he would not, however, escape the royal wrath:

> *The Queen fears that the detective department is not so efficient as it might be. No doubt the recent murders in Whitechapel were committed in circumstances which made detection very difficult; still, the Queen thinks that, in the small area where these horrible crimes have been perpetrated, a great number of detectives might be employed and that every possible suggestion might be carefully examined and, if practicable, followed.*
>
> *Have the cattle boats and passenger boats been examined?*
>
> *Has any investigation been made as to the number of single men occupying rooms by themselves?*
>
> *The murderer's clothes must be saturated with blood and kept somewhere.*
>
> *Is there sufficient surveillance at night?*

These are some of the questions that occur to the Queen on reading the accounts of these horrible crimes.

This extraordinary letter landed, via the Prime Minister, on Henry Matthews' desk. He held it in his trembling hands as if it were a Royal Warrant of Execution—ordering his own head on the chopping block. For a moment, he had visions of himself being rowed down the Thames to Traitor's Gate as Sir Thomas More, one of his historical heroes, had been. Queen Victoria was as certain of her royal prerogative as Henry VIII had been. Had she and Henry Matthews lived three centuries earlier, his fears might well have become reality save for one major difference. He knew that he did not possess a martyr's courage and thus would have done anything to keep his head firmly planted on his shoulders.

He gave instructions to his secretary that Aubrey Carsonby was to deliver Her Majesty's indictment to the man on whose desk it belonged. Let Sir Charles Warren quake in his boots and fear for *his* head.

⇥[16]⇤

AUBREY STOOD IN the centre of Blue Ball courtyard and gazed at the star-studded night, a London rarity. The stars' placement appeared random, as if, in a fit of rage, an earthbound god had hurled them skyward into the indigo vastness. But Aubrey did not believe their placement to be random. Nor did he find the complexity of the cosmos overwhelming. Aubrey was a child of Darwin; he had studied the sensational Huxley-Wilberforce Oxford debate in which the scientist and principal defender of Darwin's theories, Thomas Huxley (a "bulldog" as the popular press had dubbed him), had demolished Bishop Wilberforce in 1860. The Bishop had spoken first, his tone bantering and scoffing: "There is nothing to this idea of evolution. A rock pigeon is what a rock pigeon has always been . . . and as for this notion of man as ape," he paused and smiled at Huxley in insolence and mockery, "is it through your grandmother or grandfather that you claim descent from a monkey?" The overflow audience had been stunned by this personal attack. But Huxley had known in that moment he would win the day. He stood, and with grave dignity quietly replied: "I am not ashamed to have a monkey as an ancestor . . . no, not one iota of shame have I experienced . . . but I would be ashamed to be related to a man who used his status, his station in life, his great gifts, if he used all of these to *obscure* the truth!''

Aubrey had read varying accounts of the reaction to that historic exchange, for no one present could doubt Huxley's meaning. The audience had jumped to its feet in a ground swell of thundering approval. At that moment, Huxley had formed the creationist's coffin and driven in the first nail. Twenty-eight years later, nail after nail had been added, although others, among them William Gladstone and the naturalist Louis Agassiz, had tried diligently to pry loose that coffin's lid.

Aubrey was a great admirer of Thomas Huxley and shared his cornerstone belief in "the application of scientific methods of investigation to all of the problems of life." Huxley's basic premise was that man is a very special species of animal, endowed with a moral sense and freedom of will—that he is set above animals not for following nature but for departing *from* it.

Lost in these thoughts, Aubrey began to wander down St. James's Street, sometimes turning into small side passages. Everything around him was constructed of portland stone or substantial brick. Yet, because of architectural skill and the softening effect of the colours, beige, orange-pink and ivory, an illusion of weightlessness was created, enhanced by the façades of intricate stonework, terra-cotta friezes, gabled windows and balustraded balconies. In the moonlight, the buildings had a dollhouse quality, as if a sudden gust of wind could instantly flatten them.

Aubrey was devoted to this part of London. Everything a gentleman could possibly want, from Havana cigars at Robert Lewis's and top hats at Lock & Co. to fishing tackle at the House of Hardey, was available within a few hundred yards of where he stood. These establishments, the nearby clubs, the elegant residences, crowded with moments of history and great names, together created an atmosphere that gave him faith in himself, in his fellow Englishmen and in mankind itself. They stood as a counterbalance to Whitechapel and its drab gin shops and squalid doss-houses. His side of London, the side against which he measured himself and his civiliza-

Mark Clark

tion, rested on the solid ground of the West End, while up there somewhere in the blackness of the night stood Whitechapel and the East End, as if Hell and Heaven had exchanged positions. At this thought, he looked east in the direction of Whitechapel, wishing that he could levitate the entire neighbourhood from the earth's surface and blow it, and the monster it held, out over some ocean, there to let it sink to the bottom of the sea.

Aubrey continued his meandering stroll, passing 4 St. James's Place. A brass plaque had been mounted beside the doorway which announced that Frederic Chopin had departed this residence to perform his last public concert in Guildhall. Reading this announcement caused him to pause in his walking, and a Chopin melody almost immediately came to mind. He turned his gaze to the end of the street, which was enclosed by the grounds of Spencer House, an imposing Palladian-like mansion. As he looked at the candlelit portico, an idea began to form in his mind: the theory of evolution was a solid bedrock on which to build not only a history of mankind but to advance, by analogy, an explanation of all natural phenomena, be it placement of the stars or investigation of the human psyche. The splendour of the universe awed him—but so did the "Golden Arrow" rocketing along at 95 miles an hour or Isambard Brunel's breathtaking Severn bridge. Any number of things could awe, but none defied essential explanation. If man could venture into space, he could count and catalogue the stars, then encapsulate them into a rational theory. The complexity of the Ripper creature challenged, even obsessed him; he was daunted but far from defeated.

Aubrey had been reading an article by Casare Lombroso, an Italian physician and author of scientific papers startlingly original in their explanation of criminal behaviour. Could he not link Lombroso to Darwin . . . and Lombroso and Darwin *together* to the Ripper? And in so doing, follow in Huxley's footsteps concerning his application of science to an actual problem "in life"?

In a state of controlled excitement, he returned to his rooms.

A few hours later, Charles was sitting in his study reading a letter that had been delivered to him by Aubrey Carsonby's manservant. It read, in part:

What sort of mind is capable of such atrocities? What could possibly motivate him? Is he sexually insane? Does he derive some kind of physical gratification from mutilating women? How does he live with himself? This is where, I confess, I am stumped. For unless he is a hermit or a recluse—which I do not believe him to be—he must venture into society. He must purchase his food, his toiletries, his newspapers, whatever. My point is that he must have human contact, however fleeting, and during that contact be seen as a man of ordinary sensibilities and deportment. Surely a man of your training could detect some clue as to the duality of his personality. Perhaps the shopkeeper, the layman, would remain ignorant, but under the scrutiny of a professional such as yourself, could he escape detection?

I realize I have strung together a list of questions. The investigation to date has relied, entirely without fruition, on physical evidence. The truth of the matter is that what physical evidence there is has proved to be of precious little use. Everyone says the man is a lunatic, demented by some terrible disease process affecting his brain. That might be true, but where does it leave us? For if his dementia is so pronounced, how has it managed to escape detection? Could Hyde be seen in Jekyll?

I am interested in the psychology of this man but have neither your training nor your expertise. If we can draw a psychological portrait, we must be one step closer to his eventual capture.

I start with Darwin: "There can hardly be a doubt that we are descended from barbarians. The astonishment that I felt on first seeing a party of Fuegians on a wild and broken shore will never be forgotten by me, for the reflection at once rushed into my mind—such were our ancestors. These men were absolutely naked and debauched with paint, their long hair was tangled, their mouths frothed with excitement, and their expression was wild, startled and distrustful. They possessed hardly any arts and, like wild animals, lived on what they could catch; they had no government and were merciless to everyone not of their own small tribe. He who has seen a savage in his native land will not feel much shame, if forced to acknowledge that the blood of some more humble creature flows in his veins.

"Many may be excused for feeling some pride at having risen, though not through their own exertions, to the very summit of the organic scale, and the fact of having thus risen, instead of having been aboriginally placed there, may give him hopes for a still higher destiny in the distant future. But we are not concerned here with hopes or fears, only with the truth as far as our reason allows us to discover. I have given the evidence to the best of my ability; and we must acknowledge, as it seems to me, that man with all his noble qualities, with sympathy which he feels for the most debased, with benevolence which extends not only to other men but to the humblest living creature, with his godlike intellect which has penetrated into the movements and constitution of the solar system—with all these exalted powers—man still bears in his bodily frame the indelible stamp of his lowly origin."

Now I move to a man you might be familiar with, Casare Lombroso. He is Italian and, like yourself, a physician and scientist. He describes himself as a criminal anthropologist. Please read this excerpt (keeping in mind Darwin from above). It describes Lombroso's l'homo deliquente.

"This was not merely an idea but a flash of inspiration. At the sight of that skull (of a famous criminal), I seemed to see all of a sudden, lighted up as a vast plain under a flaming sky, the problem of the nature of the criminal—an atavistic being who reproduces in his person the ferocious instincts of primitive humanity and the inferior animals. Thus were explained anatomically the enormous jaws, high cheekbones, solitary lines in the palms, extreme size of the ocular orbits, handle-shaped ears found in criminals, savages and apes; also, insensibility to pain, extremely acute sight, tattooing, excessive idleness, love of orgies and the irresponsible craving of evil for its own sake, the desire not only to extinguish life in the victim, but to mutilate the corpse, tear its flesh and drink its blood."

My purpose is no doubt transparent: to apply scientific

criteria to the "Ripper" case. To date, traditional methods of detection have proven miserable and embarrassing failures. Five thousand constables, men and officers of the most highly trained and proficient police forces in the world, are held at bay by a single miscreant. Our police are scoffed at and held up to ridicule by the press; in public, they are openly taunted and laughed at. Where the customary and the orthodox fail, recourse must be made to the unconventional. Recourse has yet to be made to science—because men of science are not yet seen as having a role in the detection and apprehension of "criminal man." (The eyeballs of the last victims were photographed in the apparent belief that the Ripper's image was imprinted on the retinae at the instant of death—a mad superstition!)

Lombroso's stroke of genius is to bring to the forefront the physical signs or stigmata of the born criminal.

Criminals are evolutionary freaks of nature: they are trapped in the past, as it were. For whatever reason, they have not passed through the various evolutionary stages that have led to civilized 19th-century man. Criminals are throwbacks to our primitive past. Modern society condemns their behaviour, yet these men are driven to act in the manner of an ape or savage. Acts of mutilation are second nature to these individuals.

A study of the anthropological factors of crime provides the guardians and administrators of the law with new and more certain methods in the detection of the guilty. Tattooing, anthropometry, physiognomy, physical and mental conditions, records of sensibility, range of sight, etc. can give the police scientific guidance in their inquiries, which now depend entirely on their individual acuteness and mental sagacity.

Charles put the letter down, though he still had a few pages to read, and walked to his bar to pour himself a large measure of brandy. He recalled an old adage, something about brilliant insight and crackpot invention being born in the same blinding flash of inspiration. Darwin was no crackpot. His theory of evolution had penetrated every facet of 19th-century life. No scientific examination into human behaviour was complete without reference to his *Origin of Species*, published in 1859 (and his later and less known

Expression of the Emotions in Man and Animals). Charles was forced to acknowledge that Aubrey was not far off-track in invoking Darwinism.

The great scientist's impact had been felt in Charles's own field as well. British psychology was essentially "evolutionary-based"—an examination of human behaviour within the context of "survival of the fittest." All behaviour was believed to be explainable in terms of an individual's adaptation or maladaptation to his environment. *Even my own work is Darwinian,* Charles thought. Lucie Rhinegold had split into two organisms in a fight for survival. She was a mutant product of the process of natural selection.

But if Aubrey's starting point was fundamentally sound, what of this Italian? The name Lombroso was vaguely familiar—and then Charles remembered: Lombroso was a corresponding member of the Society for Psychical Research.

Charles returned to Aubrey's letter and reread the Lombroso excerpt. It was obvious that his theory was derived from the study of human skulls. Phrenologists had been reading personality, intelligence and character into the human face and skull shape for decades. Facial angles, prognathism and cranial capacities were all said to be valid indices of various human traits. Charles thought this was quackery, yet Lombroso was a medical doctor and scientist, and his theory that criminals possessed distinguishing physical traits did make some sense to Charles. As Aubrey had said, or rather asked: "Could Hyde be seen in Jekyll?" Thus, could the Ripper be seen in his "sane self"?

He returned to his chair and the letter, thinking in idle speculation about John Castrain and Fredrick Rhinegold. Rhinegold was not overtly threatening, but that signified nothing. He had a nasty temper, as had been attested by his shortness at their last encounter. Charles had kept his statement that he was the Ripper. He had done nothing with it because he did not believe his patient's husband could be the man all London sought. He stepped into his office and retrieved Rhinegold's notepaper. The handwriting was a continuous scrawl, the "R" in Ripper large and vigorously drawn. *What would a graphologist make of the handwriting?*

Charles wondered. It was rumoured that Ripper "letters" were being submitted to the scrutiny of handwriting experts in an attempt to learn something of his character. This was another meaningless exercise to Charles's mind, in the same league as phrenologists and the photographing of eyeballs. But what about John Castrain? He was a different matter. Castrain actually scared Charles. There was a tension in his body and eyes that sent a chill through him.

Experiencing a quickening of interest, he picked up Aubrey's letter to finish it:

I now draw your attention to the witnesses at the inquest of the Swedish woman, Elizabeth Stride. There were three: Brown, Smith and Marshall. The coroner made this statement: "The police stated, and several of the witnesses corroborated this, that although many couples are to be seen at night in the Commercial Road, it was exceptional to meet them in Berner Street. With regard to the man seen, there were many points of similarity, but some of dissimilarity, in the descriptions of the three witnesses; but these discrepancies did not conclusively prove that there was more than one man in the company of the deceased, for every day's experience shows how facts are differently observed and differently described by honest, intelligent witnesses. Brown, who saw least in consequence of the darkness of the spot at which the two were standing, agreed with Smith that the man's clothes were dark and that his height was about 5 feet 7 inches, but he appeared to him to be wearing an overcoat nearly down to his heels; the description of Marshall accorded with that of Smith in every respect but two. They agreed that he was respectably dressed in a black cutaway coat and dark trousers and that he was of middle age and without whiskers. On the other hand, they differed with regard to what he was wearing on his head. Smith stated that he wore a hard felt deerstalker of dark colour; Marshall that he was wearing a round cap with a small peak, like a sailor's. They also differed as to whether he had anything in his hand. Marshall stated that he observed nothing. Smith was very precise and stated that he was carrying a parcel, done up in a newspaper, about 18 inches in length and 6 inches to 8 inches in width. These differences suggested either that the woman was, during the evening, in the company of more than one man—a not very improbable supposition—or that the witnesses had been mistaken in detail."

Now Charles, please read this description: *"He is not easy to describe. There is something wrong with his appearance; something displeasing, something downright detestable. I never saw a man I so disliked, and yet I scarce know why. He must be deformed somewhere; he gives a strong feeling of deformity, although I couldn't specify the point. He's an extraordinary-looking man, and yet I really can name nothing out of the way. No, sir; I can make no hand of it; I can't describe him. And it's not want of memory; for I declare I can see him this moment."*

The above is a nondescription of none other than Mr. Hyde.

Is the *"sense or impression"* conveyed by this excerpt not one and the same as that conveyed by the coroner's remarks? The genuine inability of the fictional witness to describe Hyde is one and the same as that of the three foregoing witnesses who tried to describe the Ripper. They were unable to do so because he is not one of us. He defeats not our memories but our ability to see him. And I believe he knows this. Yet now we know what he looks like, thanks to Lombroso. I am determined to have an artist visit the three witnesses, have him also read Lombroso and, so inspired, draw a face which I believe will be that of the Ripper. We have tried everything save try to draw a portrait of the villain's face.

Please let me have your honest opinion of my theory. It is almost dawn. I have been up all night and wonder if I have rambled or stumbled up a blind alley in my tiredness.

With many thanks,
Aubrey Carsonby

Charles poured himself another brandy, sat back and began to review the gist of Aubrey's letter. The calipers of science were ceaseless in their quest to measure everything that fell within their grasp. Brains, bones, fossils, whole cemeteries had been exhumed and the skulls measured. A cottage industry had developed in the quantification of brains: how wide, what weight, how richly convoluted. Collect—classify —catalogue had become the battle cry of the scientist, amateur and professional alike. Immersion in minutiae had become an intoxicating delight. Charles paused in thought: *Am I not guilty of such obsessive curiosity myself?* he wondered. Perhaps "obsessive" was too strong an indictment. A scientist was driven to investigate, to make deductions and draw conclusions—but it was also his duty to society to do so. Charles picked up his pen and began to write: *Ours is an age that demands description and definition of all things—to everything there must be an order, a harmony, a delicate but natural balance. And if man searches for that hard enough and long enough, he shall find it. So, too, has the Ripper fallen under the scrutiny of men of learning. Yet, as physically he defies their manhunt, psychologically he defies definition. So reprehensible are his deeds, he exists outside a society to which frame of reference is everything. He cannot be explained, yet he demands explanation.*

Charles put down his pen, walked to the window and stared at the moon-shadowed Thames. Then he moved to Rossetti's painting and, after a moment's reflection, returned to his desk. *In many disquieting ways, public curiosity about his fiendish exploits runs hand-in-hand with insatiable curiosity about his victims. Not so much about the prostitutes themselves but about the nature of women in general. They stand in some sort of odd balance, the Ripper, destroyer of women, and the object of his destruction, the women themselves. For like the Ripper, they demand but defy explanation.*

Putting aside his pen, Charles felt tired but satisfied. Actually, the feeling was more of a burden lifted than one of satisfaction. Aubrey's letter had touched on a sensitive area of his mind, one he had not known to be sensitive. He had not spent much time speculating about the Ripper, yet obviously the man's deeds had provoked subconscious thought, and in jotting down some observations Charles had clearly assuaged an inner curiosity. Feeling more relaxed than he had in several days, he poured himself a nightcap and crawled into bed, wishing it was Lydia's body and not brandy that warmed him.

✦✦✦[17]✦✦✦

LYDIA ARRIVED HOME from Toynbee Hall and was greeted at the door by her mother, who was on her way out to tea. "Where have you been?" she asked, before Lydia had had an opportunity to remove her hat.

"At a meeting with Mrs. Barnett."

Her mother looked at her sharply. "Again?"

"Yes, again."

"You spend considerable time with her."

"Actually it is the other way around, Mother. It's she who spends considerable time with me. She is helping me prepare for my talk on the role of women in modern society."

"You spend far too much time in Whitechapel," her mother snapped, as she pulled on elbow-length gloves. "Your studies at Cambridge will suffer."

"My volunteer work is of great importance to me."

"You could do volunteer work closer to home. I know of several charitable organizations that could use the resources of a diligent and clever young woman. You must understand, Lydia, I worry not only about your reputation but about your safety, particularly in these days of . . . social unrest. You place yourself in physical jeopardy by constantly visiting the East End. Your father is of a like mind."

"I appreciate your concern, Mother, but I can assure you that I am in no danger. I'm home well before dark—and I have made a commitment I must honour."

"You have other unspoken commitments, Lydia," her mother said tartly. "They, too, must be honoured. The people of Whitechapel are not for you, no more than Belgravia is for them. Already, you are the object of unflattering rumours and are gaining a reputation as some sort of an adventuress. The family name suffers as a result."

"Adventuress," Lydia said, not bothering to conceal her incredulity. "According to whom?"

"According to the gospel of good and common decency," her mother retorted and huffed out the door before Lydia could respond.

At the top of the stairs, Lydia was met by Charlotte. "I hope you don't think me rude," her sister said, "but I overheard your conversation with Mother."

"I'm not surprised," Lydia said. "I'm sure the whole household heard."

"Lydia, you do rage. You must calm yourself. No useful purpose can come of such vituperativeness."

"I was not being vituperative. I merely stated where I had been and what I was doing." She walked down the hallway and entered her room, Charlotte in step behind her.

"I have never accused you of self-centredness, but you have crossed the threshold, Lydia. I find your behaviour—oh damn," she said suddenly. "You are my sister! How can I speak to you so . . . so harshly?" Her eyes began to well with tears. "Now you will think me a silly ninny, crying. How you abhor female tears. You should have been a man. Brother rather than sister . . . oh dear Lord, what nonsense I spout. I mean no hurt. I love you, for all your strange ways, your . . . modern convictions. I don't profess to understand them, but they are yours, they are your right . . . but only so long as they don't do you or our family harm!" Charlotte pulled a handkerchief from her sleeve. She touched each eye quickly and slumped down on Lydia's canopied bed.

Lydia had never seen her sister look so forlorn. *What am I to do?* she wondered. Charlotte was simple-minded. She could no more relate to the wretchedness in Whitechapel—

and to Lydia's involvement at Toynbee—than she could to the man in the moon. At the same time, Lydia knew her sister possessed every attribute man admired in woman: common sense, submissiveness, an intuitive sense of home and family.

A wave of affection swept over Lydia. God protect the man who would dash her sister's heart to pieces. *Aubrey is Charlotte's perfect match,* Lydia thought, for it was impossible to believe he could ever be unfaithful. But Charlotte had convinced herself she loved Charles, and so Aubrey stood no chance. Besides, he was considered more a family mascot by the Carlyles. He was attentive, dependable and good-humoured, marvelous qualities in a pet—but Aubrey lacked both the imagination and aggression necessary to advance his quest for Charlotte's hand. Aubrey, and Charlotte, needed a helping hand.

Lydia sat down and wrapped a protective arm around her sister's shoulders. "You are attracted to Charles?" she asked.

Charlotte bowed her head. Indistinctly, Lydia heard: "As I could be to no other man."

"And what of Aubrey?" Lydia said. "I know he is greatly attracted to you."

"Aubrey? Instead of Charles?" Charlotte's voice was incredulous. "That is like the moon next to the sun. What is there to compare? I see Charles, I swoon. I see Aubrey, I want to pet his balding head."

"But there is more to Aubrey than you think. He is bound to be a success at his career. He is clever, witty, has a delightful sense of humour, one I find rare in a man. He is generous, considerate—"

"Then *you* make a play for him, Lydia." Charlotte lifted her head and turned to face her sister. They were separated by not more than six inches. Charlotte's eyes still showed traces of her tears, but there was fight in them Lydia had never seen before.

Soft Charlotte might be, but not all cream puff, she thought. Charlotte meant to fight for Charles, but the spectre of defeat was still present deep in her black, staring pupils.

Charlotte looked frightened but not panicked. Lydia knew

her sister was making a declaration: *You might well win him—but I shall not meekly bow in defeat. You want him: you must win him.* But when she spoke, her voice was soft and composed.

"Charles needs me, needs a wife. He's in the grip of great mental stress. I don't know why, perhaps it's his work. Aubrey is obsessed with the murders in the East End. Do you think Charles is too? The thought of that monster, the . . . Ripper, makes me ill. He scares me—sometimes I get a cold chill, as if he were here! Of course, that's nonsense, childish imagination. Only weeks ago, I would never have said such things, but now. . . ." Abruptly, she pulled away from Lydia. "Now nothing is as it was."

Charlotte half turned toward her sister. "You all take my sweet disposition for granted. But I have my ups and downs, my tempers and moods too. I'm no different from anyone else." In the late afternoon sunlight, her hair glowed, forming a halo of golden light that softened her already delicate features. She paused as if to collect her thoughts, then spoke softly: "Something is disturbing the equilibrium of our home. I cannot tell you why I feel this way, but it frightens me. I sometimes think it has something to do with . . . with you," and with a visibly trembling lower lip, she suddenly darted from the room.

Several hours later, Charles and Aubrey arrived at the Carlyle residence in separate hansom cabs.

Although it was the middle of the week, Aubrey had slept the better part of the day. He had been awakened by Toby and had "come to" imbued with a sense of accomplishment. His communication to Charles was not simply a letter but an exposition of a scientific theory. Although a compilation of other men's inspiration, he had been ingenious in assembling their unrelated, individual efforts into a workable concept. To Aubrey's mind, his deductions were wholly of his own invention.

He had quizzed Toby concerning how he had busied himself that day. The servant had merely grinned, continued shaving his master and answered good-naturedly, "nothing of much account, sir. Not like you, plumbing the mysteries

of the universe and such.'' Aubrey, eyes closed, a warm
towel wrapped around his face, had smiled inwardly at the
compliment, thinking of the hymn that proclaimed each man
in his rank at ''God's Gate.'' Toby was a servant by divine
authority and he, Aubrey, was somewhat closer to the Gate
by reason of the same God-appointed hierarchy. Where he
had spent the day recuperating from a night of soul-
satisfying, intellectual investigation, Toby had no doubt
spent the day in the pursuit of idle pleasure. In fact, Aubrey
was right. Toby had lured a dollymop up to his room, where,
almost beneath his master's sleeping nose, he had ''frigged
the effing 'ell out of her,'' as he later reported to Sam, his
best friend and fellow manservant.

Aubrey greeted Charles heartily in front of the Carlyle
residence. He was looking forward to a private conversation
when his letter could be properly discussed.

''How delightful to see you,'' he said as Charles stepped
down from his cab. ''Should be a wonderful evening. Think
of it. The two most handsome men in all of London with
London's two most beautiful women.''

''I couldn't agree with you more,'' Charles said, respond-
ing with more good cheer than he actually felt. ''At least in
reference to the Carlyle sisters.''

''And what of us? We're not two ugly dogs, you know.
Well, at least you're not. I might be an ugly dog, but I'm also
a damned determined one. I mean to have Charlotte for my
wife,'' he said, realizing in the same breath that he was being
more garrulous than was his wont.

Preparing his ''Lombrosian letter,'' as he described it to
himself, seemed to have had a cathartic effect, and the
resulting emotional buoyancy was manifesting itself in his
giddy disposition. ''But, of course, that's no secret. Except,
perhaps, to Charlotte herself.'' Aubrey paused at the steps
and put a detaining hand on Charles's arm. ''Should I make
my intent clearer? Your experience with women far out-
weighs my own.''

''Oh, I doubt that, Aubrey. Besides, I've never been in
love.''

''You depreciate yourself, old friend. I know your reputation. But I shan't press you for your secrets of the trade—or,

should I say, secrets of the heart? Do you think we could meet for lunch tomorrow? The quail eggs at Brooks's are superb.''

''I'm sorry, but I leave for Paris tomorrow. I've been asked to consult on a case at the Salpêtrière. Pierre Janet himself has made the request,'' Charles glibly lied. ''It's a request I can't refuse.''

Aubrey could not conceal his disappointment. Charles added as he stepped up to the Carlyles' front door, ''Sorry, can't be helped. You can buy me that lunch of quail eggs upon my return,'' and he reached for the brass knocker—a snarling lion's head—attached to the Carlyle door.

Upstairs, Lydia was in a state of considerable anxiety. This was the first time that she and Charles would be together with others since they had consummated their mutual attraction. Would Aubrey or Charlotte, through some mischance or misspoken word, recognize that she and Charles had become lovers? Such an eventuality seemed unlikely. Aubrey was too absorbed in Charlotte to recognize a miscue, but her sister was a different matter. Lydia knew she would have to be very careful in what she said and did and hoped Charles would be as discreet.

Charlotte rapped lightly on Lydia's door. ''They've arrived,'' she said. ''Are you ready or shall I go down alone?''

''I'm ready,'' Lydia said, opening her door.

''I'm sorry for this afternoon, Lydia. I probably said some unkind things. I feel under considerable strain these days, and my behaviour has suffered as a result. Even now I feel somewhat lightheaded.''

''There is nothing to forgive, Charlotte. You merely spoke your mind. You said nothing that gave offence. Let's join them downstairs and try to make the evening as much fun as possible.'' She took her sister by the arm. ''And now that the evening is upon us, will you tell me what entertainment you have so secretively planned?''

Charlotte smiled at her as they began to descend the stairs. ''Sorry Lydia, it's a surprise I intend to keep until the last moment. Don't worry, your curiosity will soon be satisfied —and pleasantly so, I hope.''

The sisters joined Aubrey and Charles in the drawing room, where a large crystal bowl had been filled with champagne- and cranberry-flavoured punch. That was the first surprise of the evening, at least for Lydia. It seemed out of character for Charlotte to have selected an alcohol-based refreshment, especially champagne. And her first words, after initial pleasantries had been exchanged, almost caused Lydia to spill her drink in surprise.

"Did you know that, according to the law in ancient Greece, criminal proceedings could be taken if one married too late—or even unsuitably?"

Charles and Aubrey looked at Charlotte in astonishment, and Lydia wondered where on earth her sister had come up with that piece of historical arcana. She gave Charlotte credit for knowing the difference between hollandaise and amandine sauce, even between liberal and conservative politics, but she honestly did not think Charlotte knew who had come first, the Greeks or the Romans. It seemed as if the punch had gone straight to Charlotte's tongue, bypassing her brain and common sense.

"Wherever did you unearth that fact?" she asked her sister.

"Why, in the *Daily Telegraph*," Charlotte replied without hesitating a beat. "They run an advice column. Readers send in letters and a Mrs. Mona Caird responds."

"And she mentioned this Greek law?"

"No. One of her readers did . . . in a discussion on experimental matrimony."

"Experimental matrimony? How intriguing," Charles said, casting a bemused glance in Lydia's direction. "What does this Mrs. Caird imply by experimental?"

"I'm not certain," Charlotte responded, "but she has provoked a storm of controversy. The Archbishop of Canterbury is highly indignant that the *Telegraph* even condescended to publish the correspondence."

"What about our laws?" Aubrey asked. "It's against the law to . . . *experiment* in matrimony."

"What law is that, Aubrey?" Lydia asked.

"I'm not aware of any such statute," Charles said.

"I speak not of statute law but rather the law of the

church . . . and, might I add, the law of circumspect morality.''

"Well spoken, Aubrey," Charlotte said. "But we mustn't miss the point, must we?"

Aubrey looked at her in some confusion. "Which is?" he asked.

"That all bachelors should be imprisoned if they postpone marriage to an unreasonable age."

"And what is an unreasonable age?" Charles asked.

"Oh, not much past the middle thirties, I should think," Charlotte answered as casually as she could.

Aubrey made a show of mopping his brow. "Well, in that case, I have at least a year of grace," he said to much laughter.

"My period of grace is over, I fear," Charles said. Simultaneously, the Carlyle sisters looked at him to see if he were serious or joking, but his blank expression told them nothing.

Two servants appeared, each bearing a silver tray. On one were cold canapés of caviar, shrimp and mussels; on the other tray, hot hors d'oeuvres of skewered chestnuts and sautéed chicken livers.

"These are mouth-watering," Aubrey said. "I must confess that I'm famished. This is the first food I've tasted all day. I hope you won't think me a glutton if I overindulge," he said, as he reached for a biscuit crowned with caviar.

"Eat heartily," Charlotte said. "You will need all of your strength for the evening's entertainment."

"Which is?" Lydia said. She looked at Aubrey and Charles. "She has even kept the secret from me, and my patience is at an end."

"Very well," said Charlotte, "I shall put you out of your misery." She nodded her head to signal a servant, and a moment later he returned with an unmarked box that he handed to Charlotte. "The candles, please," she said, and all of the candles in the room save one were snuffed out. The single taper was placed on a nearby table and drew the room in softly muted tones of light and shadow.

"How romantic," Lydia said. "You have truly piqued my curiosity, Charlotte."

"And mine," Aubrey said. "What is in the box?"

Charlotte said, "All of you close your eyes," and then opened the box and removed the planchette. "You may now open them."

"Why, Charlotte, this is indeed a *novel* amusement!" Aubrey declared. "My sisters and I played with one of these several years ago. . . . we had loads of fun," he added.

Lydia examined the board with interest. "I've never seen one."

"I have," Charles said, picking it up. "It's called a planchette, and it has a very curious history. It was probably invented by the Chinese several centuries ago. Theirs doesn't look quite like this one, however. They sprinkle a table with flour or dust, then a straw basket is turned turtle, a stylus or chopstick—instead of a pencil—is inserted through the interstices of straw, and a simple but effective planchette is the result."

"How does it work?" Lydia asked.

Aubrey picked up the planchette and turned it upside down. "This leg is a pencil. See the wheels on the other legs? Now observe this." A servant had spread a large piece of paper on the table at which they all sat. Aubrey turned the heart-shaped instrument right side up and glided it across the paper, leaving behind a straight line. "What we do, either together or singly, is place our fingers on the planchette like this." Aubrey spread his thumbs and fingers on the wooden surface. "We then ask a medium—a spirit, if you will— questions. He, or she, guides the handwriting of the planchette in answer."

Lydia looked at her sister opposite. In the candlelight, her face looked almost white. *So that is your game?* She smiled to herself. But no, she was mistaken to think of this as a "game." To Charlotte, the planchette was both a weapon and a divining device. *And she truly believes it will work,* Lydia thought in wonder.

Charles was speaking: "It has its medical uses, as well. Actually, it can put on quite an amazing performance, something called automatic writing. Say, for instance, you lightly hypnotize a person and place a planchette under his, or her, palm. The hand, or the planchette, have it as you will,

will produce sensible messages. There is a reported case from America in which not one but a series of novels were dictated in such circumstances.''

"And who claimed royalties, Charles? The medium or the alleged author?'' Lydia asked, tongue in cheek.

But Charles ignored her. "Would you like to hear something even more astounding? Under the same conditions, a hypnotized person, with a small planchette placed under each hand, has written two different messages simultaneously. The left-hand message was in 'mirror-writing,' or backwards.''

"That's impossible,'' Lydia scoffed.

"On the contrary, it's a proven hypnotic phenomenon. The French use automatic writing as a diagnostic technique to uncover their patients' repressed thoughts.''

"I believe it's possible,'' Charlotte said. "All sorts of supposedly impossible things are, in fact, quite possible. Not everyone is as skeptical as *you,* Lydia. For instance, the Queen believes in mediums: they say she communicates with the Prince Consort . . . and he's been dead for years.''

"Yes, that's true. They say she even lays out his clothes and has his bed turned down every evening,'' Aubrey added.

"And his full chamber pot is emptied every morning,'' Lydia added, somewhat sarcastically.

"Have any of you heard of Madam Blavatsky, the Russian spiritualist?'' Aubrey asked. "I've taken a look at her *Secret Doctrine.* A remarkable, if eccentric, work. She claims much of it was written not by her hand but by the spirit of her mentor, a Master Morya, whom she met right here in London at the Great Exhibition.''

"I've heard of her,'' Lydia said. "They say she holds court like a monarch, that she is impossibly obese, that she rolls the most dainty cigarettes with fat fingers and that . . . well, it isn't polite to say this—''

"Say it, Lydia. Politeness has rarely been your impediment lately,'' Charlotte interjected.

"Very well. They say she doesn't care in whose face she farts,'' Lydia said bluntly.

She saw Charlotte wince and heard Aubrey gasp, but she continued. "What is it about her that is so newsworthy? I've heard that she keeps visitors waiting in front of a large cuckoo clock—''

''What's so extraordinary about that?'' Charlotte interrupted again.

''Nothing, really, except the clock has no chains or weights. In fact, it appears to have no internal mechanism whatsoever. Yet, punctually on the quarter-hour, a bird pops out and hoots.''

Charles had been quiet during all of this talk, but suddenly he spoke: ''She was investigated by a committee from the Psychical Research Society and was found to be something of a fraud. I've seen photographs of her in which ectoplasmic substances appear to be oozing out of her body—''

''How grotesque,'' Charlotte said.

''What was the substance?'' Aubrey asked.

''Oh, some concoction she had prepared. It had the viscosity of very thick gelatin. She apparently hid it in sacks underneath her dress, then, at the right moment, she squeezed it out.''

''What exactly is ectoplasm?'' Charlotte asked.

''According to Madam Blavatsky, it's the actual life substance of the spirit,'' Aubrey said. ''No doubt she is something of a crank, but people like Yeats are devotees. I know she's uttered some things that could have sprung from the tongue of Oscar Wilde.''

''For instance?'' Lydia asked.

''Well, she is supposed to have said, in reference to the general stupidity of mankind, that there is another smaller globe stuck on top of the North Pole . . . so that our planet is, in reality, shaped something like a dumbbell.''

''What nonsense,'' Charlotte said.

''In a more serious vein,'' Aubrey continued, ''she has founded the Theosophical Society. According to her doctrine, it's based on the accumulated wisdom of the ages. I suggest that she be our medium, *in absentia*, for the evening.''

''But she's not dead, Aubrey,'' Charlotte said.

''The medium isn't supposed to be, it's the spirit that is supposed to be dead, at least in our world.''

Charlotte looked unhappy. ''I don't think I like this Mrs.

Blavatsky." She had not intended or foreseen this sort of complication. She had thought to call upon the spirit of her clergyman grandfather. If a dean couldn't look into Charles's heart and tell her the truth, what spirit could?

"Not to worry, then," Aubrey consoled her. "The planchette, *sans* Mrs. Blavatsky, will suffice nicely for us. Now," he continued, "to the best of my knowledge, the spirit world forms a whole that surrounds us even as we speak. We are neither far from it, nor it far from us—"

"Aubrey, you're scaring me," Charlotte said.

"Don't worry, Charlotte, we are all safe and sound, here in the heart of London. What spirit could hurt us here?"

"Jack the Ripper," Charles said, before he could stop himself. Charlotte gasped, and Lydia looked at him in surprise.

"Jack the Ripper?" Aubrey paused for a second. "How original. About the only thing that hasn't been tried is—"

"Aubrey!" Charlotte snapped.

Aubrey was instantly apologetic. "I am sorry, Charlotte. Of course. It was a ghastly suggestion. And Jack isn't dead anyway—"

"No, just a handful of poor prostitutes. Let's talk to them. Perhaps they'll identify—"

"Lydia!" Charlotte sounded almost hysterical now. "Not you too!" She stood up, her ruby earrings glowing like two fireflies. "Dawkins! *Dawkins!*" she screamed. "Lights! We must have lights. Where are the candles?" Charlotte struggled to control herself. "We shall play whist," she said to the three faces staring at her. "Dawkins! Oh, where *is* he?"

The old servant, his breath laboured from having run up a flight of stairs, finally entered the room. "Yes, ma'am?" he inquired in consternation.

Charlotte thrust the planchette at him. "Throw this damn thing out!"

"Yes, ma'am," Dawkins said, startled by her vehemence. What had happened? He had seen Miss Charlotte in near hysterics before, but he had never heard her swear, and what shocked the old servant most was her tone of voice. Never, in all her 22 years, had she ever raised her voice at him.

-++[18]+++-

LYDIA STOLE DOWN the stairs from her bedroom and stepped outside into the moonlight. Not wanting to be seen, she quickly crossed the courtyard and entered the stable. She reached for her saddle in the tack room and carried it to Maude's stall. The horse whinnied softly at the sight of her, and Lydia hastily slipped a cube of sugar into the mare's mouth. She saddled the horse and led it out of the barn along the shadowed perimeter of the courtyard wall, wincing at each clattered footstep that Maude took. The gateway was latched but unlocked from the inside. She pushed the wooden door open, and it groaned loudly. For a moment, she froze, but then Maude scraped a hoof against the cobblestone and shook her head in an exclamatory snort. Lydia tugged hard on the reins, and Maude responded so quickly that her momentum almost sent Lydia into the laneway. *My God!* Lydia thought in nascent panic. *We shall wake the dead.* She looked back at the house, but it was as black and silent as a mausoleum. *Shall I close the door?* she asked herself. *What if someone spies it open? They would investigate and find Maude missing—and if Maude were found missing. . . .* She turned back and, as silently as she could, closed the courtyard door.

Quickly mounting Maude, she guided her down the laneway to the street and cantered south in the direction of the King's Road and Chelsea. Her mind flew back to the evening of planchette and Charles's abrupt announcement that he was departing for Paris in the morning—*this* morning. He had made no mention of his plans to her, and she found that shocking. Nor did she appreciate the fact that he had chosen a social gathering to make his disclosure. For the better part of two hours, she had been forced to restrain her anger—and her tongue—while she went through the motions of playing cards. Once that test of patience had been endured, Charles, with Aubrey in tow, had left with a perfunctory and formal goodbye. And, as the two men's hansom cabs pulled away, her mother and father had returned from seeing *Yeomen of the Guard*. She had been forced to listen to her parents' recounting of the operetta before going to her room. After what seemed like an interminable period of time, she had ventured downstairs and out to the stable. Recollection of the events brought her anger back to a boil. *What insufferable masculine arrogance*, she thought as she directed Maude into Cheyne Walk—yet an hour later, she was lying in the crook of Charles's arm, angry not at him but at herself for surrendering to the physical desire that had swept over her when he had brushed aside her protestations and taken her into his arms. *He uses me, and I don't resist*, she thought in self-disgust. *He's like a narcotic: I hate him but crave him at the same time*.

"You take risks," he said suddenly in the darkness.

"You don't leave a woman much alternative."

"How so?" he asked.

"Your abrupt departure for Paris," she said. "When does your train leave?"

"Seven o'clock."

"There you are. Nine, ten hours' notice does not leave much time for prudence. You must learn to be more considerate of your lovers."

After a moment's silence, Charles said, "You can come to Paris . . . to visit me."

"You are naïve. Have you never heard of chaperones? And already, I'm criticized for spending too much time away from home—too much this, too much that. Only this morning, Mother insinuated I was a 'dangerous adventuress.' If I were to go to Paris, I would only confirm her worst opinion of me."

"And what would you think of yourself?"

The question disconcerted Lydia. "Perhaps I am an adventuress," she said. "What do you think?"

"Perhaps you are," Charles said. "If so, you are a very beautiful one." This remark reminded Lydia of the Parnell Inquiry dinner and Sir James Hannen's remark concerning the threat posed by beautiful women. "And if I were not beautiful?" she asked.

"But you are," Charles said, "if you weren't, I would never have invited you to Paris."

"Or to your bed?"

Charles turned to face her. "Or to my bed," he said, softly kissing the nape of her neck.

"Please stop, Charles."

"Why?" His tongue traced the curve of her collarbone to the hollow in her neck, then in the same slow and deliberate motion, slid down between her breasts.

Lydia put a hand in his hair and halted his progress. "I want to talk," she said.

"We have talked," Charles objected, a hint of anger in his voice.

"How long will you be gone?"

"A few weeks. Until after the Symposium."

"Why must you leave now, today?"

"I explained the circumstances," Charles said as, without warning, he slipped a finger into Lydia and gently began to massage an inner fold of skin he knew brought her great pleasure.

She grabbed his arm at the wrist, wanting to stop him, yet savouring the sensation. *He has snared me again*, she thought, fighting her tumescent desire. *I must stop him. I can stop him*. Out loud she said, "Stop."

But he ignored her.

"I said 'stop!' " She was still gripping his arm and tried to push it away.

"Am I hurting you?" he said, and bent to kiss her.

She grabbed his hair with both her hands, but his neck and shoulder muscles went rigid and she couldn't budge him as his tongue darted in and out, stoking the fire he had started. At her hesitation, his hands slipped under her buttocks and she felt herself lifted. She leaned back on her pillow in defeat, wondering if she was a slave to her own pleasure . . . or to Charles's.

Charles was again mesmerized by John Castrain, who was delivering what amounted to a Shakespearean soliloquy. His memory of Lydia and their lovemaking was continuous with the appearance of Castrain. It was as if Lydia had disappeared into one room, and he had stepped out of another.

"Nature averse to crime?" Castrain shook his head. "I tell you, Doctor, nature lives and breathes by it; in fact, yearns with all her heart for the furtherance of cruelty. We do evil when we shed a little blood, quench a little breath at the door of a perishable body." Castrain shrugged. "This we do, and we call it crime. But is it unnatural?" Again, he shook his head. "If we could be one with nature, we could continually do evil with all of our might. A few murderers are nothing . . . nothing when one accepts that the whole universe is evil."

He suddenly slumped in his chair, exhausted from the performance, and Charles had to admit it had been a *tour de force*. Yet he knew Castrain's calm state could change into one of excitement without warning. That was one of his most identifiable symptoms: calmness one moment, catlike alertness the next. *He is an actor,* Charles thought, *cast in two roles in which he is forced to play one upon the heels of the other. No time for costume change, there is merely a second to switch mental personas before the curtain is raised again*.

So far this evening, he had made several bizarre observations. He had spoken of a Russian sect, the *Skoptzies:*

"Self-described white doves, they actually castrate themselves. The Bible states: 'And there be Eunuchs which have
made themselves for the Kingdom of Heaven.' But we
mustn't mock those Russian zealots. We have our own, the
Malthusians. The more fanatical of that 'sect' observe the
practice of infibulation—a surgical technique, as you are
aware, in which the foreskin is drawn over the head of the
penis and sewn tight together.''

There had been other observations: "Sex is itself innately
violent, an act of physical violation. Sexual energy is
volcanic. Cap the cone of a volcano and the primal forces of
nature will find an outlet. They are explosive; they will not
be denied. They may lie quiescent for a time, but they will
erupt. You have read Krafft-Ebing, of course. His *Psycho-
pathia Sexualis*. He writes of 'dark, incomprehensible urges'
that explode—his very word—into sexual expression. And
did you know that Havelock Ellis's wife was a lesbian? Can
you imagine such treachery?''

Castrain laughed harshly. "Do you mind if I smoke?''
From his dinner jacket, he took a package of cheroots.
"Matches?''

"On the mantel,'' Charles told him.

Castrain stood with difficulty and attempted to light the
cigar, but he could not manage that simple task. He could
strike a match to flame, but he could not bring the flame to
the tip of the cheroot because of his shaking hands. "Oh,
Christ,'' he finally said, "I don't want to smoke anyway,''
and angrily threw the box of matches across the room. It
struck the wall and broke open, spilling on the carpet, but he
did not offer an apology. He returned to his chair and, at
once calm and rational again, asked Charles if he had a
brother.

The question disturbed Charles. He was attempting to
cultivate a patient-physician relationship with Castrain, but it
was difficult, if not impossible, to do so when the man kept
asking personal questions. "No, I don't have a brother,'' he
replied coldly.

"My brother and I are twins. May I recount a brief story?
I have seen Siamese twins, in one case joined at the skull.

But I've read a fascinating case history of two such twins joined at the breastbone. As they aged, they developed a murderous hatred for one another. Indeed, the more dominant rendered fierce beatings to the weaker. It seemed that the aggressive twin could never achieve his heart's desire, which was entirely homicidal—because he knew that a fatal blow would be fatal to himself as well. Yet, in time, his rage eventually consumed all reason, and with a butcher knife, he fatally stabbed his twin and in so doing killed himself.''

As Castrain continued, Charles started thinking about his twin brother. During his childhood, Charles's mother had taken him often to the Randall plot. A stone Calvary Cross had been mounted on the grave site of tiny Jonathan Randall. It was exactly six feet tall, so ordered by his mother because ''he would have grown so in stature.'' The inscription was starkly simple:

> ### ERE HE BREATHED
> ### GOD CLAIMED HIM
> ### AS HIS OWN

Twelve years later, his mother had been laid to rest beside her stillborn son. His father had erected a granite tombstone almost dwarfed by Jonathan's cross. On it was inscribed the Latin phrase: *Sit tibi terra levis*—Light lie the earth upon thee.

But that had not been his father's first choice. Charles had found on his desk a scratch pad of possible inscriptions, some of which had been crossed out and rewritten. Two lines of one such epitaph had read:

> Harlotry Brooks No Heaven
> Heaven Brooks No Harlotry

John Castrain interrupted his train of thought: ''You've heard of Urania Cottage, the home for fallen women? Founded by that great benefactress Angela Burdett-Coutts, aided and abetted by the likes of Dickens and Gladstone. The very best of the Magdalene homes in all of England. My mother spent her formative years at Urania Cottage. Yes, she was a fallen woman, a soiled dove. But a rescued one. They cleaned her as best they could and put her back up on her pedestal. So well did they do their work, she was immaculate when she was placed back in society. Not a speck of dust from her filthy past was to be seen. Oh, I'll grant you, it was there: how can you wash away original sin? You can't. It's like blood: scrub as you might, the stain of past sin remains. You just can't see it—unless you are like me. I can see sin. But Father couldn't. No, to him she was as pure as the Virgin Mary. She was a clever witch, kept her past to herself. Father never suspected a thing, although she was very vague about her past. Oh, she was beautiful, an enchantress. I can see her now. I am her son, you understand, yet she aroused such emotion in me! Delicate like a piece of Dresden china, yet sensual like . . . like her.'' And he suddenly stabbed a finger at the Rossetti painting.

Charles was held spellbound by Castrain's words, by the emotions that flickered on and off across his face like the shadows thrown on the wall by the fire near which he sat.

''She was an orphan, a governess, a lady's companion. What did it all add up to? Respectability and evasion. How does one discredit an orphan? Yes, she had the disadvantage of having no reputable bloodline. Father's line was well established, centuries old, in fact, but he chose to ignore their different backgrounds. How could he not? She had completely bewitched him, as she would me when I first emerged from her . . . her womb. Do you know what it is like to emerge from the womb of a whore?''

Charles was about to speak, but Castrain held up his hand. ''Would you like to hear some statistics about Urania Cottage alumnae? From a group of 47, seven left to return to their parents, nine ran away, seven unregenerates were expelled, three 'relapsed' on the long passage to Australia.''

Castrain stood up and began to pace. ''You see, once their redemption had been completed, the graduates of Urania were sent, like criminals, to our far-flung colonial outposts, there to find husbands and start families. But tally the figures: of 47, 19 were known to be failures, and let us say, to be fair, three of the seven who returned home also fell back into their ungodly ways. That makes a total of 22 failures. History says nothing of these. I describe them as the reality, not the reclaimed whores of popular fiction, who in remorse turn their back on vice to establish respectable lives. My mother was one of the latter group. She didn't end up in Australia or Canada or America. She started in an English gutter and ended up in an English manor, the scullion maid became the lady of the house . . . and my father was duped like the village idiot . . . until her gutter past was revealed.''

Castrain returned to his chair. He looked at Charles with his peculiar, penetrating eyes. ''Angela Burdett-Coutts was no simple philanthropist. She didn't just give to Urania Cottage and look the other way, her soul more secure on its passage to a just reward. She took personal interest in her charges, followed their careers, as it were. She was a house guest of my father.

''Can you imagine my mother's horror and Burdett-Coutts' stupefaction when each was introduced to the other? Even Balzac could not have invented such a plot. And what of poor father standing somewhere between the two women, caught between horror and disbelief, yet in the same instant comprehending the enormity of the betrayal, the monstrous cruelty and irony of it?''

Castrain leapt to his feet again and laughed harshly. ''But that is life, isn't it? A series of quiet interludes broken by a series of nasty surprises. Like the activities of this . . . this fellow in Whitechapel. Let me read you something,'' and he fumbled in his pockets until he found a thin sheaf of papers. His hands had stopped shaking. He began to read in a calm, measured voice, as if he had suspended any emotional connection with the material he held in his hand. ''I have begun to raise a fund, to which I invite contributions from your readers, with a view of powerfully bringing the teachings of Christianity to bear on that dark corner in Whitechapel that has been disgraced by such hideous crimes. If the Gospel of Our Lord can change the cannibal inhabitants of the Fiji Islands into a nation of Christian worshippers, it is sufficient, and alone sufficient, to turn the darkest spots in London into gardens of the Lord.' It is signed 'The Dowager Lady Kinnaird, One, Pall-Mall East.'

"Now Doctor, please bear with me one more moment. I must read you this response to the good Lady Kinnaird's proposal," and he thumbed through his papers until he found the one he wanted. "Listen to this," he said and began to read, " 'Will you kindly allow me to reply to many correspondents who have desired to be informed of the best way to befriend the poor women in Whitechapel and Spitalfields, whose miserable condition has been brought before the public so prominently by the late murders.

" 'I was for ten years rector of Spitalfields, and I know full well the circumstances of these poor creatures and have been constantly among them by day and by night. A night refuge has been proposed, and it was but natural it should suggest itself as a means of benefitting the class. In my judgement, it would serve no good end, and I earnestly hope nothing of the kind will be attempted.' " Castrain paused and raised a hand in emphasis, " 'I am sure it would but *aggravate* the evil,' " he continued. " 'It is not that many of these women are to be found in the street at night because doors are closed against them. Another night refuge is not required. It would attract more of these miserable women into the neighbourhood and increase the difficulties of the situation. What is needed is a home where washing and other work could be done and where poor women who are really anxious to lead a better life could find employment. . . . R.C. Bedford, Bishop Suffragan for East London.'

"May I impose upon your good graces for a drink?" Castrain suddenly asked. At Charles's move to oblige him, he said, "I can manage," and he walked to the liquor cabinet and poured a large brandy from a crystal decanter. He then returned to Charles. "One last reference"—he held aloft a letter—"and my point shall be made. This is in reply to the bishop; it's from a vicar: 'Will, then, a "laundry" such as the Bishop of Bedford proposes be of any benefit? I say that it will, but not, in my judgement, to the extent which the bishop so sanguinely anticipates. It will no doubt save a few; and that is something for which to be thankful. But far more

will have to be done than can possibly be achieved by the
laundry system now suggested. The drink traffic of East
London will have to be grappled with. Legislative restric-
tions of a drastic character will have to be introduced to
lessen the temptations and to reduce the facilities for
drinking.

" 'The whole public house system demands reform, not
merely in regard to the hours but also as to harbouring or
encouraging prostitution in and from them. The police
should be freed from the supervision of the public house
system and a separate force of detectives in plainclothes
constituted to supervise and to prosecute, both for drink
offences and acts of prostitution. This is important. Steps
must also be taken to punish the men as well as the
women—' "

Castrain suddenly threw the paper to the floor and gulped
rather than swallowed his brandy. "Can he be serious?" he
asked rhetorically. "By the blood of Christ, I believe he
means to be. Damn fool!" Abruptly he stood, grabbed the
paper at his feet and crushed it. He then threw it into the fire
where it almost instantly turned into a bright ball of flame.

"The vicar blames the evil of whores not on the women
but on the men," Castrain said. "He is completely muddled.
Nature is the evil and women are the instruments whereby
nature enforces its will. The Lady Dowager—another Angela
Burdett-Coutts—the bishop and the vicar, all of them miss
this essential truth. They are determined to rescue as many
whores as they can. For every one *he* takes from the street
they will place 10, 100, 1,000 in one of their Urania
Cottages . . . and from such a place will go forth women
such as the whore who betrayed my father," he said.

Charles woke to find himself sitting in his study, bathed in
early morning light. He shook his head and massaged his
bleary eyes, looking around the room as if to confirm he was
alone. He noticed the matches scattered in the corner and the
empty brandy snifter on a table. The snifter rested on a
square of paper, and he reached for it. It was Fredrick
Rhinegold's Ripper confession, and Charles was instantly

puzzled as to how it had ended up underneath Castrain's glass. He had no recollection of removing it from his desk, nor any memory of discussing it with Castrain. Charles suddenly felt the cold in the room. The fire had died sometime during the night and had not been revived. He had obviously fallen asleep, and Castrain had taken his leave without awakening him.

Charles stood and shivered. *I shall be glad to leave London*, he thought, walking to his bedroom, *to leave behind the mad ramblings of John Castrain, the ubiquitous Aubrey Carsonby, Lucie Rhinegold and her alcoholic husband, even the alluring yet possessive Lydia Carlyle. Yes, Paris will do me good*. In his bedroom, he began to pack, noting that his train to the Continent left Victoria Station in little more than an hour's time. In his haste, he forgot about the Rhinegold note, which remained on the table in his study.

▸▸◾[19]◾◂◂

HYDE PARK WAS covered in early morning mist. Sir Charles Warren was standing in a small thicket near the Serpentine, shivering from the damp chill that was made worse by a raw northeastern wind. He tightened his knotted scarf and pulled at his deerstalker so that it protected his ears as much as possible. He was tempted to start stamping his feet to warm himself but resisted because he did not want to give his position away. He consulted his pocket watch and was astonished that less than five minutes had passed since he had last checked it. *Where are those damn dogs?* he wondered for the umpteenth time.

That very question was being asked by a small cadre of men standing outside the copse. The dogs they referred to were Burgho and Barnaby, two champion bloodhounds owned by Mr. Edwin Brough of Scarborough, whom the Commissioner had contacted. Warren had thought of employing the dogs to track the Ripper, but it had been stipulated that, before they were hired, they first undergo a trial in Hyde Park with the Commissioner himself serving as the quarry. The Commissioner had been given a 15-minute head start. The bloodhounds were then released and had not been seen since, although an occasional distant baying had been heard causing excited anticipation that the dogs had found the scent.

"What do you think has happened to them?" Aubrey asked Mr. Brough, a thick-set man with a bristly pair of side whiskers.

"I don't know, sir. You must keep in mind that the frost is a thick one. It deadens the scent, you understand. It's the very worst of conditions for hounds . . . worse than rain."

"But it's been almost an hour. We aren't more than a mile from where they were released. And the Commissioner's path here was hardly circuitous."

In fact, Warren had made but two detours, a loop around a duck pond and a diversionary trek through a thicket of beech trees, before entering his present hiding place. Aubrey thought that if the hounds had relied on eyesight, they could have followed the Commissioner's footprints, which were clearly visible on the frost-laden grass.

Mr. Brough scratched at his whiskers, removed his hat and stroked at his longish hair. He then brought a handkerchief to his red nose. "Patience, sir," he said. "The bloodhound is not a machine. He's a damn clever animal, but he must be given his head . . . which takes time. Barnaby and Burgho are the very best of hounds; trained from birth to the clean shoe, they were. Burgho's head is nearly 12 inches long. A very astute and indefatigable hound, he is."

Aubrey didn't know what a "clean shoe" meant; nor could he fathom the import of a hound's head size as opposed to the sensitivity of its nose. *How in God's name were the dogs supposed to track the Ripper anyway?* he wondered. The scent, if one could be identified, was days old. And even if it were recent, how could one man's scent be detected among the comings and goings of thousands of people, whose shoes tracked blood and filth all over Whitechapel? Aubrey considered the scheme as harebrained as any yet conceived by Sir Charles. "Well, if they don't appear soon, the Commissioner will catch his death of cold, and if he doesn't, I shall," he said with a loud sneeze.

Mr. Brough cast Aubrey a disdainful glance. "Bless you," he said unsympathetically.

Aubrey turned to Inspector Abberline, who was also present as a witness to the possible utility of the bloodhounds.

"Well, Inspector, what do you think? Will they find him?"

"The day's young yet," Abberline said with faint humour.

After a moment, Aubrey asked, "What do you think he looks like?"

"Beg your pardon, sir."

"Describe the Ripper as you imagine him."

Abberline stared at Aubrey for a second. "I believe he looks like you or me," he replied.

"Do you really? I can't imagine him being of ordinary appearance. Have you heard of the Italian theorist, Lombroso? He believes criminals have distinctive features that set them apart from the rest of us. He calls these features stigmata . . . prognathic jaw, prominent cheekbones, dominant cranium, that sort of thing." Aubrey paused and watched a flight of starlings take to the wing, startled by the bark of a dog. "Do you think that's them?" he asked hopefully.

"I hope so," Abberline said. "Sir Charles must be freezing."

"Yes, mustn't he," Aubrey replied. After another moment's reflection, he went on, "So you don't think there is anything to this Lombroso fellow? You don't believe that criminals bear distinguishing features?"

"I've seen many a criminal, sir; more than I care to count. If you took a dozen of them and lumped them together with a like number of ordinary citizens, I couldn't tell them apart from the law-abiding. Make my work a damn sight easier, if I could."

Aubrey thought about Abberline's observation for a moment. He had not discussed Lombroso with anyone, having decided to await Charles Randall's comments upon his return from Paris. In the meantime, he had delved further into the Italian's writings. Lombroso had produced a work entitled *Criminal Man,* which included a frontispiece featuring a panoply of criminal faces, categorized according to the nature of their crimes. To Aubrey's untrained eye, there were physical similarities among the felons, most prominently heavy brows and dark, brooding eyes. Each face was latent with menace, and he therefore found untenable Abberline's categorically stated opinion that criminal man and law-abiding citizens looked alike. Nevertheless, he decided not to pursue the matter because he did not think the detective's background sophisticated enough to appreciate the anthropological complexities of Lombroso's research. Instead, he asked Abberline if the police had developed any new theories.

"A new theory pops up every day," the Inspector told him.

"What do you think of the Queen's suggestion about the cattle boats? Isn't it true that they arrive on the weekend and depart on Sunday or Monday? All of the killings have occurred on either a Friday or Saturday."

"They have, sir, but I don't think our man is a butcher. Although some of the pathologists dispute whether or not the Ripper is a doctor, the evidence points to his having had some medical training. If he's not a doctor, then maybe he's a nurse or a hospital attendant. I interviewed a Polish Jew and asked him if he knew whether or not any of his countrymen had been nurses in their homeland. He described a fellow who is called a *feldscher,* a kind of barber-surgeon. They're a bit backward over there. Apparently, a *feldscher* assists during surgery and also cuts hair."

"Did he name a specific individual?"

"No, but we've put out enquiries in the Jewish community. If any immigrant was so employed, we intend to have a word with him."

"There is a rumour afoot that a graphologist has been retained to examine letters purportedly written by the Ripper," Aubrey said. He was also aware that since the first murder, Scotland Yard had received an avalanche of mail about the Ripper and that it had been necessary to assign three detectives full-time to the task of sorting and evaluating it.

Abberline nodded. "A waste of time, in my opinion.

Analyzing handwriting will bring us no closer to his identity, no more than this . . . *exercise* will," he said, inclining his head in the direction of the thicket where the Commissioner of Police remained in hiding.

"But I think we're close to the end of it," he added.

Aubrey reacted with surprise. "How so?"

"If you discount the third murder, during which he almost certainly was interrupted, the killings from the first in Buck's Row to the fourth in Mitre Square are progressively more savage. That indicates to me his madness is progressive . . . that he's close to the brink of complete insanity. He'll kill at least once, perhaps twice more, then we'll have him."

"What makes you so certain?"

"He won't be able to disguise his madness. He'll babble about his deeds to someone. That's why this case is so damn difficult. He's a solitary sort, lives by himself, no doubt. He confides in no one, trusts no one—and therefore, there is no one to tip us off. Nine out of ten times that's what solves a murder. The killer says something to someone that arouses suspicion. That gets back to us, and we're on our way to an arrest." Abberline paused as if to soothe an agitated inner temper. "People blame us," he continued, "because they don't think we're clever enough to capture him. I tell you, Mr. Carsonby, it's not cleverness that traps a madman—it's luck, pure and simple," he said with a note of finality and frustration.

As Aubrey listened to Abberline, he remembered that Charles Randall had reached an identical conclusion several weeks before.

He was disinclined to agree with the pessimism of the detective, but he had great respect for his friend's scientifically trained mind. Yet, acknowledging that Charles's conclusion was the same as Abberline's gave equal offence. Aubrey was tempted to say that it had nothing to do with luck and that human events are not decided by chance; nor is the fate of an individual—certainly not someone with as reprehensible a past as the Ripper. To believe otherwise was to display a deplorable lack of moral conviction. That a working-class detective lacked that conviction did not surprise Aubrey, but he could not view Charles in the same light.

This disquieting line of speculation was interrupted by the sudden emergence of Sir Charles Warren, stomping out of the trees in evident displeasure. Aubrey heard Mr. Brough clear his nose and throat, then mutter under his breath, "Can't expect the impossible out of a pair of hounds, can we now?" To which, on Aubrey's other side, Inspector Abberline responded in a whisper, "nor man, Mr. Brough, nor man," after which he spat on the ground and stepped forward to meet the Commissioner, whose angry question had a brittle quality in the cold morning air.

Lydia was sitting in a first-class coach, bound from Cambridge to London. Tonight, she was to deliver her speech at Toynbee Hall. She leaned back on her headrest and watched the scenery flash past with relentless speed. October had given way to November, and if she half-closed her eyes, the world outside the train was a streaking blur of late-autumn colours. The imagery perfectly summed up her life since Charles had left for Paris. Her emotions had run together and formed a grey, dismal outlook on life. But Charles's departure had not, and did not, cast the longest shadow.

Lydia could predict the onset of menstruation with the accuracy of a tidal forecast. When first one week and then another passed and she was still late, she knew with an intuitive certainty that she was pregnant. Her first reaction had been one of nauseating panic, followed by vehement denial; but the panic and denial had gradually given way to acceptance. She had been tempted to telegraph Charles in Paris, because on his shoulders rested her hopes for a solution to her problem, or condition, as she had come to think of it. But she did not know where Charles was staying, and she was uncertain about how to word the telegram. She could not baldly state that she was enceinte. She had formulated a message that read, "Condition worsening. Please return soonest. Lydia." Certainly, she thought, he would read between the lines. But she had decided, since she was still in the early stages, that she could wait for Charles's arrival home, which was expected this long weekend. So she had burned the message.

As the train clattered along, Lydia pulled an advertisement out of her purse:

Ladies Only

THE LADY MONTROSE
- MIRACULOUS -
FEMALE TABULES
Are positively unequalled for all FEMALE AILMENTS. The most OBSTINATE obstruc-tions, Irregularities, etc. of the female system are removed in a few doses.

The message could not be plainer. The Lady Montrose's tabules were abortifacients. The temptation to purchase some had been strong, but she had resisted doing so because of the stories she had heard—that they did not work and could be dangerous to one's health. She replaced the advertisement in her purse, wishing she had burned it with the telegram message, and opened the notebook that contained her Toynbee Hall speech. A brief excerpt from the latest *Illustrated London News* was clipped to a page:

"The Life and Letters of Mrs. Shelley, the wife of the famous poet, is a forthcoming work that promises to be of great interest. Shelley's wife was the daughter of Mary Wollstonecraft. She was, herself, as clever and uncommon a woman as such a parentage should have made her. *Franken-stein,* her singular novel, has passed into a classical place in English literature. Her first connection with Shelley was not free from blame; but during her long life as his widow she held an unblemished position, and her son, Sir Percy Shelley, who has authorized and aided the writing of the 'Life,' feels with all justice that by telling the truth about her, he is rendering homage to the memory of a mother to whom he was devoted."

Lydia had noted with surprise that Mary Wollstonecraft was the mother of Mary Shelley, who at 19 had written her famous tale of gothic terror. She had researched Wollstonecraft for her Toynbee Hall presentation because George Eliot had written about her feminist views in a favourable light. But spurred on by the *News* article, Lydia had found a biography of Mary Wollstonecraft, and it had given impetuous direction to her address, the opening remarks of which she quickly reviewed. Then, because she was alone in her compartment, she read aloud:

> "I am here tonight because of two women, one present, one no longer with us, save in spirit: they are Henrietta Barnett and Mary Wollstonecraft. Both are women of courage, of conviction, of commitment and of uncommon persuasive power. For each, in her own way, helped me to overcome my fears and gave me the strength to stand before you.
>
> I have been asked to speak about the 'new' woman. At the time, I had no further to look than Mrs. Barnett, for it struck me that she was better qualified to address you than I.
>
> I am new because I am young—19—but because I am young, I am not certain that I am 'new' in the sense that Mrs. Barnett intended. But then I discovered Mary Wollstonecraft, who wrote about the status of women a little less than a hundred years ago. And what I read in her *Vindication of the Rights of Women* seemed, although almost a century old, fresh and original and full of the vigour of the new. She was only 19 when she wrote that the inferior status of women is nurtured from the cradle."

Lydia stopped rehearsing for a moment. Wollstonecraft had said that women, like men, inherit roles that distort their nature, her example being a nobleman whose position prevents him from pursuing a life of normal social intercourse (the ageing Prince of Wales immediately sprang to Lydia's mind) and, as in the case of women in general, is consequently unable to develop his full potential as a human being. Lydia was certain that this explained something of the nature of Charles Randall, his solitariness and unwillingness truly to share himself and his thoughts with another. *He is a maverick,* Lydia thought as the train slowed and entered the brick sprawl of London's northeast suburbs. *And so am I.* Lydia closed her notebook and prepared her luggage for arrival, thinking in the back of her mind that she would attempt to force more openness and intimacy from Charles —once the matter of her pregnancy had been resolved.

As Lydia's train pulled into Liverpool Street Station, Charlotte was stepping up to Charles's home—in a state of some trepidation—an envelope in hand. She desperately wanted to see him again, and the only way to fulfill that desire was to invite him to Cadogan Square. After considerable debate, she had decided she would ask him to a tea at which only she would be present. This resolution had required courage on her part, as had the decision to deliver the invitation personally. She did not know whether Charles had returned from Paris, but the possibility of meeting him at his home, or rather, as she had corrected herself, at the *threshold* of his home, filled her with nervous anticipation. She knocked on his door, at first timidly, then with more authority. She waited a moment, experiencing a sharpening sense of disappointment. She had mustered the courage to come and, irrationally, she believed that fact alone was sufficient to make Charles appear before her. Growing bolder, she tried his door.

To Charlotte's surprise, it slowly swung open, and as it did, her enterprise faltered. But it swiftly reasserted itself, and she stepped into the hallway intending to leave her invitation in a place of prominence. Once inside, however, a keen sense of curiosity overwhelmed her reserve, and she began to explore further. She walked down the hallway and peeked into a room. On the floor, she spied a piece of paper, and this offended her fastidious sense of neatness. She hesitated but then walked over and knelt to pick it up. She had not intended to read it, but could not help doing so. *I am Jack the Ripper,* she read, and the paper dropped from her hands.

⋙[20]⋘

AUBREY ARRIVED HOME in Blue Ball Yard to find an extraordinary communication from Charlotte awaiting him: *We must meet as soon as possible. Please notify me, and I will attend your premises at the specified hour.*

"Did she appear agitated, Toby? Under some duress?" Aubrey interrogated his manservant.

"A trifle under the weather perhaps, sir."

"In what manner?"

"She was a touch pale, Mr. Aubrey," Toby said and then added, "I wonder what might be ailing her?"

Aubrey did not take kindly to his servant's sly tone. "That is none of your business, Toby. Obviously, she has suffered some emotional setback. I wonder if it concerns her sister? She is something of a renegade, fancies herself a modern woman."

"They're the troublesome kind," Toby acknowledged.

"Yes, they are, but we waste time." He quickly wrote a note and handed it to Toby. "Take this to Cadogan Square. See that it is delivered into the hands of Miss Charlotte. Wait for a reply, then return here forthwith. Have you got that?"

"Yes, sir."

"Then be off," Aubrey said, "and Toby—" the servant hesitated, "straight there, straight back, no diversions. Understood?"

"Understood, Mr. Aubrey," the servant said with a trace of resentment, and he disappeared out the door.

While Toby was delivering his message, Aubrey read and reread Charlotte's note. He concluded that only an event of the utmost gravity could have prompted its writing and prompted the quite unprecedented step of its being delivered personally. *What the devil is this all about?* he wondered.

Within the hour, he had his answer, and to his further astonishment, Charlotte returned with Toby.

"I'm sorry for this intrusion," she said. "I know it must appear unseemly—"

"Not at all," Aubrey interrupted. He turned to Toby who, all ears, hovered nearby. "That will be all," he said. "In fact, I won't be needing you for a few hours. You may leave the house."

"May I remain in my room, sir?"

"No, you may not," Aubrey said curtly. "You must have some outside business that requires your attention. Please see to it at once."

Toby bobbed his head. "Very good, sir," he said in sudden submission and left.

"He's a good servant," Aubrey explained. "Just a bit headstrong on occasion. Now, please come in and tell me what has happened."

Charlotte fumbled in her purse and handed him a slip of paper. "I found this in Charles's house. I dropped by to leave an invitation," she hastened to add, "as I intended to do here."

"Good God!" Aubrey said, after a moment. "You say you found this in Charles's house?"

Charlotte nodded her head quickly. "As I recounted, I was delivering an invitation—"

But Aubrey wasn't listening. "It must have been written by one of his patients. How extraordinary . . . yet is it so extraordinary?" he said, more to himself than to Charlotte. "Charles is home from Paris, then?" he asked suddenly.

"I don't know. His door was ajar. I found it . . . on the floor."

"Have you shown it to anyone else?"

"No. But it must be given to the police. I didn't know what to do with it. I thought better of giving it to Mama, and Father is not home. Nor is Lydia."

Aubrey said, "You knew what to do, Charlotte. You came here. You knew of my official involvement in this matter, and you are to be commended for your astuteness in communicating this"—he held aloft the slip of paper—"to me. You may be assured that it will receive the immediate attention of the police. In fact, I myself will place it in the hands of Inspector Abberline, after I have seen you home."

At Scotland Yard, Abberline read the note and then looked up. "You say you *found* this, Mr. Carsonby?"

"How it came into my possession is, for the moment, irrelevant."

"On the contrary, sir, it is relevant. We've received over 1,000, perhaps 2,000, pieces of mail in the past month alone. We have three detectives whose full-time task is to evaluate letters such as this," he said, tapping a finger on the notepaper.

"But surely they aren't all confessions."

"Of course not." Abberline picked up a letter from his desk. "This lady writes to us from the Isle of Wight. 'In confidence,' she starts, 'I believe him to be a large ape belonging to some wild-beast show who regularly escapes to satisfy his jungle lust for blood.' And we have this from a former metropolitan constable now living in Cleveland, Ohio. 'He is badly disfigured by disease,'" Abberline interrupted himself, "the next part is underlined," he said, and continued with the letter, " 'possibly his privy member has been destroyed, and he is now revenging himself on the opposite sex by these atrocities.' " He put the letter aside. "I could go on."

"That won't be necessary," Aubrey replied. "I take your point but in doing so, return to my own—the correspondences you quote are obviously from cranks. What I brought you was found in a physician's office, one who specializes in treating the mentally unsound. It's my theory that he is unknowingly treating the Ripper.''

"What is this doctor's name?"

"Charles Randall."

"Why isn't he here?"

"He's in Paris, at a symposium."

"When is he expected back?"

"Any day, I believe."

After a moment's deliberation, Abberline said, "We can't simply search his house. And what would we hope to find?"

"For God's sake, man!" Aubrey exclaimed. "A list of his patients. Case notes. Addresses."

"Without his permission?"

"Inspector, that note may well represent the first genuine clue to the man's identity. It can't simply be ignored."

"We won't ignore it, sir. I'll have a detective speak to Dr. Randall upon his return from Paris, which by your own admission is imminent."

Abruptly, Aubrey stood and reached for the incriminating notepaper. "I shall speak to higher-placed authorities, Inspector," he said ominously, and before Abberline could protest, he donned his hat and left.

On the pavement outside, Aubrey fumed. "Damn the man's intractability!" he said aloud. To what higher authority was he to turn? Neither the Home Secretary nor the Commissioner would pay him the slightest heed. And Sir Robert Anderson, Abberline's immediate superior, would take no positive action. He was an administrator not a policeman, and since his abbreviated holiday in Switzerland, he had left the Whitechapel investigation in the hands of department detectives without having displayed any of his own initiative in dealing with the case.

Aubrey started to walk in the direction of Whitehall, and as he did, James Monro's name crossed his mind. Monro had been the head of the CID for four years before resigning after his confrontation with Charles Warren. His resignation had been a severe psychological blow to the department's detectives because, like them, he was a trained police officer, and subsequent events, particularly Warren's ineptitude, had done nothing to restore their morale.

As Aubrey continued walking, it occurred to him that James Monro was the other phantom in the Ripper drama. He was never heard or seen, yet to all accounts, he was playing a role, however circumspect, by keeping an eye on the CID's operation. Aubrey had had no contact with him and, to the best of his knowledge, neither had Robert Anderson. *Shall I contact Monro?* Aubrey asked himself. He stopped and mulled over the pros and cons. *What would Charles think? Would he be angered that I put a patient's note directly into the hands of the police?* But Aubrey quickly checked himself. He had already taken that step. The only way to redress the situation was to return the note to Charles and solicit his permission.

He came to a temporizing decision and flagged down a hansom. "Cheyne Walk," he said to the driver. There was a chance his friend had returned early.

At the channel port of Dover, Charles gratefully set foot on English soil for the first time in three weeks.

His crossing from France had been a storm-tossed one, and he could feel the lingering effects of the seasickness he had suffered mid-passage. He had two options: to stay in Dover for the night or to catch a late train to London. He decided on the former and retired to an inn where he had stayed on previous occasions.

Lydia's presentation at Toynbee Hall concluded to resounding applause. The small lecture hall was crowded to overflowing, with women standing in the aisles and lining the back wall. As she finished speaking, Henrietta Barnett rushed up and clasped her hands. "Well done, Lydia! A splendid talk. You inspired us all," she said in congratulation. "You must have some tea. There are people I want you to meet." And then she spontaneously hugged Lydia, who did not know how to respond except to hug her back and whisper, "Thank you, Mrs. Barnett . . . you are a mother to me."

At the end of the evening, Lydia left Toynbee Hall feeling better than she had in days. *Is it the praise?* she wondered. *Or the warmth I feel toward these women? Or is it simply the knowledge that Charles will soon be home?*

Her parents had sent a carriage for her, and as she stepped into it, she instructed the coachman to drive by the Chelsea Embankment Road, from which she would be able to see if lights burned in Charles's home.

In Cheyne Walk, Aubrey instructed the hansom driver to wait and then strode up to Charles's house. When no one responded to his knock, he tried the door and found it unlocked. Hesitating for only a second, he stepped into the hallway and struck a match, lighting a taper in a holder. Then he walked into Charles's study, placing the candle on his desk. He realized that what he was about to do was highly irregular and illegal. But this was counterbalanced by the gravity of the Ripper's crimes and the small deceit that the Home Office had sanctioned his invasion of Charles's privacy. Having thus dealt with his conscience, Aubrey began to sort through Charles's records.

He was surprised to find his own letter marking a journal entry in which Charles had committed his thoughts concerning Lombroso and his observations about the Ripper's relationship to womankind. Obviously, Charles was preoccupied with the murderer, and this fueled Aubrey's sense that he was onto something—or *someone*. He interrupted his reading and went out to the hansom, gave the driver three shillings to remain standing by and then returned to the house.

Lydia's carriage pulled into the Embankment Road. She saw the hansom parked in front of Charles's house and immediately concluded that he was home from Paris. Directing the coachman to pull in behind the hansom, she stepped out of her carriage, ran up the steps and knocked on the door.

At the sound, Aubrey's heart leapt to his throat. For a second, he was paralyzed, not knowing whether to answer the door or ignore it—then he heard it turn on its hinges. In an instant, he was on his feet, candle in hand, dashing to the rear of the house.

Lydia heard his footsteps and started. "Charles?" she called out.

At the back door, Aubrey heard nothing. He fumbled at the latch and stepped into the laneway. As quickly as he could, he ran to the front of the house where his hansom stood in wait. He climbed into the cab and shouted, "Away!" then sat back so that he could not be observed from the street or the house.

Inside, Lydia walked to the rear of the house and found the door wide open. She called Charles's name again, puzzled by the silence that continued to greet her. *What is going on?* she wondered. She closed the door and retraced her steps to the front porch. Outside, she noticed that the hansom had vanished. She walked quickly to her carriage and asked the coachman who had entered the cab.

"A gentleman," he said. "He appeared in great haste."

"Did you recognize him?"

"No," the coachman answered, although the person he had seen had stirred a vague sense of recognition.

"Can you describe him?" Lydia asked.

"Sorry, ma'am. I didn't have the opportunity to see his face."

"Would you recognize Lord Longerdale if you saw him?"

"No, ma'am, I wouldn't."

"Very well, take me home," Lydia snapped in exasperation.

Aubrey's heart was still pounding when he stepped out of his cab in St. James's Street. He walked into Brooks's, ordered a sherry, swallowed it in a single gulp, then had his glass refilled. He sat down in a comfortable leather chair and tried to relax. *I panicked,* he thought. But another part of his mind rallied in defence. *You acted prudently,* it said. *You had no idea who the visitor might have been. It could have been him, the Ripper.* At this chilling thought, Aubrey swallowed another mouthful of sherry. "Damn and tarnation," he muttered under his breath. "Why does life have to be so complicated?"

Unable to contain his agitation, he began to walk about the club. He stopped for a moment in the card room and watched a game of faro. As they laid down their cards, the players discussed the outbreak of reciprocal blackballing that had plagued the club since the introduction of the Home Rule Bill for Ireland in Parliament. But that contentious discussion failed to hold his attention, and he continued to wander. He paused in front of a glass-enclosed cabinet that contained Brooks's most famous historical artifact, Napoleon Bonaparte's death mask. Although the mask's expression was sombre, it was also peaceful, as if in death Bonaparte had found a peace he had never been able to achieve in his momentous but strife-torn life.

Aubrey had a steward refill his glass and then he returned to his chair. After several moments of reflection, he decided he would bide his time for another 24 hours. If Charles had not returned within a day and a night, he would deliver directly to James Monro the letter Charlotte had found. He would also advise him that, according to Charles's appointment book, only one male patient had visited him within the last several weeks, a John Castrain.

Lydia Carlyle
Mary Ann Kelly

monday, november 9th

◆◆[21]◆◆

CHARLES TRAVELLED FROM Dover to London on a late-afternoon train, not bothering to alert anyone as to the time of his arrival. As the train passed through the countryside on its way to Victoria Station, he reflected upon the Paris Symposium which had been a great success. Experts from all over the world had attended, among them the Americans William James and Stanley Hall, founder of the year-old *American Journal of Psychology*. But it was two Frenchmen and a pair of Viennese doctors whose papers had captured the Symposium's attention.

Pierre Janet had presented a paper entitled *L'automatisme psychologique*, in which he argued that the principal consciousness is not fixed but movable, and that past traumas and strains which a person may not be aware of can become buried and forgotten, finally existing in the mind in a parasitical state.

Janet's countryman, Alfred Binet, had delivered a presentation on *Les altérations de la personalité*, in which he postulated that unconscious thoughts reveal the existence of an intelligence other than the self, an intelligence that acts without our aid—even without our knowledge.

And two obscure physicians from Austria, Freud and Breuer (Charles could not recall their first names), had presented a paper on "psychic traumata," shocks that fall into an individual's memory, the only cure for which is a "hypnoid" state during which they can be drawn to the surface and allowed to be worked out.

Each of these papers spoke to Charles in a meaningful, gratifying way—even, inexplicably, in a personal way. They bore out his conviction that England was removed from the mainstream of psychological research; that, in London, he lived as an island unto himself. Paris had reassured him that his own ideas and research did not belong to the arcane rites of witchcraft. His office in Chelsea might exist to some degree in isolation, but Paris had proven that it was not completely cut off from the rest of the world.

Paris had also provided a much-needed change of scenery, pace and faces. No Lucie Rhinegold, no midnight visits from John Castrain. Yet, he had enjoyed only a single night of entertainment on the eve of his return to England. He and Fritz Steinpatz, a German fellow who was investigating the working of the left and right brain hemispheres, had their hotel concièrge provide two *filles de joie*. It had been a memorable evening of champagne and whoring . . . "as the Parisiennes behave, so we must," Steinpatz had put in. They had spent almost the entire night in a drunken stupor, swapping their high-class whores back and forth like two jockeys their mounts. "We harding them ride," Steinpatz had said, in inebriated and fractured English. The Berliner had been right, and Charles had enjoyed every moment. French whores did not pretend to be something they were not. They existed to gratify the sexual urges of men: it was a commercial transaction, and they gave good value for money received. They did not aspire to marriage or, by some other subterfuge, attempt to legitimize their status within society. The French had found a place for them, and there they existed in a state of relative contentment.

From Victoria Station, Charles took a hansom to Cheyne Walk. His first surprise was that his door was open. He realized that he had left London in great haste but could not imagine he had done so without taking the precaution of locking up. Mystified, he secured all of his luggage inside the hallway, then made a quick inspection of his office and study, observing with relief that everything appeared to be in its place. He then climbed the stairs to his upper-floor bedroom where he found a second surprise—a woman in his bed.

"Welcome home, Charles," Lucie said.

Charles stepped back in amazement, "How did you get in?"

"The door was unlatched."

"But how did you know I was to return today?"

"I didn't. But I've driven by every day for the last week. This afternoon I noticed the door was slightly ajar and I assumed you had returned, so I entered. I heard your hansom and came up here."

"And into my bed?"

"Yes. I left you a note, but obviously you've had no chance to read it. I've left Fredrick. I've become a courtesan . . . does that shock you?"

Charles sat down, uncertain of how to respond. He had been home only a minute, and a woman—a beautiful woman, for he could not help but take in Lucie's bewitching attractiveness—lay in his bed. "You are a patient," he began.

But Lucie interrupted. "I *was* a patient," she corrected him. "But I am no longer. You cured me. The other Lucie is dead and gone, buried in my past. My marriage was a joyless, sexless one. I wasn't meant for the marriage bed . . . no more than you are. You don't mind me calling you Charles, do you? I am naked in your bed and to address you as Doctor Randall seems . . . well, it seems somehow inappropriate," she said.

Charles looked at her, unable to find his voice. She had always stirred strange emotions in him, desire and lust, yet somehow at the same time, dislike, even a sense of aversion.

"You desire me," Lucie said. "I have seen it in your eyes for a long time. A doctor can desire a patient. He does nothing improper so long as he doesn't cross the bounds. You didn't. Your behaviour was irreproachable. But now I am just a woman and you a man. Please, come to bed.''

She turned on her side, pulled back a sheet, and as she did her chestnut hair fell on the pillow, the sound somehow magnified by the silence. He stared at her large, full breasts. The nipples were hard, and he wanted to reach out and touch them—yet something held him back.

''You must feel no embarrassment or shame,'' she said. ''I told you, I have become a courtesan. I am mistress to a duke. His identity shall remain my secret. He treats me like a princess''—she reached to an emerald earring—''and I treat him as the most princely of men. He says I have resurrected his love life. That is grand passion speaking, of course, and I take his compliments as such. But I do give him pleasure, and he pleases me. But I ramble on, as if I haven't spoken for years—and that is precisely how I feel, like a mute who has, by some miracle, suddenly been given a voice. I wish to pay for your help and kindness, for you are my miracle—''

''But there is no need—'' Charles intervened.

''I must insist. But the manner of repayment must be of my imagination. A man can give a woman so much,'' she said. ''Jewellery, furs, money . . . a name, a title, a reputation. But what can a woman give a man? Precious little, it seems. Perhaps a child, as long as it's an heir, but I don't believe men like children. There is only one truly unique gift a woman can give a man.'' She removed the sheet and revealed her entire body. ''As you can see, I employ no artifice or female stratagems of seduction: I want to make love to you. I know I am forward, but''—she shrugged her shoulders in a helpless gesture—''what else is a woman to do?''

Lydia arrived at Cheyne Walk well after dark. Although no lights were burning, intuition told her that Charles had returned from Paris. She remained seated in her cabriolet in a state of indecision. To the west, beyond Cheyne Walk, the lights of Cremorne could be seen and, across the river, the lights of Battersea. George Eliot had lived almost opposite where Lydia sat, and she wondered if the famous novelist had ever watched, as she was doing, the black-silver mercury of the Thames and the distant white-gold shimmer of Cremorne and Battersea.

Charles's house appeared as uninhabited as it had last night. Yet she was puzzled over a change she could not at first identify. She studied the bedroom windows, which were nearly as large as French doors and opened to a small wrought-iron balcony and a panoramic vista of the river. The drapes had been moved, either opened slightly or not fully redrawn. Someone was in the house.

She left the cabriolet, walked up the laneway and found the side door unlocked. Upon entering, she saw the luggage in the doorway and walked upstairs, where she found Charles asleep. His bed was disheveled, and he was in a state of *deshabille*. A white nightshirt rode high up one thigh, the other leg was bent at the knee. She watched for a moment, arrested, not by Charles but by the masculine aura he managed to cast even in sleep.

Suddenly, his face grimaced as if in pain or at an unpleasant memory. She heard his teeth grind, and a groan emerged from deep within his chest. He began to thrash about, throwing his head from side to side, as if he were trying to free himself from the grip of some imaginary monster. . . .

Could Lydia have seen into Charles's mind, she would have been terrified herself: the river dream had diabolized Charles's sleep. A translucent cloud of sparkling dust hung over the falls. And then a vibrant rainbow appeared, narrow beams of sunlight refracted by the prism-like cloud. The splendour of the rainbow—seemingly fired by internal light—captivated him. His enthrallment was such that he had ignored the current. Alarmed, he now began to pull for the bank; only with the greatest exertion did he manage to gain shore. How close had he ventured to the edge of the falls? It seemed but a few yards. The river nymphs had appeared but only in a murky kind of twilight. They, and the rocks on which they rode like jousting knights, had been framed by the arching rainbow. But he had distinctly heard their voices. They had called out his name. . . .

He sat up in bed, attempting to collect his racing thoughts,

and became aware of a peculiar sensation in his left ear. He
touched it, and to his astonishment, he felt warm moisture.
Reaching for his pillow, he found it damp, and he could still
hear someone calling his name. He vaguely recalled the visit
with Lucie Rhinegold. She had slipped out from beside him,
put her fingers to her lips, then touched his cheek. "Goodbye," she had whispered, and she vanished. He could still
smell her perfume, could still hear her calling his name. But
he ignored her. Suddenly he wanted to be back in the
river—and that is where he found himself.

This time, there was no fear. He was swept toward the
chasm where the river suddenly narrowed, preparing for its
drop into the abyss below. Night descended on the river, but
the darkness was not total. Suddenly, he viewed the world
through a reddish-orange filter.

At this moment he *let go*.

The current dragged him below the surface, where it
jostled and buffeted him so that he performed acrobatic
twists and somersaults. He reached out to steady himself,
clutching at weirdly shaped objects. They were spongy,
could be squeezed, crushed in fact, so that whatever their
substance, their warm fluids ran freely through his fingers.

Never had he felt so fearless, so exhilarated. "I want to
joust with you!" he screamed.

Lydia heard this scream and was instantly alarmed. She
had watched, in growing consternation, as Charles sat up and
reached for his ear. She had called out his name several times
but to no avail. She now feared that he was suffering from an
epileptic fit. She grabbed him by the shoulders, but still he
would not awaken.

In the river, Charles felt as though he had sprung loose
from the gravity of society. The high and mighty principles
by which people governed themselves were not his. He would
spit blood in society's eyes and blind it. At that moment, he
shuddered awake, screaming in the darkness of his room.

He felt a virulent fireball of rage and hatred swell up inside
his head. For a split second, he seemed to black out, but
consciousness immediately returned. Then it faded as quickly again; his peripheral vision narrowed and greyed, then

rapidly expanded. Everything was startlingly clear. Everything was larger than life. He could see for miles, and the colours were brilliant. There was a woman standing directly in front of him. He was sitting on the bed. Whose bed? Who was this whore? Had he just fucked her? Was he about to fuck her?

She appeared startled. "Are you all right, Charles?" Lydia asked.

Her eyes really were enormous. They were hard, the pupils enormous and black. He disliked them immensely. He had never liked whores' eyes. They took without giving. They were vacuous, calculating, sizing him up, pricing him to the nearest farthing. Should she go for more? Would she lose him? Where was the risk? What was the price of his flesh? What had been the price of his father's flesh?

"Charles?" The shouted name jarred him. *Who was Charles?*

Lydia moved towards him, making a gesture with her hands. Yet at the same time, she was terrified. She had once witnessed a cousin's epileptic attack. He had lain on the floor, convulsing violently and grotesquely, but a threat to no one save himself. That was not the nature of whatever possessed Charles at this moment: his eyes were filled with murderous rage.

He pushed an arm out, catching all of her face in the palm of his hand. He dug his fingers in and shoved her violently away. She fell backwards with a shriek and lay spread-eagled on the floor, stunned.

He tore at her clothes. Still groggy, Lydia looked up at him from the floor, shocked by his attack.

He knelt between her legs and thrust a thumb into her vagina. He could feel no resistance. He rotated his thumb and in so doing her uterus seemed to swell, to grow before his eyes—it seemed to want to swallow him.

He pushed and his arm sank into the softest, warmest, moistest substance he could imagine. His mind began to spin dizzyingly . . . he confronted a tunnel, a circular opening; a sun seemed to shine from within: a blood-red sun, yet it was also warm with wonderful tropical colours, tangerine, apricot, orange. But there was violence inside this sun, as there was within the seething sun that stood above the earth like a fiery god—but abruptly, the tunnel and the sun and the river vanished. There was only blackness. For an instant, he thought he had somehow been sucked up from the earth into the vastness of cold black space.

He felt a hand in his face. It was cold and claw-like. With great strength, it shoved him back. His head struck something, and there, in front of him, was a face he was certain he recognized. But somewhere a mental door slammed shut, and he could remember only the image of the face white with terror. It belonged to a woman, and she was haemorrhaging like the river. Her legs seemed to be running with blood, and all of a sudden, she collapsed on the floor.

He washed the blood from his hands and dressed in the clothes on the bedside table. He walked up to the Battersea Bridge and hailed a hansom, ordering the driver to Aldgate Pump. From there, he walked to the Minories, a small mercantile street southwest of Whitechapel.

He changed in his flat to a black suit, black cape and a soft black felt hat. The most recent *Times* at the top of the stack on the floor was over three weeks old. He took it and made a flat scabbard. Then he unlocked the dresser drawer, removed the knife, honed it and slipped it into the newspaper.

Outside, he began to walk the crowded streets of Whitechapel. He stopped at a church behind the London Hospital in Whitechapel Road and read the cornerstone:

BY ONE UNKNOWN
YET WELL KNOWN

What does this oxymoronic message signify? he wondered. It symbolized perfectly the ambivalent state of the human mind.

Fifteen minutes later, he found himself on the steps of Christ Church, Spitalfields, directly opposite the market. On an impulse, he slipped into the church and climbed a stairway to the sacristy. At either end of the room, there were two massive castiron fireplaces. A wooden door, small and arched, led up the steeple to the belfry. He climbed the winding stairway by touch, for the darkness was complete.

In the belfry, a circular commemorative shield had been mounted, gold leaf legible against lacquered black:

CUMBERLAND SOCIETY

On Monday
Dec. 29th, 1845 the under
mentioned members of
the above Society rang in this
Steeple a true Peal of
Grandsire Triples
consisting of 5,040 changes in 3 hours
and 24 minutes being the first Peal
on these bells.

God Bless you all, you merry Christian gentlemen, he thought to himself. *I trust from Christ to kingdom come and back your bells were heard.*

He climbed the cramped staircase until he arrived where the bells themselves were hung. They were black and looked like giant hooded bats. On his knees, through slatted wood, he could see lights blazing all over London, save for the dark asymmetrical shapes of the numerous parks and the broad, black course of the Thames.

Directly beneath him, the fires of Whitechapel burned like the thousand campfires of an invading army. He could see toy soldiers and toy camp followers, women and children, moving from bivouac to bivouac.

Caligula's Rome has become Victoria's London: this thought struck him with great force. For could he switch cities and centuries—virtuous British monarch for debauched Roman emperor—Rome, not London, would be his home; Caligula not Victoria, his spiritual and moral example.

In Whitechapel, a pagan god had taken brick and mortar, vision and purpose and constructed *his* ideal paradise. From his vantage point, he could turn in any direction and identify in swift succession a dozen dwellings in which the seven deadly sins were practised, without respite or remorse, every hour of every day: gin palaces crowded with gin soaks; opium dens with wasted Malays and Chinamen; sweatshops with children already decrepit from age; and brothels by the hundreds. Inside those brothels, a virgin—often bartered by mother or sister—could be purchased for a shilling; but those virgins were conspiring waifs, their virginity resurrected as in the blink of an eye by the magic of needle and thread, of nimble fingers and elastic hymens. A stitch here, a stitch there, and a virgin was miraculously restored to maidenhood: another shilling pocketed, another fool satisfied.

But the soldiers of the Christian God had not meekly turned their cheeks to such depravity. Missionaries of every conceivable faith and denomination—Anglican, Methodist, Rabbinical, Presbyterian, Salvationist—had joined the battle against the heathens. Their adherents walked side by side with followers of that pagan god: prostitutes, muggers, thieves, murderers, rapists. The former traded in souls and salvation, the latter in the commerce and coin of earthly pleasure. And temples of worship stood side by side with dens of iniquity, often sharing a common wall in a perverse yet oddly symbiotic relationship, as if good had to feed off evil and evil off good.

If a detached observer surveyed the battleground, and read the faces of the soldiers of each army, he arrived at a startling, heretical conclusion: the pagan god had gained the upper hand. The Christian God, although not defeated, was bloody and badly bruised, reeling from overwhelming assault. Victory was beyond His grasp; at best He could hope for a kind of spiritual stalemate, claiming some converts but conceding the majority as souls lost to the enemy.

An inner voice told him that he should be outraged at this triumph of evil over good. But the truth of the matter was he experienced neither shock nor outrage but rather a strange kind of kinship with the paganists. Or perhaps, more accurately, not kinship with them as fellow human beings but rather with the primitiveness of their behaviour, their unthinking carnal lusts.

Having arrived at this conclusion, he stood and descended the stairs to street level and was almost immediately accosted by a prostitute.

"Will you come with me?" she asked.

"Where?" he inquired, feeling, rather than hearing, the familiar drumming in his head.

"A short distance. I have a room."

He was surprised. "Your own room?"

She nodded. "I do quite well," she said, with an Irish lilt. Her accent sounded familiar, as a voice from the not-so-distant past. A small bell of alarm sounded. He looked at her more closely. She was young and pretty, although her face was also dissolute. She was a whore after all, and hatred rose like bile in his throat. But he grinned and said, "I'll follow you."

She led him to a room in Miller's Court off Dorset Street, not far from the Convent of Mercy. He sat on the only chair in the miserable room, which was no larger than a wardrobe closet. A single, nondescript landscape print decorated the wall, its colour as anemic as the washed-out and flaking paint. It hung from a nail. She had not taken the trouble to hang the picture so that the nail and wire were hidden. A small fire burned and crackled quietly, throwing tortuous shadows around the room—the flames of hell, he thought with a wry smile. Never had he felt so calm, so at peace—and, at least for the moment, so patient. No one would interrupt his work here.

He let her go about her petty rituals, the disrobing of her female vanities. She fussed with her hair, which had been drawn up beneath a bonnet.

"Do you like it down?" she asked, watching his face in the shadows. She removed some pins, and a lock of hair uncoiled and dropped to her shoulder.

He shook his head.

"You are a quiet one," she said.

Slowly, childlike, she undressed. She did so with great

deliberation, neither self-consciously nor lewdly. As each piece of clothing was removed, it was neatly folded and placed at the foot of her narrow bed.

"There is nothing quiet about me," he said.

"You're a gentleman, aren't you?"

"How do you mean?"

She shrugged her pretty shoulders. "Educated, cultured . . . probably from a good family. Rich. You're from the West End, I can tell, despite the shabby clothes. Why do you wear them? So nobody will know?"

"Know what?" he asked, restraining his hatred and his fury.

"That you're a gentleman. Nothing to fear here, even with the Ripper about. Gentlemen are fast and furious around here. . . ."

She paused as she unfastened a stay. "I once had a gentleman friend like you. He kept me in style for a time, gave me money for food, clothes and the like. Then he took me to Paris. Stayed a week, had his sport and buggered off. I stayed on."

"Why did you come back?"

"The froggies drove me crazy. Their cigarettes, the smell. And the cheap wine. It gets to you—you're always pissing. I missed gin. Froggie men like to diddle but don't like to pay."

She was beginning to prattle. She was vivacious in a crude country way, and this offended him. Soon the gaiety would be wiped from her face.

She stepped out of her last petticoat. "An Englishman, whatever else you might say, knows the score—payment for services. He'll try and gyp you, cheat you, pass a farthing for a sixpence if he can, barter like a fishmonger. Whatever. But he knows he must pay. That's the difference, and God bless it, I say."

She finally stood naked. The firelight danced on her body, turning it white and orange and yellow. Her eyes seemed black and flinty, glinting like pieces of coal. He imagined her a witch, naked at the stake, flames leaping up from her feet. And she was smiling.

"Do you like it?" she said leeringly.

He closed his eyes, the blood pulsing into his temples. He could hear the roar of the falls, the rush of the river. An effusion of warmth washed around and over him. He slipped into the river and immersed himself in the blood-warm water. The roaring filled his ears. The current was very, *very* fast.

Still, she stared at him. *All of her*. Her nipples, her navel like the eye of a cyclops, even her knees, her bush—where flames seemed to tangle with the thick mat of coarse hair. She was all eyes, like his dying mother. May she burn in hell.

He could see fire burning *inside* those eyes, as if she were consumed by a conflagration that needed the oxygen from the outside world to survive. But such witchcraft would never work with him. He heard, or rather felt, the snarl emerge from his throat. She mistook the sound as a groan of passion. A witch she might be; a seer she was not.

He started to laugh, threw back his head and roared. That startled her. The laughter rolled over him in dizzying waves. He felt weak at the knees, lightheaded, yet consumed by murderous intent. When the lightheadedness emptied from his brain, he felt intoxicated, drunk on the pleasure of anticipation. Pleasure shaded into hatred; hatred into pleasure, so that his state of mind became a hybrid, a synthesis of pain-pleasure: as if two distinct elements of nature had been bound together to form a lethal and never before seen mutation.

The newspaper was beside him, and he reached for it.

"What are you doing?" she asked, her voice suddenly anxious.

"Lie down," he commanded.

Instantly, she did as she was told. She knew men, knew they could be punishing in their assaults. Did he want to do more than fuck her? Humiliate, hurt her? Men could be animals, wild, enraged beasts. Best to obey, to submit to their will. The wildness would pass. Then he would probably weep in regret.

He stood over her, and ran his fingers along her throat. The apparent tenderness momentarily shocked her. She could feel her heartbeat against his fingers and it was a strange, intimate sensation. She felt lifted out of her own body. He was a very peculiar man. He frightened but fascinated her. His eyes were mesmerizing.

He knelt at her side, ignoring the smell of gin on her breath. With his free hand, he brushed the hair back from her neck. The other hand gripped the knife. "Close your eyes," he whispered hoarsely. "Close them tight . . . *very* tight."

It was a fine neck, white and soft. He pressed two fingers against the carotid artery, feeling the persistent throbbing flow of blood. For a moment, he rested them there, counting her pulse rate. It was elevated. By what? Sexual excitement? Did a common whore feel sexually aroused? He briefly felt her forehead. It was cool but moist to the touch. Her face was flushed. He let the back of his fingers brush her neck from the jaw line to her collarbone. He heard a low animal sound. *Silly bitch.* Did she think this was some kind of foreplay?

Her eyes flashed open; she turned her head, lips parted, inviting. With a terrible fury, he ripped the knife across her throat. Her eyes widened in amazement. The blood gushed upwards, fountainlike. And still her eyes stared, still very much alive, still astonished yet terrified.

"You deserve to die," he hissed at the eyes, "*all* of you."

He put a hand to her breast feeling the erratic, fluttering beat of her heart, feeling the sudden frantic surge of adrenaline as the heart recognized and momentarily fought the onrush of death, and feeling, too, within that same brief second, its acceptance of its fate: a faint, rapidly weakening pulse. All of this he sensed through the thin skin and tissue of her breast, as the final, feeble flow of lifeblood trickled across the hand still gripping her neck.

Aubrey arrived at Charles's house and was disappointed to find it in darkness. It appeared that Charles had delayed his departure from Paris. On the other hand, Aubrey reasoned, the hour was late and perhaps his friend, fatigued by his journey, had gone to an early bed. So he stepped down from his hansom and walked the length of the laneway, where he found a cabriolet and horse tethered to a hitching post. He went up to the back door and found he could push it open. He rapped on it with his cane but heard no response. He was confronted once again with the dilemma of whether or not to enter the house. He rapped on the door a second time and listened—and thought he heard a sound, low and indistinct like a moan. He stepped into the hallway, paused, and heard the sound again coming from an upstairs room. He immediately started down the hallway and collided with a suitcase— so Charles *was* home. But before that fact could really register, he heard the sound again, this time more desperate. In growing alarm, he ran upstairs and entered Charles's bedroom. He found a woman sprawled on the carpet and rushed to her side, astounded to recognize Lydia Carlyle.

"Lydia!" he said. "What in God's name has happened to you?"

She reached up and clutched at his coat lapel. "Charles," she whispered through clenched teeth, then fell back unconscious.

He stood on Waterloo Bridge, watching the flow of the river. He felt sated, yet at the same time, strangely empty, as though he had been purged of all emotion.

Moonlight fell on the river and mixed with the brownish water to form a golden liquid.

His memory of the room in Miller's Court was awash with blood. If he closed his eyes and scrubbed hard, the blood temporarily receded, and he could see the woman's face— which he had disfigured—on the bed. He opened his eyes and looked at the river. Other faces floated past, his mother and father's, even by some chimera, the adult face of his brother, who was the spitting image of someone he also recognized as John Castrain.

He closed his eyes again and thought he heard voices, women's voices. The river was rising, beckoning to him. He remembered its scented warmth and the elixir-like effect it had on his mind and body. Suddenly, he was overwhelmed by the most profound sadness and loneliness and felt the presence of the river rushing in to fill the void. Unhesitatingly, he climbed over the fence and fell into its welcoming embrace.

AFTERWORD

THE TRUE IDENTITY of Jack the Ripper has provoked endless speculation. Candidates include George Chapman (Severin Antoniovich Klosowski), a surgically trained Polish immigrant, Queen Victoria's grandson, the Duke of Clarence, and the Victorian painter, Walter Sickert. Readers interested in these and other theories are directed to Donald Rumbelow's excellent *The Complete Jack the Ripper*.

Wherever possible, I incorporated genuine historical documents and records, including letters and scientific papers, into the narrative. Parts of William James's letter describing his patient, Ansel Bourne, are reproduced verbatim; the case history of Mr. "S" is an actual one; Lucie Rhinegold is a composite portrait drawn in part from case studies described by the French psychologists Pierre Janet and Alfred Binet; and John Castrain, a figment of Charles Randall's imagination, was developed from the description of a patient who suffered from syphilitic dementia.

I confess that on several occasions I "rearranged" history in the interests of maintaining the story's momentum. For example, *The Dean's Daughter* opened at the St. James's Theatre a month later than portrayed; and the Lady Montrose tabules became available more than a year later (they were fake; women who ordered them were blackmailed by the manufacturer who threatened to reveal their pregnancies).

One final historical note: upon the discovery of Mary Kelly's body, Sir Charles Warren resigned as Commissioner of Police and was replaced by James Monro. Henry Matthews continued on as Home Secretary and was eventually knighted.

Visitors to London who wish to capture a glimpse of what the East End looked like 100 years ago are advised to start their tour at Liverpool Street Station. From there, a five minute walk through narrow streets will take them to Christ Church, the Convent of Mercy and Spitalfields Market. Nearby is Hanbury Street which, of all the murder sites, remains most like it was in the late 19th century.

One facet of East End London that has remained constant is its affinity for immigrants. French Protestants, Irish Catholics and Polish Jews have now given way to Middle East Muslims.

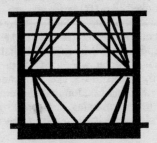